THE SWEET SECOND LIFE OF DARRELL KINCAID

CATHERINE ROBERTSON

ISBN: 978-0-473-58708-6

Cover design by Callum Robertson @inklinewolves

Chapter One

I WAS in love with happy endings until approximately a minute and a half after I'd written my ninth. I typed the last full stop and waited to feel the usual regret that I could no longer lose myself in my characters' lives. But what I felt was nothing like regret, apart from its first letter. What I felt was rage.

It was so strong that I sat there, blinking at the page in astonishment. Normally I'd expect to feel a twinge of wistful sadness, as if I was saying goodbye to best friends who were heading off to live overseas. And without wishing to sound like a complete tragic, that's exactly what it was like. I loved having these imaginary people in my head. I loved their fantasy world — that of uber-wealthy alpha males with commitment issues and private jets meeting their match in determined young women with excellent legs. I make no apologies. In my world, that's how we roll.

My characters really did come alive in my head, although I confess I stuck with a limited range of physical types. My men were either forty-plus, suave and with a hint of past tragedy, or late thirties-ish with a whiff of danger. My women were without fail mid-twenties, big-eyed brunettes.

In my ninth book (*Bought for the Billionaire's Private Collection,* in case you were wondering), she = Daisy Ridley, he = *The Thomas Crown Affair*-era Pierce Brosnan. Previous book, *The Emerald Magnate's Auctioned Mistress,* he = Henry Cavill, she = Emilia Clarke. I didn't do blondes for some reason. Resentment, probably.

They talked in my head, too. Often — too often for Tom's liking — their conversations would wake me up in the middle of the night. I kept a notebook and pencil handy, because experience had proven that if I didn't write it all down immediately, the only thing I'd be able to remember in the morning was that her chest was heaving and when, quite frankly, did it not? I'd also be left with a lingering suspicion that it was the best dialogue I had ever written, possibly the best in any romance written in the entire history of time. Which would make me Miss Ornery for the rest of the week. Unless I had total recall at three a.m. the *next* night, whereupon I'd sit bolt upright, switch on the light, grab my notebook and scribble furiously until I had it all down, whereupon I would punch the air and yell, 'Yes!' Which would always make Tom sit upright and yell, 'For the love of Christ! Will you shift those imaginary bastards into the same fucking time zone!' Of course, in the morning the dialogue would never be as good as I'd convinced myself it was when I couldn't recall a word of it. But I was usually so pleased to have remembered it that I didn't care.

I loved picturing the settings. Houses, cars, clothing, accessories — all so deliciously desirable and completely unattainable for peasants like me. I think if I ever stopped writing, the Condé Nast magazine empire would crumble. I buy a scrapbook for each of my romances — I prefer nice, classy ones with textured paper, but I'd settle for ones with the Wiggles on them if that's all that was going down at the stationery shop. Into them, I glue-stick glossy pictures of Greek villas, crisp white against azure sky; razor-sharp, minimalist New York penthouses; chicly faded belle époque Parisian apartments;

stately English homes with lawns the size of a county; red Ferraris, silver Bentleys and Riva boats with piped cream leather seats and polished wood; classy bling, like Patek Philippe watches and Cartier emerald earrings; and all those movie-star photo spreads from *Vanity Fair*, which give me clothes and hair and faces to shamelessly plagiarise. To be safe, you can change one thing about them — eye or hair colour, for instance, but in truth, I imagine the chance of someone famous recognising themselves in print is minimal. If you're going to be paparazzi'd, you really want to be caught reading *A Brief History of Time*, not *The Sicilian Marquis' Reluctant Virgin*.

I loved seeing my name on the covers. My parents called me Darrell, which as far as I know has never been a girl's name. But having done battle on its behalf for several years in the playground, I've grown quite attached to it. And my married name was Kincaid, which meant I didn't need to invent a pseudonym for my books. Romantic fiction authors often write under assumed names. Not necessarily because they find their real names embarrassing; more that when you've finished with Lord Valentin Ripley swooping upon Lady Alethea, Duchess of Boscastle, signing off as Susan Hughes can feel a tad pedestrian. Much better to be Suzanne Hughendon or Susannah Highfield or the like. Darrell Kincaid has a certain rhythm to it. And in this woman-heavy industry, you can generate a bit of interest by being thought a bloke.

And the bit I love— that I *used* to love most? The bit where it all works out. When my hero and heroine finally admit they are destined for each other. The happy ending.

But not this time. As I typed the last full stop, then read over my last few pages, I was overwhelmed by a rage so intense I wanted to go out and provoke some unsuspecting person into being rude to me, just so I'd have the excuse to smack them one. At first, I thought — this is nuts: I'm just tired. It was true; I had been tired all the time since . . . But as

I read again the bit where billionaire Pierce admitted that no Impressionist masterpiece could hold a candle to Daisy's beauty and that Monet wasn't everything, I realised I wasn't tired. I was so complete and utterly enraged that it's a miracle my laptop wasn't suddenly replaced by a scorched hollow with the faint echo of a sound that can only be written as 'Woomph'.

How *dare* my characters be happy? How dare it all work out for them? How dare romantic fiction be so patently, manifestly and absolutely unlike my own reality? How dare they, in short, have everything I did not?

I needed a break. I made myself a cup of tea and spread butter on two digestives. I nearly added a slice of cheese to each but decided against it. That's one of the things Tom and I could never agree on — digestive biscuits with butter and cheese. I'd always considered the combination a type of superfood, like goji berries or wheatgrass, only edible. Tom said he would rather eat his own sick. 'It's wrong,' he used to say. 'Pure D wrong. Go and eat it in another room. A room in another *country*, preferably.'

Other things Tom and I could never agree on:

Kate Bush. Tom thought Kate had been designed by a committee formed exclusively for the purpose of frightening small children. His evidence was her mad cat-lady's hair and the opening note of *Wuthering Heights*, which has been known to resurrect dead people. I thought this was a bit rich coming from a man who listened to a Scottish pirate metal band with a tattooed midget bass-player called Alestorm (the band, not the midget bassist). But I suppose he had a point. Even so, Kate has been a great comfort to me.

Running. My God, it's tedious. And it hurts. And I'm convinced it undermines the structure of your boobs. Tom (who, let's be clear, had no boobs) ran every day, for miles. He loved it . . .

Reading. I don't feel fully dressed unless I have a book in my hand. I read all the time, even when cooking and occasionally when driving. When they invent a way to read in the shower, I'll have reached Nirvana. Tom read running magazines and occasionally the *TV Guide*. Yet somehow he wasn't the mentally stunted ignoramus you'd expect. He knew a lot. Where he picked it up, no idea. There were times I would have liked to have a cultured discussion — I have a degree in English literature, which I suppose goes to show how much one of those is worth. The closest we got was watching a rerun of *Brideshead Revisited*, when Tom said, 'Hey, doesn't that guy do the voice of Scar in *The Lion King*?' He was right. Why is it your memory hangs onto stuff like that . . . ?

Tom died. There doesn't seem any point in being less blunt about it. He died over a year ago. Nineteen months and fifteen days ago, to be rather pathetically exact. He dropped dead and I mean that literally. He had just completed a half marathon. It wasn't called that; it was called a fun run. (I don't need to comment. This whole story is a study in irony.) Tom crossed the finish line (see?), checked his watch, and collapsed. The first aid crew was promptly by his side and he was promptly loaded into an ambulance and rushed to hospital, where he was promptly pronounced dead. My fit, young husband had just run twenty-one kilometres in a personal best time of one hour, twenty-two minutes. It took him less than ten minutes to die.

The correct medical term is sudden cardiac death. It wasn't a heart attack; it was a heart malfunction. In older people, the cause is usually heart disease, fatty build-up and all that stuff we're warned about by Jamie Oliver. In younger people, it's most often an undetected abnormality — a dodgy heart rhythm, a weakness of the valves. Undetected meaning that the first hint of there being anything wrong is when something triggers it. Something like adrenaline released during intense physical activity, for example. And then it's like flicking a light switch — the heart just shuts off. Sometimes it can be restarted, but not in Tom's case. His heart was buggered, and no one knew. No one had the slightest idea.

And I wasn't there. At the finish line . . .

You see, I met Tom when I was twenty-three and he was twenty-four. We were married a year later. When he died, we'd been married ten years.

Which is the point of this story. When you're in the first throes of love, you're thrilled to get up at crack of dawn and hang out for hours watching hordes of stringy, sweaty people pound past you, so you can be there to applaud and hug one of them, even though the amount of sweat dripping off him is, quite frankly, repulsive. But after ten years, you'd rather stay in bed, read a book and hug him after he's returned and has showered and changed. So I wasn't there when he died. I was at home. Reading Barbara Pym.

I had the book in one hand and was still glancing at it when I opened the front door. There were two policemen on my doorstep, looking absurdly young and not very happy to be there. I don't remember what they said. All I could think, when they took me inside, sat me down and told me, was how difficult it must have been for them. While one was talking to me, I noticed the other one take off his hat, drop his head and run his hand over his hair. Poor boy, I thought. You poor boy, having to do this. They took me to the hospital. And I really, *really* don't remember much about that at all. Except that Tom didn't look peaceful. He looked dead. Sort of collapsed and grey and strangely featureless. Like a skin shed by some alien. Not like my Tom.

I spoke at the funeral. Everyone remarked on how well I held myself together. I do remember that I had no intention of crying — my grief was for Tom alone, so it seemed right to keep any tears just between him and me, as it were. It was a very good speech, apparently. I have no recollection of it at all . . .

You'd assume that my life changed dramatically that morning. In fact, it was extraordinary how much of it continued as normal. I continued to write my books. I continued to live in our house. My relationships with friends and family kept on pretty much as they always had. True, I was suddenly several hundred thousand dollars richer from Tom's life insurance. But that was still in the bank, mainly because I couldn't bring myself to spend a cent of it. My own earnings were enough to pay the mortgage and I had only myself to feed.

Of course, the loss of Tom was a change. Ridiculous to say otherwise. Better writers than I have described what it's like to lose someone you love. All the things you do that, in any other circumstance, would peg you as unhinged but that here and now just seem poignant. Like keeping their unwashed clothes, so you can bury your face in their 'Motörhead: No Sleep 'til Hammersmith' t-shirt and inhale their familiar scent. Like playing old video clips and listening to their voicemail message, because you crave that ache of familiarity and because you're terrified that you'll forget what they looked and sounded like. Like refusing to throw out any of their stuff, even their sports bag, which you *know* has a blackened dead banana in it. Like continuing to share the morning coffee between two cups, being careful to pour the last into his cup because he always liked the kick from those strong, treacly dregs. Like remembering to record the London Marathon, even though he'd never see who won.

But — and how can I explain this? — the lack of Tom in my day-to-day life was not the worst of it. It was the lack of Tom *from now on* that was destroying me. That's why my happy ending enraged me so much. Because a happy ending isn't an ending at all — it's the start of the rest of a perfect life. We, the readers, know that. We can play out the rest of the story in our minds as clearly as if we had a sequel to hand. It's not the happy that's important — it's the ever after. I missed Tom with every ounce of my being, but his absence had not altered the basic structure of the life I lived. What it *had* altered was everything we — Tom and I — had expected would happen next.

Don't get me wrong. We hadn't developed some soulless 'Life Plan', with actions and milestones and all that. All the details of our future might not have been fully worked out, but the sense of it, the look, the shape, the *flavour* of it, certainly was. We knew how our future would feel, and we knew how we would feel about each other. We would live a full life together, and together, we would happily and contentedly grow old.

We'd done pretty well so far. Thanks to Tom, I'd finally made it as a published romance author. Before I'd met Tom, my stories existed only in my head, which was where I used to escape to with a frequency that didn't do a whole lot for my ability to, say, arrive places on time or recall what someone had been saying to me for the last fifteen minutes or indeed remember who they were. Tom persuaded me to start setting my ideas down on paper. It was he who sent my first story off to a weekly woman's magazine, which to my astonishment, accepted it and even paid me for it. I remember Tom flicking through one of the tragically huge stack of copies I'd hoovered up from the stationery shop with a bemused look on his face. 'So, let me get this straight,' he said. 'There's a whole bunch of recipes for cake, the latest celebrity gossip tosh and four pages on how to knit a potholder.' He shook his head. 'Why don't they just cut to the chase and tell their readers how to knit a bloke who looks like Henry Cavill and knows how to bake?'

But he encouraged me to write more, and when I'd written and submitted my first full-length romance to a series of publishers, he pulled me out the funk that I sank into with every rejection letter. 'It'll happen,' he said. 'Not every firm's going to be staffed by morons.' And he was right. The night I got the call, we blew a stack of our savings on dinner at the flashest restaurant in the city, where Tom insisted on addressing the maître'd as 'My good man' and we were almost kicked out for rolling around with laughter when the wine waiter called the pinot gris 'audacious'.

Not long after that, our savings took another hit when Tom scored his dream job as a marketing manager for the national sports body in charge of running. And not long after that, we bought our first house in the area we liked most. It was a bit of a trek to the city, but we were bounded by sea on one side and a forest park on the other. It was peaceful and smelled of ozone and pine. The perfect spot for running *and* writing. Good for body and soul. Good for the two of us.

We were so happy with the house, and with each other. We were a good match, Tom and I. Of course we argued, but no disagreement ever felt terminal, or even, after a night's sleep, that important. We enjoyed each other's company. We enjoyed talking to each other and we enjoyed the life we were building together. Tom made anything seem achievable. Mainly because he truly believed anything was. I know now that if it hadn't been for his single-mindedness and his unwavering self-belief that I would never have become a writer. I'd still be retreating into my head and trying desperately to remember the name of the person in front of me.

We were really looking forward to the next stage, too. The plan was that within two years, we'd have saved enough money to take six months off work, rent out our house and travel around the world. When we came home, we'd start earning again and then we'd have children. Two, at least. We knew we'd be leaving it late — I'd be thirty-seven, thirty-eight by then. But we knew heaps of couples who'd started at that age and even later. We'd be fine, we thought. And then we'd get a dog. We could never agree on the dog. I wanted a big, woolly, cream-coloured retriever thingy. Tom wanted a chihuahua. It seemed an unusual choice for a man who believed the air guitar was a real instrument, but he insisted that chihuahuas were cool. They had attitude, he said. They were the tattooed midget bassists of the dog world, whereas big woolly cream-coloured retrievers were Ed Sheeran.

In any case, after we'd had children and sorted out the dog, I thought I might have a go at becoming a fully-fledged 'proper' author. Tom said that if I did manage to crack the bestseller list big-time, he'd go back to university and do a degree in sports coaching, because what he had always wanted to do was teach people how to run . . .

Do you see? It was all out there, waiting for us. The rest of our life together. It was as real to me as if I could already see and smell and touch it. And now it had gone. My perfect life had stopped the moment Tom died. It was like watching a genie disappearing back into its bottle with a petulant swoosh because you were too slow in making your wish. You are left staring at the stopper, your first reaction one of shock and surprise. But then it dawns on you that the genie will never re-emerge, that your wish will never be heard. You have lost your chance forever. And the regret that follows is almost unbearable.

I kept on. Kept on living in our house, writing my books and avoiding my parents. But I was going nowhere. My half-brother Simon gave me a book by a man who looks like one of those toads Australians like to stamp on but who is apparently a guru. The book was all about living in the now. I know Simon meant well; I know he was trying to help. But without a future, there is no now. It's hollow, empty. When Tom's heart stopped beating, so did the heart of my life, the vital centre that held everything together. Everything that brought my life *alive*, all the joy and affection and laughter and connection, had been plucked out and stripped away. Everything that kept my life in motion, the hopes and dreams, the loving creation of our shared future, had frozen in mid-stride.

Last night, I woke at three in the morning and sat bolt upright in bed. But there was no punching the air with joy. There was only my breath coming in gasps, my heart hammering as if a freight train had thundered past, inches from my head. That's because instead of imaginary conversations between book characters, it was my own life that I was clutching for, desperate to grasp and to hold.

I realised that with nowhere to go, I was in fact going backwards. I was slipping — back to the place I was before I met Tom. Back to when I let myself be bumped along by circumstance because I was never present, never in charge. I realised that if I stayed on this track, I was in danger of waking up one day and finding myself aged seventy-nine, and about to share a tin of pilchards with a cat named Mr Higgins.

I needed to do something — go somewhere — and quickly, before it was too late. Trouble was, I hadn't the foggiest idea where to start.

Chapter Two

LADY MO: No, no! Spent six months at Catchpole London before begging for a transfer to the Charlotte office! London is as grey and depressing as my mother's latest perm! Why not pick somewhere romantic? Like Paris? Surely one cannot bypass the home of Fabrice?

DARRELL: All French I know comes from the song *Lady Marmalade*. Do not want to ask for bread and end up with an unidentifiable bit of cattle beast. Besides, London is home of 1930s fabulousness! Debutantes! Gentlemen's clubs! (like Whites, not like Stringfellows.) Tea at the Ritz! In Miss Marple, they are always going up to town to buy glass cloths and meet at Lyons Corner House. And anyhow, Fabrice was a regular visitor to London, remember? Though he probably wasn't there to buy glass cloths.

LADY MO: Are you aware Lyons Corner House once owned by Nigella Lawson's family?

DARRELL: Nigella aka Lucky Cow?

LADY MO: Same. Although name is Nigella, so…

DARRELL: Forgetting MY name? Anyway, back to London. Where did you live whilst there?

LADY MO: (suppressing shudder) Dalston. Dodgy part. Flat was the size of a raisin box and smelled like the inside of a rubber boot recently occupied by a farmer's damp woollen sock. Surely there are other options? Prague, for instance? Looks like fairyland on Living Channel travel shows.

DARRELL: Prague? Wait. Googling now . . . All right. Prague is beautiful, I'll give you that. However, weather stats indicate it also to be cold as buggery. Google also provided image of Vaclav Havel. Looks like a dying horse. If Vaclav a typical Czech man, then Prague is a no go.

LADY MO: Is a man a mandatory part of your new life?

DARRELL: Yes. Also children. Also a career as bestselling author. And a big woolly cream-coloured dog.

LADY MO: Could it benefit you to relax your parameters just a smidge?

DARRELL: Girl can dream, can't she? (Hint: a good friend would not burst bubble.)

LADY MO: But British men are not the stuff of fantasy! British men are stunted! Weazened! Have teeth that look like joke ones you buy for Halloween!

DARRELL: Yes, but you say that in retrospect of being married to Chad, who looks as if he should be attracting small planetary systems into his orbit.

LADY MO: True. Chad not perfect, though.

DARRELL: ???!!

LADY MO: Harry is perfect. Chad is runner-up. Oo! Idea! Why not come here? Charlotte is a very cool city! Nowhere near backward as the rest of the US South!

DARRELL: You have scooped the perfect life there. With my luck, only suitors will be a man with no front teeth and a banjo wearing a singlet that says 'When I die bury me upside down so the whole world can kiss my ass' or a man sporting a navy blazer with gold buttons and a smile that can only be described using the word 'glint'.

LADY MO: Chad has a navy blazer. But he only wears it when his mother makes him. How about New York? Only short plane trip away from me and my perfect life.

DARRELL: If Sarah Jessica struggled to find a man, what hope for me?

LADY MO: Aware that *Sex and City* is fiction?

DARRELL: Lines blurry.

LADY MO: Also aware that Fabrice lives only in the train station of the mind?

DARRELL: As I say. Blurry . . .

LADY MO: Sigh. Well. Let me know how it goes. And for God's sake, don't live in any part of Dalston.

MICHELLE LAWRENCE (NÉE Horton) was my best friend at school. She got married three years ago to an American investment banker named Chad, and the pair now lived in Charlotte, North Carolina with their first child, Harry, an adorable eighteen-month-old blonde bruiser. Until taking maternity leave, Michelle had been climbing the ranks of a successful law firm called Catchpole, Laycock and Lobb, which managed to sound both faintly rude and entirely English, but which in fact was owned by loud, short Jewish New Yorkers. Despite her previous ambitions, Michelle didn't seem to miss work at all. She was delighted to be a Mommy and quite happy to spend, it seemed to me, an inordinate amount of time watching Dr Phil.

She was convinced she had the perfect life, and let's face it, who was I to doubt her? She'd married into old money, which enabled her to have a house that looked like Tara in the best part of Charlotte, a holiday house in Maine, and a mother-in-law whose neck veins bulged at the slightest breach of social protocol. Michelle became Lady Mo online purely to wind up Mrs Lawrence Senior, who thought any word ending with 'o' sounded like it came out of the mouths of rappers, a breed she placed slightly higher than feminists (but much lower than Democrats). Michelle was waiting for the moment her mother-in-law's pearl choker stopped living on borrowed time and exploded into the four corners of the marble foyer.

Despite his terrifying family and his sit-com joke name, Chad seemed a decent enough bloke, even though my actual acquaintance with him had been limited to Michelle's emails and a few fuzzy digital photos. He didn't seem to be a shagger-arounder, he tolerated her obsession with Dr Phil and he was entirely besotted with their son. He was handsome, too, in the way that you'd expect of a man named Chad. Blonde. Square. Teeth. You know the type.

I was a little surprised at her choice because our romantic ideal had always been a short, dark Frenchman. When

Michelle and I met at age fourteen, I was in the classroom reading Nancy Mitford's *The Pursuit of Love*. Michelle swooped upon me. 'Fabrice,' was all she said.

My God, yes. Fabrice, Duc de Sauveterre. Fiction's most perfect man.

He was based on a real-life lover of Nancy Mitford, and even though he clearly was the great love of her life, she had the awareness to make it an honest portrayal, infidelities and all. Trouble is, that's what makes Fabrice such perfection. Although he conforms to many aspects of the Ultimate Romantic Hero — aristocratic, moneyed and a confident seducer — he is also a short-arse. He is humorous but prone to pomposity. He is courageous but also vain. If Nancy had not made him so human, girls like Michelle and I would have confined him to fantasyland years ago. We wouldn't have deluded ourselves that he could be there, on some railway station in Paris, waiting for us, if only we stepped off the right train . . .

Other fictional things Michelle and I always wished were true:

Magic: When I was fourteen, I wanted magic powers for two reasons only: instant beautification and exacting revenge on mean girls. The idea of using my powers to vanquish evil would have had no appeal, even if it had ever occurred to me. Twenty years later, I was slim enough. Well, let's more accurately say I had an acceptable body mass index, helped along by being reasonably tall. I was pretty enough, too. Thick, dark curly hair, big grey eyes, good skin. Not as radiant as I was when I met Tom, but I didn't feel a need to shriek 'Ai-eeee!' whenever I looked in the mirror. So what would I do now with magical powers? Transform myself into a bestselling author? Chances are I would bungle the spell and end up as Barbara Cartland in her final days, being slowly crushed by the weight of four decades' worth of turquoise eye shadow. Sigh.

Time travel: For me, there is only one place you'd want to travel to: 1930s England, but in the mode of Nancy Mitford and *Poirot* and not, say, *A Handful of Dust* or even *Brideshead Revisited* (mainly because I never got over my disappointment that the book did not include the feverish, sweaty shag-fest between Charles and Julia that was in the TV series). No, to me the 1930s is all about great clothes, hats and gloves, young men called Teddy who drive open-top Bugattis and say 'What ho!' Tennis and garden parties. Country house japes. Jaunts to Monaco and Cap d'Antibes. But where would I travel to in my past? Could I have done anything to prevent what happened to Tom? Was that worth even thinking about? I wasn't sure on either count.

Large, loving, eccentric families: Michelle and I bonded first over Fabrice and secondly over the astonishing dullness of our domestic circles. Michelle's parents divorced when she was twelve and her father went to live in Canada. Michelle's mother muttered bitterly but did nothing interesting, such as take to gin or teenage boys. Michelle and her mother lived in relative harmony in a nice house in a respectable suburb, supported by funds sent monthly from the Yukon or wherever Mr Horton had ended up. My own parents married in their forties, and did not intend to have me at all. My father had never married before; my mother was a widow. She already had one son, my half-brother, Simon, who was nineteen when I was born and had left home. That meant I, like Michelle, was effectively an only child, which is why one of our greatest fantasies was to be surrounded by the kind of families that seem to exist only in novels. The Radletts: Nancy Mitford's thinly fictionalised portrait of her own large, rambunctious, adventurous and oh-so-posh family. The Honeychurches in *A Room with a View*: Lucy and her brother Freddy, that lovely mother and all those people coming and going, all that humour and affection. Don't get me wrong. My parents were kind, intelligent, good-hearted people. But they were not socially gregarious, adventurous or overtly affectionate. My father would never send his daughters out to be hunted by baying hounds, like Nancy Mitford's 'Farve'. He was a retired dentist alert to ubiquitous (in his opinion) crimes of grammar. My mother was mildly animated by only two things: Pringle cardigans and the correct way to prune a shrub. Eccentricity, to my parents, was not an appealing quality; it was the first sign of an inevitable slide towards exposing oneself to young women in public parks, or yelling incoherent abuse at passing cars on your way back to your home and your fifty-three cats. My parents were careful people who had arranged their lives to suit, and who were not keen on disruption of any kind. Tom's death was a disruption, but one they understood. Mum's first husband had died of pancreatic cancer, rather slowly and awfully. I think, when Tom died, she wanted to give me more than a quick hug and the usual clichés of consolation, but found it beyond her. I didn't mind. Sometimes what you know is unsaid says enough . . .

Anyway — back to my big move. The idea had come to me, as you may have already guessed, at three in the morning. In the cold light of day it seemed nothing but terrifying. But after a mental struggle where I reminded myself that Fabrice only found Linda because she ventured abroad, I decided I'd do it. I mean, why not? There was nothing for me here. Nothing but memories that made me sad. If I was to make a new start, why not in a new place surrounded by all-new people? London was the place that popped immediately into my head, along with numerous images that I knew to be at least ninety years out of date, but which proved clinchingly seductive nonetheless.

The reality, of course, was that I knew no one there. I had no idea where I should live and no idea where to start looking. Normally, now that Tom wasn't here to lend me a spine, I would have given up the task at once as too enormous. But, somewhat to my surprise, I didn't. Instead, I emailed my friends overseas and asked them for advice.

It wasn't Michelle who answered first. It was Adam, who

had studied English with me at university and now worked as a script editor in Los Angeles. Adam's specialty was horror movies, mostly ones that went straight to video. He cared not a jot because he got paid the same, regardless. And he had a great life, surrounded as he was by buff, bronzed, gay aspiring actors. The only thing Adam had in common with them was that he was gay, but he was 'in the business', so despite being gangly, white and skinny, he got laid all the time.

Adam's email said he had a friend in London, who had recently got married to some 'fabulously rich bloke' but who hadn't wanted to give up her independence entirely and still owned a house in North London that she would be prepared to rent out for the pitiful amount I had proposed. The catch was that she was having the place renovated.

Clare says — continued Adam — *that if you don't mind men hammering around you, and I know I wouldn't (please note that clichéd jokes like this are the mainstay of my writing career), then you're welcome to take it. She'd just love to have someone in there because she is very attached to the house, and can't bear to see it empty and unloved. Note she is not actually crazy but five months pregnant and thus a seething tempest of hormones. If you are keen, here are her details . . .*

I have to say, I wasn't keen. Hammers and flashes of builder butt were a far cry from tennis and Teddy. I waited until lunchtime to see if anyone else had any leads, but my inbox remained empty. So I gave in and emailed Simon. He did do a lot of traveling, even if it was usually straight up a rock face. Simon, now fifty-three, was a scientist who studied waves and tides. He isn't as bad as that might make him seem. True, he has a stringy beard and a possibly pathological attachment to Birkenstock sandals, but he also likes to take off to Patagonia and suchlike places with the sole aim of clambering to the top of stark and inhospitable mountains. He can suspend himself from a rock ledge by one hand and knows how to survive an avalanche. If the world was faced with disaster in the next few years, I would be bunking down with Simon and his sandals.

Know anyone in London? said my email.

He emailed me back. *I know the Queen. Does that count? Of course, I'm not sure she's all that familiar with me. May I ask why you want to know?*

No. He couldn't. Because that would mean I'd have to tell my mother. Ours might not have been the closest family in the world, but I suspected it was easier for her nerves to have me nearby. I'd heard her complain often enough about Simon's jaunts to Kathmandu and Machu Picchu and suchlike. No, that's not true — she didn't openly complain. Just came out with statements like, 'Well, I assume he's kept up with his vaccinations' or 'Perhaps it's a good thing after all that he never married.'

Actually, to be honest, the reason I didn't want to tell my mother wasn't that I thought she would find it unsettling. The reason was that *I* was unsettled. To be completely frank, I was a wreck.

My God! The money required to shift countries! In my books, all my heroines had to do to be whipped off around the world was to get a job as a billionaire's marketing manager. Right now, there didn't seem to be any such vacancies currently available (and yes, tragically, I did look). So what I had to do was as follows:

- Email my editor to check if payments would still be the same if moved to another country. Answer yes, i.e. in New Zealand dollars, as per contract.
- Research the average rental of a half-decent two-bedroom flat in a half-decent part of London (as judged via Google images and reference to Agatha Christie).
- Research what I could rent out my house for. Ring

property management company, who suggest much lower figure, due to soft rental market.

- Work out the exchange rate between British pounds and New Zealand dollars.
- Downgrade expectation to one bedroom and/or studio flat.
- Look at cost of flights from here to London. Think about going off and having a little cry.
- Ring up and ask bank if I could break the term deposit that I had put Tom's life insurance money into (feeling sick throughout the entire conversation). Answer, yes 'but penalties apply'.
- Find out how much 'penalties' amount to.
- Downgrade expectation to room above pawnshop and/or all-night takeaway.
- Go off and have a little cry.
- Check inbox once last time to see if anyone has come up with offer better than Adam's.
- Go to bed at half-past eight because knackered.

And then, of course, I woke up again at three a.m. convinced that the move was impossible because I would run out of money, be kicked out of my rental and, friendless and penniless, end up starving on the street or dying of hypothermia or being stabbed by some drug-crazed homeless person, whose makeshift home I'd trespass on in my desperate search for food and shelter . . .

With all those mental gremlins clamouring for my attention, it took me a while to work out what I was really terrified of. And it was far worse than any fear of starvation or stabbing by a random loon. I was truly, deeply afraid that what Tom and I had was not to be repeated in my lifetime. I was afraid that it was true that there was someone for everyone, and my someone had been Tom and that was that. I was afraid

Michelle was right and that my dream lover did, and always would, exist only in a dream.

I ate my breakfast in the kitchen that Tom and I had painted over a weekend. I'd wanted a brighter green, but Tom had said a softer colour would work better and he'd been right. I could see out the French doors to the small back garden. It was autumn and I knew that in a couple of months, all the flowers would be gone. But I also knew that in spring they'd all be back again, as they had every year since Tom and I bought this house.

I knew the routine of this life. I knew what I was in for. It would be so much easier to do nothing. I wouldn't have to worry about money. I wouldn't have to try to find someone new — and to risk discovering that there was no one. That Tom had been it . . .

So that was my choice. Leave and take all those risks. Stay and do — what? Slide inevitably towards old age and pilchards?

I checked the details Adam had sent me again. And emailed a woman I didn't know about a house I really wasn't sure I could afford.

Chapter Three

THE PLANE LANDED at five-thirty in the morning. Customs wasn't the aggressive nightmare I'd been led to believe (but this had come from Simon, who, Lord love him, does sport the kind of beard that has customs agents reaching for the snappy gloves), and after a brief scrimmage through the crowds waiting for loved ones who weren't me, I found myself in the airport proper. It was now twenty-five past six. I'd been told that the Heathrow Express would take fifteen minutes to drop me at Paddington and from there it would be, at this early hour, no more than twenty minutes by cab to Islington. I had arranged to meet my new landlord — landlady, I suppose, although that conjured up a vision of housecoats, cabbage and disapproval — at nine o'clock. So by my jet-lagged calculation, that left me with two hours to kill.

I considered spending it in the airport, but the entire place seemed to be dedicated to funnelling you into the exit chutes as quickly as possible. And there were soldiers with machine guns. I'd never seen machine guns in the flesh, so to speak. They made me feel guilty and anxious, even though I knew that all I had in my jolly orange wheely-case was a sponge bag and as many clothes as I could fit, and in the backpack I took on board a flight pillow shaped like a Polish sausage and all four volumes of Anthony Powell's *A Dance to the Music of Time*, which had proved heavy going in more ways than one. I decided to catch the Heathrow Express and see what Paddington Station had to offer.

The answer was an ethereally brilliant vaulted glass roof and a few half-decent snack bars, but nowhere I'd feel comfortable sitting for two hours. Stations and airports are the places between. They're neither where you've come from nor where you want to go. I found myself a cab and asked him to take me to any café within walking distance of my new home that would be open by the time we got there.

When we stopped, my heart sank. Two minutes earlier, we'd zipped into a big street lined with shops and restaurants, and busy with vehicles and commuters now that the working day had properly begun. But then we'd hurtled off down a side street, where there was nothing but slightly grubby terrace dwellings and, on one corner, a rather forbidding-looking school. The school down the end of my street back home had low wooden fences, a wide-open entranceway and a big, well-kept grass field. This school had a cracked concrete court and bars on the windows.

At that corner, the taxi had turned sharp left and braked only seconds later. We pulled into a small cul-de-sac parallel to the main road, a piece of waste ground in front of us and a row of dingy shops beside us, culminating in what did appear to be a very small café. On the main road were more terraced houses and what looked like a huge council estate. The only vaguely attractive building anywhere was a church a little way up the road, alone on a scrubby island of green, sheltered by a few nice trees. I realized that if the taxi driver had got it right, my new house must be close by. I began to wonder what I'd let myself in for.

'You're dahn there,' said the driver. I had felt the need to make nervous chat on the way, and as a result had told him where I was going to live. He was pointing down a small side street off the main road, lined by a short row of terraced houses on one side and the massed squat blocks of council estate on the other. The houses looked neat enough. So for that matter did the estate. Which made me feel half a degree better.

'It used to be bleedin' rough, that estate,' said my driver, who was clearly straight out of Central Casting for the role of wry, street-wise Cockney. 'It's been cleaned up. Notser bad now. And 'ere's the caff,' he added, nodding to our left. 'Pair of Eye-talians. They do a good brew.'

'Are you from around here?' I asked.

He turned. He was in his early fifties, grey hair smoothed back in a thinning Teddy-boy quiff, skin roughened and yellowed by years of dedicated smoking. He hooked his thumb over his shoulder.

'I might 'ave been one of the reasons they needed to 'ave a clean-up,' he grinned. 'But I came right in the end. Want a hand with yer bags?'

I hesitated a fraction and his grin widened. 'Like I said, it's notser bad now. You won't 'ave any trouble.'

But as the cab rumbled away, I could see he'd stopped grinning and was now laughing. For that reason, I eyed up his choice of 'caff' with some mistrust. Its entrance was a flap in a plastic tent-like arrangement attached to the front of the building. Then tent's purpose was obviously to provide shelter for the small number of tables within it. Presumably in summer, it was taken down. Or not — I'd heard that British summers were notoriously crap. It was early May now and the forecast was for about thirteen degrees. The temperature had a fair way to go before it reached that.

It occurred to me that I was both cold and starving. New Zealand was twelve hours ahead so seven o'clock meant dinnertime. And in three hours it would be bedtime. In truth, after close to thirty hours traveling, I wanted to go to bed right now. But it would be another two hours before I could meet my landlady. I wheeled my jolly orange bag into the café and ordered a strong double espresso and big fat ham and cheese croissant.

Of course, when I looked around properly, I saw there were no free tables. There weren't many tables to start off with and all of them already held one or two people. At the back, near the door to the bathroom, there was a table for four, with only one man at it, sitting in typical man fashion with the newspaper up in front of his face. I dithered for a moment, but decided I was too frazzled to be unselfish. I strode up to the table and pulled out a chair. One corner of the newspaper was lowered, and a dark brown eye appeared, its eyebrow raised in enquiry.

'Can I sit here?' I said.

'Sure.' The voice was gruff and deep, but seemed friendly enough in a neutral, 'I couldn't give a monkey's' kind of way.

The newspaper went back up. I sat down. My coffee came, delivered with a smile and a '*Buon giorno*' by what I deduced was one of the 'Eye-talians'. He was in his late forties, balding, nice looking. I decided I liked him.

I also liked his café. Now that I had time to look around, I could see it was a deli, too, its floor-to-ceiling shelves packed with pasta and olives, canned tomatoes and boxes of panettone, bottles of wine, olive oil and balsamic vinegar. There was a gelato freezer and a counter full of fresh-made baking, salads and pasta dishes. My heart lifted a degree more. This was quite civilized really. A civilized wee oasis surrounded by crud.

My croissant came. I'd ordered it toasted, and it was golden warm and oozing with cheese. Too ravenous for the niceties of knife and fork, I picked it up and stuffed it in my mouth. It was delicious, and I may have given a little moan of pleasure because there was a rustle and the newspaper was lowered again. I found myself face to face with two brown eyes and eyebrows now knitted in a frown.

I brushed stray buttery crumbs off my cheeks. 'Sorry,' I mumbled. 'Starving.'

But my table companion was staring at my croissant, not at me. He muttered something that I could have sworn was 'Fucking unfair'.

'Excuse me?'

He stared at me, still frowning. 'Bacon?' he demanded.

I checked. 'No. Definitely ham.'

'Mmph.'

He raised the paper again. Clearly that was the end of what could hardly be called a conversation. I glanced around to see if there were any free tables, but there were none, and there was a constant stream of people in and out the door. I got the impression that this timeslot belonged to the pre-work crowd, the lucky ones able to sit for a while, others with longer journeys or earlier clocking-in times stopping only to grab a cup of coffee and a paper bag of something to keep them going. I imagined that around eight-thirty the work crowd would start to thin. And then who would come in? Too early for mothers and babies — they're more mid-morning if my friends who've bred have told me right. Who then?

I finished my croissant and surreptitiously picked up all the crumbs with a dampened fingertip. I checked my watch. Barely seven-thirty! An hour and a bloody half to go! The shops wouldn't be open and after my conversation with the cabbie, I didn't feel safe wheeling my suitcase around the neighbourhood. I guessed I could always smack any mugger across the head with my book-laden backpack — probably the most enjoyment I'd get out of the *Dance* quartet — but decided I wasn't keen to put that theory to the test.

It made me think about my last conversation with my parents. It was at their house — after I left home, they'd bought a newer, smaller place. It is very tidy and everything matches, including my parents. There is one spare room, but it will never be for guests. My parents don't do guests. My mother is the kind of person who has guest soaps that remain intact and unused for decades. My mother *dusts* her guest soaps.

Anyway, I digress. My parents took my news well. I suppose they had little choice; I am thirty-four after all, not seventeen. But they weren't thrilled. My mother said, 'Well, I imagine security is much tighter now since those last bombings.' My father said, 'I do anticipate that the New Zealand dollar will fall still further against the pound. But I expect you have made provision for a suitable financial buffer.' Then he offered me a dry sherry. As you can probably guess, I accepted. I may even have downed it in one gulp . . .

I checked my watch again. Seven thirty-three. Sigh. I stared at the newspaper my table companion was holding up. I know it's rude to read other people's papers but it wasn't as if he could see me, having erected The Great Wall of *Guardian* between us. But the headlines — every one of them — mentioned people I'd never heard of. I found that completely depressing. Not only did I have to start my own life from scratch, I had to get to know a whole different bunch of politicians, media people and minor celebrities. The page was like a code I had to figure out how to break before I had any chance of feeling as if I belonged here. I felt like sinking my forehead onto the table in despair. I would have, too, if there'd been enough room.

Suddenly, the paper was snapped up into brisk folds and slapped down onto the table. My companion was revealed as a broad-shouldered man in his mid-forties, with dark, close-cropped hair and a strong-featured, olive-skinned face. Not handsome as such — not handsome at all really, but attractive in the way that self-confident people are. He was wearing a smart black suit, a white shirt and plain blue-striped tie. He exuded affluence and impatience in equal measure. I could not even begin to guess what he did for a living. To be honest, he looked like the kind of shadowy underworld figure whose life would be turned into a movie starring Robert de Niro or, if budget was an issue, Ian McShane. In either case, there would be a dead pizza delivery boy and at least one ear-slicing scene.

Gangster-man, too, was checking his watch. He blew out a breath, as if it was nowhere near the time he'd hoped it was. Then, to my consternation, he looked right at me.

'I could go home,' he said. 'But then I'd have to come back. Which would be a waste of fucking time.'

He sounded just like the cab driver — straight out of *East-Enders*. In my mind, Ian McShane just lost the role to Ross Kemp.

'I see . . .'

'I can't order another coffee because it's bad for my nerves and I can't order any food worth eating because it's bad for my arteries. How's your cholesterol?'

'I — have no idea.'

He wagged an admonitory finger at me. 'You should do. That's the problem. You think you're young and invincible and then — whammo. You hit forty and you're fucked. Always pays to get checked out early. You don't want any nasty surprises. Death, for example. God's ultimate I-fucking-told-you-s—'

He stopped short because he'd seen my face. Myself, I had no idea how I looked at moments like these; I was always too busy concentrating on just trying to breathe. But from his reaction, which was identical to that of many, many people before him, I suspected I went very pale, very quickly. There may also have been a light sheen of sweat. My palms certainly felt clammy enough.

'Jesus,' he said, wide-eyed. 'What brought that on?' He leaned forward with a frown. 'You're not pregnant, are you?'

The surprise of it actually made me laugh. And I started to breathe again. 'No!'

'My wife's pregnant. Five months. Her moods are — well, unpredictable doesn't go halfway there. It's like being stalked by a ninja assassin; one minute you're whistling in the sunshine, the next you're diving for cover into the nearest ditch. She cries at the drop of a hat. I can't let her read the paper anymore, or watch the news. Someone gave her *The Velveteen Rabbit* at her baby shower and she started crying just looking at the cover. I hid it. I mean, God help us if she'd got all the way to the end.'

'Congratulations,' I managed to say. 'About the baby, I mean.'

'Yeah—' He grinned, and went unexpectedly and rather charmingly pink. 'Thanks.' Then he frowned. 'What did I say to I upset you?'

'Oh—' Now it was my turn to go pink. I avoided his eye. 'No, I'm just jet-lagged—'

But then, of course, I reached for my coffee cup and sent it flying. I'd forgotten to give my hands time to stop shaking. There was hardly any coffee left, but it proved too much for the flimsy paper napkin, which instantly began to disintegrate. Even though it was futile, I kept on dabbing. Silently, my companion extracted a white handkerchief from his pocket and handed it to me.

It didn't stay white for long. I glanced at the stained ball of cotton in my hand and bit my lip in apology.

He waved his hand briskly, impatiently. 'Keep it.' Then he said, 'Jet-lag doesn't usually send you into a funk like that. What's up?'

Jeepers. I couldn't decide if I found his directness irksome or a relief. But it was clear he wouldn't give up until I answered. So I did—

'My husband died.'

He sat back, surprised. 'Accident?'

'Duff heart. No one knew.'

'How long ago?'

'Quite a while. But I still get hit by—' I went pink again. 'I don't know what they are really. I call them grief bombs.'

He stared at me. 'I'm sorry. I'm really sorry. That's fucking terrible.'

Time for the awkward pause. It always came at this point. When the other person tried to think of a way to shift either the conversation to another topic — or themselves towards the door.

But then he said, 'If Clare died, I'd go as far away as possible. Probably spend the rest of my life holed up in some cave in Azerbaijan, wallowing in misery and yak's piss.'

'Are there caves in Azerbaijan?'

He blinked at me, then grinned. 'I have no fucking idea.'

He gestured at my empty cup. 'Want another? Nerves say I shouldn't but I say fuck 'em.'

I tested my own nerves and found them to have settled. I was, in fact, feeling remarkably chipper. For that, I believe I owed a big thank you to this large, strange man's directness. Most people would sooner pluck out their eyeballs than talk about stuff like this. But then, I suspected that the man across the table wasn't even a little bit like most people.

I smiled at him gratefully. 'I'd love another. Thank you.'

When he stood up, I realized that he was not only broad but also very tall — at least six foot four, I'd have said. In his black suit, he was quite a formidable presence, but the Italian man at the counter greeted him with relaxed cheer and they chatted away. My companion was obviously a regular — and, I had to concede (with some disappointment) no gangster. There'd definitely be more cringing and nodding if he'd been dodgy. Also a pinkie ring.

My mind started to turn him into a character in a book. This is a terrible habit and one I need to watch. I only do it with people I don't know very well and it's for the best that we remain unacquainted — because I have met the odd person again and begun talking to them about something they'd done, only to realise that that something was a product entirely of my own invention and they didn't have the first clue what I was on about. Quite embarrassing. Not to be recommended.

Hard to stop, though. Fantasising, I mean. By the time he returned to the table, I had mentally made him over so he now looked like a taller Henry Cavill, given him a murky past — how *did* he make his fortune? — and decided he was locked up emotionally, in denial about his deep love for an innocent, beautiful school teacher (Emilia Clarke with a bun and glasses). I was musing on a name for her — Clare wasn't bad, but I was leaning towards something even more old-fashioned and intellectual, like Margaret—

He'd said something. I knew he had because he was looking at me both expectantly and a little askance. Lost in my own head, I had heard not a word, and was quite surprised to find he looked nothing like Henry Cavill.

'Sorry?'

He continued. 'I said, my wife was supposed to meet some bloke this morning, but she had to go to work instead and asked me to do it. I swore she said it was for eight o'clock, but she insists she told me nine. I'm not about to argue with her; I'm too attached to my parts. But only bacon and coffee are going to make it worth hanging round here any longer, worse fucking luck.'

A small bell rang. 'Wait. Your wife is called Clare?'

'Yeah. Why?'

'I may be the bloke.'

He regarded me for a beat. 'I can't even—'

I stuck out my hand. 'My name is Darrell. Unusual, I know. Not sure of my parents' rationale, but there you go—'

He returned my handshake. 'I'm Patrick. My parents were Irish. Don't have to be Einstein to make that link.'

I clocked his dark hair and eyes and olive skin. 'You don't look very Irish.'

He hesitated a second. 'Romani. Once known as Gypsies.'

'Really? How romantic!'

'If you classify dirt poor and socially untouchable as romantic, then — yeah.'

Mentally, I slapped myself. I could be a real moron sometimes.

He saved me by changing the subject. 'So you're OK to live with all the building work going on?' It seemed more a question of my sanity than anything.

'I can't afford not to.'

He nodded. Despite his affluent appearance, I got the distinct feeling he knew exactly what it was like to count his pennies and find there simply weren't enough.

'You done with that coffee?' he asked.

As he'd drained his in one mouthful and was already half out of his chair, my answer could only be 'Yes.'

'Right,' he said. 'Let's go to the house.'

Then he lifted my wheely-case with one hand as if it were no heavier than his newspaper and headed to the door. I hurried behind him, trying to keep pace with his long strides. The nice Italian called after us, '*Ciao*. See you tomorrow.'

I'm sure he meant the man in front, his regular customer, and not me. But as I took a last glance over my shoulder at the small café, I wondered. If I came here again — who else might I meet . . .?

And then I realized a really big man had just taken my wheely-case and if I didn't get a move on I mightn't see either of them again.

Chapter Four

LADY MO: The house is gorgeous! I love those little square Georgian terraces. How many bedrooms?

DARRELL: Only two. Mine has a big white squishy bed in it. I feel like the Little Princess. Before she got imprisoned in the attic, of course.

LADY MO: Lovely colours — all that soft greeny-blue in the living room. Chad's mother insists on calling it the parlour, which is why I always call it the lounge. Her neck veins bulge but she can do nothing to me. I am mother of the Heir.

DARRELL: My mother has what she calls a drawing room. I think it has been occupied by actual humans only twice in living memory. And never by dust. Any sensible dust speck would be far too afraid.

LADY MO: Thank God and Gloria Steinem that we don't feel compelled to keep our houses like that. Although the apple porridge layers on my kitchen table are reaching critical mass. I may have to get out the blowtorch. Speaking of which – when is your gorgeous house due to be demolished?

DARRELL: Not all of it's going to be demolished. Just the kitchen and bathroom.

LADY MO: Bathroom singular? What will you do when out of action? Shower at gym?

DARRELL: Ha! (Hollow laugh.) Cannot afford library membership let alone gym.

LADY MO: What then? Rent a Portaloo? Dig a hole in the back garden?

DARRELL: Why this fascination with toilet arrangements?

LADY MO: Harry is starting potty training. It's very exciting!

DARRELL: For you . . .

LADY MO: Point harsh but taken. Changing subject now. Assume you Googled your landlord?

DARRELL: Of course. He is fabulously rich. Made a fortune in property.

LADY MO: Google images show a scary huge man. Is that 'property' with inverted commas? Like 'waste disposal' or 'gentleman's entertainment'?

DARRELL: Admit his looks suggest that as a possibility. But he is far too lovely.

LADY MO: Sudden passion for huge and scary??!!

DARRELL: No! Loveliness refers to his personality! He makes me laugh. Swears like trooper. Feel I could talk to him about anything.

LADY MO: Yikes! Besotted?

DARRELL: Fortunately not. I'd be fresh out of luck if I was. He is COMPLETELY besotted with pregnant landlady wife. No. Sigh. My affection stems from a whole other source. It is like the time when you were eleven and the wallflower at the school dance and a boy finally asked you to dance and you were so grateful that you followed him round like a big-eyed puppy until you drove him nuts.

LADY MO: I never did that. That is sad. Is your point to make me pity you?

DARRELL: No. Point is that pathetic gratitude is making me latch on to anyone who is nice to me. Italian men at café are also nice. I order more coffees than I can afford just so they will be nice to me for bit longer. Also having bursts of affection for a dodgy bloke on a bike who has twice yelled obscenities at me while riding by.

LADY MO: Explain the affection aspect?

DARRELL: At least he noticed me! I am feeling invisible. Swallowed up by big city.

LADY MO: Why not look for another gorgeous house but in a small picturesque English village? You could have Miss Marple as a neighbour and a humorous address such as The Tit's Nest, Upper Todger?

DARRELL: Have you seen country cottage rental prices??? Only affordable picturesque village = in farthest part of Scotland where if frostbite won't get you, mutant midges will.

LADY MO: Then I will adopt the 'no-sugar-coating' tone of Dr Phil, and instruct you to get off your butt and go out and meet people.

DARRELL: I would if not prevented by one thing. Namely cowardice.

LADY MO: You met Tom. He was a complete stranger.

DARRELL: We met each other. I didn't do anything to make happen. It just happened.

LADY MO: When I met Chad he was surrounded by bimbos. I waded through and punted them out of the way. Bimbos had no chance. Nor did Chad for that matter.

DARRELL: But what if I introduce myself to someone and find them so boring I crave to slit my wrists?

LADY MO: Won't know til you try. Ha, ha, ha!

DARRELL: Wow. You're the best friend a girl could ever have.

LADY MO: Will be your only friend if you continue to be a big girl's blouse.

DARRELL: Point harsh but taken. Sigh. All right. I will get off my butt and be brave.

LADY MO: Atta girl! If he knew or cared that you existed, Dr Phil would be very proud.

YOU MIGHT BE THINKING that 'romance writer' sounds intriguing and possibly even glamorous. In my head, it is both those things. In practical reality, it is a job, as it is for most writers who don't have '#1 Bestseller!' on their book covers. Which is, as it happens, most writers. My job is to create a product that people want to buy. I need to put in regular hours and deliver to a deadline. I'm paid adequately but not a lot. I could be paid more if I promoted myself better, or if I wrote single title instead of category romances, or if my category was one of the hot favourites, such as paranormal urban fantasy—

Sorry. Let me explain. Romance fiction is split into two basic types — category romance and single title. Category romances are 'categorised' by a specific theme or genre. The first romances were all in one category: Boy meets Girl. Now, the categories include Contemporary (sex and modern realism), Romantic Suspense (sex and mystery), Historical (sex and codpieces), Paranormal (sex and non-humans), Young Adult (thinking about sex), and Traditional (absolutely no sex as it spoils the lovely story).

Category romances are sold as a packaged line, each identified by a name like *Captivate* or *Smouldering Liaisons*, which is essentially a key to how filthy the books are. A whole new set of books per line is issued around every three weeks, so they don't stay on the shelves long.

My books are in the Contemporary category, part of a packaged line called *Love Magnates* (yes, I'm sorry, but I had nothing to do with it). As a category romance writer, I am one of a pool of a few thousand worldwide. Most of my fellows are very happy to write categories. Some of us — me included, though I'd done nothing about it — aspire to move up to single title.

Why? Because unlike category romances, single titles are just that: stand-alone books that stay on the shelf as long as they continue to sell. If you want to make a name — and more money — then you need to write single title. It could mean the difference between seeing your books on the *New York Times* bestseller list and in the airport bookshop bargain bin marked down to 99p.

So how do you become a single-title writer? The easiest way is to be invited to do so by your publisher. If you've shown promise in your category romances, you might be asked to step up. So far, I hadn't been.

I could blame it on the Hipster. She is my editor, one of many employed by my publisher. Her name is — it sounds like I make this stuff up, but I kid you not — Hippolyte McManus. She hails from Queens, in Noo Yawk. I speak to her by phone maybe twice a year, and when she ends each call, she always says 'It's been real'. The rest of the time, we email. It is she who calls herself the Hipster. It says much about her personality that she never notices that I don't.

I am contracted to write three books a year. That might sound like a lot, but my kind of book is only fifty thousand words long — around half the length of a single title, and a fifth the size of a Jilly Cooper, bless her. There is precious little research to do, apart from compiling my Condé Nast scrapbook, which I can do in an evening over a few glasses of wine. My sentences need not be literature, just literate. Usually, it would take me about five weeks to finish my first draft. Then I'd sit on it for a week, re-read it to check that it wasn't *total* bollocks, and send it to the Hipster. She'd dash back an email with a list of questions — why does Pierce take the call from his ex on page eleven? Why is Daisy so polite to him when he's being such an asshole? And what's with the damn tiara — has anyone worn a tiara since Lady Di croaked? I'd do my best to explain and/or rewrite until she was happy with it. Then I'd be sent a few advance copies of the published book. Then I'd be paid.

But this time I was a bit anxious. I'd sent her *Bought for the Billionaire's Private Collection* before I left New Zealand, and normally by now we'd have started the toing and froing. An editor of action, was the Hipster. But maybe she'd had a deluge of manuscripts? Maybe she was away?

There was undoubtedly a good explanation. And let's face it — pretty much anything beyond the act of breathing made me anxious right now.

Which meant that, despite Michelle's pep talk, there was no way in hell I'd have the gumption to introduce myself to the other regulars at the café. I'd gone there frequently enough now to identify which people were regulars — but I hadn't yet been brave enough to even catch an eye. All I did was hide myself behind my book.

Like a coward.

A chicken.

Book, book, book . . .

It was even more pathetic because my presence had taken the total of regulars from three to four. As in me and three others. You'd think I'd have the balls to say hello to three people. Ha! You'd be wrong!

And if you weren't questioning my level of balls, you were probably asking: why the hell was she spending all this time in a café when the sights of one of the greatest cities in the world lay waiting and as yet unseen? Fair enough, and I had no good reason. I only had a bad one, which was the same as before: cowardice. I felt so tentatively connected to this new place that even venturing off to neighbouring Highbury seemed like a risk. I felt as if I was only just starting to become visible – the Italians knew my name now, the girls in the next door chemist said 'Hi' – and if I left for too long, they might forget about me. I simply could not go off and be an anonymous sightseer without knowing I could return to a place where people acknowledged my existence. They might not know me personally yet – but they at least made me feel I was alive and not some invisible, nameless ghost.

That's why I never really relaxed at the café. I was vigilant, observant – no one who came in escaped my notice. I began to know who worked in the shops and businesses next door. There was the chatty woman, who I think was from the NHS doctor's surgery next to the chemist, who bought a custard tart for 'Dr Graham, he *does* love his tarts' (actually, I did make that up; sorry, but it was only a matter of time), the guy who looked like an architect (black polo-neck jersey, black-rimmed spectacles, smug expression) who'd take away a half-decaf soy latté, and an elderly man, most likely the vicar of the church up the street, who every morning collected a ham and cheese croissant and a sticky bun. Bearing in mind Patrick's warning, either his cholesterol was excellent or he was looking forward to passing on.

I never saw my landlord. He was at the café early, when he was there at all. I knew this because I had now met my landlady, his wife. Clare told me this when she came round to visit me. Her motivation for dropping by, it quickly became clear, was less to check out her new tenant and more to find out if I had designs on her husband — which would, of course, leave her no option but to stab me through the heart.

It was the day after I'd moved in. The house came mostly furnished, so all I'd had to do was unpack the clothes I'd bought with me in my orange suitcase, find a place for my laptop, and put my four Anthony Powells in the bookshelf, where they sat surrounded by empty space. Before I left, I'd had a moment of book-separation panic, and seriously considered packing them all up and shipping them over. But then I had a reverse panic about them being diverted to Abu Dhabi or hefted overboard if the ship needed to shed ballast in a storm. I calmed myself by reasoning that I could always buy more books, or if that proved too expensive, I could join the library. All the same, on that first day, the empty bookshelf gave me a twinge. Even the *Dance* quartet didn't deserve that kind of treatment.

I got myself a mobile, so I could ring to get the power put on. This, amazingly, was done by the end of the day. I had thought Britain to be a nightmare of bureaucracy, where dead people moved faster, but apparently not. I was all set at home. Now all I needed was a bank account, a National Insurance number, and to register with the tax department as self-employed, and I would be a fully paid-up, contributing member of society.

I should add, just in case you're worried, that not any stray rooster from New Zealand can rock up and live here. We *are* allowed to work here until the day we turn twenty-seven, whereupon Immigration comes knocking at our flat in Earls Court or wherever we hang out now, and tells us to sling our hook back home. After that, we need a British passport. I had one because Dad was born in Guildford. Thank you, Dad. If not for him, my choice of escape venues would have been limited to Bondi Beach, three tiny Pacific atolls or Scott Base on the Antarctic ice shelf.

Anyway, back to the visit from the landlady. She knocked on the door at seven forty-five in the morning. Fortunately, thanks to jet-lag, I had been up and dressed since five. Ever since the day the young policemen came around about Tom, I've found knocks on the door unnerving, and all the more so when they occur early. So I was already a bit unnerved when I answered the door. My anxiety increased tenfold when a very beautiful pregnant woman with glossy chestnut hair said accusingly, 'You know, I thought you were a man, too.'

Without introducing herself, she walked right in. 'I mean — I *know* Adam said "she", but I thought he was talking about "one of the girls" in the gay sense—'

She paused in front of the bookshelf and frowned at my Powells. 'Are those mine?'

'Er, no, they're—'

She strode through into the tiny kitchen and lifted the lid of the kettle to check if it held water. She opened a cupboard and started to reach for a mug. Then her hand paused in mid-air and slowly she turned. 'This isn't my house.'

'Well—'

She cradled her face in her hands and shook her head from side to side.

'Oh, my God—' she said in a muffled voice.

She dropped her hands and gave me a smile that was part sheepish, part annoyed, as if some of this was my fault.

'My brains are mush,' she said. 'And I've no idea if it will get any better. Who knows what level of mental disintegration I have to look forward to?'

'My friend says it reaches its peak when you're breastfeeding. Soon as you stop, your faculties start to come back.'

'Right. Well, that's as good an argument for bottle-feeding as I've ever heard.'

She smiled, less frostily this time, and stuck out her hand. 'Let's start again. I'm Clare King. And I'd love to be able to assure you that I won't barge on in again, but anything's possible.'

I shook her hand. 'I'm Darrell Kincaid. And I'm sorry I'm not a man.'

'Darrell is an unusual name for a girl, isn't it? Was it one of those family names that are supposed to be passed down through the male line but are inflicted on girls when there are no boys born? Like it was on Richmal Crompton?'

'I don't think so. To be honest, I've never asked my parents. I always felt they might be concerned I didn't like it.'

'Surely they've been asked by other people?'

'No. My parents are not the kind of people other people ask personal questions of. If you see what I mean.'

'Yes. I think I do. Are they in favour of doilies?'

'Also antimacassars.'

Suddenly, my landlady's eyes widened. She strode to the mantelpiece where I'd placed a couple of photos, including one of Tom and me. But that wasn't the photo she picked up.

'Oh my God, what a gorgeous baby. How old is he?'

'That's Harry. He was about nine months there. He's—'

I got no further. She clasped the photo to her chest and I saw her eyes well up.

'He's so — *beautiful . . .*'

'Yes, he—'

'I can't believe how beautiful babies are,' she whispered. 'They're so *perfect*, and so *tiny*, and so *vulnerable . . .*'

Her voice petered out and she stood there, hugging Harry's photo to her, tears running silently down her cheeks. I was tempted to size up the distance to the nearest exit. But I deemed it more prudent to say, 'Um . . . Would you like some tea?'

It seemed to do the trick. She heaved in a breath. Then she glanced down, realised that she was holding the photo in a death grip and hastily placed it back on the mantelpiece. She ran a finger under her eyes and then began to rummage in her coat pockets.

'Shit. I don't have a tissue—'

My bag was on the table next to us. I pulled out the white handkerchief and handed it to her.

'It's covered in coffee,' I apologised. 'But I think that corner's OK.'

She took it with a wan, grateful smile. But as she held it up to her face, her expression hardened.

'This is Patrick's,' she accused.

'Oh. Yes. He lent it to me yesterday. Sorry, I was going to—'

'*Why* did he lend it to you?'

'Um . . . I spilled some coffee. Hence the coffee stains.' I made a conciliatory face. 'I was going to wash it and give it back to him.'

'When?'

Jeepers. I shrugged. 'At the café?'

'He's hardly ever there,' she said, immediately. 'And if he is, he's there *very* early. He'd be long gone by now,' she added, to drive home the point.

'OK.'

Her fist tightened over the balled-up handkerchief. 'I'll give it to him.'

'OK.'

She looked down as she pocketed it, and then, like before, she froze. Slowly, she raised her eyes to me. Her expression was wary.

'You may find this hard to believe,' she said, 'but before I got knocked up, I was calm and lucid. I had a sense of humour and everything.'

'That's all right. My friend Michelle went mildly bonkers, too. She was convinced the mailman was staking out her house on behalf of an illegal adoption network.'

'I accused the cable TV man of installing secret cameras for paedophiles. Actually, I didn't believe that at all,' she added, 'but it was a great release of hormonal tension to watch him grovel and plead.'

We grinned at each other.

'Tea?' I asked again.

'Why not?' she replied. 'It'll give me a chance to show you exactly how this house is going to be ripped apart.'

Chapter Five

THE PEOPLE *I fantasised about meeting at the Italian café:*

A woman with a huge shambolic house stuffed with flowers and dogs and people. Called Hattie. (The woman, not the house.) She would be upper class and absent-minded and would call me 'darling Darrell'. She would include me in all her mad family's get-togethers, including Christmas. She would try to set me up with her charming wastrel younger brother, Jago, more for his sake than for mine. But while Jago and I would have a brief fling (can't decide whether the sex should be frantic and mind-blowing or companionable and giggly), his tragically self-destructive nature would lead him away from me and possibly into either a Turkish prison or a motorcycle crash in the Mongolian desert.

An older man with connections in publishing. He would be dapperly dressed and find me deeply interesting and charming but not enough to want to jump my bones. He would offer to read my books and would come to the café the next day brimming with excitement about my unique 'voice' and my intelligence and wit and humour. He would set me up with an agent friend, who would immediately take me on and win me a three-book contract with Black Swan. He would take me to tea at Claridge's, where they do over thirty kinds of cake. Possibly, he would die and leave me his Nash Regency house and his collection of small Impressionist paintings.

Fabrice, Duc de Sauveterre. Enough said.

But as we all know, due to my chicken nature, the most I'd got to know about the regulars at the café was that they came regularly. We all had our separate tables; we all had our separate and individual little morning routines. I would bring a book and nurse my double espresso for as long as decently possible. Real names wanting, I had given them nicknames. Big Man sat out in the tented area, smoking and staring into space. He was, as you've probably guessed, a big man. Not quite as tall as landlord Patrick, but more solid. I placed him in his early fifties and decided he must have been handsome in his youth, but that age and endless cigarettes and perhaps circumstances (he didn't appear to be all that well off) had turned a strong chin and jaw jowly and etched rows of lines under his eyes. His physique was that of a strongman gone to seed — not fat, exactly, but he was certainly carrying more weight than was good for him. His hair was military buzz-cut short and every day, without fail, he wore a godawful blue polyester bomber jacket that looked as if it hadn't been washed in years. He never read, not even the paper, just stared out through the plastic sections of the clip-on tent. I'd tried this myself and you cannot see a thing. The plastic made the world outside as blurry as a pavement chalk painting in the rain. What was he staring at then? I couldn't tell by his expression; it was neither sad nor thoughtful. I could describe it as neutral except that it wasn't that, either. In some not immediately obvious way, Big Man radiated 'go away' vibes, though I'd hazard a guess that he'd phrase it more succinctly. I'd heard him order coffee only a couple of times. His voice was gruff and his method of expression terse. The normally voluble Italian brothers — I knew *their* names now: Mario and Vincente — seemed to know their customer wasn't up for idle chitchat and they served him politely, but quickly and quietly. If there was to be a first person I approached, I'd make a wild stab that it would not be Big Man.

Mind you, I wasn't sure that Mr Perfect was any less intimidating. One, because he had a voice that made Prince Charles sound like Dot Cotton and two, because he was the neatest human being I'd ever seen. For me to be that tidy, I'd have to be encased in resin, like a dead beetle. Mr Perfect — what else could I call him? — was, I guessed, in his mid-forties, and looked as if he'd stepped out of an advertisement for Patek Phillipe watches or Armani. It wasn't that he was spectacularly handsome, although he was certainly a good-looking man. It was more that everything about him was clearly a cut above. Like landlord Patrick, he wore a suit that fitted him too well to be anything but bespoke. Unlike Patrick, he had clearly never known anything but affluence. He appeared to have no paying occupation — I'd never seen him with a mobile phone — so I could only assume he was a man of independent financial means. It would certainly explain why he was so freakishly tidy. His shirts were unfailingly pristine, with knife-sharp cuffs and collars. His ties were always in a perfect Windsor knot. You could have eaten off his shoes. He didn't actually dust off the chair with a handkerchief before he sat down, but I got the distinct impression he wanted to. When I saw him eat a croissant without shedding a single crumb (a feat that surely should have been acknowledged by some worldwide authority), I decided he was an even less likely prospect for introduction than Big Man.

Regular number three was a woman. I'd nicknamed her Miss Flaky, as all she drank was herbal tea, and all she read were self-help books with the kind of titles that make you throw up a little in your mouth. She was around forty and almost, but not quite, beautiful. She had amazing long blonde hair, big blue eyes and the porcelain skin of a Renaissance Madonna. But the reason she wasn't beautiful was because she wore the most hideous clothes in Christendom — Edwardian-style high-necked, ruffled blouses in beige or cream and ankle-length skirts that looked as if they'd been made from blankets that had been rejected by one of the more desperate refugee camps. These items were inevitably covered by one of two long, shapeless cardigans — one in dead-leaf brown with leather buttons and a maroon one with a stringy knitted belt. From the neck up, she was lovely. Full length, she looked monkey weird.

I suppose I had no right to feel disappointed. I mean, what had I really been expecting? That there'd be someone here who'd tick all the boxes of a perfect match? That our eyes would meet across the room and there'd be an instant connection, like there had been with Tom? OK, Tom and I weren't in a room as such; we were at the bus stop. But there *was* a connection. I dropped my change and he picked it up for me and bammo! It wasn't a lightning bolt of lust, a *coup de foudre* as the French say. It was more a jolt of recognition. An acknowledgment of each other, and how right we'd be together.

Yes. All right. I suppose I had been expecting that. Or at the very least hoping for it.

But if it was going to happen, it certainly wasn't going to happen here with this lot. That little bit of hope had been crushed like one of Big Man's fag butts under the heel of his crappy vinyl shoe.

What then? Should I still try to make contact? Let's face it — I had precious few other opportunities to meet people. The one person who'd been keen to chat with me lately had only initiated conversation because he wanted to sell me a copy of *The Big Issue*.

I *couldn't*, though! And it wasn't just that I didn't have the balls — although, admittedly, that was a large contributing factor. My problem was that everyone was so — separate. We all sat at separate tables, with at least one other table between us. Big Man sat alone in the smoking section, Miss Flaky in the far corner by the panettone, Mr Perfect in the middle, and me by the front door. Mario or Vincente greeted all of us with their usual bonhomie (or whatever is the Italian equivalent), but so far, none of the three had acknowledged me, or either of the other two. Not even a nod. I supposed that the reason they chose this timeslot was for its lack of other people, so they could read, or smoke and stare, in relative peace. Separately. Alone.

I started fantasising about a major event occurring, which was the only catalyst I could see for any kind of shared conversation. A car crash right outside. Or the chemist's going up in flames. Eventually, I had scripted a full *Die Hard* moment, in which a car catapulted into a helicopter, which crashed onto the chemist shop, and the whole block burst into flames. Yippee kay-yay . . .

I should have remembered what my mother always said. Be careful what you wish for.

This time, I was expecting the knock. Landlady Clare had rung the night before to tell me she'd be coming round at seven-thirty in the morning with the builder. I felt my heart sink. I'd been in the house almost three weeks now and there'd been no mention of ripping out kitchens and bathrooms. Secretly, I'd hoped her baby brain had wiped the whole notion from her head. But no—

Clare was on the doorstep with a man who to all intents was a smaller, slimmer version of her husband. The same olive skin, the same dark eyes and close-cropped hair. Except this man was younger — same age as me, I guessed — and much better looking. Landlord Patrick was attractive because he exuded energy and confidence, but he wasn't really handsome. This man had similarly strong features, but they were more refined. I also noticed he had a small gold hoop in one ear.

'This is Anselo,' said Clare. 'He's Patrick's cousin.'

'Hello.' I smiled and extended a hand.

Anselo did not smile, and he gave my hand only a cursory shake. Righty-ho. Either he didn't like women in general, or he just didn't like the look of me. Or perhaps he didn't like the fact that he'd have to work around me. I suppose it would be a bit of a nuisance to have someone watching you. You might actually have to build something.

'Anselo and I are just going to run over the plans this morning,' Clare explained. 'Is that all right?'

'As long as you don't mind me eating toast in front of you.' I gestured for them to come inside. 'Cup of tea?'

'Yes, *please*,' said Clare.

But from Anselo, all I got was a curt shake of the head.

Jolly good. On top of angsting about money and why I hadn't heard from my publisher, I was now going to have share my house with a man with no charm and no conversation. If I'd been made of sterner stuff, I would have seen that as the perfect excuse to sit at my computer and bash away at another book, confident that Hyppolite's lack of contact was a mere glitch. But as we all know my stuff was considerably stern-lacking, I decided it was the perfect excuse to get out and stay out. Which I did.

And I entered a café that was a complete zoo. There were people everywhere!

'What happened?' I asked Vincente, the younger brother. 'Are you giving away free coffee?'

'It was a fire alarm in building next door. All the people from the doctor's and chemist's have to leave until the fire truck turns up.'

'But it was a drill, right? Not an actual fire?'

Vincente shrugged. 'Someone pressed the alarm. Maybe some crazy looking for drugs.'

'Does that happen often?'

'Not *so* often.'

Good to hear.

I ordered my usual espresso and then looked around for somewhere to sit. I had half-hoped Mr Perfect's table might have a free chair, but no — there was a man with him. He was about forty-five, with curly brown hair that could do with a brush and a good trim. He wore a shirt under one of those Fair Isle woollen vests that were big in the nineteen forties, and Dickensian wire-framed spectacles behind which he squinted and blinked like a small, irritable mammal roused from hibernation. I was a little surprised to see that he and Mr Perfect were intently engaged in conversation. I had not thought Mr Perfect keen on conversing with anyone.

As I turned on my heel, I realised there was not one free chair anywhere inside. Even Miss Flaky's table was packed; she had all the girls from the chemist with her Feeling a little foolish and obvious, I walked quickly out into the smoking area. No free chairs there, either. Great. My only options seemed to be to push back into the café and swap my cup for a takeaway one, or keep walking, cup in hand, back to the house.

Then I spotted the chair. It was at Big Man's table. He was in the far corner, and the chair was tucked tight between his table and the wall. If I wanted to sit there, I'd have to ask him to get up and shift the table outwards. I could see why someone else had not already tried this. Big Man's whole stance — the leg slightly outward, the arm crossed over the chest, the set shoulders — said 'piss off'.

I glanced down at my coffee and saw the lovely rich crema on the top was starting to fade. It meant it was getting cold. After two weeks of sussing out the prices of food, public transport, phone calls, etc, I was less panicky about my finances, but I knew there was very little sliding room. If I wasted this coffee, I could not have another today. Suddenly, I became extremely pissed off. How dare some stupid person set off the fire alarm during *my* coffee time? How dare everyone decide to come here instead of schlepping up to the high street? Didn't they know walking was good for them? How dare Big Man be such a rude prick?

Fuelled by burning outrage, I strode right up to him, nodded at the spare chair and said, 'Can I get in there?'

At first, his eyebrows rose a fraction in surprise. Then his face settled back into its usual neutral (read hostile) expression. He stared up at me and took the time to blow smoke sideways out his mouth.

'If you like,' he said.

'I'll have to pull the table out,' I told him.

I was no longer feeling so fired up. Close up, he really was quite intimidating. It was his lack of response, I decided. You couldn't tell what he was thinking, and as such, you had no idea what he might do. He might do nothing. Or he might crush you with one giant fist. It was all rather unsettling.

Without a word, he stood up and tugged the table out just far enough to let me squeeze through the gap. Then he sat back down, angled his body away, and ignored me. I felt another surge of irritation. How hard is it to be even a *tiny* bit polite?

'Thank you,' I said pointedly.

His eyes slid sideways, but all he did was tap his cigarette on the edge of the Campari ashtray and stick it back in his mouth.

Fine. I pulled my book out of my bag and began to read. I'd re-read every Agatha Christie I could find in the library, and I'd now migrated to more nineteen thirties crime fiction with Margery Allingham. Her detective's name is Albert Campion. It's a pseudonym, as he is keen to hide his real identity — that of the scion of a seriously posh family from whom he is now estranged. His father may have been a viscount. Marvellous. I was hooked . . .

My ability to lose myself completely in a book used to drive Tom insane. 'I've been talking to you for the last ten bloody minutes!' he'd yell. 'You haven't heard one word!' I'd reply, 'If I'm reading, you know you need to get my attention *before* you start talking. What did you say?' He'd fold his arms and say, 'No, I'm done now. Forget it. Piss off back to bookland.' And I'd shut my book and wait until he'd sulked for five minutes and then we'd be right. Living with Tom was a breeze, now that I thought about it. I couldn't imagine what it would be like to have a relationship that was all *sturm und drang*, slammed doors and the silent treatment. All right, I admit, I wrote a lot of that in my books, but in reality, it would be awful, wouldn't it? But perhaps Tom was the only man on earth who was that easy-going. Or who loved me enough to want to always be kind . . .

Lost in the book, I don't know how long it took me to realise that my table companion was no longer smoking and ignoring me, but collapsed forward and emitting grunts of pain.

'Are you all right?' I said.

He shook his head so briefly, I wasn't sure whether it was an actual 'No', or disbelief at such a stupid question. Panic growing, I looked up and around. The smoking section had emptied out since I started reading. I jumped up and squeezed out from behind the table, scraping my hip against the wall. I sprinted into the café and, as I looked around, realised I had not even the beginning of a plan. Both Mario and Vincente were out the back. Mr Perfect was still in conversation with the man at his table. Miss Flaky was still sitting with the pharmacy girls. I rushed up to them and said, 'Quick! Where's a doctor?'

The girls and Miss Flaky stared up at me, wide-eyed. The man at Mr Perfect's table rose and said, 'I'm a doctor. What's the matter?'

'The man! Out there!'

I grabbed him by the arm and almost shoved him towards

the door. To his credit, he didn't resist. And as soon as he saw Big Man, he snapped into full emergency assessment mode. It took him about ten seconds to work out what was wrong.

'Call an ambulance,' he instructed me. 'This man is having a heart attack.'

I'm ashamed to say that I froze. It was the phrase 'heart attack' that did it. If it had been 'stroke' or 'pulmonary embolism', I would have been fine. But those two words transported me instantly back to a knock on the door and two young policemen and the endless drive to the hospital and—

'I'll call one.'

Mr Perfect was standing at my shoulder. I turned and looked up at him. I don't know what expression was on my face, but I saw his eyes widen a little, and as he spoke into his phone, he reached out and touched me briefly on the arm.

He lowered his phone. 'They'll be here in five minutes, Alastair,' he said to the doctor.

'Good. Can we clear these tables away?'

As if they'd been waiting for the summons, Mario and Vincente appeared. With practiced speed and precision, they folded and stacked away the few tables and chairs. The doctor sat beside Big Man, who now had his head down on the table, resting on his folded arms. He was still in obvious pain. I could see he had both fists balled up tight, and he was breathing fast and roughly.

Once the smoking section was cleared, Mr Perfect asked, 'Alastair, is there anything else you would like us to do?'

The doctor shook his head. 'Nothing. Keep the gawkers away, that's all.' He glanced at Big Man. 'It's a relatively minor one. He should be right as rain in a few days.' His eyes travelled to the ashtray. 'Whether he stays that way, of course, will be up to him.'

'And are *you* all right?' I heard.

Mr Perfect was half-smiling, half-frowning down at me. But I had lost the power of speech. All I could do was nod.

'You might be more comfortable if—'

I felt his hand close over mine which, as I only then became aware, was holding onto the door jamb in a white-knuckle death grip. Gently, he loosened my fingers. His hand was warm and his skin more calloused than I'd expected from a man who always appeared so impeccably groomed. He held my hand for a moment, and then released it.

'I'm sorry,' I said, and then because my brain was mush, added, 'I didn't think you had a phone.'

The non sequitur didn't seem to faze him, I suspect because he was too well bred. All he did was give me a small, wry smile.

'I try not to,' he said. 'I keep it buried in my pocket, for my broker mainly, and for the odd occasion such as this, when it might become necessary.'

'Thank you for calling the ambulance. I—' I stopped, hot with embarrassment at how I'd gone to pieces.

'No need to explain.' He smiled. 'If there'd been blood involved, you would now be stepping around my prone body.'

'I don't wish to interrupt your chat,' came a voice from behind us, 'but does anyone give a damn about how much pain this man is in?'

It was Miss Flaky, and her tone was as much of a surprise as her accent. She was American. And despite her fluffy blonde appearance, she came across as forthright and sharp. Bossy, even. Goes to show you never can tell.

Mr Perfect turned and said, mildly, 'Naturally. But I feel that my lack of formal medical training ill equips me to contribute in any more meaningful way.'

He called to the doctor. 'Alastair? Concern has been raised about the need for analgesic relief. Is there anything to be done?'

The doctor raised his head, but at the same time came the wail of a siren. It turned out to be the fire engine, arriving what I would consider far too late to save anyone, had the next-door building been indeed on fire. But immediately behind it was the ambulance. Its own siren noise terminated mid-yelp as it braked hard and disgorged a crew of three. There was a minor kerfuffle as the fire crew and the ambulance crew worked out where they each should be, but soon a purposeful-looking trio was jogging towards us.

The doctor stood. 'Right. All of you. Inside and keep out of the way.'

We obeyed. Mr Perfect, Miss Flaky and I stood in the doorway of the café proper, with the chemist girls behind us and Mario and Vincente behind them, muttering low words in Italian that I assumed were prayers, but which could have been curses. I mean, who knew how much trade they were losing with this disruption?

The ambulance crew was amazingly quick and efficient. In minutes, they had Big Man on a gurney and were wheeling him outside, the doctor close behind. I'm not sure any of us did it consciously, but as one we all moved outside to see what was happening. Big Man was in the ambulance now, being hooked up to all manner of bleeping equipment. The doctor remained on the footpath, issuing instructions and asking questions. It was clear he did not intend to go with Big Man, but wanted to ensure all care was taken.

Once the doors were shut and the ambulance on its way, he turned, and saw us gawping. He walked up and said, 'Does anyone know that man? Does he have any family here?'

'He's not a patient of yours?' asked Mr Perfect.

'No. Not on our books.' The doctor made a wry face. 'I suspect not on anyone's, by the look of him.'

One of the chemist girls piped up. 'His name's Hogan.'

'Hogan—?' said the doctor.

'Mr Hogan,' she added helpfully.

'Yes, well, I'd assumed he wasn't Admiral of the Fleet Hogan. Any idea of his Christian name?'

The girl shook her head. 'He gets his cigarettes from the

shop next door. I was in there buying my *Heat* magazine and I heard them call him Mr Hogan.'

The doctor sighed. 'Better than nothing, I suppose. Anyone know where he lives?'

'There, I think.' Mario pointed across to the council estate. He shrugged. 'At least, I have seen him come out from gate.'

'Right. Well, the hospital may find identification on him. In any case, he should be well enough to tell them himself tomorrow.'

He spoke directly to Mr Perfect. 'Friday?'

'Absolutely.'

And the doctor started to walk away.

Miss Flaky said sharply 'Is that it? Is that all you're doing for him?'

The doctor paused. 'What else do you propose I do?'

'Surely somebody should *be* with him? How can you leave him to face such a traumatic situation on his own?'

The doctor blew out a breath. He glanced at his watch. 'I had a fully booked surgery this morning. What with one thing and another, I am now well over an hour behind. Even so, I will see them all because they are my patients. Mr Hogan, should that be his name, is *not* my patient. As such, my obligation to him is limited. He will be in good hands at St Regus'. If you're so concerned, feel free to pay him a visit yourself.' He nodded at the rest of us. 'Thank you all for staying out of the way. Good day to you.'

He strode off without a backward glance.

'I don't know about you,' said Miss Flaky, 'but I think that's pretty raw.'

Mr Perfect's smile was courtesy itself. 'As Alastair suggested, you'd be welcome to visit the man. Would you like me to take you? I have a car nearby.'

For a second, her eyes shot daggers at him. But her reply was cool. 'Thank you, but that won't be possible. I have a full schedule of appointments for the week.'

'What a pity.'

I hid a grin. Miss Flaky's mouth did a brief twitching dance of displeasure. She nodded to Mr Perfect and to me, and then walked away at a dignified pace, blonde head held high.

I looked around. Mario and Vincente had hastened back to the café. The fire engine had rumbled off, so the chemist girls were drifting reluctantly back to work. I was alone with Mr Perfect.

He extended his hand. 'I'm Claude.'

Of course, he was. Suddenly, I felt embarrassed about my name. But I could hardly avoid telling him. I shook his hand and tried not to blush.

'I'm Darrell.'

Not even a faint quiver of surprise. He really *was* well bred.

'The reader,' he smiled.

He'd noticed! This time, I couldn't help blushing. And I couldn't think of one sensible thing to say. So I just grinned and stood there, like a red-faced grinning loon.

'Well—' he said, in the ensuing pause. 'I must say goodbye. I'd like to say that I, too—' His voice acquired a hint of an American twang '—have a full schedule of appointments for the week. But sadly, I have only the one, and if I don't leave now, I will have lost my chance for even that.'

'I have to go, too,' I lied. 'It was nice to meet you.'

Inwardly, I cringed. I was sure it wasn't done in Mr Perfect's circles to say things like that. I'd read my Nancy and Jilly. 'Nice to meet you' belonged to the lower middle class and the aspiring proles.

But he said, 'Yes. Indeed.' And, to my surprise, added, 'I'll see you tomorrow.'

I waited to see which way he went before I headed off myself. Nothing more embarrassing than saying goodbye and finding you're both walking the same way.

I was passing the entrance to the council estate when I pulled up short. My encounter with Mr Perfect — now to be known as Mr Claude Perfect — had lifted me onto a small pink-tinged cloud of pleasure. But at the gate to the estate I stopped, and started to think about Big Man. My rosy cloud disappeared behind a pall of gloom.

Miss Flaky, despite her obnoxious way of delivering it, had a point. Big Man, in pain and probably scared witless, was potentially about to face some major medical intervention, all on his own. I thought about the question of family and suddenly became convinced that he had none. If he had a wife and kids, wouldn't he have asked the doctor to phone them? And what wife would let him wear that godawful jacket for so long?

I thought about how I'd frozen when the doctor asked me to call the ambulance. Big Man probably wouldn't have seen that, but then again—

I thought about the day Tom died, and how I had not been there. I couldn't have done anything to help him — that's what they'd all told me. Was that true? I'd never know . . .

I stood there, outside the gate — a big iron one that was rusted permanently open — and came to a decision. I was only a minute's walk from my front door, but I turned around and walked all the way back to the café. And I asked Mario and Vincente to tell me the best way to get to St Regus' hospital.

Chapter Six

'HE TOLD us he had no family.'

'No immediate family. I'm his cousin.'

The receptionist nurse person, a tall, rather glamorous black woman, gave me a long look. 'You're from Australia.'

'New Zealand. I'm from the distant New Zealand arm of the family.'

'And how did you know he was here?'

'The neighbours told me. I was supposed to visit him today.'

The woman gave me an even longer look. 'Well, you can't visit him now.'

My heart lurched. 'God! Why not? Has he—'

At my obviously genuine distress, the woman finally softened. 'No, no, don't you be worrying. He's in surgery, that's all. He won't be fit for anything for at least two days. You come back the day after tomorrow. Leave your contact details here. I'll make a note that you're coming.'

Eek. I wasn't sure I wanted my lie to be committed to paper. But then it hadn't been a very big lie. Most of it, in fact, had been almost true.

And deep down, what worried me more was whether I'd

have enough courage to come back. What would I say to him, after all? What would he say to *me?*

I decided I'd wait and see how I felt on the morning of the day in question. I told myself that no one but me would know if I wimped out. But I didn't find that terribly reassuring.

When I returned to the house, it was quiet. No landlady. No builder. I assumed he'd be back tomorrow, but for now I could enjoy the peace and privacy and lack of surliness.

I fired up my email and found three new messages in my inbox: one from Michelle with the subject line 'NEWS!!!', one from Simon, subject line 'How's Blighty?', and one from H McManus, no subject line at all.

As is my wont, I opened the least worrying one first. Simon wanted to know how I was, whether I'd been to Greenwich yet, and whether he could crash for a night or two if he managed to con his bosses into letting him go to some international wave science conference on the Faroe Islands in a few months' time. He did not mention my parents, for which I silently thanked him. I said I was fine, that Greenwich was about middle on my as yet un-begun list of sights to see, and that if he didn't mind using a Portaloo he was welcome to stay. I hit send, and opened up Michelle's email.

There were only two words in the subject line, all in capital letters, followed by fifty thousand exclamation marks. The email had a few more words. She was pregnant again. It was a girl. And for a moment, I didn't know if I was happy for her. But after I'd given myself a firm mental slapping, I decided I was. I didn't want Michelle's life. What I *did* want was a bit of her luck. Tom had come easily to me, just as Michelle's good fortune had come easily to her. It just didn't seem fair that her luck was continuing, whereas mine— Well, I'd been working hard lately to try to push that kind of thought aside. There was no rational reason, I'd been telling myself sternly, why I couldn't be lucky again. I mean what had *I* done to be singled out by the gods of misfortune? Didn't I deserve a good life as much as anyone?

I was happy for Michelle. I sent her an email to tell her so. I made sure to include fifty thousand and one exclamation marks.

Then I took a deep breath and opened Hippolyte's email. I read it through, and then I read it through again. I checked that it was addressed to me, and found it was addressed not only to me but also to a whole lot of other people. I recognised some names as those of other romance writers.

The email said she had resigned to take a senior position at a top New York publishing firm. She said we'd be reallocated to one or other of her colleagues, who'd be in touch sometime in the next few weeks. There might be some hold up with any books currently being reviewed and she apologised for any inconvenience. Then she said it had been real and wished us all the best.

Oh shit.

Shit, shit, shit, shit, shit.

Exclamation mark.

The following morning, there was no knock at all. He just walked right in. He and another bloke.

I was in the kitchen, making tea and toast. I could see why Clare wanted to renovate. The kitchen was tiny; two people standing at opposite benches would be less back to back than bottom pressed to bottom. If you opened a cupboard door, no one could get in or out of the room.

Adjoining the kitchen was a small courtyard. Clare's plan was to knock the kitchen and courtyard into one, roof the whole lot and put in large skylights. The new, big kitchen would be open to the dining room. Right now, the old, tiny kitchen was down the end of the hallway that ran parallel to the stairs. When you came in the front door, you looked straight down to it. The two builders had just closed the front door. They couldn't miss me.

Technically, I was dressed, if you count a t-shirt and a pair of boy-leg underpants as an outfit. The t-shirt was an old one of Tom's. It had a cartoon lightning bolt on it and the words 'Captain Awesome'. The underpants were my own. I'd always been practical in my choice of knickers. Comfort first. Looks second. I was beginning to doubt the wisdom of this, especially as this pair had started off pale blue but long since faded to dishwater grey. They had also lost quite a lot of their elasticity and were hence a tad baggy around the edges. I suspected I looked a little like Steptoe, which wasn't, let's be frank, the look I was aiming for. Then again, I was glad of the coverage. My bum wasn't exactly bikini-ready, if you know what I mean, even in the dim light of morning.

Not that I would have had the slightest option, even if I'd been oiled up and buck naked. The only way to the bedroom and more clothing was back down the hallway and up the stairs by the front door. Where the builders were. I braced myself and tried to act as if I was always very comfortable to be caught half-starkers and with no makeup. Like I was part Swedish or something.

Anselo came in first, lugging a toolbox. He didn't smile at me, but he did nod, which I suppose was a step up courtesy-wise. Behind him was a very young man, no more than eighteen, with amazing colouring: dark red hair, freckled coppery skin and coffee brown eyes. He too, I noticed, had a gold hoop in his ear. In fact, he had several.

He also, without asking, dragged a chair from the living room and used it to prop open the front door. I resented this. Even though this wasn't my house, I was the one living here. The furniture and I both had a right to be treated in a less cavalier manner.

I was torn. If I protested, I'd draw attention to myself and my old-man underwear. But if I didn't, this could be a bad precedent. If I didn't set the rules of engagement now, it'd be too late—

'Any chance of knocking next time?' I said, still from the safety of the kitchen. 'And that chair may not be Chippendale, but I don't think Clare wants it damaged.'

Anselo stared at me. Then he said something to the boy, who went outside and came back with an old towel, which he draped over the chair back so it was protected from the pressure of the door. Then both of them went outside again, presumably to unload more stuff from their truck or van.

I walked quickly down the hallway, hoping to make it upstairs before they came back. But I had only just set foot on the first stair when they reappeared in the open doorway. I had to turn to face them.

'Morning,' I said. Someone had to say something.

Anselo's expression suggested he'd be counting the minutes until I left them alone to do their work. The red-haired boy just stared at me, without much interest. If I'd been sixteen, blonde and busty, things might have been different. But then again, who knows?

'This is Tyso,' Anselo said.

Yet another member of the odd names club.

I gave the boy a small wave. 'Darrell.'

Anselo blew out a short breath, as if talking to me was a waste of his time. 'We're bringing in some materials. We'll store them outside in the courtyard.'

As if that was his cue, Tyso headed back out the door. I noticed that along with the gold earrings, he had a green handkerchief knotted around his neck. It occurred to me that I knew nothing about the Romani people, apart from the crossing the palm with silver thing and the baking of hedgehogs between bricks thing. Which are probably apocryphal and almost certainly racist. I mean, how much meat would you get off a hedgehog?

I knew Patrick had mentioned the Romani connection, but I had no idea how recent or distant it was. Were the hoops and handkerchiefs the real thing or just for show; a way of advertising their claim to a long-lost heritage, like those Americans in Irish pubs who can only be dissuaded from singing 'Danny Boy' with a punch in the head?

'Another cousin?' I asked Anselo.

He frowned, surprised. Then he scowled. 'I got this job on my own merits,' he said.

Jeepers. It was too early for this sort of shenanigans.

'Are you always this touchy?' I asked him.

He blinked, taken aback. But before he could confirm or deny, his offsider clattered through the door with an armload of wood and metal bits and forced us to step aside. At that moment, I caught a glimpse of myself in the hall mirror and just about swallowed my tongue. The Steptoe pants weren't the worst of it. I looked like I'd tried to cut my own hair, and there was a big smudge of yesterday's mascara under one eye. I assumed that these two would be turning up this time every morning, and I vowed that from tomorrow, I'd be ready for them. Today, I decided that the best thing to do was run. Which I did. Up the stairs and into the safety of the bedroom.

When I felt presentable enough to venture back downstairs, the front door was closed and the chair replaced, and there were drop sheets along the hallway. I could hear a faint, tinny sound of music. The two men were out in the courtyard, along with a half-ton of building stuff and a portable Bluetooth speaker. It was emitting some standard rock fare that I did not recognise. The singer sounded as if he should have been more attentive while zipping his fly.

Anselo glanced my way as I approached. The only reason I'd come down was to snoop, so I pretended I'd actually come down for a glass of water. The door to the courtyard was propped open. I stepped into the doorway.

'You can use the kettle,' I said. 'If you want tea.'

Anselo nodded. I assumed that was his way of saying thank you.

I really wanted to ask him what his schedule was — when all the big work was going to be done, when I was going to have to live on takeaways, or toast grilled in the open fire because there would be a big pile of rubble where the stove was. Anselo mistook my lingering as having another purpose.

'You want the music down?'

'Oh! No—' I frowned. 'What is it?'

Over his shoulder, Anselo said. 'Tyso? What is this shit?'

'Nickelback.'

Anselo and I exchanged a look and, to my astonishment, he grinned. I know it's a terrible cliché to say that someone was transformed when they smiled, but Anselo's smile was a corker. At the risk of making him sound like a horse, he had excellent teeth, straight and even and white. His eyes changed from wary to alive and amused. I was quite amazed at the difference. People can have natural good looks, but to me it's their personalities that determine whether they are attractive or not. Tom was always smiling. He always looked as if he was genuinely happy to be alive, genuinely pleased to see you, and you could not help but respond to that.

Anselo said, 'We take turns. If I had to listen to Tyso's music all day, I'd be taking to the speaker with a bit of four by two.'

Tyso straightened up. 'If I had to listen to yours, I'd be shooting myself in the head with the fucking nail gun.'

'Don't fucking swear.'

Tyso winked at me. I decided he was a naturally happy boy, too. But then, he was young. He had a job. What did he have to worry about?

'And what does your boss listen to?' I asked him.

'Old boring shit.'

I looked at the boss. 'That true?'

He shrugged. He'd stopped smiling. 'I suppose,' he said, and stepped away from me, towards the toolbox.

I could have been offended. But I had seen a flash of discomfort in his eyes. I sensed he had not intended for the familiarity to go so far and now wanted to quickly restore the distance between us. I wondered if it was personal, but decided it wasn't. He was probably emotionally constipated with everyone.

In any case, sharing a house with a monosyllabic builder was the least of my worries. It was café time, and I would be seeing Mr Perfect — could I ever call him Claude? — for the first time since we'd introduced ourselves. My worry was that I had no idea what the protocol was now. Should I invite him to sit with me? Should I feel free to invite myself onto his table? Or should I just wave and smile? Composedly this time, not like a loonish fool.

The latter seemed the best option, although I really, *really* wanted to talk to someone about being abandoned by my editor. I'd woken up at three panicking about it. My rational side had reminded me that I had a contract for this book. There might be a delay but they could not, by rights, refuse to continue working with me on it. My gremlin side had asked if I'd actually *read* my contract? Was there some fine print that gave them an out? Could they delay indefinitely? And what would happen to me if my money did not come through as expected?

I knew the answer. It was dead simple: I'd have to pack up and go home.

And, you know, a couple of weeks ago, that might have seemed like an OK deal. But now? Now, what I feared would never happen in a million years just had. I'd met someone! And he was handsome, older (in a good, Pierce-like way, not a creepy, pervy way), posh, and possibly very, very wealthy.

I tell you, if I was writing this story, this is what would happen: Mr Perfect would turn out to be the scion of an aristocratic family from whom he is now estranged. He would have reached an emotional turning point in his life, and be looking for greater meaning than merely watching his wealth accumulate and jetting between his Monegasque chateau and his Manhattan penthouse. The usual parade of well-bred, flawless women now filled him with nothing but ennui, and he would be initially intrigued by and soon violently attracted to a sparky young brunette who combined refreshingly normal good looks with a certain amusing colonial charm.

Ideally, she'd also be a virgin and have the lissome grace of a willow sapling. But then we all have to get used to disappointment, don't we?

Chapter Seven

LADY MO: Either you are pulling a leg with bells on it, or it is his name — like Duke Ellington or the Dukes of Hazzard.

DARRELL: No, no! He's an actual duke! As in — of Wellington!

LADY MO: And — how could you fail to mention — de Sauveterre! Though he was a Duc, of course. No 'k', otherwise he would be a waterfowl.

DARRELL: I dreamed of meeting Fabrice in London. Despite of course knowing he is fictional. Mainly. Seems uncanny.

LADY MO: Seems like ridiculous plot straight out of one of your smutty books. Does he have a fake tan and a diamond Rolex?

DARRELL: I will have you know that all my heroes have natural tans and wear Patek Philippes!

LADY MO: Chad has a natural tan. But had to settle for a James Bond Omega. What does your Duke wear watch-wise?

DARRELL: His cuffs are so neatly tailored, I have not yet spotted which watch. And I now have to confess vital piece of information: he is not actually an actual duke. His father — who was an actual duke — disclaimed the title in 1960s.

LADY MO: Dad didn't want to be a duke?? Was Dad mad?

DARRELL: Possibly. Wanted to go into politics and the law was that he couldn't be an MP if he was still a duke. Not true, now — law changed. Probably by dukes. But was the case then.

LADY MO: Yikes. So can your man reclaim the title? Or is the dukedom lost forever, like Amelia Earhart?

DARRELL: Hmm. Do not know. Regarding himself, the man is evasive. From the crumbs of information he gave me I have managed to glean the following: Father's political career was a washout. Father is now dead. Family seat was sold to pay humungous inheritance tax. Mother lives somewhere along Thames (assume not on barge). Younger sister lives in Milan and works in an art gallery. Younger brother lives in LA and works in film. My man lives here and does not work at all far as I can tell. He has a broker, so probably lives off a big pile of investments.

LADY MO: As eldest son, he probably got all the moolah.

DARRELL: Seems unfair to the youngest son? Not to mention the sister.

LADY MO: Posh people care not a jot about that sort of thing. They are all freaks.

DARRELL: What's with the harsh words? You used to *love* posh people! You wanted to live in the Mitfords' Hons' Cupboard! What happened?

LADY MO: Met real posh people. They are highly irritating. Haw-haw like donkeys. Expect you to know everyone they know. Possess hyphenated last names with ridiculous pronunciation that bears no resemblance to the actual spelling. And have vomitably twee nicknames like Bitsy and Onky.

DARRELL: No real person is called Onky!

LADY MO: Ha! Wrong! Worked with bloke called Maurice who married into old money. His wife's proper name was Monica, but she insisted he call her Onky, just like the rest of her family of in-breds did.

DARRELL: What did she call him?

LADY MO: Moo-Moo. Their conversations sounded like a chorus of 'Old MacDonald' performed after serious head injury. Posh people are freaks. Mark my word.

DARRELL: Speaking of names — what are you going to call the baby?

LADY MO: Haven't decided yet. Chad wants to call her Matheson. Will humour him for now, but he has no hope in hell.

DARRELL: Wrong person to comment. At least he doesn't want Britney.

LADY MO: No fear. He would be struck out of the will immediately. Chad's mother has ban on all names ending with 'ey'. Also Joanne, for some reason.

DARRELL: Fair enough. Names are for life, not just to make it easier to spot your suitcase on the baggage carousel.

I HUNG around outside the hospital for a full half hour, psyching myself up to go in. To be scrupulously honest, the actual psyching up part took only around ten minutes — the rest of the time I filled with daydreaming about Mr Perfect.

My God! The man was almost a duke! The only title above that was king! And he was nothing like Michelle had warned he might be. I needn't have worried about protocol; he'd immediately invited me to join him at his table. He'd even bought my coffee. He was courteous and amusing, and he didn't expect me to know anyone called Binky or Bertie. He even seemed interested in my stories, such as they were, although I spent most of my time trying to divert him back to the subject of himself, which he bore with good grace even if he wasn't terribly willing to divulge—

Your Grace! That's what I'd have to call him if he were a duke! Instead, he asked me to call him Claude, which was not unreasonable considering it was his name. It occurred to me that he hadn't told me his last name, but I supposed there'd be plenty of time to find that out.

Which led me to think: where to now? He seemed to enjoy my company, but did that mean he was interested in me? Was I, for that matter, interested in him? He was handsome (tick), single (tick), perfectly groomed with perfect manners (tick, though to be fair, I'd never cared that Tom had been neither), and the son of an ex-duke (let's face it — ticks into infinity). True, there had been no connection, as such, between us. But I suspected he was too buttoned up to give off any real sexual vibes; he would see that as. . . impolite.

No, to me there appeared to be only one major hurdle. If I liked him, what on earth did I imagine I was going to do about it? In three weeks I hadn't even worked up the nerve to say hello. Asking him out would be like attempting to conquer Everest when, in reality, you were too feeble to work a cheap Stairmaster. I'd never had to worry about this with Tom. We met, we fell in love, we got married — it all happened as naturally and as easily as breathing.

I gave up thinking about it, and started to wonder again if Big Man was married. It would be embarrassing enough to explain to *him* why I had come, let alone to a Mrs Big Man. I had a story worked up that might sound plausible: I had been deputised by Alastair the doctor to see if he was all right and whether he needed anything. Why the doctor should choose me, I had no answer for. With luck, it wouldn't occur to Big Man to ask.

To once again be scrupulously honest, there was one more reason I was delaying. I don't like hospitals. In fact, I hate them. They bring me out in a cold sweat, and I find myself dragging my feet, searching frantically for excuses to turn and run. I'd only been to a hospital twice since Tom died, not counting the visit to St Regus' reception yesterday. My mother had an operation on her varicose veins and Simon was bowled off his bike by a car. Neither was in bad shape when I went to see them — Simon had only a fractured collarbone and my mother was as usual, apart from a particularly unattractive pressure stocking. But the smell, the colour of the walls, the drip machines and metal beds — every time I looked anywhere, a picture flashed in my mind of the room where they'd put Tom. A nurse that day gave me a cup of tea, filled with so much sugar my fillings buzzed. To this day, I cannot drink tea with sugar.

I paced for another five minutes and then made a decision. I would go in. Secretly, I was hoping that the note the receptionist nurse had left said, 'This woman is a fraud. Expel her immediately.' But when I got to reception, another woman said, 'Oh yes. He's in Ward 12. You can go on up.'

I found Ward 12. It was full of people — men — in various states of consciousness. Some seemed to be sleeping. One looked as if he wouldn't be waking up. One was a boy, not yet out of his teens. His mother was with him. I assumed, if these were all heart patients, that the boy had some congenital defect. I found myself feeling absurdly, tearfully grateful that he was here — safe, well, alive . . .

'Can I help you?'

A man with sticky-out black hair was in front of me, squinting. He was in his late thirties and sounded Irish. He was wearing a grey chunky-knit jersey, a shabby old tweedy jacket and tan cords. He did not look like a medical professional. He looked like he was trying to piece together his movements for the last three days.

He squinted at me more closely and frowned. 'Are you all right?'

'Yes!' I replied, too brightly. I pressed on to cover it. 'I'm looking for B— er, Mr Hogan.'

'Are you now?'

I couldn't quite read his tone. Was he saying he didn't believe me?

'You're a relative?' he continued.

Suddenly, I couldn't cope with pretending any more.

'Actually, I'm not,' I sighed. 'I was just on the spot when he had his heart attack and I was worried about him. I don't think he has any family and—'

I ran out of steam and stood there, waiting for Mr Squinty to send me packing.

'So, you know nothing about him?' He seemed more curious than put out.

I shrugged. 'He smokes. He may live in a council estate. He sits at my local café at the same time I do, every morning. He never has anyone with him — I don't think he's very sociable. He always wears the same godawful blue jacket . . .'

Mr Squinty said nothing for ages, which was extremely disconcerting. Then he nodded, slowly, as if he was thinking something through.

'Does he know you?' he asked. 'Would he recognise you, I mean?'

'Yes. Almost certainly.'

'Good,' he said. He put his hand firmly on the back of my arm. 'Come with me.' A few beds down, he added, 'I'm Gabriel Flynn, by the way.'

'Darrell Kincaid. You're a — doctor?'

'Tone of doubt noted and granted. I am a doctor, but of psychiatry.'

'A psychiatrist? Why does—?'

But Dr Flynn stopped abruptly, and I almost cannoned into him. His tweed jacket smelled faintly of cigar smoke. I found it strangely comforting.

We were at Big Man's bed. He was hooked up to a drip and to a machine that I assumed was monitoring his vital signs. He was lying with the sheets pulled tight across his chest, as if a nurse had recently re-made the bed and not been too fussed that there was someone in it. His arms were above the sheets, but I noticed that they were just lying there limply, as if he had lost the power to move them. He was staring up at the ceiling and seemed oblivious to our presence. His gaze was so intense that instinctively I glanced upwards. But the ceiling was uniformly plain and bland. White tiles with a slight texture. Nothing that seemed to require prolonged scrutiny.

'I'm back,' said Dr Flynn, in a voice that was cheerful but a little too loud — the kind used by a preschool teacher who desperately wants another job.

'And I've brought a visitor,' he continued. 'Her name is Darrell, and she was worried about you. Although God knows why, when you're clearly right as rain.'

Big Man did not respond to the dig. He may as well not even have heard it. He kept on lying there, unmoving, staring at the ceiling.

I raised my eyebrows at Dr Flynn. I expected him to take me aside and explain, but he spoke right up. Either it was a psychological tactic designed to provoke or discretion was simply not his thing.

'Yes,' he said, 'our Mr Hogan has been like this since he was given the all clear from the surgery. He won't move. He won't talk and he won't eat.' He addressed Big Man directly. 'The nurses are becoming more than a fraction annoyed, Michael. And believe me, if you saw some of the instruments they have at their disposal, I myself would be wanting to stay on their good side.'

To me, he said, 'It's common for people, especially men, to go into a bit of a despond after heart surgery — brush with mortality, loss of sexual power and all that. But this reaction is more like a severe post-natal depression. Quite interesting, really, from an academic point of view. Pain in the jacksie from a practical one. Because if he doesn't improve—' He gave a brief, resigned shrug.

'What?' I asked, perturbed. 'What happens if he doesn't improve?'

'Well, there's a joyous spectrum of possibilities. Committing him to the loony ward is a likely start. Then there'll have to be a feeding tube inserted, because we are duty-bound to not let him starve. Plus catheters and all that palaver for when the food we force into him inevitably makes its way out. Then if he continues to refuse to help himself, we will probably resort to ECT.'

'ECT? You don't mean — electric shock therapy?'

'I do indeed mean that.'

I was horrified. 'I thought that had been *banned?*'

Dr Flynn looked mildly surprised. 'No, no. It's still in use. Highly effective, in fact. Not pleasant, of course, even though we do stick you with an anaesthetic beforehand. But apart from the risk of chunks of your memory being erased, side effects are on the whole minimal.'

I stared down at Big Man. The odd blink had been his only detectable movement during this whole exchange. But unless the surgery had gone very awry, I knew he must have heard every word. If *I'd* been the subject of Dr Flynn's bald prognosis, I'd be down the corridor, gown flapping, running like the bare-arsed wind.

'You said if he doesn't improve soon—' I asked. 'How soon is soon?'

'Tomorrow, I'd say. Can't keep him in here much longer.'

'What can we *do*?' I said.

It was a general cry for help, not directed to anyone in particular. But Dr Flynn said. 'Glad you asked. I want you to sit here and talk to him.'

'But . . . about what?'

'Anything you like. What do you do for a living?'

'I write romance novels,' I admitted, a little reluctantly.

Dr Flynn grinned delightedly. 'Really? My God! I always thought they were written by the kind of woman who keeps dolls on her bed. Do you keep dolls?'

'No.'

'Teddies?'

'No!'

He chuckled. 'Well, that's grand, then. You'll have yards of material.'

And he started to walk away! I grabbed his arm.

'Are you serious? You want me to sit and talk to him?'

He paused. His smile had gone. 'I want to keep him in the world,' he said. 'And I can't do it on my own.'

I let go his arm. 'How long should I stay?'

'Long as you can,' he replied. 'Long as you can . . .'

He nodded to me, stuck his hands in his grubby tweed pockets and strolled off.

I looked around to see if anyone else had overheard our conversation, so I could ask if I was hallucinating. No one seemed to be even the slightest bit aware of me. I looked down at Big Man. He didn't seem to be aware of me either, but I knew now that was because he was ignoring me.

I found myself in an ambivalent emotional state. Part of me was full of admiration for his ability to sustain such extraordinary pig-headedness, and part of me was becoming increasingly irate — for much the same reason. What did he think he was going to achieve by this? And what on earth made him do it in the first place?

'I want to keep him in the world.' It was an odd thing to say, but Dr Flynn wasn't exactly conventional. Then again, I hadn't had much to do with the psychiatric profession. I'd been offered grief counselling after Tom died, and did one session with a well-meaning but intense woman who seemed to want me to cry. *I* wanted someone to cheer me up. I thought that was the point of grief counselling — to make you feel better, not worse. But this woman seemed to think crying would be good for me, a healthy release. In my opinion, Tom's death was so dramatic that tears seemed a particularly useless reaction to it.

Keep him in the world? Perhaps Dr Flynn had meant that Big Man needed to be reminded that the world existed, hence the need for a running commentary from me. It made a certain sense: difficult to stay locked in your head with someone yabbering non-stop beside you. There was a chair against the wall. I pulled it out and sat down. And began to talk.

I told him everything. I didn't intend to, but once I'd started, I found I couldn't stop. At first, it was all light-hearted — stories of my parents: my father's personal crusade against random apostrophes ('Surely all but the most egregiously obtuse can distinguish between a plural and a possessive?'), my mother's reaction when Pringle branched out of knitwear and went all modern ('Of course, I bought from them at the right time, when they still had royal patronage.'). Stories about Simon: that he was considering applying to the *Guinness Book of Records* for the most number of cavity-searches performed by international customs on a single individual. Stories about my name: the lists I'd made as a young child of super-girly alternatives (my favourite was Fifi Honey-Belle, and this was *years* before Bob Geldof had daughters). Stories about me and Michelle: the book of love spells we got from the library. We performed the least disgusting — most required us to use our menstrual blood — by chanting a few lines and sticking lemon peel in our bras. It didn't work, unless some poor random male is still finding himself inexplicably riddled with lust for two unknown teenage girls whenever he makes a gin and tonic. I found it harder to talk about my writing because I still hadn't heard if my publisher had assigned a new editor to me, and felt a rising bubble of panic whenever I thought about it. But then I started to talk about coming to London, the hoops I'd had to jump through to leave home, my constant freak-outs about money, the house that was infested by grumpy Romani builders — and rather like a piece of film run in reverse, I gradually worked my way back to the event that had triggered it all off.

But I didn't come right out with it. I couldn't. I paused, and sat there. I'd been talking for at least an hour, and the silence sort of rang around me. So when there was a movement in the bed next to me, I jumped. My eyes had gone down to my hands, where I'd been unconsciously rubbing the space where my wedding ring used to be. When I looked up, Big Man was staring right at me.

I stared back, mouth open a little in surprise. Then, before I could stop them, the words just came out.

'He died,' I said. 'My husband died. Tom. My husband. He's dead.'

I shut my mouth with a snap. I could feel my face start to flame with embarrassment at the stupid way I'd blurted it out, and because of the way Big Man continued to stare at me. His expression was similar to his usual one, but this time, hostility was definitely winning over neutrality.

Then I jumped again. Because Big Man spoke. His words were slow but absolutely distinct.

He said: 'Lucky bastard.'

Dear Reader, I slapped him.

Dear God. I leapt up and slapped a man two days out of heart surgery right across the face.

I stared down at him for one horrified moment, my hand poised above the cheek it had just struck, the cheek on which a livid white imprint was now turning red.

And then I turned. And I ran.

I had just enough presence of mind not to run in the tube stations in case someone thought I was a bag snatcher, but I ran all the way there and all the way from the last tube stop to my house. I threw open my front door, slammed it shut behind me and clattered up the stairs. In the bedroom, I came to a sudden halt, and that's when my knees gave way and I sank down onto the floor and curled up into a ball. My breathing was ragged and gasping, and I could not seem able to catch any air.

I thought — I really *had* thought — that I'd coped as well as anyone whose partner had died. I thought I had passed through all the stages of grieving — shock, denial, anger and sadness — and come out the other side still sad, but ready to move on. How wrong I had been. Look what had been lurking inside me all that time, just waiting to be released. Some person, some *thing* I did not recognise. Some kind of furious, maddened monster. I had never hit anyone in my life. I'd never had brothers or sisters my own age, never got into playground scraps or catfights. I'd never had physical arguments with a boyfriend, couldn't even *imagine* having one . . .

I heard the bedroom door creak, but I did not raise my head until a voice said, 'You all right?'

I'd left the house that morning before the builders arrived, and to be honest, the obvious thought that they'd be here hadn't occurred to me when I'd run in as if pursued by the hounds of hell. I must really have given the pair a start if the boss had felt compelled to come up and check on me.

Anselo's expression was a wary frown, and he seemed poised as if ready to bolt. It was clear to even the meanest intelligence that I was nowhere near all right. But to spare him, and myself, I have to admit, from any further discussion, I replied, 'I will be.'

I thought he'd nod and beat a hasty retreat. But he frowned down at me for a moment more and said, 'You're not hurt? No one tried to—?'

I almost laughed. Little did he know that today's top candidate for unhinged smack-down artist was, in fact, my good self.

'No. I'm not hurt. Just upset.'

This time he did nod, but continued to hover in the doorway. 'You want — tea?'

It was the last thing I wanted. I felt like food and drink would choke me. I shook my head.

I was desperate for him to leave me alone, and I think he sensed that. He nodded again, once, and carefully shut the door.

After a while, it was too uncomfortable to keep sitting on the floor. I hauled myself up into the bed and lay there until the sky outside the window was completely black. When I eventually made my way down to the kitchen for a glass of water, there was no one there.

Chapter Eight

'YOU CAN BE thin on the outside but fat on the inside. A thin person can still have sky-high levels of cholesterol and arteries clogged worse than the M twenty-fucking-five.'

'Tremendous. Any other happy fact you feel compelled to impart?'

'Don't get me started on bowel health.'

'If that is an offer, let me accept it.'

'Do you know how much half-digested red meat could right now be backed up in your colon?'

Mr Perfect sank back in his chair and shot me a despairing look. 'How did we get started on such a conversation?'

It was kind of him to suggest it had nothing to do with me, when in fact it was entirely my fault that we were discussing his lower bowel.

It was my fault because I'd had no sleep, no breakfast and had been walking the streets since six in the morning, because I did not want to have to pretend I was OK to Anselo. The probability that he would actually *ask* if I was OK was low, but still — I didn't want to see him. I walked for over two hours, down to the canal and all the way up to Highbury Fields and back to the café. By then, though my feet were killing me, I was thinking that I felt marginally better. But as soon as Mr Perfect saw me, he said, 'Are you all right?'

I hesitated. 'Don't I look all right?'

'I'd have to say that you look a little peaky.'

He was standing, waiting for me to take the chair he had offered me at his table. For a second, it occurred to me that he might be only being polite because now that he'd started, he felt compelled to continue. Then I decided that I gave not a crap. If I didn't sit down right now, I'd have to saw off my feet to stop the pain.

'A late night?' he ventured, as he resumed his seat. 'Or is something troubling you?'

I came *this* close to telling him. But as the story formed in my head, I realised how bad it sounded — and I did *not* want to jeopardise this relationship before it had even made it to the starting line. My book reading had informed me that posh people married the non-posh for only two reasons — one: an injection of funds, and two: to counterbalance the odd wayward chromosome. Not that I was leaping ahead to marriage, you understand. That would be entering crazy-woman territory. But if I were him and I heard my story, I'd be drawing a thick black line through my name on the suitable spouses list. And as my mother always said — better safe than sorry.

I was saved by Mario, who placed my cup of coffee in front of me. I offered him a grateful smile and said to Mr Perfect, 'Nothing that this won't fix.'

A voice beside us said, 'It could be your zinc levels.'

Mr Perfect and I exchanged a quick, alarmed glance. Then he shifted his seat to the side, so the two of us were now facing the adjacent table. Miss Flaky had a pot of some biological-smelling tea in front of her, and a book whose title I couldn't quite read, but which included the word *Authenticity*.

Miss Flaky continued, 'Zinc deficiency is one of the least

recognised causes of sleep disturbances. It can also lead to loss of appetite and mild anaemia. How are your fingernails?'

'My fingernails—?'

'Are there white lines present?'

I checked. 'No . . .'

'That's a common sign, but not the only one. I'd suggest you ask the pharmacist next door to do a zinc check for you.'

'Does it involve giving blood?' I suddenly remembered Mr Perfect's gore-phobia and shot him an apologetic glance. 'Sorry—'

'That's quite all right. I can hear it mentioned. I just can't look at it.'

'The zinc check is simple. All you do is hold some liquid zinc sulphate in your mouth for a few seconds. If you can taste it, you probably have a deficiency.'

'And then what?'

'Supplements. You should be taking some kind of multivitamin, anyway. Our modern diet is woefully inadequate nutrition-wise, plus we're constantly under assault from environmental pollutants, genetically modified foods, chronic stress, etc. A lack of folic acid alone puts us at risk of cardiovascular disease, not to mention breast and colon cancer—'

'What a good idea.' Mr Perfect broke her flow. 'Let's *not* mention those. Why don't we, in fact, change the subject entirely?'

Miss Flaky gave him a look. 'Men are often uncomfortable discussing their health. It seems to be a little threatening to them.'

Mr Perfect spread his hands. 'I am entirely comfortable with the state of my health.'

'Oh really? And you were last checked when?'

'As I recall, when I was ten years old. I had my tonsils removed. I'm sure you'll be pleased to know that my recovery went without a hitch.'

'Oh my God—' Miss Flaky was slowly shaking her head.

'The tonsils are a vital lymphatic barrier between us and infection. We should be thankful for our children's sake that barbaric Victorianisms like tonsillectomies are now rarely performed.'

'I've never had a day's illness since!' Mr Perfect protested.

'How do you know?' Miss Flaky asked. 'How do you know what state your cholesterol is in? Your blood pressure? And what about your prostate?'

'I could go out there now and run five miles with ease.' Mr Perfect's tone was still light, but I did notice he was sitting up straighter in his chair. 'I'd want to be more suitably dressed, of course—'

Miss Flaky gave him a grim smile. 'That means nothing. Your aerobic and muscular fitness is no indication of your true inner health. You can be thin on the outside but fat on the inside . . .'

And that's how we'd got to red meat backed up in the colon. That's why, when Mr Perfect asked me how the conversation had started, he was really asking for my help to make it stop.

I grinned at him and said, 'My landlord is about your age. His cholesterol level is crap, apparently. But I think he considers bacon a condiment.'

'Isn't it?'

'Why don't you see your doctor friend?' I asked, amused to see his normally suave self rather flapped. 'He'd be happy to give you a once over, wouldn't he?'

'Possibly. But on my part, if Alastair had to ask me to assume the position, I'm not sure our friendship would survive.'

'They can check for prostate cancer with a blood test these days,' said Miss Flaky.

'Can they now? Fascinating—'

Mr Perfect was on his feet, lifting his jacket from the back of the chair. 'Well, this last hour has simply *flown* by. But I must go. Good day to you both.'

And he walked rather quickly out of the café.

Miss Flaky said, 'It's the penis delusion.'

'It is?'

'They think that as long as *that's* still working, they're fine. As if their johnson is some barometer of total health. And when it fails, that's all they care about. They can have a lipid level that would rival a tallow factory, type two diabetes and gout, but as long as they have access to those little blue pills, as far as they're concerned, they'll live forever.'

I found myself struggling for something to say. Mainly because what *could* you say to that? But also partly because all this medical talk was reminding me, with sharp prods of guilt and discomfort, of what I'd done to Big Man. And of what I hadn't done — which was to return to the hospital and apologise.

So I pretended to check my watch, and said, 'I have to go, too.' I stood and slung my bag over my shoulder. 'Um — bye.'

Miss Flaky glanced up at me briefly, and her mouth twisted into a moue of — I couldn't tell what. Resignation? Disgust? Then she picked up her book and started to read. Fine. Next time, I wouldn't even bother with goodbye.

Outside, I took a deep breath, as if somehow I might inhale some courage along with the oxygen. I knew I should start walking towards the tube. I knew I had to face Big Man sooner or later — mainly because I suspected that if I didn't go back and apologise, he might come looking for *me*. In my mind, I heard the ominous crack of a set of giant knuckles.

But then I spotted him. Mr Perfect. Claude. He was in the churchyard of all places, standing under a tree. His jacket was draped elegantly over his shoulder, secured by one finger, a pose that made him look even more like an advertisement for Armani.

Should I go up and talk to him? Was this my opportunity

to take this friendship a step further? He didn't look as if he was waiting for anyone, or had anything pressing to do — so the only stumbling block, really, was that I had jelly instead of a spine . . .

Right! Damn it! If I didn't act now, I never would. As I started to walk towards the church, I thought I heard a faint cracking, as of knuckles. I shoved it into the far recesses of my mind and focused on working out what the heck I should say.

He noticed me as I was crossing the road to the tiny green island on which the church sat. I was close enough to see that he had some reaction, but not close enough to see what it was. Whatever he'd felt, he had a smile on by the time I reached him.

'*Let not ambition mock their useful toil*,' he said to me. '*Their homely joys, and destiny obscure.*'

A small bell from years back gave a faint chime. 'Thomas Grey?'

'Well done.' He glanced around. 'Though this could hardly be described as a country churchyard. But perhaps it was once. In the seventeenth century, Islington Green did mark the boundary of the city . . .'

I was stumped. This wasn't exactly going as planned. Admittedly, my plan had consisted pretty much entirely of me saying hello, and then winging it from there. Even so, I hadn't expected to be plunged into a discussion around poetry and history. My thoughts were on a path that was leading more towards a cup of tea and a sandwich.

'Well,' he said, in the pause. 'I had better cease loitering. Not that anything more productive awaits me, but—'

This was it. It was now or never. I blurted it out. 'Would you like to do something?'

He blinked at me. 'Do — *something*?' He picked out the word much as if it were a foreign object in his food.

I blushed. 'Oh, well, I just thought — maybe — you'd like to—'

He was staring at me with undisguised amazement, and I couldn't go on. My heart sank. I'd blown it. I prepared to crawl away in shame, like the worm I was—

But then he said, 'You know, there *is* something I've always wanted to do.'

My eyes shot up, half-wary, half-hopeful. His own expression was hard to read. If I were to label it with any emotion, I'd have to choose mild curiosity. But that was *so* much better than contempt that I experienced a heady rush of relief.

'What have you always wanted to do?' I asked.

I have to confess my thoughts had by now made a quantum leap from tea and a sandwich to a private jet and a fruit platter in the Maldives. I was picturing myself in a lacy dress with no underwear, like Renee Russo in *The Thomas Crown Affair*, and Mr Perfect in a tuxedo, with his black tie draped loose around his neck and his shirt buttons open, revealing a hint of manly chest—

'I think the nearest stop is London Bridge,' were the words I managed to catch.

He smiled at me. 'You don't mind walking, do you?

I thought I coped very well. I nodded appreciatively when I saw the sign that said London Dungeon. I smiled when the woman in the ticket booth told us to 'have a horrible time'. I didn't panic in the mirror maze or shriek like the rest of the group whenever we were leapt out on or had objects thrust at or dropped on us. I even managed a brief glance at the photos of eviscerated prostitutes in the Jack the Ripper room. It wasn't until we were sitting in the Sweeney Todd barbers' chairs that I finally said, 'Is this sort of thing not — beneath you?'

He looked across. 'Beneath me?'

'Well, you are really quite posh.'

'Which is why, generally speaking, I can do anything I please.'

'And this pleases you?'

'It's terrific!'

'You wouldn't prefer something a little more — cultured?'

'No. Be quiet. That chap with the razor is about to speak—'

At the gift shop, he offered to buy me a purple paperweight shaped like a skull. I declined. Then we were back out on the street, blinking in the bright light.

For a minute or so, we just stood there. Mr Perfect seemed a little at a loss. It occurred to me that he wasn't a person who directed his life with a great deal of proactivity. Which was potentially an issue, because neither was I. That's what I'd relied on Tom for. I was all right once I got started. But sometimes the only thing that would get me to that point was a big toe up the backside.

'I, er — I suppose we should wend our way back,' he said.

I couldn't help feeling a stab of disappointment. But I hadn't offered any better suggestion, had I? And what did I expect – that we'd go onto drinks and dinner? It's what I *wanted*, but even the most rose-tinted wishing glasses couldn't disguise that this had been a very platonic outing. The only time he'd touched me was when our fingers met while rummaging through a basket of imitation poison rings.

Still, it was a start. And some people don't like to be rushed . . .

Speaking of which— I checked my watch. It was three o'clock. I should have been on my way home from St Regus' hospital, but that would have to wait until tomorrow. Or the day after. Or never. Never would be good.

'And what is the time?' Mr Perfect asked me. 'I don't wear a watch, I'm afraid."

'It's just after three. Why? Are you meant to be somewhere?'

'Me? No . . .'

He stared away from me, up the street. There wasn't much

to see up there, as far as I could tell; brick walls and more road. I used the opportunity to take a good look at him. He was wearing a dark grey suit and a pale shirt with a thin striping of light blue or grey, crisply formal attire that had drawn some bemused looks in the Dungeon. His hands, I had noticed before, were well manicured. Not fussily so, but you could tell they received regular attention. On the middle finger of his right hand, I saw he wore a ring. It was platinum, I thought, and looked more like a woman's wedding band than a ring for a man. His mother's, perhaps? I took my ring off on the morning of Tom's funeral. But the mark on my finger stayed there for weeks.

I looked up at Mr Perfect's face in profile. He was certainly handsome, but in spite of excellent bones, I had to admit that he somehow lacked definition. He had a face you'd be hard-pressed to describe in a witness statement. It occurred to me he'd make a perfect spy; there was a kind of courteous blandness to him that would let him blend into any situation. If it weren't for his expensive clothes, he could pass by entirely unnoticed.

In my mind, the theme to *Smiley's People* started to play. Then I realised the orchestra music wasn't in my head at all. It was coming from my companion's jacket.

'I think your phone is ringing,' I said.

He gave me a look. 'I know. I'm trying to ignore it.'

Sure enough, it stopped. But instantly, it began again. With a sigh, he reached into his inner jacket pocket and drew out the small, plain Nokia. He glanced at the screen and raised an eyebrow, not so much in surprise, I thought, but in resignation.

He pressed the call button. 'Yes? What?'

I could hear the thin yap of a voice on the other end, but could not tell if it was male or female.

Claude said. 'I am *not* always in. Occasionally, I am also out.'

More yap, to which he replied: 'At least an hour.' And then: 'Well, you must do as you please.'

He ended the call and replaced the phone in his pocket. Then he met my eye and gave me a small smile.

'That was my brother. He is outside my front door, and considerably irritated that I am not on the other side about to open it.'

'I thought he lived in LA?'

'He does. Unfortunately, not all of the time.'

I decided to risk a personal question. 'Do the two of you not get on?'

I regretted it. His expression immediately iced over. 'Our relationship is amicable enough.'

Then he sighed, and added, 'Marcus and I — and our sister — were all at boarding school by the age of eight. My brother and I were at different schools; our father thought Marcus needed more — structure. So for years, we only saw each other in the holidays, and even then, Marcus usually chose to stay at friends' houses, rather than at home. I don't blame him. Our father by then was not a — happy man . . .'

I thought about telling him that I'd never really known my brother, either. But our situations were so distant that it seemed futile to try to connect them.

I glanced up and found to my relief that he was smiling at me. 'Time to go, I think,' he said.

When I opened the door to my house, there were no builders, for which I gave a sigh of relief. I wanted peace and quiet to think about the day — about what it had meant. I hoped it meant something. I hoped at least it was a start.

Along from the tube, at the corner of the high street, we'd paused to go our separate ways. To my surprise and pleasure, he had bent and kissed me goodbye, quickly but firmly, on both cheeks.

'I really enjoyed myself,' I told him, and mentally cursed myself for sounding far too eager.

'Yes,' he said, as if the concept was quite new to him. 'We must do it again someday. I've heard LEGOLAND is rather good, too.'

LEGOLAND. Well, as I said — a start.

I went into the kitchen to make a cup of tea, and found that someone had placed wildflowers in a drinking glass on the bench. Landlady Clare must have been, to check on progress, and brought them from her garden. They were limp now, drooping over the side of the glass, their brief lives almost at an end. Not wanting to see them dead in the morning, I picked them up and chucked them in the bin.

Chapter Nine

I HAD LEFT the house at crack of dawn, hoping that my surge of courage would last as long as it took me to do the deed and apologise to Big Man. It had lasted until about four paces from the front door of the hospital, where I'd now been standing for a good twenty minutes. Every time I worked up the nerve to take a step towards the entrance, I bottled and took a step right back again. Dancing the Hoky-Chokey, like a coward.

'Hello there!'

Oh God. The Irish shrink was heading my way. My first thought was to turn and run. He had to know what I'd done! Perhaps he'd been keeping a lookout for me? That smile he had on was just to lull me until he could get me in his clutches and whistle for the fuzz—

Too late. He was by my side. He had on much the same outfit as he'd been wearing the other day: the hairy tweed jacket, cords and a homespun jumper the texture and colour of porridge. He smelled even more strongly of cigars this time. It must be torture for his poor patients, for whom the smoking zone was at least ten miles in any direction.

'Glad to have caught you, Miss Kincaid,' he said cheerfully. 'Whatever by all that's holy did you do to our friend Mr Hogan?'

I felt the blood drain from my face. My mouth opened but I couldn't utter a word. I gaped at him, like a goldfish.

'I came back that evening,' he continued, seemingly oblivious to my discomfort, 'to find him tucking into meat and two veg.' He paused. 'I assume it was meat, not always easy to tell. Anyway, begob, as we don't say, what silken words of yours effected such a radical transformation?'

My mouth was still open, but now for quite a different reason.

'He was *eating*?' I finally managed to say.

'Masticating steadily.'

'And he didn't say anything to you? About — well, about me?'

'Not a word. Hence my current interest in your side of the story.'

My mind was churning furiously. If Big Man hadn't said anything, then should I? I had a microsecond's worth of moral dither, but then I wimped. My mother always said that discretion was the better part of valour, and why, quite frankly, should I not believe her?

'I just talked to him,' I said, with a small shrug. 'As you suggested.'

'But what did you talk about?'

'Family. Friends. Childhood. Nothing exciting.' I gave him an apologetic smile. 'I actually thought I'd bored the poor man senseless.'

My pants were about to burst into flames at any moment with all this fibbing.

Dr Flynn seemed disappointed. 'You didn't get him all gingered up with a racy summary of one of your plotlines? The odd gobbet of red-hot dialogue?'

'Definitely not.'

'Hmm. Well, perhaps I'm smarter than I think.' He

shrugged. 'Or his appetite was stronger than his willpower — who knows?'

I frowned. 'Didn't he say *anything* to you?'

'He said "Yes", and "No". More accurately, he explored variations on the theme of grunt. I didn't push it. He has quite the off-putting face on him. Reminds me of my grandmother, Nanny O'Byrne. She had a face that could make a train back up and take a dirt road.'

He gestured towards the hospital entrance. 'Why don't we see what you can elicit from him this time? I assume that's where you were headed?'

'Oh! Um—'

But I could hardly pretend otherwise. And, even though I was filled with relief that Big Man hadn't ratted me out, I without doubt still owed him an apology. He may not have thought a face slapping worth mentioning to Dr Flynn, but I doubt he'd be so reticent with the actual slapper. So to speak.

I squared my shoulders. 'That's exactly where I was headed. Is he still in Ward 12?'

He was. Dr Flynn led the way and I reluctantly followed. When we arrived at Big Man's bed, I'm ashamed to say I hid behind the psychiatrist's hairy tweeded back.

'Good morning, Michael!' Dr Flynn greeted him cheerfully. 'I see that you have already enjoyed breakfast. Nothing fried, of course, and only a mere smear of polyunsaturated spread on your toast, so perhaps "enjoyed" is overstating it. But nevertheless, good that you are eating.'

I was still hiding, so I could not see Big Man's reaction to all this. But I did not hear even a grunted reply, so I assumed he was not brimming with newfound enthusiasm.

'And guess who I've brought to visit—?'

Dr Flynn glanced over his shoulder and stepped to one side, so that I was revealed. I very nearly clapped my hands over my face, like a small child who hopes that if they can't see you, you can't see them. As it was, Big Man's eyes and mine locked immediately. I saw his widen the tiniest fraction before his expression settled into its usual grim blankness. He did not say a word, and I couldn't think of one either because all the brainpower I usually required for speech was being channelled into not peeing my pants.

'Sadly, I can't tarry,' said Dr Flynn. 'I have an exciting day ahead, filled with actual bona fide cases, as opposed to those who simply wish to put our meagre psychiatric resources to the test en passant, as it were.'

I saw Big Man's eyes shift fractionally and somewhat balefully towards the smiling Irishman. But again no word or grunt. I had to admire his self-control. I was also really hoping it might continue, so I could say my piece and flee without having to listen to a single recrimination. It occurred to me that I didn't like myself too much at the present. I had always thought of myself as a decent human being. If I wasn't exactly a model of rectitude, then at least I was clear about what was right and what was wrong. Yet here I was acting in a manner that I could only describe as weaselly.

Suddenly, I realised Dr Flynn had left us, and that I was staring along the length of the ward at his retreating back. Then I realised what *that* meant. I was alone with Big Man. I braced myself, and looked down at the bed.

He was looking right back at me, and I had to steel myself not to whimper. Instead, I moved over to the visitor's chair and sank down into it. His eyes followed me. I felt like a small mammal caught out in the open with a raptor circling above. There was no escape.

It was clear that if anyone was going to speak, it would have to be me. At least a hundred opening lines entered my head and were all discarded as insincere, trite or grovelingly pathetic. But I had to say *something*.

'I'm sorry.' My voice caught and I had to clear my throat. 'I'm sorry I slapped you.'

There was an excruciatingly long pause, during which all

he did was stare. Then — finally — he spoke. His voice was gruff and deep and distinctly north London.

'It hurt.'

I sank my head in my hands. 'Oh God,' I said, my voice muffled.

Then I sucked in a huge breath and sat up again.

'I'm sorry.'

'Course,' he added slowly, 'after having my chest hacked open and sewn back up, and then having all these fucking tubes stuck in me, the pain was sort of relative.'

I was so mortified, I could no longer look at him. I wanted to crawl under his hospital bed and curl up in a foetal position.

Because the blood was pounding in my head so loudly, I didn't immediately identify the sound coming from the bed beside me. It was sort of a hoarse wheeze, and my first thought was some medical emergency — Big Man couldn't breathe. I stood up, startled, ready to call for help.

He didn't need help. He was laughing.

He paused as I shot out of my chair. Then he caught the look on my face and started again.

I couldn't think what to say. Frankly, I wanted to slap him a second time.

'It's not funny!' I said. 'I thought you were serious!'

'I was serious! That smack fucking stung!'

'I've been wound up like a top about this!' I protested. 'That was the worst thing I've done! Ever!'

He stopped smiling. 'I didn't mean it the way you think,' he said, quietly.

'You didn't mean what?'

'What I said. That made you slap me.'

'Oh—' I felt my face flame again. 'What *did* you mean by it then?'

He stared. 'Why are you here?'

His expression was bordering on hostile again. I wasn't sure now where this conversation was headed.

'I came to apologise,' I replied. 'And — to see how you were.'

'Why? You don't know me from Adam.'

I began to bridle at his tone. 'You're not a *complete* stranger! And you had a heart attack right in front of me! Wouldn't it be weirder if I *wasn't* concerned?'

He settled back against the pillows. 'Well, you've done your duty now. I'm all right. I accept your apology. So why don't you piss off?'

I did the goldfish gape again, but almost instantly forgot my shock as I was swamped by another rush of fury. How dare he be so *unbelievably* rude? What had I done to warrant it? Nothing! He was a prick! A pig-headed, big-headed prick!

My hands were shaking, so I took hold of my bag strap and clutched it tight to stop them. I took a deep, slow breath, and I rose from my chair in the most dignified manner I could muster.

'Why don't I?' I snapped. 'I wouldn't want to tire you, what with your constant stream of other visitors. Friends and family, all queuing up to see you.'

My God, the look he shot me! It was one of such pure, unadulterated venom that I took a step backwards.

But all he did next was turn his head away, settle further onto the pillows, and close his eyes.

I stood there, the last bursts of anger swiftly being overcome by a growing remorse. I was appalled at my behaviour. At how quickly I'd become furious with him — for the *second* time. He may well be a rude pig, but he had also just had a large brush with mortality. I should be making allowances, not leaping down his throat.

I hovered on the spot for a moment, but his eyes remained firmly closed. As far as he was concerned, I'd already gone for good.

I thought about whispering, 'I'm sorry.'

But I turned and walked away without a word.

. . .

It was only one o'clock when I returned home; I knew that the builders would be there. I opened the door quietly and glanced down the hallway, ready to offer a, with luck, casual-sounding hello. But although I could hear the bustle of activity down in the courtyard, no one's head popped out to see who'd come in. I might as well not have bothered.

I went upstairs and checked my computer. There was nothing, not even a message from Michelle updating me on the potty progress. I would have liked an update. I would even, in my current mood, have liked to see photos.

I considered emailing my publisher, but decided against it. I did not want to sound desperate — the whiff of neediness is unattractive in any circumstance, not only a romantic one. Besides, I'd had no regular contact with anyone at the firm except Hippolyte, and a little gremlin in my head had me worried that no one else would actually know who I was. I had not produced any startlingly good sellers that might have got me on someone senior's radar. I had not actively promoted myself. Most romance writers not only had their own websites, but also newsletters and even their own merchandise — bookmarks and calendars and suchlike. I had nothing like that. I didn't even talk about my writing much on Facebook. That was probably why I was in this situation. I had not made enough noise to not be ignored.

I sat on the bed and tried to work out my best strategy for survival. I did not want to go home. But if my publisher reneged or did not get around to finding me a replacement editor any time soon, what should I do? What might I be *forced* to do?

Normally by this time, I would be most of the way through my next book. But the limbo I was in with my publisher had sapped my confidence, and all I had were a few tentative plot outlines, a couple of character sketches and one line of dialogue that I didn't think was all that good. It had been ages since I'd heard my 'imaginary bastards' talk in my head, and I was having trouble remembering what sexy conversations between men and women were like. I was having trouble remembering how to write full stop because I just couldn't focus. Which was ironic because, let's be honest, I had very few other demands on my time. Perhaps that was it? I had too much time?

It occurred to me that this was a truly pathetic excuse. If I had time, I should be finding more productive ways to fill it than fiddling around with scraps of not-very-good writing and fantasising about getting it on with a Duke.

It occurred to me that I *could* use the opportunity to finally, once and for all, embark on a "proper'" novel. But oh, the thought of it! A proper novel would have to be at least a hundred thousand words. My little books were half that size and, up until now, I could dash them off with relative ease in a matter of weeks. A "proper" book would need much more application. To come up with the theme, the plots and sub-plots, to make the dialogue fresh and contemporary, to make each character believable and likeable, and then to put it all on paper — how long would that realistically take me? A year? How could I support myself financially for that long? And what if, after all that effort, it was a failure? What if I simply did not have what it took?

I fingered the raised surface of the white damask bedspread, or counterpane, as Mr Perfect's family probably called it. I had not until now thought about this being landlady Clare's old bed. I wondered for a fleeting second whether she and Patrick had—

And then I banished such a thought from my mind. Not only did it make me sad, it was also icky.

The whine of a circular saw came up through the floorboards. Someone was busy at least. Someone knew what he needed to do . . .

I decided to go downstairs and make a cup of tea. It would also, now that I thought about it, be a good moment to have some buttered digestives and cheese.

Anselo was bent over one of those horse things, cutting wood with the saw. He had earmuffs on, so was oblivious to me. Tyso was facing away, measuring something. I slipped into the kitchen unobserved and flicked on the kettle.

I was reaching into the dishwasher for a clean mugs when a voice in my ear made me jump.

'Milk and two, thanks.'

Tyso was grinning at me.

'You'll be lucky if it's not two spoons of cyanide,' I warned him.

'Foxglove,' he said. 'That's the thing. Drops you dead and everyone thinks it's a heart attack.'

I raised an eyebrow. 'Romani lore?'

'Nah, I saw it on *Midsomer Murders*.'

'Right—'

I looked past him, into the courtyard. His boss had stopped cutting wood and was now stacking it. There was an efficient certainty about the way he worked. He had a goal. He had a plan to get there. He did not faff about. I admired that, but at the same time, I found I resented it a little. Why did someone like him have it nailed (if you'll pardon the pun)? Why was it so impossibly bloody hard for me?

Tyso followed my line of sight. Fortunately, he wasn't able to follow my line of thought. 'He'll have it black, no sugar,' he said. 'And leave the teabag in.'

'Really?' I made a face.

'Yeah, he's not keen on sweet things.'

I would never have guessed.

Tyso handed his boss the mug, and nodded towards the kitchen to indicate that I was there. To my surprise, Anselo slung the earmuffs around his neck, left his assistant and came to stand in the kitchen doorway. He was possibly about to say something when a burst of rock music made him glance back over his shoulder.

'If that's Linkin fucking Park again,' he said, 'I will shove this mug up your backside.'

'Why do we have to have *your* bloody music?' Tyso whinged.

'Because I will kick you in the slats if you play any more of yours.'

Muttering, Tyso went off to adjust the playlist.

I met Anselo's eye and grinned. 'And who says the youth of today have no motivation?'

I started to butter the digestives and caught him staring. 'Want some?' I asked. 'They're really good with cheese.'

He shook his head, as mutely appalled as if I'd offered him a love potion made with menstrual blood. I wondered idly if Anselo knew any Romani love spells? Perhaps I could use one on Claude?

Digestive in hand, I gestured to the courtyard. 'How's it going?'

He glanced behind him, as if he'd temporarily forgotten it existed. 'All right.'

'On schedule?'

He screwed up his mouth. 'Yeah. Well. Her nibs changing her mind every five seconds hasn't helped.'

'She's pregnant. It makes you a bit — erratic.'

The driving guitar intro of The Velvet Underground's *Sweet Jane* sounded out. Tyso returned, his face a picture of youthful despair.

'It could be worse,' I told him. 'I could force you to listen to my music.'

He eyed me warily. 'Can't be worse than this, can it?'

'Kate Bush?'

He frowned. 'Who?'

'I inherited a poster of her from my older brother,' said

Anselo, with a slightly wistful expression. 'She was wearing a pink singlet.'

'I've got a pink singlet with her face on it,' I confessed. 'I'm a bit of a Kate nut. I saw Wuthering Heights on a best of the 80s TV show. It rocked my world. I bought up every album and never looked back.'

'I've never heard of her!' Tyso clearly found this disturbing. In his world, it was the old people who hadn't heard of stuff.

'I can't imagine you liking Kate Bush,' I said to Anselo. 'She's not exactly a rock legend.'

He eyed me evenly over the rim of his mug. 'I didn't. I just liked the pink singlet.'

I laughed. And this time, he gave me a proper grin, a sparkler like the other day.

Then Tyso said, 'Is that someone at the door?'

We all stopped to listen. He was right. There was a knock.

We all stood there. The two men stared at me until I said, 'Oh. Right—' and went to open the door of what was now, if only temporarily, my house.

There was a man outside. In a sweaty courier's uniform. He had a bunch of flowers in his hand. Yellow roses.

'Darrell?' he said.

'That's me.'

He gave me a sceptical look. 'Yeah?'

I smiled. 'My mother wanted a boy. She also thought she was Joan of Arc.'

He'd lost interest. 'Right, yeah.'

He shoved the flowers at me. Once I'd taken them, he hightailed it for his double-parked van, leapt in the cab, did a screeching u-turn and disappeared up the street.

I closed the front door and carried the roses to the kitchen. Tyso whistled when he saw them.

'Oo-er,' he said. 'Who's got an admirer, then?'

'It's probably a mistake,' I said.

I mean, who did I have in my life who would send me flowers?

Tyso peered at the layers of paper wrapping. 'There's a card!'

He made a grab for it, but I held the bunch up out of his reach. 'Bugger off!'

'Tyso.'

The boss was back in the courtyard and the tone of his voice was unambiguous. Tyso made a quick face at me, and headed back to work as ordered.

I ripped the card from its staples, and opened it. It said 'Thank you'. There was no name, only an initial, which appeared to be a C.

Claude. Oh my God. How amazing.

I hunted in the kitchen cupboards for a vase but had to settle for a measuring jug. I was about to take jug and flowers out to the table in the front room when I caught Anselo watching me. I smiled, but he dipped his head quickly and started up the circular saw again. Work to do. Deadlines to meet.

I set the jug of flowers on the table. They were so pretty. The yellow glowed like sunshine against Clare's greeny-blue walls. She had good taste, my landlady, and for the first time, I felt genuinely glad to be in her house. Even the whine of the saw didn't bother me. Even the thought of Big Man didn't bother me as much. I'd made my apology; he'd told me to piss off. That, I supposed, was that.

I was so buoyed up, I spent the next few hours jotting furiously in a notebook, working out ideas for a new novel. I knew it might not come to anything, but if I didn't start, I'd *guarantee* it got nowhere.

And, for the first time in months, I slept right through the night.

Chapter Ten

I SLEPT SO WELL, I slept through the alarm. I was woken by the bang of the front door. Curses. Builders were back in the house and I wasn't ready for them.

I snuck into the bathroom and had a quick shower. Normally, I'd wrap myself in a towel for the return journey to the bedroom, but this morning I decided to take no chances. My legs weren't fat exactly, but I did hate my knees. They were like two sacks of small spuds. The knobbly kind. Not the smooth kind you use for salads.

Tom used to roll his eyes whenever I moaned about my knees. 'They're knees, for Christ's sake,' he'd say. 'They're meant to be functional, not decorative. Has a poet ever written an ode to knees? I don't think so.'

'That means you think they're ugly,' I'd pout.

'No-o,' he'd reply slowly. 'It means I think you're a dickhead.'

Then he'd fend me off while I tried to thump him.

One day, about three years into our marriage, I found a card on my pillow. On the front was a cartoon pair of large, naked boobs. Inside, Tom had written:

This is what poets really think about when they write. But since you insist . . .
Ode to Knees:
I love your knees
They are the bees
My eyes they please
And they're fun to squeeze
Lol.

Love, Tom XXXXX

Even so, I'd exposed my knees once to the builders, and I wasn't keen for them to get a second chance to look more closely. I took my clothes into the bathroom and changed there. Being still slightly damp, I struggled to pull up my jeans and when I passed the mirror at the bottom of the stairs, I wasn't pleased to see that my face was flushed and my hair frizzy. Oh well. It was only Anselo.

As it turned out, it was only Tyso.

'Where's your boss?'

He made a sour face and hooked his thumb towards the front door. 'On the phone.'

'Trouble at mill?'

'Trouble with his stuck-up girlfriend.'

I felt a jolt of surprise. For some reason, I had never thought about Anselo having a girlfriend. But why not? He was good looking and in regular employment. He was hardly a sparkling conversationalist, but then again, some girls prefer the strong, stunned type.

I dropped two slices of bread into the toaster and tried to picture what kind of girl would fancy Anselo. I failed. I would have to get the low-down from Tyso.

'You don't like the girlfriend?' I asked him.

'She's a cow.'

'A rude cow? A selfish cow? An actual cow? Like a Jersey?'

'A stuck-up cow.'

'What does she look like?'

Tyso shrugged. 'Blonde. Skinny.'

I hated her already. I was beginning to hate Tyso, too, for his complete inability to give me any information worth a damn.

'What famous woman does she most closely resemble?'

Tyso frowned as he thought. 'That old chick. The dead one,' he said eventually.

The toast popped up. I refrained from throwing it at his head.

'The Princess one,' he added. 'Who died in the car crash.'

'Princess Diana?'

'Nah, the *other* one. The one in the really old movies my mum watches.'

'Oh-h. Princess Grace?'

'That's her!' Tyso snapped his fingers. 'She looks like her.'

'Good lord . . .' I buttered my toast thoughtfully. 'Is she rich?'

'She's an architect. Lives in St John's Wood.'

I assumed that was Tyso's idea of a yes.

Anselo and a well-heeled architect who looked like Grace Kelly. The more I thought about it, the more it failed to compute.

I made two mugs of tea and handed one to Tyso. 'Didn't he want a nice Romani lass, then?'

Tyso made a face. 'We haven't been proper Romani for years. My granddad said there was serious harassment in the sixties, kicking us off our sites and all that, and my family just got sick of it. We're *didikoi* now,' he grinned.

'Diddy-what?'

'Those who don't live as Romani any more. *Didikoi* is also what you are if you marry outside the tribes.'

'Like Patrick? Anselo's cousin?'

Tyso gave me a knowing grin. 'He was *didikoi* before. His

Mum is Roma but the Kings weren't. They were Irish. Travellers.'

'What's the difference?'

'Whoa!' Tyso's eyes opened wide. '*Big* difference! Travellers are a whole different tribe. Even have their own weird language.' He gave me the knowing grin again. 'Us Hernes are proper Romani. Patrick King's family are nothing but pikey tinkers.'

'You snob!' I accused him.

Then I asked, 'Herne? Is that Anselo's surname, too?'

Tyso nodded. 'His dad and my dad were first cousins. His aunt is Patrick King's ma.'

'So even though you don't live as Romani, you still stick together?'

'Yeah.' Tyso's grin was positively wicked this time. 'Thick as thieves, us.'

It occurred to me that, fascinating though this was, I'd been distracted from my original purpose.

'So why don't you like Anselo's girlfriend?' I asked quickly.

Tyso shrugged again. 'She's a cow. Likes to dress him up and take him places.'

The mental pictures this evoked were, quite frankly, disturbing. But before I could ask him to tell me whether he meant Glyndebourne or something out of *Eyes Wide Shut*, the front door slammed. The dress-ee was here.

Hastily, Tyso replaced his mug on the bench, jumped into the courtyard and snatched up a hammer. I soon saw why. Anselo's face was like Alex Ferguson's on a bad day at Old Trafford. Someone's head was at risk of connecting with the blunt end of a hurled boot.

I waylaid him with a smile. Just to see what would happen. 'Tea?'

He scowled and shook his head, ready to push past me. But then he paused and, seemingly with some effort, met my eye.

'No,' he said, and added, 'thanks.'

'Tequila slammer? Semi-nude bar-girl optional, of course—'

I saw the corner of his mouth rise ever so faintly. 'No,' he said. 'But that doesn't mean it's a bad idea.'

'Maybe later?'

He frowned, studying my face.

'Yeah,' he said. 'Maybe—'

I could fully understand his uncertainty. I mean, my God, what was I *doing*? I didn't want to go for a drink with Anselo; what *possessed* me?

Maybe it was nerves? That was Michelle's fault. I'd messaged her about Claude and the flowers, expecting her to be as over the moon as I was. But she was really quite down-beat about it. Posh people may have good manners, she'd told me, but that doesn't mean they care. Good manners can be, in fact, a substitute for actual emotional commitment. Well then, how do I find out whether he's just being polite, I'd demanded? Ask him out again, she'd replied. And be upfront — make sure he knows it's a real date and not a play-date like the last one . . .

That had to be it. Nerves had temporarily fried my brain, and now I'd dropped myself right in the poop. But Anselo wouldn't consider it a serious invitation, would he? Not from me. And besides, he had a girlfriend, didn't he? A rich, beau-tiful one to boot . . .

Anselo's phone beeped. It was still in his hand. He glanced down at the screen. Then he almost but not quite looked back up at me and said, 'I have to go somewhere. Later.'

'Understand,' I nodded. I was relieved, but then again—

No. No! I *didn't* want to go for a drink with Anselo! That was nerves, goddamit!

I searched for an excuse to scarper, but Anselo beat me to it by turning his back on me and stepping into the courtyard. As he did, I heard his phone beep again. This time, he didn't glance at it, but shoved it deep into a pocket in the side of his tool bag.

I went to the door and grabbed my coat. There seemed no need to say goodbye, so I didn't.

As soon as I entered the café, I spotted a man in the smoking section. For an instant, I was on high alert. But, of course, it wasn't Big Man. How could it be? It was far too early for him to be out of hospital. And this man was too well dressed. He was wearing an extremely nice mid-length grey wool coat with a herringbone pattern. His trousers were a darker grey and he had one highly polished black brogue propped casually and somewhat arrogantly on the neighbouring table's chair. He was sitting in the far corner angled away from me, cigarette in one hand, phone in the other. His hair was dark and touched his collar, but I could not see his face.

To be honest, confronting Big Man would have been the least of my worries. I had no *clue* what to say to Claude. Should I say anything at all? Let's face it, it would be a whole lot easier and less potentially humiliating if I let *him* make the next move.

Claude had seen me come in and was rising to pull out a chair for me. I took a moment to study his face — was he happy to see me? — but I couldn't see anything past his usual pleasant, bland courteousness. Perhaps that was what he was always like with women? Perhaps that was as demonstrative as he got?

I had a sudden vision of what Tom would be doing if it were him I was meeting. Well, for starters he wouldn't be pulling out a chair for me. Not because he was a rude bastard, you understand, but because he always saw us as equals. If there was stuff to be carried, we'd both do it. Whoever went through a door first held it open for the other. No, Tom wouldn't have offered me a chair, but he would be standing, so that as soon as I got close enough, he could hug and kiss me soundly, no matter where we were or who was looking.

All Claude touched was the back of my chair. But he was smiling at me. That was something, I suppose.

As I sat down, I glanced over at Miss Flaky. She had her head in a magazine this time. It was about natural health. I swear there was a headline on the cover that suggested it was beneficial to drink your own wee.

I glanced back to see that Claude's gaze had also been drawn in that direction. Miss Flaky's eyes stayed on her magazine, but I saw her she straighten her spine just a fraction and I *knew* she knew that he was looking.

And then Claude became aware that *I* knew he was looking, and he turned back to me with a quick smile.

'Well—' he said, lifting his cup, as if in salute. 'Another juncture in the quotidian progression of our lives. Another coffee spoon to measure by.'

I have to say, a suitable response didn't leap instantly to mind. But, mercifully, he went on: 'Thank you for the other day. I enjoyed it.'

'Thank *you*,' I said hastily. 'I should have thanked you yesterday, but I, um, had something I had to do . . .'

'That's quite all right,' he replied. 'We must do it again some time.'

I waited a fraction, but it was clear no more concrete invitation was about to be issued. Michelle's warning about politeness flashed annoyingly in my mind, and I knew she was right: if I did not ask, clearly and unambiguously, for a date, then I might not get one. I'd be left with nothing but a lingering waft of something vaguely pleasant as good manners swept on by me and vanished up the street.

I was girding up my nerve when a voice right behind us made me jump. 'Am I interrupting something?'

The chair beside me was pulled out and down into it

thumped a man. I registered a hint of herringbone and a whiff of nicotine. And then I saw his face.

I was still staring when I realised someone at the table was speaking. It was Claude. But '—met Darrell' was all I caught before he stopped.

Claude had introduced me and I had not heard a word. This was bad.

The face was smiling. It was a smile that suggested he knew exactly how furiously my brain was churning.

'Hello,' he said.

His voice was lazy, amused. He was laughing at me.

It was a fair call. I do not think I have ever been as gobsmacked as I was at that moment. I could not speak but neither could I shut my mouth. I was less goldfish and more one of those clowns in an arcade, mouth fixed shock-wide open on a slowly rotating head. It was tragic.

In my defence, you weren't there and you didn't see him. It was as if all my book hero types — yes, all right, all two of them — had risen from the page and merged into one ultimate, superlative hero type. He was Pierce Cavill. Henry Brosnan. Cav Peirsnan. Briny — well, you get the picture. He was about thirty-five, olive-skinned and hazel-eyed. He had a classic handsomeness that was only enhanced by a slight pugilistic twist to his nose and mouth. You could picture him posing for a painter of Greek vases, wearing nothing but sandals and a dead lion. But it wasn't his looks as much as the presence of him that was creating all the havoc within me. He *throbbed*, *pulsated* with sexual energy. I could see now why certain actors really had what it took to mesmerise audiences. Like everyone was with Polly in *Love in a Cold Climate*, you were simply *compelled* to gaze and gaze. Which I was doing. With a humiliating and comprehensive lack of subtlety.

'Your espresso, signor.' Mario placed a cup and saucer in front of him.

'Mario,' said Claude. 'This is my brother, Marcus.'

'Ah!' beamed Mario and spread his hands wide. '*Fratello.* Welcome. Whatever you need, you just ask.'

And he bustled off to tend the counter.

Marcus grinned at his brother. 'Can he have somebody whacked for me?'

'Don't be a vulgar bigot.'

'Don't be a humourless git.'

I watched him rip the top off one sachet of sugar and then two more, and dump the contents into his small cup of coffee. The men's brief interchange had been enough for me to sweep my scrambled thoughts into a rough heap. They weren't ordered, but they were at least in one place, instead of pinging off all four corners of my brain.

Claude's brother. Marcus. My goodness. *Not* what I had expected at *all.* I mean, they were so *completely* unalike. Colouring, features and, above all, the fact that beside his brother, Claude exuded all the wattage of a fridge light. Then again, it wasn't really fair to compare them on that score; if sexual energy could be harnessed, the younger Perfect could power a mid-sized European nation.

God, he was looking at me again. And he was still grinning.

'Your name is Darrell,' he said. 'Was there an error at the hospital? Did your parents receive the wrong child and decide to make the best of it?'

What could I do but reply? Well, I could sit there like an idiot, I suppose, but that didn't seem like the best option. I prayed my voice wouldn't come out all high and squeaky—

'I have no idea why my parents named me Darrell. It could be worse. They could have named me Kevin.'

He laughed! I did a little mental hoppity-skip of relief. Not only had I not squeaked, I'd actually managed to crack a joke! Nice one, me!

Marcus slid a glance at his brother. 'Yes, I'm always

grateful that our father didn't choose to afflict me with a humorous handle. As he did Claudius here.'

I blinked at Claude, surprised. 'Are you really Claudius?'

Claude gave me a resigned smile. 'Our father considered himself something of a Latin scholar. I suppose it, too, could have been worse. I could have been Horatio.'

'Or Pontius,' said Marcus.

'Or Tiberius,' I contributed.

'Our sister is Augusta.' Marcus drained his coffee. 'No wonder she became a dyke.'

'Marcus—'

Claude's voice held a warning tone. I wasn't exactly sure why. Did he object to the crudeness of the term "dyke"? Would "daughter of Sappho" be more to his taste?

Marcus rolled his eyes at me. 'Claudie gets in a bit of a lather when I talk about the family in public.'

'That is *not* unreasonable—' Claude retorted.

'Despite the fact that as regards our family,' Marcus continued, 'not a single person on this planet gives a flying fuck.'

'That's not the point,' said his brother.

'Isn't it?'

'It isn't. No. The point is that I am entitled to my personal privacy, and if I choose to favour discretion then you should respect that.'

Marcus said, 'And what if I choose the opposite? Do I get any respect in return?'

Claude clicked his tongue, irritated. 'You invariably choose the opposite. For any stance I take on *any* subject, you assume a contrary position.'

Marcus paused. 'No, I don't.'

Then he burst out laughing.

His brother did not join him.

'Oh, come on, Claudie,' protested Marcus. 'Lighten up. That was quite a passable joke.'

He turned to me. '*You* smiled. I saw you.'

My eyes shifted guiltily towards Claude. 'Um . . .'

Marcus grinned. 'Don't panic. I won't make you choose sides. You can stay on Team Claudie. It's certainly safer.'

I glanced at Claude but he was avoiding my eye. Suddenly, I resented Marcus' presence. I would have no chance now to ask Claude anything, let alone something as personal as would he like to go out with me? And I resented the 'safer' remark, too. I mean, that wasn't a bad thing, was it? I decided that the younger Perfect was, let's face it, a bit of an arse.

The arse was leaning back in his chair and surveying the interior of the café. I saw his eye light upon Miss Flaky. As he watched her, his expression shifted from interest to frowning disbelief.

'Why on earth,' he said, making no attempt to lower his voice, 'is that woman dressed like that?'

Miss Flaky didn't raise her eyes even a millimetre. But in steely tones, she said, 'I can hear you.'

Claude shifted in his chair to face her. 'I must apol—' he began.

Marcus overrode him. 'Of course, you can wear anything you like, but I'd very much like to know what's behind it. Is it some sort of religious thing?'

Slowly and deliberately, Miss Flaky closed her magazine. She bent to pick up her bag, then rose from her chair and started to walk towards the door. At our table, though, she halted, looked Marcus right in the eye and said, 'I don't have to justify myself to the likes of you.'

'Sound decision,' said Marcus. 'The likes of me don't deserve much. I will resign myself to never knowing why you deliberately wear clothes you know are terrible. Because it *is* a deliberate choice, isn't it?'

I expected Miss Flaky to be annoyed. I didn't expect her to react as if Marcus had stabbed a dagger into her very core. But instead of him, she turned on Claude.

'You should keep your creatures under a bigger rock,' she said. 'So they can't crawl out.'

Claude shot out of his chair. 'I am so—'

Miss Flaky didn't stay to listen. She wheeled around and stalked out the door, her blanket skirt swishing and snapping around her feet.

Claude remained standing, staring after her, his usually ramrod-straight figure sagging a little. Then he looked down at his brother.

'Could you, just once, not behave like a complete shit?' Claude said to him.

Marcus gave an astonished laugh. 'Claudie! You said "shit"!'

'You insulted a woman you don't even know. You commented on her appearance, which is *none* of your business—'

'I asked her a fair question that was, at worst, tactless,' said Marcus. 'It was her choice to be insulted.'

'Rubbish. You were deliberately and offensively provocative.'

'Then, I'll apologise next time I see her,' said Marcus. 'In the meantime, could you relax and sit back down?'

But Claude removed his jacket from the back of the chair, nodded once to me, and walked out without a backwards glance.

I rose from my chair, but Marcus sighed, and said, 'Don't bother.'

I glared at him. 'Why not?'

Marcus looked up at me. 'He'll be fine. He loves any excuse to fuck off on his own.'

He nodded at my chair. 'Let's you and I talk, instead.'

I resented that he seemed confident I'd agree, but I couldn't deny that his invitation had appeal. He was an arse, but he was still also very much Pierce and Henry. Pierce Arse-nan. It was hard to resist.

A little warily, I resumed my chair. 'Talk about what?'

He pursed his mouth. 'Anything. I don't know. Are you shagging my brother?'

I did the goldfish again. 'What—?'

'Shagging. Or as they say in my beloved new homeland, "parking the beef bus in tuna town".'

I had to laugh. 'That is *terrible*!'

'Yes, it is. Are you?'

'No!' I was blushing, damn him. 'We've only just met!'

'Personally, I've never found that to be an obstacle.'

He shot me a conspiratorial grin that was pure charm, and I felt the soles of my feet tingle. Immediately, I gave myself a sanity slapping. He was *completely* out of my league. In fact, compared to him, I was in a league where they gave out oranges at half time.

Fortunately, I was blushing again. It gave me an excuse to resume hating him. He helped that along by adding, 'I didn't really expect you to be banging Claude, by the way. I don't think Claude's old boy has had a glimpse of daylight since Nursey last changed his nappy.'

'Why are you so horrible to him?' I demanded.

He hesitated. 'Because he makes me feel inadequate. Because he considers me of slightly less value than a dodgy three-quid note.'

'Behave better and he might think better of you.'

He recoiled in mock horror. 'You sound like my mother.'

I made a face. 'I sound like *my* mother. Perhaps they're related?'

Even though I'd only meant it as a joke, I was struck with the sudden depressing realisation of how impossible that was. If Claude was the son of an ex-duke, then so was Marcus. My mother's most notable ancestor was a Norfolk vicar who, in the mid-nineteenth century, had invented a more effective way to wrap cheese.

'What brought that on?'

Marcus was speaking to me. I wasn't sure when he'd started, or how much I'd missed.

'Sorry?'

'The sudden glum downturn of the mouth. Was it my crack about Claude's old boy? I'm not saying there's *no* chance he'll get it out for you—'

'I dislike you intensely,' I said. 'I may even hate you.'

'Excellent,' he said. 'Let's go out.'

I blinked at him. 'What?'

'Out. Let's go out. Tonight. You and me.'

'Why? What for?'

He lifted his hands. 'Why else? So I can get you drunk and into bed. We'll have drunken hate sex. It'll be superb.'

This time, I wasn't blushing. Blushes are generally confined to your face. What I had was happening to my entire body. Even the ends of my hair were hot and pink.

He was laughing at me again. My resentment came storming back.

'Stop being an arse!' I said. 'It's not kind and it's not fair!'

Then he was no longer grinning.

'You're right,' he said. 'I'm sorry. Claudie does tend to bring out the worst in me. But I should choose to put it away again more quickly, so to speak. I'm sorry,' he said, again. 'Can we start afresh—?'

'Why?' I frowned.

'Because I don't want you to think I'm an arse. And because you're cute and funny, and I would genuinely like to go out to dinner with you.'

The words 'cute' and 'funny' began looping round my brain, waving frantically for attention like small children on a merry-go-round. But I still couldn't quite shake the notion that he was taking the mickey.

'I don't know . . .'

'Tell you what,' he said. 'We'll all go. You, me and Claudie.'

'Really?'

He spread his hands. 'Why not?' The grin was back. 'I could help you get *him* drunk and into the sack. Could be the best thing that's ever happened to him.'

'You're doing it again,' I warned. 'How can I trust you?'

'Because I may be many things,' he replied, 'but the one thing I am not is a liar. I've never seen the point in it.'

With some surprise, I realised that he was right. He had been tactless and rude, but he had not been dishonest. If anything, he could do with being a little more insincere.

The irony of the situation struck me. I'd come into the café this morning trying to work up the nerve to ask Claude for a date. Now here I was wondering whether to accept an invitation from his brother. Which would result in me going on a date with Claude. Sort of. In a way.

Oh, what the hell.

'Where did you have in mind?'

Chapter Eleven

LADY MO: Two men and a date! Like three men and a baby! But not really, of course, due to the lack of baby. Which is good because, let me tell you, baby is big cramp of style on a date.

DARRELL: More like three men in a boat. I am all at sea, and feeling queasy.

LADY MO: Pourquoi? That is French for WTF? You are going on a date with the dishy ducal duo! Before, it was just like you were observing an amusing spoof of one of your whimsical smut-fests. Now, you are a main character! Life is imitating art! Well, not that your books could ever be classified as art, of course,

DARRELL: Thank you.

LADY MO: My point is not to pour scorn on your endeavours, though that is always good fun. My point is that if I were in your shoes, I would not be queasily half-hearted about it! I would be excited to the point of internal combustion! Like my first date with Chad. Had to put an ice pack on my face to calm the flush.

DARRELL: Chad is a nice person, though. I'm not so sure about ducal the younger.

LADY MO: Oh ho! Telling! Mention of ducal younger before ducal elder! Has object of your futile fantasy shifted?

DARRELL: Might I remind you that he called me cute *and* funny!

LADY MO: Leaving aside the fact that makes you sound like a Zhu Zhu Pet, may *I* remind you that only three seconds ago you wanted to boff toff one, not toff two!

DARRELL: Not sure toff one wants to boff me. Or anyone for that matter . . .

LADY MO: Will be very strange date then. Which is par for the course for posh freaks. But at least you'll get a free dinner out of it.

DARRELL: Toff two says he *does* want to boff me. But he boffs anything with pulse, I suspect . . .

LADY MO: Hello! Are you seriously considering doing ducal younger? Or have you embarked on magic carpet to la-la land? Tell the truth because despite my cynicism re your fantasies, I have glimpsed the possibility of living vicariously through your hot sex escapades and if promised raunch does not eventuate, I will hunt you down and commit murder.

DARRELL: Sigh. Don't know. I am hardly his type. Combo of us is all wrong — like hot pink and mustard yellow.

LADY MO: Actually, I have a Hermès scarf with touches of hot pink and mustard yellow. Looks quite swish, if I do say so.

DARRELL: All right then — maroon and teal.

LADY MO: Accept that is a shuddersome combo. My mother wears maroon stretch-waisted pants with teal high-neck jumpers. And dark blue cardies with matching slip-on shoes. Will never give in to teal and maroon when I am older! Will wear silver and look like Helen Mirren!

DARRELL: Arghh!! Hitting forehead against desk in despair! Had not yet thought of clothing requirement! WHAT SHALL I WEAR??????

LADY MO: What is your current choice of posh clobber?

DARRELL: Sod all. Only flash frock = plunging red halter-neck I wore for tenth wedding anniversary shindig.

LADY MO: Recall the pics. Very nice frock, too. But if you wear it, it will indicate your willingness to give blow job. Is that the signal you wish to give out?

DARRELL: What do you THINK?

LADY MO: In that case, I suggest something simple and classic with a hint of sexual unavailability. No spangles or sequins or gauzy mesh that makes it obvious you're not wearing underwear. Black is always good.

DARRELL: Always thought little black dress = sexy?

LADY MO: Is very sexy but only because it conveys taste and restraint. A black dress says sex is all very well, but for now could you just light my cigarette?

DARRELL: Don't smoke. But do get the point. Black makes no promises, but at same time doesn't say no. One problem. Don't have a black dress. Also don't have any money.

LADY MO: Black dress or kneepads. Your choice. Sorry. Must dash. Harry has woken up. Cannot type while Harry is breakfasting. Apple porridge splatters infiltrate keyboard and cannot be removed except by initiation of nuclear device. Remember – if hot sex happens, I expect a report before sweat has dried! (Blow-by-blow if wearing red dress.)

DARRELL: May have died from humiliation by then.

LADY MO: Have fun! Report immediately. Bye-ee!

WHEN I WAS SIXTEEN, my father astonished me by saying, 'We all have choices.' I was less taken aback by the philosophical nature of his statement — my father generally preferred more concrete pronouncements, such as 'Those who spell barbecue with a "q" have absolved their right to be treated as functioning members of society' — than by what it said about him. Did he really believe that? As far as I could see, there had only ever been one path my father could have trod, the safe one. Career. Wife. Suburb. All safe. Car? A Volvo. Investments? Bonds. Secure, respectable and unlikely to cause comment — those were my father's criteria for every aspect of his life. If he had been offered a V-necked sweater in any colour other than navy blue, he wouldn't have even picked it up to check the size. Looking back now, I think both my parents made exactly the choices that suited them best and they were happy with them. But at sixteen, I hated the thought that the only choice was a safe and dull one. At sixteen, I desperately wanted more.

Yet standing in the last clothes shop I'd visited, the most expensive one by miles, I realised my genes were more powerful than I'd suspected. I'd been to all the high street shops and I'd found some nice enough black dresses at a good price. But they were all made of fabric that had a sheen of cheapness on it. Few were lined and you could feel the seams against your skin. Darts were puckered and obvious, hems were uneven. If I'd been going out with friends, I wouldn't have hesitated. High heels, a big, bold necklace, perhaps a belt and any of the dresses would have been fine. But I wasn't going out with friends. And I wasn't going to the London Dungeon. I was going out with men who were in a whole different league and who would expect a certain minimum standard. For the same reasons Julia Roberts had to go shopping on Wilshire Boulevard and Eliza Doolittle had to have a bath, I knew that if I rocked up tonight in a high-street dress, I would not fit in. I would embarrass the pair of them. I needed a dress like the one on the rack in front of me. It was a simple, classic, almost nineteen-forties-style dress with three-quarter sleeves, a sexily demure neckline and a skirt just above the knee. The fabric was light and velvety soft, and cut on the bias so I knew it would feel slinky and gorgeous. It was the perfect dress. It was also two hundred and fifty pounds.

Technically, I had the money. It was there, in the bank. But during my panicky phase, I had calculated how long all my money should last me, and then, as now, it did not seem long enough. *Technically*, if my book money came in, I could afford to splurge at least once. But I couldn't be sure that it would. And I couldn't bring myself to take the risk.

I walked out of the shop empty-handed. And sat on a bench in Islington Green and cursed Michelle for making it impossible for me to wear the red halter-neck, and cursed myself for being my father's child, and cursed the fact I was going to settle for a dress that would probably make me sweat in all the wrong places and ride up whenever I walked.

'Have the builders driven you out?

It was Clare, my pregnant landlady. With a small grimace, she lowered herself onto the bench beside me and let out a sigh of relief.

'I was quite fit once, you know,' she said to me. 'Decent core body strength. Good aerobic stamina. But it's beaten me.' She pointed at her bump. 'Sapped every last bit of energy and muscular capacity. How can something that weighs barely three kilos do that to you?'

'My friend says it all comes back,' I told her.

'Does it?' She gave me a hard stare. 'Tell me the truth. When this thing is out, am I going to look like one of those people who've lost vast amounts of weight, all yards of skin folds sagging like damp washing down to my knees?'

'I'm pretty sure you won't.'

'Ha! *Pretty* sure!' She glared at a passing pigeon. 'I should be at work right now. But when I woke up, I had gastric reflux so bad I thought someone was in my stomach trying to shove a fist-full of vindaloo all the way to my tonsils.'

I grinned. 'That goes away. So do the swollen ankles and the grossly inflated boobs.'

'Oh.' Clare sounded disappointed. 'I quite like the boobs.'

'Not the pregnant boobs. The breastfeeding boobs. The ones that make you feel, so I've been told, like you have two *Hindenburgs* filled with milk strapped to your chest.'

'Patrick would love that,' she muttered darkly. 'He'd care

not a jot if I turned into a grotesquely swollen bovine, just as long as I had huge boobs.'

She gave me another hard stare. 'Did the flowers look all right?'

My heart gave a sudden lurch. 'Flowers?'

'The roses!' she said impatiently. 'I used to buy yellow roses for myself every week. They looked so good with the colours of the house. I thought you might like them too.'

So, it had not been Claude. I was jolted with disappointment. But what else could I say but, 'I did like them. Thank you. It was — very kind.'

'You're looking after my house,' she said quickly, as if embarrassed. 'And these stupid hormones are making me prone to expansive gestures. Most unlike me. I usually favour quite another kind of gesture.' Then with an accusing tut, she added: 'You didn't say — are you here to escape the builders?'

I resisted pointing out that she hadn't let me answer. 'Not at all,' I replied. 'I'm buying time to avoid buying a dress—' I gave her the potted version. I was honest-ish about my financial state, but I did leave out Michelle's prediction about what would happen if I wore the red halter-neck.

'I'm hoping,' I finished up, 'that if I wait here long enough, someone will cast a size-ten vintage Chanel from a passing car. Or take pity on me and press the exact cost of the dress I want into my hand.'

Clare frowned at me. 'Where did you say you were going again? On this date?'

'The Anderson? It's a hotel—'

'Yes, I know it.' She gave me a sideways look. 'It's very glam. A place to be seen.'

'Dimly lit glam like a jazz club?' I asked, hopefully.

'That would rather defeat the idea of being seen, don't you think? The restaurant is reasonably subdued. But the bar is all white walls and arty lighting. The bar itself looks like one of those novelty ice cubes that glow in your drink.'

My heart sank. I was done for. Burning shame would be mine tonight . . .

Clare was eyeing me up and down, somewhat critically I thought. 'You and I are about the same size,' she said. 'Well, not *now*, of course. But I might have some dresses that will fit you. Are you interested?'

Is a shipwrecked man interested in not smelling like shark treats?

'That would be *enormously* generous,' I told her.

'How could it be anything but?' she said. 'Look at the size of me.'

I wasn't exactly sure what kind of house a rich London property developer should live in, but this one didn't even feature among the contenders. I suppose I'd expected either something with a lot of glass and black and chrome furniture overlooking the Thames, or a mock mansion with fake columns and the latest in video surveillance.

Clare and Patrick's house looked like the Big Bear version of mine. Admittedly, there was no council estate across the road, only other houses like it. And the street was quiet and leafy — no man on a bike yelling obscenities. And the cars parked along it were sleek, black Audis and Mercedes, instead of a brown Vauxhall Cavalier and a rust-pitted Austin Princess. But apart from that, Clare's old house and Clare's new house were very similar.

Clare was rummaging in her bag for her keys.

'You might be thinking it's a bit creepy that Patrick's house and mine are only ten minutes apart, like we were part of some neighbourhood sex-swapping circle.'

It hadn't occurred to me in the slightest, but that didn't matter because Clare pressed on.

'Actually, we met at the Italian café. We were both early-morning regulars there—' Clare wrenched her bag open wider and glared into it. 'Where *is* that bloody key?'

Suddenly, the door swung open. A very large man loomed at us, causing me momentarily to catch my breath. But, of course, it was Patrick.

'What the hell are *you* doing here?' demanded his loving wife.

'A seagull that was either very unwell or in the pay of my enemies decided to shit all over my suit.' He let us in and shut the door behind us. 'I came home to change.'

'Don't you have minions to do that sort of thing for you?' Clare asked.

'What? Shit on me? Sometimes it seems that way.' Patrick grinned, bent and kissed her cheek. 'How are you feeling? Better?'

She glowered at him. '*You*—' She gave the word special emphasis '—have *no* idea.'

Patrick grinned at me, unabashed. 'I have no idea,' he informed me. 'How are you, Darrell? Or shouldn't I ask?'

'Darrell,' said Clare before I'd even opened my mouth, 'is going to borrow a dress. A dress I *used* to fit into to. A dress I *used* to look sexy and desirable in. A dress that will be going to Oxfam after this thing is out because of all the sagging skin folds I will be left with.'

I saw Patrick wince a little at the use of the word 'thing'. But, in tones that were obviously meant to be hearty and reassuring, he said, 'You'll be back in shape in no time. You're young. You're fit.'

Clare's look would have reduced a lesser man to a small smoking pile of ash. 'Oh, so I'll *need* to get back in shape, will I? Because you wouldn't want a wife with skin folds, would you now? No, I'll need to slave for *hours* in the gym each day, won't I, stopping only to plug the baby to my breast at perfectly timed intervals because God forbid I should do anything as un-maternal as bottle feed! And then, after all that, me and my toned arms will be put to work making you a three-course gourmet dinner, which I will serve wearing a glamorous dress unmarred by baby spit or breast-milk leakage, because that's what *real* women do!'

Patrick said, 'You forgot a couple of details. When I come home, I'll expect the house to be spotless and the fridge well stocked with beer.'

Then he burst out laughing, drew his wife to him and tenderly kissed the top of her head.

'I hate you.' Clare's voice was muffled by his shirt.

'Yeah, yeah.'

He kissed her again. And for a moment there, I thought I was going to die. Literally expire from the pain that ripped through me. I suppose I could be grateful it was only the second grief bomb that had struck me in Patrick's presence. Now, just like at the café, I froze up but I did not cry. A grief bomb never resulted in tears. It was as if they stripped me of even that small release. When they hit, it felt like everything that kept me warm and hopeful and alive was extracted from me abruptly and all at once, leaving me shivering in a skin that was now paper thin and unable to protect me.

Clare and Patrick. So different from Tom and me. But the love — that was exactly the same. And I missed it so badly, I did not think I could bear it.

Patrick released his wife from his embrace and she turned to me, her face relaxed and happy.

'So? Shall we go and raid my wardrobe?'

I once heard a comedy skit on the radio, in which a British journalist in the Antarctic kept stating how glad he was of his Harris tweed. As I sat on a tall chair at the bar at the Anderson, which was less than half full at this early hour, I was very glad of Clare's Matthew Williamson pleated georgette cocktail dress. I had no idea what it had cost her, but suspected that two hundred and fifty pounds didn't even come close. The dress was not proper black but I thought Michelle would approve. The filmy fabric had a black ground, covered by a swirly, feathered pattern in the shimmery colours of oil on water. It had a high, straight-across neckline, softened by ruffle-edged short sleeves. Clare had leant me a wide, black patent belt that cinched in my waist. The skirt fell above the knee, which I was afraid might be a deal-breaker. But Clare pooh-poohed my fear of bulging knees. 'Wear it with opaque black stockings,' she said. 'They suck in everything. Add black high heels, and you'll look as though your legs go on forever.'

That wasn't quite the case, as I saw when I looked in the mirror. But the rest of my reflection definitely passed muster. Someone who knew more about fashion than I did would probably be able to point out how the superior cut led the fabric to fall in such a flattering way, and how the overall look was so 'now' and yet also so classically timeless, blah, blah. All I could do was be very, very grateful.

Still, I wished that Marcus and/or Claude had offered to pick me up from my house rather than meet me at the bar. Clare was spot on — this was a glamorous place, for glamorous, socially confident people. The walls were covered in white gauze curtains. The long, wide bar did indeed glow, lit artily from within. The tall chairs around it were silver and white, and on each rounded back was painted a single large eye. It was if the bar itself was assessing you as you came in. I wondered what would happen if you were found wanting. Would the eyes close slowly, as if in pain?

I had arrived just after eight, hoping like hell that Marcus and Claude would already be there. They weren't. I'd found a chair and, doing my best not to touch the painted eye, I'd managed to get up on to it with reasonable grace. Clare had offered me another dress — a tight black sheath. I was glad I hadn't been able to wrestle my way into it; I would never have got onto the chair, let alone been able to sit down.

A barman slid across to greet me and present me with the cocktail menu. I hoped no one saw my eyes bug out as I clocked the prices. There was nothing under fifteen pounds! The dress I'd been planning to buy from the high street only cost fifty-five! And I'd have been able to keep that!

But I couldn't sit there and take up space. I ordered something called a Lady Killer. It was sixteen pounds — I didn't want the barman to think I was forced to go for the cheapest drink on the menu. I paid with my incredibly low-rent green Visa, but the barman took it without a second glance, instead of, as I'd feared, carrying it off by one corner as if it was a dead mouse.

As I waited for the drink to arrive, I worked hard to give the impression that I was perfectly at ease sitting here on my own. That required me to seem cool and aloof, completely uninterested in the bar's other patrons. In truth, I was dying to gawk. But being unable to, I had to settle for a peripheral sense of what type of people were here. The buzz of conversation was animated and familiar, as if most people knew each other. Body language was assured. Perfume smelled expensive. There were no flashes of garish colour; clothes were clean and stylish. I was not aware of anyone taking the slightest bit of notice of me. That was either a good sign: I was fitting in; or a bad one: I wasn't interesting or pretty enough to draw attention.

As the minutes dragged, I found it harder to keep up the aloof act. My cocktail had long since arrived and though I had sipped at it slowly, it was nearly gone. Surreptitiously, I checked my watch. Eight-twenty. Past the point of not quite on time, and into the category of undeniably late.

I have never been purposefully stood up by a date. There had been a few times where he'd been delayed or we'd cocked up the venue and missed each other, but those had been genuine mistakes. I had never been left alone by someone who had no intention at all of turning up. My heart started to beat faster. All the trouble I'd been through today! All the worry and effort! The humiliation of borrowing another woman's dress! And I'd just spent sixteen bloody quid on a drink I didn't even want!

I bet it was Marcus' fault. Claude would no more be unpunctual than he would wear unpressed trousers. I decided I'd give them five minutes, and then I'd leave. And I knew I'd be angrier at myself than at Marcus. What was I thinking, accepting an invitation from an arse? I should have *known*—

'My God, you look amazing.'

He was standing at my shoulder, his head on a level with mine. Before I could say anything, he kissed me on the corner of my mouth and for a second I went all weak and woozy. Until I glanced over his shoulder and failed to see his brother.

'Where's Claude?'

'Ah—'

'What do you mean "Ah"? "Ah" is not good, in any circumstance.'

'Even when doctors ask you to say it?'

'*Especially* then!'

'Mm . . .'

'And "Mm" is worse!'

My resentment intensified a hundredfold as I watched Marcus take a seat. Whereas I'd had to clamber, he sort of flowed onto the tall chair beside me. Then he offered me a brief apologetic glance. 'Claude couldn't come.'

'Why couldn't he? Did you actually ask him? And what kind of time do you call this?'

'Any preference for which question I answer first?'

But then the barman slid over and asked Marcus what he'd like. He said, 'Peroni.' And the bar man slid away again.

'That's a beer,' I pointed out. 'It's not on the menu.'

Marcus shrugged. 'I'm a beer man.'

'It's not on the menu,' I said again.

He eyed my cocktail. 'Would you prefer a beer?'

My glass was empty but I had too much pride to order another. And not enough money, of course. Which helped with the pride thing. 'No,' I replied. 'But I didn't know I had a choice.'

His mouth twitched, as if I amused him. 'You look amazing,' he said again. 'That dress is superb.'

'Greaser.'

He grinned. 'Guilty. But I do mean it.'

He looked pretty darn superb himself, I reluctantly had to admit. He was wearing a grey wool jacket that had a faint white stripe. Under it he wore a shirt in a lighter grey and a chunky tie just a shade darker. The trousers were dark grey and quite slim fitting. With all that grey on grey, it could have looked dull, but it all came together to make him look rather like a raffish schoolboy. One risking a caning for the unacceptable length of his hair.

However, I would sooner order another sixteen pound cocktail than tell him he looked good. 'Why couldn't Claude come? You didn't ask him, did you?'

He was no longer smiling. 'Actually, I did. Look—'

His beer arrived, with a glass. He ignored the glass and took a quick swig straight from the bottle.

'Sorry,' he said. 'Parched.' Then he frowned. 'Look, you can tell me it's none of my business, but did you seriously have designs on Claude or was that just a bit of banter between us? Sometimes I lose track.'

I could feel the humiliating rise of another blush. Yellow roses leapt to mind, which didn't help. But this time the jolt was more one of embarrassment than disappointment. Deep down, I knew those flowers could never have come from Claude. Just as I wasn't really surprised that he was not here with us tonight.

I avoided Marcus' eye, but I did at least answer honestly. 'My designs weren't very serious . . .'

'Good. Because Claude is as clamped tight as an oyster

and has not the least intention of being shucked any time soon.'

'Is that what he told you?'

He sighed. 'It's what he demonstrates with every facet of his life! I'm not entirely convinced it's what he really *wants*, but—'

'What do you care about what he wants?' I was feeling hard done by and it was making me spiteful. 'All you do is wind him up.'

'Because when I'm around him, I feel deficient. And it manifests itself in very bad behaviour.' He sighed. 'It always has . . .'

'You don't think—?' I stopped.

Marcus gave me a look. 'What? That Claudie's a closet arse-bandit?'

Obviously, this evening would be one continuous blush-fest. 'Well—'

'He isn't. Believe me, I've had enough passes made at me by the real deal to know the signs.'

I did believe him. Mainly because the fact that he was willing and more than ready for any kind of sexual activity was obvious to all but the blind. Even then, it was possible they could scent it. At that moment, he was taking the opportunity to check out the room. His appraisal was swift but comprehensive. I felt sure that he now knew where every beautiful woman was, who they were with, and what level of interest they had shown when he had ever so briefly locked eyes with them. I had no idea whatsoever why he was bothering to have dinner with *me*.

It suddenly occurred to me that I would have no problem asking him that exact question. Which was a surprise, as being forthright about that kind of stuff was not standard behaviour for me. Angsting and delaying about it, as I'd done with Claude, was much more typical. If Tom hadn't been the one to speak first on that bus ride, then we might never have got together at all. I wondered why it was different with Marcus? Perhaps it was because he *did* always tell the truth—?

I leaned closer to him. 'The blonde chick over there, in the blue suede dress,' I said in his ear. 'She'll ditch the old bald guy she's with in an instant if you give her the nod.'

He gave a shout of laughter. 'No, she won't,' he grinned. 'He's rich as Croesus, whereas I'm only a sap on an annual salary.'

'How can you tell that?' I frowned. 'He just looks old and bald to me.'

'He arrived the same time as I did. Only I came by cab, and he was chauffeured in his Maybach.'

'Simon Cowell had one of those.'

'There you are then.'

I eyed him curiously. 'Were you not left any money?'

He made a face. 'As it happens, I was. But I can't touch it until I'm sixty-five.'

'Sixty-*five?*'

'Our father was of the opinion that if I came into it any earlier, I might never do a single productive day's work.' He upended his bottle and finished his beer. 'He was, of course, absolutely correct.'

'But Claude got his money?'

Marcus gave me an even stare. 'Claude is the eldest son. There's a protocol, you know.'

I risked a personal question. 'Claude said your father wasn't a very happy man.'

Marcus' eyebrows rose. 'Did he? Coming from Claude, that's tantamount to a full and open disclosure.' He grinned. 'He *does* like you.'

I blushed yet again. 'Not *that* much, it seems—'

He lifted a finger and touched me on the tip of my nose. It was a gesture that, coming from anyone else, I would have found repellently twee. From Marcus, it was delightful. It made me feel like a best friend, a co-conspirator.

'He talks to you,' he said, 'so he must like you.'

I was not so sure Marcus was right. I also wasn't sure how I felt about knowing that there was no point in pursuing Claude any longer. I was embarrassed that I'd made a bit of a fool of myself, definitely. But was I disappointed—?

Marcus touched me on the arm. He clearly liked to touch, and as often as possible. 'I'm starving. Let's see if our table's ready.'

He was about to get down from his chair, but I stopped him. 'Why are you here with me?'

He blinked, taken aback. 'Why shouldn't I be?'

'Well . . .' I screwed up my nose. 'You *could* do better.'

He tilted his head to one side, and stared at me, unsmiling. 'You know, you're right. I could have that blonde in the blue suede dress if I wanted to. I could have that girl in the see-through silver thing, too. And there's also a rather handsome young man eyeing me up across the way there.' He let out a breath and leaned forward. 'I could have all of them if I chose. But the thing is, I have already chosen. I've chosen you.'

The soles of my feet were tingling again. 'Chosen me for what, exactly?'

'To relax with. To have fun with. To have, as they say, a laugh. To talk rubbish with. To get pleasantly drunk with. To have a good time with. No pressure. No demands. Does that sound like something *you'd* like to do, too?'

'Is that — it? That's all you want?'

He grinned. 'Absolutely not! Are you offering?'

'No!'

'There was a tiny wobble of doubt. I heard it.'

I bridled. 'I'm sure you hear exactly what you want to hear.'

'Indeed I do,' he admitted with a smile. 'But usually because people are actually saying it.'

'Do you ever do anything you *don't* want to do?'

'I'll put my back into a hard day's work when it's required. But apart from that, no. Why should I?'

It was a good question. And such a tough question for someone like me, brought up where the choices had been limited by the bounds of duty and safety. Even Tom; he did aim for the things he enjoyed, but he was also prepared to work for them, to wait. I wasn't at all sure Marcus knew the meaning of the word. So what was my choice here? What choice *should* I make? A safe one, or one that I wanted? Did I trust myself to know which was which?

I glanced around the bar. One thing I did know: this was *not* my kind of place.

'Could we eat somewhere else?' I asked.

He smiled. 'Anywhere you like.'

'I don't know anywhere.'

He stepped elegantly from his chair, and held out a hand to help me down from mine.

'In that case,' he said, 'there's only one place for us to go.'

Chapter Twelve

WE WERE in a pub in Holborn, so small and packed that we were practically shoulder to shoulder with the people at the table next to us. I didn't care — the food in front of me was too good. One scan of the menu and I'd decided I could always loosen Clare's belt a notch, so I ordered a game pie and a glass of red wine that was a meal in itself. Marcus had hand-cut chips and a steak that, to my amusement, he'd ordered well done.

'I thought that almost guaranteed the chef will spit on it?' I asked him. 'Isn't rare more the thing?'

'All that gore makes the chips soggy. And I refuse to waste a good chip.' He picked up three with his fingers and shoved them in his mouth all in one go. 'It may be months before I get to eat another.'

'Why is that? Doctor's orders?'

'On the contrary, I am in the rudest of health. If I die young, it will be at the hands of some jealous husband or in a hijacking incident. No, it's because I associate with people who don't eat and I want to ingratiate myself.'

'Is it really that bad?'

He gave me a look. 'No one in in Los Angeles — not one

soul, male or female — lets a food item of any kind cross their lips. Why California is the world's fourth largest agricultural economy is a mystery. Thank God for cocaine and the local all-night 7-Eleven.'

I found myself jolted into a state of unease. Cocaine and people who didn't eat were as foreign to me as the high street of Dar es Salaam. I had smoked a joint once. It made me hungry. Marcus was not only in another league romantic action-wise; he lived in a world so removed from mine it may as well have been Gallifrey.

'You did it again,' he said.

'What?'

'Your mouth turned all upside-down glum, like in a cartoon.'

I could hardly explain. 'It must have been the thought of not eating. I could never not eat, if you can see what I mean through all those double negatives—'

He raised an eyebrow. 'Disappointing. I was hoping to polish off the rest of that pie.'

'Oh, go on, then—' I pushed the plate across to him.

'Why did you choose the film business?' I asked, as he ate. 'Did you start out wanting to be an actor?'

There was a small shower of pastry crumbs. 'Christ, no!' he spluttered. 'Have you any idea how boring acting is? All that standing around waiting? Why do you think so many of them take drugs? It's solely to relieve the relentless tedium.'

He reached for his beer bottle, no glass again, and took a swig. 'No, I got into film because I followed a woman to LA and found an industry that required you to have no qualifications other than overweening self-confidence. I met that criterion with ease, plus I had charm, boyish good looks and a posh English accent.' He grinned. 'You can imagine how quickly they embraced me. I don't even mind when they insist on calling me Hugh.'

I frowned. 'You must need *some* qualifications, surely? It is a multi-bazillion-dollar business, after all.'

'There are people employed in senior positions in Hollywood,' he replied, 'who anywhere else in the world would struggle to get a job that required them to say "Can I supersize that for you?"'

'Why do you do it, then?' I asked. 'If you're so down on it?'

'Because the money's good, the weather's good and woman with enormous breasts are plentiful.' He spread his hands. 'What can I say? I am both sybaritic and shallow.'

I made a face. 'I'd never fit in in Hollywood. I couldn't be bothered with all that waxing.'

Marcus smiled and leaned forward. 'Did you know that Ruskin — you do know who Ruskin is, don't you?'

'Yes! I'm not a complete dolt!'

'Ruskin,' he continued, 'was so appalled by the sight of his wife's pubic hair on their wedding night that he refused to consummate the marriage. He'd expected her to look like a Greek statue. *Mons pubis marbelus*.' He shook his head. 'What an almighty git.'

'Jilly Cooper's women — you do know who Jilly Cooper is, don't you—?'

He grinned. 'When I was thirteen, I picked up a copy that my mother was reading and opened it to a page where the hero dropped his boxer shorts to the ground, flipped them up with one foot and caught them on his erect cock. I practised it for ages but never quite nailed it. So to speak. Anyway — you were saying?'

'They're always hairless. Jilly's women. It made me worried to the point where I actually bought an issue of *Cosmopolitan* which came with a free do-it-yourself Brazilian kit. There were four choices of stencil: arrow, heart, triangle and vertical rectangle.'

'Otherwise known as the landing strip,' he said, and added, 'My mother has one of those.'

I blinked at him. I know Michelle said posh people were freaks, but surely—

He saw my face. 'Oh. No. An actual landing strip. For light aircraft.' He screwed up his mouth. 'Pretentious cow—'

I couldn't help a little exhalation of shock. There had been real venom in those words. Marcus heard me, and his expression became partly sheepish, mostly defensive.

'She isn't my real mother,' he said. 'I don't have to like her.'

'So she's your — stepmother?' I ventured.

'No, she's my adoptive mother.'

All his ebullience had vanished. It was clear this wasn't a subject he enjoyed. But I was far too intrigued to let it slide.

'You were *adopted*?'

'Yes,' he sighed. 'Call me Heathcliff. Claude, on the other hand, is more Little Orphan Annie. Minus the spunk.'

'Claude was adopted too?'

Well, *that* would explain why they looked nothing alike.

'And Gus. Our sister.'

'Your parents couldn't have children?'

'They might have been able to if our mother had ever let our father in her bed.'

It was probably good that the waitress turned up when she did. She wedged herself with practised ease between our table and the next, and gathered up our plates. 'Can I get you more drinks?'

Marcus' sulkiness vanished with an almost audible pop. Clearly it didn't take much to restore his equilibrium; he was naturally buoyant. He raised an eyebrow at me. 'Another?'

'Oh—' I dithered. 'I really shouldn't—'

'She'd love one,' he said to the waitress. 'In fact, bring a bottle and another glass. I'm done with beer for the evening.'

'I'm not going to drink it,' I told him crossly, when she'd left.

'Why?' he grinned. 'Because you're worried you'll cave in and let me have my way with you? Which is, let's face it, exactly my plan.'

'You do realise,' I told him with some heat, 'that all your talk about being shallow does nothing to make me feel special! I could be anyone! I could be a goat, for all the sense I get that you're in any way fussy!'

'Hm,' he said. 'You're right. But does that mean that if I make you feel special you'll sleep with me?'

'No!'

He stared at me. 'Even so — it's nice to be wanted for more than a bit of fluid exchange and genital friction, isn't it?'

'Well—'

He leaned forward again and propped his forearms on the table. 'This is what I can tell you. My primary incentive for bedding you is because you wanted Claude, and I have a deep-seated, possibly pathological need to compete with him. Even when he has no idea it's a competition and without doubt couldn't care less. But I also like you. I like being with you. And I find you physically attractive. I understand if that doesn't compensate for the rest of the motivation, but it's the truth. And that's the best I can do.'

The waitress arrived with the bottle, and filled our glasses. Marcus gave her a charming smile which, to my immense gratification, she ignored.

Then he raised his glass to me. 'Here's to you.'

'Greaser.'

'It's a gift,' he replied. 'Now drink up.'

'You're not coming in.'

Marcus was leaning against the front door jamb, watching me rummage for my key.

'But I have nowhere else to go,' he said. 'Claudie won't let me in at this hour.'

'Go to a hotel.'

He glanced across the road at the estate. 'If I stagger off down the street in search of a cab, I'll undoubtedly get mugged and next morning some poor innocent passer-by will find my violated, beaten body in an alleyway.' He spread his hands. 'Still, if you're prepared to have that on your conscience . . .'

'I'll call you a cab.' I got the key in the door and began to open it.

'Good—' He pushed the door wide and strode through beside me. 'I'll wait for it inside.'

He made a beeline for my couch and flopped down on it, feet outstretched.

'You're not staying.' I picked up my phone. 'Look. This is me. Dialling the minicab company.'

He checked his watch. 'Sweetheart, it's one a.m. By the time I get to any hotel worth a damn, it'll be after two. Grant me an extra hour's precious sleep and let me crash here.'

'I don't trust you.'

'And you have very good reason not to. But I have an important meeting mid-morning tomorrow, and if I have to trek all the way back to Claude's for my clothes—

'Oh, all *right*! Jeepers. I'm too tired to argue.' I pointed to the ceiling. 'Spare bedroom is first on the right. Bathroom's on the landing. Clean towels are in the chest outside *my* bedroom, which will remain a no-go area for the entire duration of your stay. *Comprende*?'

He touched a finger to his forehead in salute. 'Absolutely.'

'I don't like the way you're smiling.'

'And again, you have very good reason.'

I put my hand on the banister and my foot on the first stair. 'I'm tired. I'm going to bed now. I'll see you in the morning. Maybe—'

Up in my room, I regretted that the door had no lock. I briefly considered shoving the chest of drawers across it, but gave up the idea as requiring too much effort. Then I sank down on the edge of the bed, kicked off my shoes and started to undress.

I don't know if any of you have this problem, but I am extraordinarily uncoordinated when it comes to the putting on and taking off of clothes. I stick my arms in the wrong sleeves or, more usually, my head in an armhole, temporarily blinding myself. I have fallen over while pulling on jeans too many times to count. Even when I double-check where the label is on a top, I must somehow breach the law of physics when I pull it over my head because it *always* ends up on backwards. I'm incapable of doing up a zip without it catching on the fabric and refusing to move either up or down. My worst moments have been when I've tried to pull off a dress in a shop changing room and found it's got stuck under my boobs and won't budge. I stand there, with my arms trapped pointing skywards like I'm in a stick-up, the skirt over my face and my knickers on show to the world, knowing that if I can't suck in enough to make it shift, I'll have no choice but to ask the shop assistant to cut me free. The only time I can imagine feeling more panic would be waking up in a coffin and finding I wasn't dead.

So I was incredibly relieved to get Clare's Matthew Williamson over my head without incident. God knows what she would have done if I'd ripped it; had me killed, probably. I laid it carefully over the back of the chair and was just reaching around to unhook my bra when I heard a creak on the floorboards outside my door. I froze, arms in the duck dance position, and listened with all my might. Another creak, the squeak of a wooden lid being opened, the clunk of it being shut. Thank God. He was only getting a towel.

I did wonder why he needed a towel at one-thirty in the morning but, frankly, I was too tired to care. I tensed as another floorboard creaked, but then I heard the sound of a door being shut. He was in the spare room. With his towel. I could relax.

I unhooked my bra, shed my pantyhose and pulled Tom's Captain Awesome t-shirt out from under my pillow. As I put it on, I felt a sharp jolt of something like regret. I realised just how long it had been since I'd been held and kissed and caressed. The remembrance of another's skin against mine was so intense and vivid that I was compelled to wrap my arms tight around myself for comfort.

I knew that in the next room was someone who would welcome me into his bed without hesitating. I also knew that it would be easy — no strings, no demands — just as he'd said. It would also, unless he was full of shit (which was possible) be rather good. But was that what I wanted?

What *did* I want? That was quite a question. I sat on the bed, staring out of the window at a night sky that was less black and more dirty yellow from the still-lit city. I could hear my head saying things like: You want a good man, someone you can trust, someone you can rely on. My heart was yelling: Hold me! Love me! Don't let me die alone!

I tried to imagine what Tom would have advised. I know he thought Hugh Grant was a wanker. But in the end, I think he would have said to me: Choose well. Don't waste time being unhappy.

I sat there a while longer until I realised that if I wanted to sleep tonight, I should really close the curtains.

With a sigh, I shuffled off the bed and schlepped to the window. I had one hand on the curtain when I froze for the second time that evening. And then I lifted my bathrobe from the corner of the closet, threw it on as I dashed to the bedroom door, yanked it open and ran through.

I'd made barely four steps when the spare bedroom door was also yanked open, and Marcus stepped in front of me so fast I almost collided with him.

'God almighty!' I gasped. And then I yelled, 'Jesus—!'

Marcus was naked. Fully naked. Not a *stitch* on him. I had *no* idea where to look, although trust me, there were plenty of options.

'What the hell's going on?' he demanded. 'Why are you running?'

'What are you *doing*?' I had my fingers splayed over my eyes. 'You had a *towel*! Wrap it *round* you!'

'Ah.' He screwed up his face. 'That towel may be just a fraction used.'

I didn't have time for this. Trying to put as much distance as I could between me and his nakedness, I sidled around him and started off down the stairs.

'Darrell!' he yelled after me. 'Where the hell are you going?'

'I'll be back!' I yelled in reply.

I ran down the stairs and out the door. I didn't bother to look before I ran across the street because everything was quiet. I dropped to my haunches in front of Big Man, who was sitting on the grass verge outside the estate, head sunk deep between splayed knees. I shook the shoulder of his blue jacket.

'God! Are you all right?'

He lifted his head so suddenly and with such a huge, rattling intake of breath that I gasped in shock.

He gazed at me, blinking as if trying to focus. Or as if he couldn't quite believe what he was seeing.

'You!' he said. 'What the hell d'you think you're doing?'

I was so relieved, I collapsed onto the ground beside him. 'Oh, thank God. You're not dead.'

'Dead? Does it look like I'm fucking dead?'

'Yes, goddamit! From up there it did!'

'Up—?' He lifted his head and went still. I followed his gaze to my bedroom window. For a moment, we both stared in silence.

'Does he know we can see him?' Big Man asked.

'Oh, I don't think he cares.'

'Hmm. I can see why.'

Marcus was wrestling with the sash window. With some effort he hauled it up and leant out on the ledge.

'Darrell, what in the love of Christ is going on?'

'What *is* going on?' I demanded of Big Man. 'Why are you sitting here?'

'I went shopping.' For the first time, I noticed the shopping bags behind him. 'It took a bit more out of me than I expected.'

'What the hell are you doing shopping at one-thirty in the morning? The all-night Tesco's is miles away!'

His stare was mutinous. 'I don't like crowds.'

'But you can't—!' I stopped and sighed. And changed the subject. 'When did you get out of hospital?'

'This morning.' He shrugged. 'A man's got to eat.'

'This morning! Don't you have *any* help?'

Big Man's expression became mutinous again, and he opened his mouth to say something. But—

'Darrell!' came impatiently from on high.

'Go back to bed!' I yelled up to him. 'I'm fine! I'm just going to carry B— er, Mr Hogan's shopping to his flat.'

'No, you're bloody not,' said Big Man. He began to struggle to his feet.

'Why can't *he* do it? Is he tight?'

'He's not well!'

'I'm *fine*!' Big Man was panting with the effort. I offered him a hand, but he slapped it away.

'Hoy!' Marcus yelled from the window. 'Right! I'm coming down.'

Clearly, he'd had practice at getting dressed fast. In less than two minutes, he was standing beside us, looking down at Big Man, who had failed to get up under his own steam.

'You can fuck off,' Big Man informed him. 'And she can fuck off as well.'

'Now, now.' Marcus had recovered his composure. I got the feeling he was now finding all this quite amusing. 'Be polite. Or spend the rest of the night on the grass.'

'I can get up—'

He tried. He couldn't. He sank back with a muttered curse and looked up at us resentfully.

Marcus regarded him, and then held out his hand. Big Man looked as if he would like to crush its each and every bone into dust. But he took it. Marcus braced himself and managed to haul the older man to his feet. I saw Marcus' expression flicker fractionally as he realised how many inches Big Man had over him. But Big Man was in no state to commit violence. I wasn't even sure whether he'd be able to walk.

I bent and picked up the shopping. It was unexpectedly heavy. I checked and discovered it consisted entirely of cans.

'Right then,' I said. 'Which way?'

Big Man looked at me, and then at Marcus, and then at the shopping.

'Fuck,' he muttered. He flipped a hand in the general direction of straight ahead. 'Second entrance. Third floor.'

Marcus stepped forward. 'And if you so much as touch even my elbow,' Big Man warned him, 'I'll deck you.'

'As it happens, I'd consider it a good night's entertainment to see you fall on your arse again,' Marcus replied, cheerfully. 'So that's settled.'

The second entrance to the council estate building was badly lit and malodorous. Marcus and I exchanged a glance.

'You go first,' he said. 'I'll provide back up.'

I gave him a look. 'My hero.'

Then Big Man said, 'Are we going to stand here all fucking night?' And in we went.

Marcus raised a finger to the lift button and paused. 'Is there any point?'

'It's working,' said Big Man. 'Well, it was when I came down.'

He was leaning against the wall. The dim light may have been responsible for his skin's grey tinge, but there was no mistaking its sweaty sheen.

I heard the rumble of the lift. The door pinged and rattled open. Marcus stepped inside, and stood against the door to keep it open for us. I held up a hand to say indicate 'just a moment'.

'Do you want to wait a bit?' I asked.

Big Man shook his head. He put a hand on the wall to steady himself upright and then walked slowly and with care into the lift.

Marcus pressed button three and the lift jerked and rumbled upwards. I did my best to ignore all the graffiti, and I was definitely not going to look any closer at the brown stuff in the corner.

'It's not all bad,' Marcus remarked. 'Sharleeze in 454 will suck cock for any motherfucker, apparently. How very community-minded of her.'

Fortunately, the lift shuddered to a halt and scraped open with a noise that made my sinuses ache. Marcus held the door open again. I looked to Big Man.

'Right or left?'

He pointed right. He was still ashen and sweaty, and I saw Marcus frown in concern. But there was no way in hell Big Man would allow him to help, so he didn't bother to suggest it. We accompanied Big Man at glacial speed down the corridor, until we came to flat 312.

Big Man felt in his pocket for his key. It took him an age to get it in the lock, but all I could do was bite my lip and wait. Door finally open, Big Man said, 'Put the bags down here. I'll take 'em in.'

'Don't be ridiculous,' I told him. 'You can barely stand.'

And I barged my way on in to Big Man's home.

Marcus, a good half-minute later, said what I was thinking. 'Christ almighty. How does anyone live like this?'

The flat was a tip. No — tip suggests some kind of order. Bulldozers shifting stuff into neater piles. Bins for recycling. A man helping you to reverse your trailer. In that respect Big Man's house was nothing like a tip. It was more like his ceiling had been opened up and all the garbage in the world had been dropped through it. You could see one chair. You could see the stovetop, such as it was. I assumed that if I went in his bathroom, I might be able to see the toilet seat. Every other available surface, high and low, was covered with crap. Newspapers, cardboard, magazines, envelopes, bills, the odd dog-eared book, used paper plates and plastic cutlery, crushed takeaway coffee cups, pizza boxes, milk cartons, Coke cans, baked bean cans, orange peel, a ripped sock, plastic shopping bags, apple cores, crumpled tissues, phone books, a broken pair of spectacles, encrusted cereal bowls, blackened saucepans, an old shoe covered with mould, things I couldn't identify covered with mould — and this was just what I saw in only one swift, appalled glance around the room.

Big Man made it to the one visible chair and sank down in it. For a moment, he hung his head, trying to get his breath back. Then he turned on the two of us a look of pure hatred and said, 'No one asked you. So you can fu—'

But I refused to let him finish. 'I can't even find a place to put this shopping,' I told him. 'You can *not* live like this!'

'No one asked you—'

'Serial killers live better than this! Jeffrey Dahmer had a nicer flat — and he had chopped-up body parts in the *vegetable crisper*!'

I heard Marcus say, 'Darrell. Let the man be.'

I turned on him. 'How *can* I? How can I let him *stay* here? For God's sake!'

'Darrell, it's his house. He's his own man. He's the one who has the right to decide.'

'But surely?' I was flabbergasted. 'Surely, if this is a council estate — don't they expect some standards?'

'If they've never received a complaint, I doubt they'd care.'

'How can they *not* have?'

Then I glanced across at Big Man and shut my mouth. No one would ever have been in here. Apart from the strong reek of nicotine, it didn't, surprisingly, smell all that bad; he must get rid of the worst of the waste. He paid his rent on time. He never caused trouble. He was, in almost every respect, a model tenant.

He was looking at me, warily, furiously. He'd kept this secret for God knows how many years, and now through no fault of his own, he'd been made vulnerable. Suddenly, my heart went out to him.

I held up the shopping. 'Where do you want this?'

He shrugged. I picked my way over debris and into the kitchenette. There was no clear bench space anywhere. I opened a cupboard and to my amazement found an empty shelf. I realised its emptiness was why he needed to go shopping. The cans in the bags were what he lived on. There were fourteen — baked beans, spaghetti, baked beans and sausages. One each day for lunch, I guessed. One for dinner. I placed them on the shelf and shut the cupboard door.

Marcus caught my eye, and indicated with a nod of his head that we should leave. Big Man was slumped in the chair, but his colour was better, his breathing more regular. Still — even though I knew his shopping would, by his reckoning anyway, last him a week, I was not at all keen for him to be left alone.

Marcus had the front door open. He said, 'Come on, Darrell. Time to go.'

'I could bring you a cup of coffee tomorrow?' I ventured.

Big Man's eyes widened briefly in surprise. Then they settled into hard anger. 'You come here again and I'll do you.'

Marcus tutted. 'No, you won't, you cantankerous sod. But don't worry. She won't come here again. Will you, Darrell?'

I didn't look at him. I didn't look at Big Man, either, as I left the flat. But all the way down the corridor and in the lift, I could feel Marcus's eyes on me.

'You'll regret it,' he said, when we once more outside the estate. 'He doesn't want your help.'

I continued to ignore him. I heard him chuckle softly in the darkness.

But at my front door, I was forced to speak. 'Oh shit! The key!'

And there it was, in his hand. 'Call me ever-prepared,' he said. 'Actually, no, it was sheer luck. I saw it on the hall table. But I'll accept your thanks, nonetheless.'

Inside, in the quiet and peace of the house, my legs suddenly started to wobble, and I had to sit down where I was, at the foot of the stairs. I lifted my hands to wipe my face and found they were all clammy. I wiped my face anyway.

Marcus let out a breath, and lowered himself onto the stairs next to me. There wasn't much room. I felt his body press against mine, and the warmth and solidity of it was astonishingly welcome.

'Was it his flat that distressed you most?' he asked. 'Or something else—?'

I couldn't answer him. I had no idea.

He hesitated. 'Would you object if I hugged you?'

That forced a quick smile from me. I shook my head, and he reached around behind me with his arm and pulled me to him, so that my head rested on his shoulder. I felt his cheek press against my hair. He smelled slightly sweaty with a hint of nicotine. It wasn't at all unpleasant.

'I can't help him, can I?' I said after a while.

'I very much doubt it.'

I stared at him. 'How can he do that to himself, though? How *can* he?'

Marcus regarded me in return. 'It's his choice. No one has forced him to live like that. So why let it bother you?'

He frowned. 'And why him, anyway? How on earth do you know him?'

'I don't really,' I admitted. 'I know his name and that's about it . . .'

'Then why? Why bother about him?'

A thought darted into my head. It said: Because he lived. Because death decided to give him a second chance—

'I have something to tell you,' I said to Marcus.

'Tell me, then.'

'I was married. My husband died.'

He was silent. I felt him take a deep breath, in and out. 'I can't imagine what that must be like,' he said eventually. 'That kind of loss . . .'

'It's hell,' I said. 'Because it seems like it will never go away. You think it's lifting and then — wham. There it is. Back again, just as bad as before. No — *worse.* If it was constant, it wouldn't be half so awful . . .'

'How long has it been?'

'Twenty-one months and three days.'

'Ah.'

'I'm sorry.'

He stared at me, genuinely astonished. 'What on earth for?'

'For putting a damper on things.'

He chuckled and tightened his arm around my shoulder.

'Angel, I've had more fun and excitement tonight than I've had in eons. Beer, chips, a laugh — topped off by a midnight mercy mission.' He turned his head and placed a gentle kiss on my temple. 'Thank you.'

The need rose up in me with such force, I had no chance of deflecting it. I grabbed the back of his neck, pulled his mouth onto mine and kissed him for all I was worth. I felt him give the briefest startled jerk, but then his mouth opened to mine and he began to kiss me back.

But after only a few seconds—

'Mmph—' He broke away. I reached for him again, but he put a hand on my shoulder and held me apart from him.

'I can hardly believe I'm saying this. But I'm not sure this is a good idea.'

The need was still so strong, I almost smacked him around the head in frustration. How dare he stop? He wouldn't stop with anyone else — it's not *fair*! I'll *make* him kiss me again! I'll *make* him sleep with me—!

As I reached out to him again, I felt a surge of sick horror. What was I *doing*? What kind of desperate saddo did I think I was? I shoved my traitorous hands in my lap, and tried to breathe.

'I'm sorry,' I managed to say. 'Again.'

He sighed. 'If it's any consolation, I'm regretting it.'

I offered him a quick wry grin. 'Well, I do have more towels.'

He screwed up his face in sheepish apology. 'Ah. Yes. Sorry about that. It was the thought of you undressing only ten feet away that did for me, I'm afraid. I'll wash it. You'll never know, I promise.'

Relief and gratitude rushed through me. I had to revise my opinion of him being an arse. Despite the fact he had no humility and — let's not forget — had jacked off in my spare bed, he really was all right. He'd been patient and kind, and he had not taken advantage of a desperate sad case when, to be quite frank, I was fully there for the taking.

'Thanks,' I said with a smile.

He smiled in return, and then checked his watch. 'Christ! It's nearly three!' He blew out a breath. 'Is it even worth going to bed—?'

I felt a clutch in my gut as the need raised its stupid head again. Wearily, I beat it back down.

Marcus was watching me. 'Your mouth did the cartoon thing again.'

I sighed. 'Did it?'

'Darrell—' He hesitated. 'One of the other reasons I like women in my bed is because I find it comforting. There's probably some Freudian urge behind it, or it could just be the result of ten years of nights on a narrow, iron-hard plank, surrounded by evil little bastards who intended to do me ill at the first opportunity.'

He saw my raised eyebrow. 'Yes, well, my point is — would you like me to come to bed with you? Only to sleep—' he added hastily. 'No hanky panky. I promise.'

I gave him a long, hard look. 'That sounds like an absolute crock, you do know that?'

'Then say no,' he replied. 'It's only an offer.'

No was the right answer. I knew that. Well, my head knew that. My heart, my gut—

'All right,' I said. 'But none of your naked shenanigans. I'll lend you a t-shirt. And I'll expect you to keep your underpants on.'

He got to his feet and held out his hand to help me up.

'And if you grope me even a little,' I warned, 'I'll cut it off with a nail file.'

'Sleep time now,' he said, as he led me up the stairs. 'You can threaten me more in the morning . . .'

Chapter Thirteen

'FLYNN. I'm pretty sure it's Flynn. Irish? Slightly nuts?'

'We have a Dr Gabriel Flynn.'

'That's him.'

'Putting you through . . .'

It rang so long, I was about to hang up. Then a voice that sounded tired and fed up barked, 'Flynn!'

Caught off guard, I began to stammer. 'Oh! Um, look, it's—'

Suddenly the voice was cheerful. 'Ms Kincaid! What can I do for you?'

'How did you know?' I asked, cautiously.

'Two and two. Charming Antipodean accent. Our friend Mr Hogan having discharged himself without proper authority. Though God knows how he managed to walk out without anyone noticing. Being the size of the average public work as he is.'

'He's not supposed to be out yet?' I felt my heart sink. 'Look,' I began, 'I'm incredibly worried about him. He's not well at *all*, and he has no one who can help him, and—'

'Miss Kincaid,' he sighed. 'Do you want me to notify social services?'

'No!'

His voice started to rise. 'Listen, if you want *my* help, I can't give it to you! I'm up to my neck in enough hopeless bloody official cases. I don't need one on the side!'

I caught a hint of something in his tone.

'Bad morning?' I asked gently.

There was a short pause. He said, 'Yes. But I'll spare you the details. No reason why two of us should be kept awake nights.'

'I'm sorry . . .'

He sighed. 'But you still want my help, do you not?'

'I'll buy you a drink.'

'I don't drink.'

'Dinner, then?' I persisted. 'It might have to be pizza, though.'

'Pizza? My sweet Lord, the luxury! I've been subsisting for weeks on cheese and onion crisps and Fanta. I think my gums are losing their once proud grip on my choppers.'

I named a wood-fired pizza place on the Essex Road. 'Seven? Or is that too early?'

'I've had ten hours sleep in three days. Make it six-thirty, and be prepared for me to be slumped face down in my quattro stagioni by six-forty-five.'

What a morning. And where to start relating it? From the beginning, I suppose . . .

When the alarm Marcus had set dragged me out of sleep at six, I realised two things. One, Marcus had shed his t-shirt and underpants in the night and was once again buck naked. Two, something akin to the fuselage of a Boeing 737 was pressed up against my bottom.

I was furious. With him for being so utterly shameless. And with myself for agreeing to this moronic plan. I should have slid out of bed right away. Instead, I sat up and prodded him hard in the shoulder.

'Wh—? Howsit—?' He jerked awake, and blinked, bleary-eyed, until he managed to focus on my face.

'What do you think you're doing?' I demanded. 'Where are your clothes?'

He lifted his head a fraction and glanced around, bemused. 'I've no idea. I got too hot, I suppose.'

I glared at him. 'You were poking me.'

'Poking you?'

I nodded towards the spot. He peered down the bedclothes, to where it looked as if someone had pitched a small tent. 'Oh. Right.' Then he grinned. 'Sorry. Beyond my control.'

He propped his palms on the bed and hauled himself into a sitting position next to me. 'Sorry,' he said again. 'Please don't bring out the nail file.'

I couldn't help it. My eyes were magnetically drawn. 'It's still there.'

He made a face. 'So it seems. I'll have to douse it with cold water or it'll be hell trying to pee.'

Oh God. I don't know what was going on with me, but I was having the internal struggle of my *life*. It was as if I was two people: a smart, sane, rational person, and a demented loon. My whole body was overheating, as if I was being filled with boiling liquid. My skin was pinking like a hot car engine. My heart — let's not even go there. I suspect the beat rate had reached a point where it was no longer detectable by known medical instrumentation.

I wanted him. I wanted him so badly, I feared for any flammable materials in the area. I wanted to grab hold of that erect monster and do terrible, filthy things with it. I hadn't had sex in so long I could barely remember. And I wanted it. I wanted it now—

I put my hand on his cock.

He jumped. 'Christ!' Then he gazed at me, wide-eyed. 'Are you sure?'

'No,' I said. 'So don't ask again.'

I ran my fingers up the length of the shaft.

He closed his eyes, 'Oh, Christ—'

And then I whipped off my knickers and straddled him. I was preparing to lower myself down when I was doused by the cold water of sanity.

'Bugger!' I said.

'I certainly can if you prefer—?'

'No!' I glared down at him. 'No, we need — you know!'

He raised a questioning eyebrow. 'What? Handcuffs? A third party?'

'Protection!' I slumped down so I was sitting on his thighs. 'I don't have any. Do you?'

'Ah, well. As it happens . . .'

He reached out sideways to my desk and lifted off it a small foil packet, which he brandished with a grin.

Then he saw my face and his grin vanished.

'I thought you might have some in your wallet,' I said slowly. 'In your jacket pocket. Over on the chair. On the other side of the room. But instead you had them right here, by the bed . . .'

'I know! But God! Please! Don't get me wrong! I never expected this! Trust me — it's one of my cardinal rules! Never expect and you'll never be disappointed!'

'Then why did you—?'

'Because one of my other cardinal rules is — be prepared. That way if it does turn out, you won't be disappointed, either.'

His expression was genuinely beseeching. 'Please. Please don't stop. I am hard as a rock here. I don't think I could bear it if had to settle for another towel.'

I hesitated for a half second. 'Oh, go on, then.'

I've never seen a man roll on a condom that quickly. And

there he was, ready. He placed his hands first on my hips and then slid them upwards under my t-shirt. The touch of him was so intensely pleasurable, I realised how much I'd been missing the feel of a man's hands on my skin.

'I think we can do without Captain Awesome,' he murmured, and he took off my shirt. 'God, look at those. Wonderful. Now, come here—'

Oh, Dear Reader, it was astonishing. And I believe that was for one simple reason — he just *loved* to fuck. Everything he did was dedicated to creating the maximum pleasure for both of us. When I came, it absolutely rocked me through and through. With some effort, I roused myself from the golden, sleepy haze and found him smiling down at me.

'Glorious,' he said. 'Now, if you're ready, I'd like to join you.'

In reply, I wrapped my legs back around him and pressed my heels into his beautiful, muscled arse.

'Right,' he breathed. 'Hold tight. Here we go—'

Afterwards, we lay locked together for a sweaty age, until Marcus finally raised his head.

'Now *that*—' he grinned, 'was my idea of a good morning.'

Then he tensed. Downstairs, the front door had opened and shut. 'What the hell?'

'Builders,' I sighed.

'Building *what*?'

'A new kitchen. And, eventually, bathroom. For my pregnant landlady.'

Marcus rolled off me and reached for his watch. 'It's barely seven!'

'Builders start early.'

He flopped down on his back. 'And put paid to any encore. Oh, well—' He expelled a long breath and sat up. 'Bathroom time.'

But as he was about to swing his legs out of bed, I grabbed his arm.

'Can I just ask you a question? Before we reach the point where I simply can't because it will be too embarrassing?'

He grinned. 'Fire away.'

'Right. First — what *is* your surname?'

'Reynolds.'

'Like the painter?'

'Yes. But no relation.'

'Are you an Hon?'

"That's two questions. But yes, I am. Technically.' He gave a quick grimace. 'Look, sorry — I really *must* go for a pee.'

I still had hold of his arm. I let go and watched him walk naked to the door — and then straight out! Did he not care that there were people in the house? I sighed. What a stupid question.

There was no way I was taking a shower with builders present, so I slid reluctantly out of bed and began to forage for a shirt and jeans. On the floor I found the t-shirt I'd lent Marcus. Two steps further on were his underpants. I picked them up. Armani.

'Right—' He was back and had at least closed the door behind him. 'I'd better get clad.' He noted what was in my hand. 'Toss me those, will you, angel?'

'You're going to re-wear them?'

'Unless you can lend me a fresh pair, I have little choice.'

'You could go commando.'

'Not with these trousers,' he grinned. 'They're wool. The chafing would be unbearable.'

He'd finished dressing while I was still buttoning my shirt. I assumed, with a stab of resentment, that getaways from the aforementioned jealous husbands had trained him in the art of the quick change.

As if reading my mind, he came up to me and placed his hands lightly on my upper arms. 'Thank you,' he said. 'You've been more generous than I deserve.'

Then he bent his head and kissed me, arms reaching

around now to pull me close. The kiss deepened. His hand began to run up under my shirt, his fingers warm and tingling on my bare skin. I felt him growing hard against me.

From below us, the screech of a circular saw wound up like a dentist's drill. Marcus and I broke apart.

'Christ,' he winced. 'The appearance of my dead grandmother would be less of a passion killer.'

'I'm sorry. But they do go home at five on the dot.'

I hadn't meant it to be a hint, but as it was, he didn't take it. He left me with my shirt still hitched up, and strode off to his jacket, hanging over the back of the bedroom chair. From the inside pocket he drew a pack of cigarettes and a silver lighter. It gave me a start; I'd almost forgotten that he smoked.

He saw my surprise and said, a little sheepishly, 'I've managed to cut down to two a day. One before breakfast, one mid-morning.'

I straightened my shirt. 'Why don't you give it up altogether?'

'Because I like it,' he said. 'But it's one of the few things in life that's definitely best in moderation.'

He glanced out the window to check the weather. 'I'll smoke outside.' He grinned — 'See you in five' — and was gone.

When I came down to the kitchen five minutes later, Anselo was at the far end of the courtyard. He looked up the instant I arrived. I waved in passing and headed to switch on the kettle. I grabbed the bread out of the fridge, shut the door and almost backed right into him.

'God, this room is tiny,' I laughed. 'Good thing we're not Sumo wrestlers.'

Anselo didn't reply. He was frowning, as if there was something on his mind.

'I — uh—' He ground to a halt.

I widened my eyes at him encouragingly, and could almost see him stiffen his sinews. 'I was wondering—'

The front door banged shut and footsteps clipped down the hallway. Marcus must have gone out more quietly than he'd come back in because Anselo's head shot up and around in wary alertness, like a deer that's scented a threat but can't yet tell how close or how big it might be.

'Wondering?' I pressed him.

But Marcus had reached the kitchen. He leaned against the wall, gave Anselo a cool once-over and then deliberately shifted his gaze to me. It was an entirely unsubtle assertion of male dominance executed with a casual arrogance designed to infuriate. I glanced swiftly at Anselo. He was rigid with anger, but steeling himself not to react. If he did, and we all knew it, he'd lose. By making the first move, Marcus had left him no choice but to walk away and seethe in silence. Yet, I couldn't avoid introducing them; they were less than a foot apart and it would be doubly insulting to Anselo if I pretended he didn't exist. Unsure if I was making the wisest decision, I said quickly, 'Anselo, this is Marcus. Marcus, Anselo.'

Marcus could have offered his hand. But all he did was nod once, in the same coolly offensive manner. Anselo nodded curtly back. Then he scorched me with a look that said, in no uncertain terms, what he thought of us both, turned his back and stalked off to where an oblivious Tyso was hunched over some drawings.

I watched him go. His whole bearing was taut with suppressed rage. I felt for him, but then again, he didn't have to let it bother him so much. He didn't have to let Marcus wind him up.

Marcus was still leaning against the wall. But now there was a smirk playing around his mouth.

'You,' I hissed at him, 'are a rude, competitive pig person.'

He stepped into the kitchen and murmured in my ear. 'Dogs piss on trees. Men one-up each other. Besides, he was such an easy target, I couldn't resist. Macho pride is a terrible handicap.'

The circular saw started up again, Anselo at the helm. There was no doubt — this was his way of saying 'Fuck you'.

'Come on,' Marcus sighed. 'I'll shout you a ham and cheese croissant at the café.'

I checked my watch. 'I'm not usually there till eight-thirty.'

'Well, then.' Marcus took hold of my arm. 'This morning you'll be early, won't you?'

By twenty past eight, the stream of workers had abated. The chatty woman from the doctor's had been in for her boss's custard tarts. The man in the black polo-neck and trendy glasses had been in for his half-decaf trim latte. Marcus conceded that he could be an architect, though felt there was also a strong possibility he ran a gallery. Either way, we both agreed that he owned an original Eames lounge chair.

At twenty-three minutes past eight, Miss Flaky entered. Marcus was scanning the newspaper, so he didn't see her. She, however, registered his presence immediately. After directing at him a laser beam of pure loathing, she caught *my* eye. I could feel myself visibly shrivelling under her scorn. If Miss Flaky considered Marcus pond scum, then I was a small dead fish rotting in the mud at the bottom.

As if suddenly aware of the vibrations, Marcus lifted his head. I half expected him to do something childish and irritating, like give her a cheery wave. But instead he slowly folded up the paper, and said, 'I'd better apologise. Claude will never forgive me if I don't.'

Vincente was manning the counter this morning. Miss Flaky gave him her order and sat down at her usual table, two away from ours. There were free tables that would have put more distance between us, but she ignored those. She was clearly not going to let the presence of pond scum deter her from her daily routine.

Marcus stood up. Watching him carefully, I was intrigued to see no trace of sexy charm. This Marcus was toned down, serious, but also, I observed, not overly apologetic. I suddenly realised that he was pitching it perfectly. Miss Flaky would be ruthless with crawlers. I found it a little unsettling. He didn't seem to have adapted his personality to suit me. Or perhaps I just hadn't noticed?

Miss Flaky knew full well he was approaching, but she made him stand for a good half minute before she acknowledged his presence. When she did, she didn't shirk. She looked him right in the eye, with an expression that left no doubt that her preferred fate for Marcus involved a pack of starving wild dogs. To his credit, Marcus didn't shirk, either.

'I had no right to interrogate you yesterday,' he said to her, 'and I apologise. But don't give Claude a hard time because of it. He's not my keeper.' He nodded once. 'Enjoy your morning.'

At our table he paused, stuck his hand in his pocket and pulled out his phone. It was buzzing. He had it on vibrate, which was the only choice once you thought about it.

'Damn,' he told me. 'I'll have to take this. I shouldn't be long.' He pressed the call button. 'Hello there—'

I watched him walk out, his conversation fading as he disappeared into the smoking section. With a sigh, I turned back — and found Miss Flaky staring at me. With her lip slightly curled.

'Are you *serious?*' she said to me.

I blinked at her. 'Serious?'

'About jerk-off there? Jesus, he'd bang road-kill if it was still a few days fresh.'

I not only gaped like a goldfish, I mouthed like one in mute astonishment.

'Do yourself a favour,' she went on. 'Dump him like the trash he is.'

I could feel my cheeks flaming. I've never been good at confrontation. To be fair, I've never needed to be. But this was *completely* uncalled for—

'I don't need to justify myself to the likes of you,' I told her. Her words. She could take them and shove it.

She stared at me, unmoved, over her teacup. Then her mouth twitched into a knowing smirk. 'Yeah, well,' she said. 'Good luck with that.'

Then she set down her teacup and picked up her book. I was no longer of interest.

I wanted to slap her. No, I *craved* to slap her. Smug, rude, know-it-all! How dare she be so convinced that her shitty opinion was the only right one? I craved for her to have no friends, and to die lonely, bitter and full of regrets.

Naturally, that was the moment Claude arrived at the table. He saw my face, and took a step backwards.

'Is, er — is this a bad time?'

'No,' I sighed. 'It's fine.'

With some hesitation, he sat. His eyes slid to Miss Flaky. She kept *her* eyes on her book. Part of me admired her self-possession. The rest of me still longed to smack her into next week.

Claude turned back and, for a moment, we stared at each other in silence. I realised that there were *quite a few* questions I wanted to ask him. But as I watched him compose his expression into a polite smile, I realised, too, that I never, ever would.

Vincente arrived with Claude's coffee. 'Another for you?' he beamed at me. 'And for your young man also? For when he is free from the phone?'

Oh Lord. Under Claude's sharp glance, I blushed instantly. 'No thanks,' I replied, every part of me willing Vincente to go away right now.

He didn't. 'Is nice to see, you know,' he continued, conversationally. 'This place, I think, is good for people to meet. We've even have one marriage!' He beamed more widely. 'Maybe it is the Italian here. Everything we do is with *amore*. Food, drink, life — all is richer when we fill with *molto amore*!'

As he bustled off, I cursed him, his *amore* and his evilly acute powers of observation. Claude was ominously quiet. I steeled myself to look at him.

'I saw Marcus outside.'

He said it lightly, but I wasn't fooled for a second.

'You don't approve, do you?' I said.

'I wouldn't call it the *wisest* choice, Darrell. But then again,' he added, 'I suppose that hardly matters.'

I was about to ask him exactly what he meant by that, when Marcus' voice at the counter made us both look over. He and Vincente were exchanging banter. Marcus said something that made Vincente shout with laughter. I glanced back at Claude and caught my breath. He was staring at Marcus with an intensity I'd never seen before and could not accurately interpret. It might have been anger. It might have been grief. I was unable to tell.

Then it was gone. Next moment, Marcus was back at our table. He sat down between Claude and me and touched his brother briefly on the arm.

'All well?'

'Of course.' Claude's reply suggested annoyance that Marcus felt a need to ask such an obvious question.

'Excellent,' he said. 'All is also very well indeed with me, as I'm sure you're both most eager to know. That sexy little French book is *this* close to being ours.'

'Book?' I had to ask.

'I'm negotiating to buy the rights,' he said, as if that actually answered my question. 'And I will have them!' He gestured skywards with his coffee cup. 'Oh yes, she will be mine!'

'Does this mean you'll be here for the foreseeable future?'

Claude asked. The pursed nature of his lips suggested that thrilled about this he was not.

'Don't panic,' said Marcus. 'I'll be jetting between here and Paris regularly for the next couple of weeks at least. You'll hardly see me.' He shrugged. 'But I can check into a hotel if you'd prefer.'

'I really don't care,' replied his brother. 'Do as you please. As always.'

A brief frown darkened Marcus' face. I could see that it really did hurt him to see evidence of his brother's low opinion of him.

My mind went back to this mysterious sexy French book. What could it be? A work by the Marquis de Sade? *The Story of O*? I had a small qualm that I had not yet told him what I did for a living. Not specifically, anyway. Over breakfast, I may have said that I wrote, but then again, I might have made it sound more as if I were a freelance copywriter, who produced — well, manuals and stuff. I didn't actually *specify* manuals, but I suspected that was the most likely outtake. I wasn't sure why I didn't 'fess up; I wasn't usually embarrassed to admit I was a romance writer. But with Marcus — I don't know. Perhaps I didn't feel it would impress him? If I was Jackie Collins, it might be different. But my books were nowhere near her league. Just as I was nowhere near Marcus' . . .

I tuned in to catch the words, '—Mother's garden party.'

Marcus was rolling his eyes. 'Christ, must I?'

'When did she last see you?'

'I don't know why you bother to ask. You know the answer. In any case,' Marcus added, 'why the hell now? It's barely spring, so we're practically guaranteed torrential rain. It'll be like Glastonbury with Pimm's. Can't she wait until summer?'

'You know she likes to show off the garden in spring. The magnolias are in peak flower, apparently.'

Marcus turned to me. 'In that case, why don't you come?'

'To—?'

'To the floral-themed hell-on-earth known as our mother's garden party.'

'Oh!'

I was plunged into a quandary. On the one hand, it was wonderfully flattering. I mean, dinner at a pub was one thing, but inviting me into his circle was quite another. On the other hand, *he was inviting me into his circle*. Which would be full of many other posh people. Not to mention his mother. I found the prospect terrifying.

Then I realised all of that was irrelevant. He was asking me on another date. I would see him again. And right now, that was all that mattered.

'I'd love to,' I told him.

He grinned at me. 'Good.'

Then he checked his watch. 'Shit. I'd better go.' He stood and said to Claude, 'Is the key in the usual?'

'Where else would it be?' replied his brother.

'See you, angel.' Marcus stooped and kissed me briefly on the mouth.

For the sake of my own dignity, not to mention sanity, I had to play it cool. I couldn't let on for a second that my insides were a churning mess of desperate questions and need.

But I think he sensed it, because he hesitated. 'I'll call,' he said.

'You don't have to.' I hoped I sounded relaxed. It was hard to tell, what with all that screaming in my head.

'I want to,' he replied. 'So I will.'

He bent and kissed me again, longer this time. But then he smiled and was off, out of the café, and soon, I assumed, down the street.

So that my face wouldn't betray me, I reached under the table for my bag. When I touched it, I realised my hands were shaking. Goddamit, this would never do. I could *not* be this desperate! It would kill me.

A distraction. That's what I needed. And that's when the

thought of ringing Dr Flynn popped into my churning mind-sea like a welcome lifebuoy.

Claude rose when I did, generations of impeccable breeding making it impossible for him to do otherwise. He had a slight frown on his face.

'Take care,' he said, and I believe he genuinely meant it.

'I will,' I said. But I wasn't sure I genuinely meant that.

Coming through my front door, I bumped into Anselo heading out. He paused for a second, then started to walk around me.

'I'm sorry,' I said quickly, as he passed. 'Marcus was rude.'

He met my eye, briefly and coolly. I suppose he'd had all morning to compose himself, but I could still sense the anger underneath.

'You're the one going out with him,' he said.

Then he pushed past and strode off to the van.

Bloody hell. I was starting to think that Tom had been the only man in the world I could rely on. That's because we were true friends as well as husband and wife. Friends don't only partially commit. And they don't hold grudges. Friends are open and loyal and kind . . .

I went upstairs and lay on the bed, and turned up Kate Bush on my phone loud enough to block the noise in my head. I lay there for ages, until I realised that if I wanted to ask Dr Flynn for a drink this evening, it'd be a fine idea to do it before evening actually fell.

Chapter Fourteen

'YOU CANNOT DRINK THAT. It'll make everything taste horrible.'

'I will drink it. I like it.'

'Why not have some sparkling water instead? At least that way, you'll be able to tell an olive from an artichoke.'

'Why do I need to? They both end up in the same place.'

'Oh, suit yourself.'

I flopped back in the chair, and watched Gabriel Flynn ignore the glass provided and drink straight out of the can of Fanta. I thought of Marcus and his beer. What was it with men and glassware? Did they believe drinking from a glass would cause erectile dysfunction or something?

'Ahhh—' he said, just to irritate me, I could tell.

'Michael Hogan,' I reminded him. 'What can you tell me?'

He stifled a belch, and said, 'Ah yes. Our Mr Hogan. A man filled to the brim with furious self-loathing.'

I blinked at him, taken aback. 'I thought it was *other* people he hated?' Like me, for instance.

'No, no. That's just a side effect.'

I leaned forward, thinking hard. 'So, when you said to me,

that first day in the hospital, that you wanted to keep him in the world — did you mean that he was suicidal?'

He broke a breadstick in two and assessed which was the bigger half. 'Ms Kincaid, are you familiar now with the concept of patient confidentiality?'

I gave him a look. 'Are you telling me you've accepted my invitation to buy you dinner, but in fact you have no intention of telling me anything useful?'

'You are asking me to be delinquent in my professional duty,' he replied. 'I could be struck off.'

'I could strike you, too?' I suggested.

'I wouldn't recommend it,' he replied. 'Did you not see how effortlessly I snapped this breadstick?'

I leaned closer and he flinched slightly. 'Are you going to tell me anything or not?'

Dr Flynn bit the breadstick and chewed it meditatively. 'I suppose I could provide hypothetical scenarios. About a purely fictional man we could call, perhaps, Mr Logan?'

'Perfect,' I said. 'No one will ever see through that.'

'Well, go on then!' he said. 'What are you mucking about for? Fire away!'

I suppressed a sigh. 'Is he — Mr Logan — suicidal?'

'Not exactly.'

'Not exactly? Surely either you are suicidal or you're not?'

Dr Flynn paused to pluck a sachet of sugar out of the container. He placed it on the table and while he replied proceeded to lay down others and pile them up crossways, as if constructing a very small log cabin.

'Let's say that, like a suicidal person, our Mr Logan wants to die. But unlike them, he does not want to commit the act himself.'

I gave a start of recollection. 'Oh, my God. *That's* what he meant—'

Dr Flynn raised enquiring eyes from the sugar logs.

'I told him my husband was dead,' I explained, 'and he said he was a lucky bastard. '

I tailed off, imprint of the slap on Big Man's face vivid in my memory, and convinced my own face was crimson with guilt.

But Dr Flynn said, 'Your husband is dead? How? Accident? Illness? Murder?'

Tact was *definitely* not his strong point.

'His heart stopped. They couldn't get it going again.'

'Yes, that will do it—' Dr Flynn sat up and pointed. 'Pass me that coaster.'

I did. He lowered it onto the sugar logs and removed it immediately. 'Too big.'

He rummaged in the pocket of his jacket. It really was a particularly nasty tweed, I decided, orangey brown and overly hairy, as if it had been woven from the beards of ancient Scots warriors. Under it, he had on a greyish jumper that was more hole than wool. When he lifted his arm, I could see a serried row of safety pins holding together the side seam. The Sex Pistols had worn more practical garments.

'Ha!' He pulled out a business card and placed it on the logs. 'Perfect!'

The card was bright pink. It had a photo of a naked-boobed blonde and the words 'Super Busty French Kisser. All Positions and Toys.' There was also a phone number.

Dr Flynn followed my gaze. There was a short pause. 'We're just very good friends,' he said.

The waiter arrived with two pizzas. He slid mine in front of me, and then looked pointedly at the space in front of Dr Flynn, which was occupied by what could now only be considered a small log brothel. Dr Flynn stared back. The waiter waited.

'Put it *down*, man!'

The waiter slid the pizza onto the far end of the table, perilously close to the edge, and stalked off.

Dr Flynn shook his head. 'A village somewhere has been deprived of an idiot.'

With one sweep of his arm, he demolished the sugar cabin and cleared the space in front of him.

'You could have done that earlier,' I pointed out.

He reached for the pizza and dragged it to him. 'I wasn't ready to earlier.'

I watched in mild alarm has he rolled one slice of pizza on top of the next, and then those two on top of a third, picked up the stack and shoved it in his mouth.

His eyes met mine in mid-bite. He chewed, swallowed. 'That's the trouble with crisps. Ten bags and a minute later you're hungry again.'

'You should get married,' I said. 'Or hire a housekeeper who cooks.'

'I am married.'

My initial shock was followed by a disappointment so strong, I had to mentally slap myself out of it. I didn't fancy Gabriel Flynn. I wasn't even sure I had the strength to be friends with him. So what was wrong with me? Was I now so desperate that I had to latch on to any passing person?

It occurred to me I was sitting across from a psychiatrist who could probably tell me. However, I would sooner poke out my eyes with a fork than reveal the mess in my head to anyone. So, I raised my eyebrows as if my only reaction was one of mild surprise.

'And she lets you go outside in clothes like that?'

'She works in military intelligence,' he replied. 'She is currently somewhere in the Middle East.'

Now, my reaction was one of real surprise. In fact, I goggled at him.

He was rolling up another pizza stack. 'And in case you've leapt to the conclusion that I can barely tie my shoes when she's gone, I also dress like this when she's home. Because I like it.'

'How often *is* she home?'

He spoke with a mouth full of pizza. 'She's been gone two months,' he said. 'She'll be back in another two.'

I frowned. 'Don't you *miss* her?'

'My God, yes. But in a way, the arrangement works perfectly. We both have such demanding jobs that I'm not sure we could do them if we were forced to tend to each other all the time, too.'

'I suppose "How was your day, dear?" isn't a question often heard in your house?'

He laughed. 'How many snipers' bullets did you dodge? How many of your lunatics smeared faeces all round their rooms?' He made a face. 'On second thoughts, that's not entirely hilarious.' He shrugged. 'Do you want the rest of that?'

He pointed at my pizza. I'd managed to eat one slice in the time he'd taken to eat the whole of his.

'You can have two slices if you tell me what's wrong with our Mr Logan. What did you mean, he doesn't want to commit the act himself?'

'He feels he deserves to suffer. He doesn't feel he deserves to release himself from it. But yet, he wants nothing more than to die.'

'Does he want someone *else* to, er, commit it for him?'

'I think he'd accept that as an option, as long it was someone he did not bear a grudge against. That he would resent. But he wouldn't mind if it was, say, a random loon with a box cutter.'

'Ick!'

'However, I think he'd prefer to die from accident or illness.'

'Like a heart attack.'

'Yes.' He met my eye. 'Our Mr Logan is not the greatest fan of the miracles of modern medicine.'

'Which is probably why he discharged himself early . . .'

I sat, staring into nothing, thinking about Big Man. I wasn't so lost in thought that I failed to notice Gabriel Flynn's hand steal over to grab another slice of my pizza, but I decided to let it slide.

'Why?' I asked. 'Why does he feel he deserves to suffer? What did he do?'

'That I don't know exactly. However, as patient confidentiality doesn't extend to information in the public domain, I *can* tell you that he was put in jail for murder.'

'*What?*' I was so shocked I began to stammer. 'What do—? Who did—?' I sank back in my chair. 'Holy *crap*.'

Dr Flynn took the opportunity to summon the waiter to bring him another Fanta and a loaf of garlic bread. The interval also gave me the chance to gather myself enough to ask the vital question. 'Who did he murder?'

'No one.'

'But you said—!'

'I said he was put in jail for it. He was acquitted twelve years later.'

'Let me get this straight. He was jailed for a murder that he did not commit? And it took them twelve years to work that out?'

'Bang on.'

'Who *did* do it?'

'No idea. My understanding is that new evidence came to light, which proved beyond doubt that he was innocent. But I'm not sure that involved finding the real culprit.'

'How do you *know* all this?' I demanded. 'Did he tell you?'

'Ha!' Dr Flynn shook his head. 'I've had patients in a coma who were more eager to chat. No, I Googled him.'

The waiter plonked down the Fanta and garlic bread with a scowl and a clatter, only to be completely disconcerted when Dr Flynn beamed and said, 'My good man, you are a prince among waiters. Thank you kindly.'

The waiter, who was all of nineteen, obviously couldn't

decide whether he was being made fun of or not. He settled for a tentative smile and then scurried away.

'Five minutes ago, you thought he was an idiot,' I reminded him.

Dr Flynn's gaze was all wide-eyed innocence. 'Did I?'

'Yes. Anyway — you Googled. Are you sure the information you found was reliable?'

'Why don't you look it up and decide for yourself?'

I tapped the tabletop with my fingers, while Dr Flynn shovelled down garlic bread at a pace that would surely take its revenge on him later. I still had a slice of pizza remaining. When the last piece of bread was gone, I silently slid it across. He folded it up and ate it in two bites.

'How can I help him?' I asked quietly.

Dr Flynn gave me a look. 'Why do you want to? You hardly know him.'

That sounded familiar. 'I realise that,' I sighed. 'And he doesn't want my help, either. In fact, he's threatened me with bodily harm if I go within fifty feet.'

'You've already bearded him in his lair?' he asked, with genuine surprise.

'I have. And it's— Oh, God. I can't even begin to describe it.'

'I can imagine. No, truly I can. His surroundings, his actions — all the equivalent of a hair shirt. A daily penance. A living death when death itself proves cruelly elusive.' He paused. 'I'm talking about Mr Logan, of course.'

For a moment, I thought I was going to cry. 'But that's it? That's why? I *can't* let him live like that! I have to do something!'

Dr Flynn chuckled. 'You're a better woman than I am, Gunga Din.'

I reached over and I grabbed his wrist. 'Help me! Where should I start?'

He started hard at me for a minute, and then blew out a

reluctant breath. 'Why don't you try to find out more about what happened to him? That may give you a better angle on your approach.'

'How?'

'You're a writer, aren't you? You must do research?'

I didn't feel that skimming through *Vanity Fair* and *Condé Nast Traveller* counted as research. But to be honest, the thought of spending time doing something other than fretting about Marcus was enormously appealing. And I could feel occupied and productive, something I had not felt for a long time.

'Can I call you again if I need to?' I asked him.

'Is there any point in me saying no?'

'Not really.'

'Hmph.' He thumped back in his chair. Immediately, he sat up again, and craned his head around the room, scowling impatiently.

'What in God's name,' he bellowed, 'does one have to do to get dessert in this joint?'

Three possible reasons why Big Man was found guilty when he was really innocent:

The jury hated him: I could just picture Big Man on the stand. Not only would he look like he'd be better known as 'Crusher' or 'Knuckles McGee', he'd *exude* hostility and loathing for everyone in the courtroom, including, I imagined, his own defence lawyer. He'd say as little as possible — quite probably nothing at all. The judge would get so impatient that he or she would start fantasising about bringing back hanging. The jury would rationalise that even if he hadn't done *this* murder, it was only a matter of time. Big Man wouldn't have stood a chance.

He was protecting someone: Don't know who. Don't know why. The man who was murdered had apparently sexually assaulted Big Man's wife. I found it hard to accept that Big Man had once had a wife, that he'd once had someone to love him. Where was she now? Did she dump him because he was found guilty? Did they have any children? Where were *they* now? How old would they be? Were they the ones Big Man needed to protect? Or did his *wife* do it?

He felt as if he was *guilty:* If he felt he deserved punishment now, then perhaps he'd always felt that way? Big Man had been twenty-nine when he was arrested. He'd been sentenced to life, but his defence lawyer had campaigned from that day onwards to have his appeal heard. It took twelve years, and I don't know how much of that might have been due to Big Man's reluctance to fight for his innocence. I don't know what the evidence was that got him off; all the article I found on Google said was that it proved Michael Hogan was elsewhere when the crime was committed.

I suppose, having looked up some of the famous appeals that took decades, twelve years wasn't that long. But to have such a large chunk of his life taken from him . . .

Big Man was acquitted and released nine years ago. He was now fifty-one. And I wasn't sure he was any better off out of jail than in.

Chapter Fifteen

LADY MO: Cannot forgive you! You promised you would email immediately, not a century and a half later!

DARRELL: Sorry, sorry. Distracted by life taking weird turnings.

LADY MO: Care not a jot for your turnings! Only one thing matters! Sex! Did you get any?

DARRELL: Yes.

LADY MO: Woefully inadequate reply! Details, woman! Starting with — which one? Elder or younger?

DARRELL: Younger.

LADY MO: Ha! And—?

DARRELL: And what?

LADY MO: DETAILS!!!!

DARRELL: Please no. Embarrassed.

LADY MO: Why are you embarrassed? Did he yell 'One for Her Majesty!' at the moment of climax? Make you spank him? Yodel 'Yoicks, tallyho!' as he leapt onto bed?

DARRELL: No!

LADY MO: Well, what? Cannot be embarrassed! You write about engorged members for a living, for Pete's sake!

DARRELL: No, no. Cannot say 'engorged'. Restricted to 'silken male strength' or suchlike.

LADY MO: Right. Listen up, buckaroo. I love my life but it currently centres on pee, poo, water retention, sore boobs, apple porridge and a map that is the property of Dora the Explorer. Chad and I have not done it since this last conception, and I am starting to look at Dr Phil with more than just academic interest. I have this one chance to shag vicariously through you. Do you comprende? (Learning Spanish from Dora.)

DARRELL: OK. Sigh. Ducal younger is very well built all over, if you know what I mean. Blissmaking in the sack, too. Did everything to me. At least twice.

LADY MO: Even—?

DARRELL: Oh, yes. Sex happened in morning because weirdness happened the night before.

LADY MO: Sneak off to brush teeth first?

DARRELL: No need. He is a man who cares not a jot about fuzzy breath. Am I done?

LADY MO: To be frank, have been more erotically stimulated by Dr Phil. Last question — was this a one-off? Or is more rumpy on the horizon?

DARRELL: No idea.

LADY MO: Really? Hm. That's not so good. Even big knob and nob status cannot compensate for you feeling like poop.

DARRELL: He's invited me to a garden party.

LADY MO: At Bucky Palais? Yeepers! Get out your hat!

DARRELL: No, at his mother's house. Or mansion. Or castle. I know nothing about her except that she has a landing strip.

LADY MO: Ducal younger's mother has a Brazilian???

DARRELL: No! Proper strip! For planes! Sheesh. Can I change the subject now? How is little Rose-to- be?

LADY MO: Rose? Where <u>that</u> come from?

DARRELL: My landlady likes them in the house. Now I'm too scared not to have some in case she pops round. I've got pink ones at the moment. They're very pretty.

LADY MO: Hmm. Rose. Rosie Lawrence. I like it! Which is all that counts as Chad has no say.

DARRELL: How's Chad? How's Harry?

LADY MO: Delicious! And being pregnant again like a breeding cow is making me once more flavour of month with Chad's mother.

DARRELL: Thought Chad's mother was scary beyond all reason?

LADY MO: Like horror movie. But strangely, she is a model grandmama. Does sweet, old-fashioned stuff with Harry, like blueberry picking and canning. Which actually means putting them in preserving jars, not cans. Ridiculous Americanisms. Do you know how many new words I had to learn when I had Harry? Diaper, pacifier, stroller — simply not right. Chad is very patient. Knows what I mean when I yell at him to put pushchair in the boot of the car. Also copes well when I refuse to ask for cream in my coffee. It is milk, goddamit! Milk!

DARRELL: Chad is a good lad.

LADY MO: Chad is the best. Erase from memory my earlier bitching. I am the luckiest woman in the whole gol'darn US of A!

WHEN I WENT DOWN to the kitchen in the morning, Anselo made a point of ignoring me. He stared coolly, then put his earmuffs on and proceeded to apply a drill to a large piece of wood. Clearly, when it came to grudges, here was a man who could hold one so long it would have to be prised from his cold, dead fingers.

I found it infuriating. For Christ's sake, it wasn't as if *I'd* insulted him! I had, in point of fact, apologised! But no! That wasn't enough, was it? I would have to be given the cold shoulder from now until sodding eternity!

I didn't realise that I was slamming stuff in time to my thoughts. The cupboards. Bang! The kettle lid. Smack! The fridge door. Bash!

I wasn't aware until Tyso's voice came from behind me. 'Um—' he said. 'Is this a bad time to get some water?'

I wheeled around and he took a step backwards. 'I'll — er, I'll come back later.'

'No, it's fine!' I snapped. 'What's wrong with you?'

He made a face. 'Not me that's demolishing the kitchen. Well, not yet, anyway—'

I sagged against the bench. 'I'm irritated, that's all.'

Tyso sidled around me to the sink. 'Yeah? Never have picked that.'

'With *your* boss,' I said, with a glower in said boss's direction.

Then I noticed Tyso was drinking out of the tap. 'What *is* it with men and glassware?' I demanded. 'Why do you refuse to use one?'

Tyso wiped his mouth with the back of his hand and shrugged. 'Easier not to.'

Fair enough.

Tyso checked to see that Anselo wasn't watching and, with a grin, whispered, 'What'd he do?'

'Oh, nothing,' I sighed. 'He's just sulking.'

'Yeah, he's good at that. My dad always said he could sulk for England. Olympic level, Dad felt.'

That made me laugh out loud. And that made Anselo look up, and catch Tyso and I together. He flipped off his earmuffs and glared at us.

'Oops,' murmured Tyso. 'I'll be in the shit now. Oh, well. Same old, same old.'

He strolled back, took up his hammer and stuck some nails

in his mouth. As he turned to the wall, he sent me a swift wink. I felt a stab of envy. How nice to be so secure in your own happiness that you could shrug off problems that blithely.

I took a cup of tea back up to my bedroom and revisited what had kept me awake most of last night. Marcus hadn't called, so to prevent myself getting in a complete demented lather over it, I forced myself to think about Big Man. Which wasn't, as you might expect, the greatest alternative. But it was better, because at least I could do something about it.

Trouble is, I still couldn't decide what. Should I knock on his door again? Should I send him a letter? Should I do what Gabriel Flynn had originally suggested, and call social services?

None of those had huge appeal. In the unlikely event that he answered his door, I imagined he'd slam it again instantly. A letter, he would rip up. And if social services appeared, he might hunt me down and kill me.

I sighed and checked my inbox, even though I knew it would be empty. On top of everything, I'd had no word from the publishers, and it was at the point where it was harder to tell myself that they needed time to get organised. By now *someone* must have given both my book and my contract at least a cursory once-over. But if they hadn't liked what they read, perhaps they were currently putting their name to a letter of rejection?

I could find out. I could call and ask someone. To be honest, I'd had that option open to me all along. But I was so dreading what the answer might be that I simply could not summon the courage to do it. If bad news was a-comin', I wanted it to take the very, *very* long way round.

It was time to go to the café. I hadn't thought my heart could sink any further, but by golly, it seemed it could. I had no idea now where I stood with Claude. I wasn't sure how he felt about me, and I wasn't at all sure how I felt about him. I was embarrassed that I'd pursued him, and embarrassed that he'd rejected me. I was embarrassed about Marcus — I was embarrassed full stop. I found the whole situation utterly humiliating.

I wondered if I should do us both a favour and tell him that he didn't have to be table buddies with me anymore. But as soon as I thought it, I realised I couldn't do it. I couldn't bear to think of there being one less person in my new life. I did not trust that nature would fill a vacuum. I could only see the hole and to me it looked too much like despair.

Despair or humiliation. Had my life really come to the point where those were my only choices?

Downstairs again, I checked my mobile before I put it in my bag. No missed calls. No messages. I grabbed my coat and opened the front door to a crisp but sunny spring day.

'Bye, Darrell!

Tyso's voice sailed down the hallway. I glanced back. He was standing in the kitchen, where his boss could not fail to see him. He gave me a cheery salute that was clearly meant as more of a wind-up for Anselo than a farewell for me. I grinned and waved back. It was nice to know that I had one supporter. Even if he was a child.

Outside the café, I had to gird myself before I stepped inside. As it turned, out, Claude was sitting with Alastair the doctor. Miss Flaky was also there — not at her usual table, but at the one right next door to the two men. For a second, I wondered why, as her usual table as free. But mostly, I was focused on the fact that Claude had company. What an enormous relief! The perfect excuse to keep a polite distance. For today, at least.

But as soon as Claude saw me, he smiled and beckoned me over. He stood as I approached, prompting his companion to throw him a look of rather pained disbelief. The doctor obviously had no time for anachronistic courtesies and intended to stay right where he was.

'Alastair, you remember Darrell?' said Claude, when he and I were both seated.

Alastair nodded curtly. 'The alarm raiser.' He made it sound lumped in the same category as every other irritating time-waster, like Jehovah's Witnesses and telemarketers. But then he added, 'I rang the hospital to check on our Mr Hogan. He's been discharged, so I assume he's still with us. For now, anyway. I can't say as I expect him to be a role model for heart-disease management.'

'That's because the system sucks.'

Miss Flaky had put down her book. I caught the words *Raw Food* on the spine. It seemed not inappropriate.

Despite a palpable lack of encouragement on our part, she went on. 'Health systems worldwide have a financial interest in keeping the people ignorant and dependent. More disease means more drugs, which mean obscene profits. And the crime of it all is that the drugs being pushed as cures are in fact the reason disease levels are at near epidemic levels. That, and the toxic processed crap that the food "authorities" are bribed into passing as fit for human consumption.'

There was a pointed pause, as we all stared at her. Alastair the doctor spoke first.

'Mr Hogan's disinclination to take physical exercise and stop smoking,' he said, 'seems to me more of a personal choice than one imposed on him by a system.'

'Cigarettes should have been banned decades ago,' replied Miss Flaky. 'But again, there's too much money in it, for the death merchants who peddle them, the governments who get their cut and the drug corporation vultures who feed off the ill and dying.'

'I see—' The doctor shifted around in his seat, so he had a clearer line of sight. 'So what you're saying is that the current system should be replaced by another system that permits us to have only what it decides is good for us?'

Miss Flaky's eyes narrowed fractionally. 'There are proven

alternatives,' she replied. 'We would all be better off if they were more widely available.'

The doctor nodded. 'And if we could force people to make better choices, things would be damn near perfect.'

'People don't make those choices because they don't know they have them.'

'I can't imagine there's one person in the first world that doesn't know smoking is bad for you. Yet around ten million Britons still smoke.' He hooked a thumb towards an empty plate on our table. 'I am five pounds over an ideal weight, and my cholesterol is marginal, but I still chose to consume two custard tarts. And by Christ, you know what?' He leaned forward. 'I relished — every — *bite.*'

Abruptly, he shoved back his chair and stood up. 'You come and tell my seventeen year old with the weeping sores that if she chose not to inject methamphetamine she wouldn't feel the need to scratch her arms until they bled. You come and tell the woman whose teenage son killed himself that she should have rejected the opportunity to have her first good sleep in months because it helped fill the coffers of drug companies. You come and tell my fifty-two-year-old father of three that he would never have been afflicted by leukaemia if he'd chosen to eat organic mung beans and wheatgrass. I'm in the surgery from eight in the morning till eight at night most days. Drop in when you find a free moment.'

And without a further word to any of us, he walked out.

Claude rose, as if to go after him. But then he sighed, and resumed his seat. 'I'll see him later,' he said to me, with a small, rueful smile. 'And I think with a bottle of single malt in hand.'

'He's a typical apologist for the system. No surprises there.'

Miss Flaky was cool and entirely unruffled. Again, part of me admired her composure. But my God, the nerve! I truly believe she'd sat at the next-door table purely for the opportunity to have a go at Alastair, in revenge for the other day.

'He is my friend,' Claude said to her, 'and by far the best man I know.'

Miss Flaky's mouth once again did the twisty-smirk thing. 'Yeah, well — having seen the calibre of man you hang out with, that's hardly an earth-shaker.'

Claude flushed. 'I find that extremely insulting.'

'You'd find gum on the sidewalk insulting,' she said. 'A speck of lint on your trousers. Your whole life must an endless stream of insults. What's one more?'

'How *dare* you?' Claude was ramrod straight in his chair.

'Give it a rest, champ.' Miss Flaky sounded bored. 'Only thing all that pent up moral outrage will give you is a bad case of haemorrhoids.'

I'd had enough. 'What *is* your problem?'

Miss Flaky raised her eyebrows. The corner of her mouth twitched. It dimly occurred to me that she loved this sort of thing, which meant she'd be far better at it than I would. But it was too late now—

She said, 'Seems to me you're the one who's upset.'

'Oh, so you can be a complete bitch to everyone, and we're just supposed to take it?'

She reached for her book and calmly opened it back up. 'Take it or leave it,' she shrugged. 'Whatever floats your little boat.'

Aware I was on a fast trip to nowhere via humiliation-ville, I took a last random stab.

'You don't like people much, do you?' I said. 'Do you hate everyone in general? Or do you just hate men?'

If you hadn't been watching, you wouldn't have seen it. The flash of rage came and went in an instant. But I had been watching, and she knew it. And because she'd hesitated , now Claude knew it, too.

'Ah,' he murmured. 'That would explain a great deal.'

'Don't patronise me!' She lunged forward and hissed at him. 'You spineless English fuck!'

From cool and composed only minutes before, Miss Flaky was now incandescent with fury. And like before, it was all aimed at Claude. I may as well have vanished into thin air.

To my amazement, Claude laughed out loud.

'I may once have aspired to a more laudable epitaph,' he chuckled, 'but sadly, that one will probably have to do.'

Miss Flaky took the only course left open to her. She stood, tucked her book under her arm, and became the second person that morning to walk out on us.

'Well, well . . .' Claude was staring at the now empty doorway. 'I wonder what happened to her?'

'With luck, something viciously horrible,' I muttered.

'I don't know,' he said, still staring. 'Sometimes I think — if there were more people like her in the world . . .'

He turned and caught my eye. Across his face, I saw a flash of what looked like embarrassed defiance. But it smoothed again so fast I couldn't tell.

He leaned forward, all trace of a smile now gone. For some reason, I felt a need to mentally brace myself.

'I owe you an apology,' he said. 'I should never have judged you. You seem a level-headed person and for all I know, you may have no expectations of Marcus, and simply be content to enjoy his company if and when he makes himself available.'

Ouch. Sucker punch. Straight to the heart.

And all the worse because I knew he was right. Marcus would make himself available if and when he wanted to. He had never promised me more. It didn't stop me *wanting* more, but that would just be something I'd have to put up with.

Still, Claude needn't have been *quite* so brutal about it.

'You don't like him much, do you?'

His whole face *completely* blanked, and he managed to reply without, as far as I could tell, moving his lips. 'I really don't care to discuss it.'

'No,' I said. 'You really don't, do you?'

I felt that the nature-versus-nurture crowd would have watched these proceedings with interest. When it came to personal stuff, Marcus spilled everything whether you wanted him to or not, whereas Claude kept the lid on tighter than an old marmalade jar. Their genes were too different for any shared upbringing to have created a closer connection. I thought about my brother, Simon. Even though we were nineteen years and half a set of DNA apart, I was very fond of him. For an emotional second, I really hoped nothing would stop him coming over; I wanted to see him very much.

Claude was looking at me a tad askance. I suspected my rush of sentiment had shown on my face.

'If that bothers you—?' he said.

'What?' I wound the conversation back. 'Oh! No, it doesn't bother me.' I sighed. 'To be honest, I'd much prefer to talk about something else.'

His relief was palpable, even through all the layers of manners. 'Right! Well! Let us indeed talk about something else.'

I waited.

'Would you like me to start?' I asked him.

'Why don't you?' he said. 'No doubt I'll pick it up as we go.'

I grinned. 'You are quite funny, you know that?'

He gave me a look. 'Perhaps I could have that as my epitaph instead? So nice to have a choice.'

It was the word 'epitaph' that did it. If Marcus had been there, he would have said I was doing it again. The glum cartoon mouth thing. And then he probably would have tried to kiss me better.

All Claude did was raise an eyebrow.

I blew out a breath. 'I need help. Well, no, *I* don't,' I added hastily, seeing his flash of alarm. 'Someone else does. I just need help figuring out how to help them.'

'Do they wish to be helped?'

'Good question. As it happens, no.'

'Pride?' he asked. 'Or circumstance?'

'A bit of both, I think.'

Claude hesitated. 'Is the person to whom we are obliquely referring our heart-attack victim? Mr — what was his name again? Hogan?'

'Yes! How did you guess?'

'When Alastair mentioned his name earlier, you did a rather good impression of a startled faun.'

'Oh.' I screwed up my face. 'That's partly guilt, and partly because he scares the bejeesus out of me.'

'Mr Hogan?'

'Him, too.'

Claude laughed. 'My dear friend Alastair does not tolerate fools, that is very true. However, in his opinion, less than one per cent of the human race falls outside that category. Which can lead to difficulties. As we have just witnessed.'

'He tolerates *you*.'

'That's because I make no demands of him.'

'How do you know him?' I asked.

'He married a friend of our family.'

Then he said, 'Let's get back to our Mr Hogan. Why don't you tell me what you have in mind, and we'll see what we can do?'

'Is that the royal we?' I asked hesitantly. 'Or are you actually offering to help?'

'In the absence of any other pressing obligation, I may as well.'

A vision flashed into my head of Big Man opening the door to Claude. I wasn't sure if I saw it as hilarious, or as an event that would have the same effect on the universe as dividing by zero.

But Claude had done more than offer to help. He had reconnected himself to my life when I was convinced he'd been *this* close to leaving. I was so grateful, I could have run up to Big Man's door right then and there and knocked until he was forced to let me in.

Then again, why rush it?

'I have two ideas about what to do next,' I told Claude. 'Please tell me which one seems the least crap.'

Chapter Sixteen

GOOD THINGS that happened this week:

Marcus called! He was in Paris, for a series of meetings with the author of the sexy little French book. He told me he'd woken the morning after he'd arrived in the hotel with, his words, an erection so substantial it made him sorry he couldn't remember what he'd been dreaming about. He assumed it had been me, because every time he'd thought of me since, his words again, he'd had to go beat himself down with a stick. I asked if any of those moments had been inappropriately public and he said yes, but he'd been concealed both times by a meeting table, so the worst consequence was being forced to sit with the kind of posture that would in earlier years have earned him a swift, exquisitely painful ear-tweak from his schoolmasters. Because I couldn't help myself, I asked about the author of the sexy French book. Turns out, she was a nineteen-year-old girl who, at age sixteen, had actually asked her prostitute mother's pimp if she, too, could work for him. She took to it, let's say, like a duck to water, and had described her encounters in her book with lyrical proficiency and a level of detail that compelled even Marcus to go outside and get some fresh air. It was the perfect combination, Marcus said, of literary mastery and utter filth. As a film, it would blow box-office earnings records sky high, and the French teen's level of fame would shift into the stratosphere. I asked if she was ready for stratospheric fame. Marcus said he felt a girl who was prepared to undertake the activities described in Chapter 5: The Circus Comes was ready for anything. There was a pause and I assumed he'd now ask me what I'd been up to. I prepared myself to give the accurate answer, which was 'sod all'. But he didn't ask. He said: 'Oh, and by the way, the garden party is themed. Nineteen thirties. We'll be expected to dress up. That won't be a problem, will it?'

Claude offered me a ride to the garden party. And grudgingly, after I'd pushed him, extended the offer to Marcus. He did not mention whether he had also invited a partner. I thought about Claude and sex. Not about Claude having sex with *me* this time, you understand, but whether he had it with anyone. Or had ever had it. Maybe the first event was so awful it put him off for life? Then I started to think about the kind of sex that would seriously put you off, and I hoped like hell that it wasn't anything like that because that was too appalling for words. With luck, he may have just found sex too messy for his liking. Anyway, Claude's sex life was the least of my worries. I had no idea what the garden party would be like and was too terrified to try to imagine it. All my years of reading Nancy Mitford had only served to make me skin-crawlingly conscious of my middle-class, doily-strewn upbringing. I was not part of the 'writing paper', 'scent' or 'counterpane' set. I may as well be done with it and stand amongst them wrapped in net curtain with 'pardon' tattooed on my forehead, shouting out 'note-paper!', 'perfume!', 'bedspread!' I tried to ask Claude about the party but all he did was sigh. He would be there, I suppose. That was something.

I summoned the courage to knock on Big Man's door and run away. The two ideas I'd floated past Claude were, from most to least wimpy, to write Big Man a letter or to front up to his flat with a cup of coffee. I settled for a medium-wimpy combination of both. I placed the takeaway paper cup outside his door, slipped a note underneath, knocked and scarpered. The note said that he'd better open his door quick before the cup was nicked, and that if he wanted me to get him anything else (beans, smokes, more beans), he could leave a note sticking out from under his door next morning (but not too far, in case it got nicked). The first time I did this I was only a bit nervous. The second time, I half expected him to snatch open the door when he heard my knock and give me what-for. The third time, I was positive he'd be lying in wait, possibly with a crowbar. But the door stayed shut. There was no note for me. The coffee cups were gone each morning when I arrived with a fresh one, but that didn't necessarily mean he was the one who'd taken them. Apart from roping in strong men to bust down his door, I couldn't see any way to discover whether he was alive or dead. I pressed my ear against the door and thought I heard the faint burble of television sound. I decided that was good enough. Until swarms of flies suggested otherwise, I'd assume he was alive. How long should I keep this up, though? When would it become obvious I was wasting my time? Big Man had proved he had bloody-mindedness beyond the reach of normal humans, so potentially he could hold out for decades. I decided to give it one more week and see then how keen I was to continue.

I did something else, too. Something I didn't feel terribly good about. I went down to the Islington Register Office and put in a request for Big Man's marriage certificate. I didn't know when he'd got married, but because I knew how old he was, the helpful woman at the counter found his birth certificate record, which she said they could use to cross-reference. We decided that he could have got married anywhere between the ages of sixteen and twenty-nine, which didn't narrow it down tremendously, but was better than nothing. I told the woman I was a relative and that Big Man (who, obviously, I did not refer to as Big Man) was terminally ill with a brain tumour that had caused him to lose great chunks of his memory. I was helping him to compile a journal record, with all his paperwork and photographs in chronological order, so he could revisit his life before he died. The woman was quite touched. I was disgusted with myself. Even more so because the marriage certificate was only the first step. What I really wanted was to use the information to see if I could find out if Big Man and his wife had had children. There had been no mention of children in the article I'd found on the internet. But somehow, the level of Big Man's anger at himself. It was as if he believed he'd let more than himself down.

I considered calling Gabriel Flynn to see whether he thought what I was doing was acceptable or a one-way ticket to hell. But I didn't. He'd told me to do research and to date that was all I was doing. Big Man need never know I'd been prying. No one need ever know.

Writing emails doesn't really count as writing, but I told myself it did, and busied myself with messages to Simon, Michelle and Adam.

The message to Simon confirmed that the offer of a bed for a few nights was still on. I said I looked forward to seeing him, which was very true. With a small start, I realised that Simon and Marcus, while different in every other respect, did have one thing in common — they liked to wander about the house naked. To be fair, I'd only seen Simon naked once, when he stayed with Tom and me one Christmas. But he had admitted it was something he did often, in his own home, he hastened to add; he'd temporarily forgotten he'd been in ours. My lasting impression of Simon naked was, fortunately, not of his bits but of the rest of him. Simon has always looked rather bent and stringy from the outside, but that morning in my hallway, I was almost shocked to see that he was as strongly muscled as any athlete. I supposed it was all that rock climbing; his arms looked like something Leonardo da Vinci drew as an anatomical study, all sinews and veins and lean, hard muscle.

I gave a small shudder. Having my brother and my lover both naked in my head was not to be recommended.

But as I hit send, it occurred to me that I knew very little about Simon's love life. He'd never married. When I was in my teens and he in his thirties, he'd had a girlfriend for several years, another rock-climbing scientist with some short, practical name, like Jan or Pam. That ended over a decade ago, and I realised I did not know who, if anyone, had filled the years between then and now. I had a moment of intense sadness at this. Why, I wasn't sure. Either I felt I should know more about my only brother, even if he was just a half, or I couldn't bear the thought of anyone being alone. I certainly couldn't bear the thought of *me* being alone. I vowed to grill Simon about his personal life when he came to stay. I hoped he would tell me he'd never been happier.

The messages to Michelle and Adam were about the nineteen thirties. Dresses and shoes, to be exact. And hair. And shades of lipstick. I've watched a whole bunch of Agatha Christie videos, I told them, and I have the vibe. But where to get? Try the vintage shops, said Michelle. Or find an old pattern. Can you sew? Actually, I can, I replied. But I have no machine here; I always borrowed my mother's. Adam said: I have slinky white satin Jean Harlow number I can Fedex to you if you like? I said: it's a garden party, not the Kit-Kat Club. Thanks, anyway. Ooh! said Adam. Just remembered! Good friend is West End theatre wardrobe manager! I quizzed: how good a friend if only just remembered? Good friend means slept with, Adam explained. Friend just means friend. Only did it once and quite drunk at time, hence temporarily slipped mind. Would he remember Adam, or memory lost forever in haze of drunken stupor? No, no, said

Adam. He'll remember. He gave me Jean Harlow dress. Here's his phone number. His name is Ambrose.

'My knees are terrible.'

'Mm-hm . . .'

Ambrose cared not a jot about my knees. He was on a mission. In front of him was a rack of clothing. There was also one behind him, and to each side. In fact, so much clothing surrounded us it was hard to breathe. It was like being trapped in the den of a dry-cleaning fetishist.

A green dress was thrown up against me and whipped away. 'No,' pronounced Ambrose. 'No puffed sleeves. Sleek must be our watchword.'

Sleek was certainly the word for Ambrose. In the stuffy, over-warm wardrobe room, he'd quickly removed his leather jacket. The tight black singlet underneath revealed smooth, buttery skin taut over a solid, gym-honed torso and arms. He was my height, no more than five seven. With his shaven head, he brought to mind the slickly padded muscularity of a seal. I thought of Adam, who was good looking enough but six foot three tall and an inch wide, with skinny limbs all a-gangle, and I had a sudden, vivid image of a spider and a fly getting it on in the middle of a web.

Ambrose mistook my shudder as a response to the dress he was currently holding up.

'Too mumsy?'

The dress had three-quarter sleeves, a belted waist and black flowers dotted on a cream background. It was quite pretty but not in the least bit sexy.

'Um—'

'The curse of thirties daywear,' he sighed, slotting the dress back on the rack. 'It makes you look like either Shirley Temple or an advertisement for Oxo cubes. Are you sure I can't interest you in bias-cut floor-length red satin?'

'At a garden party?'

'Glamour should never be curtailed by convention,' he sniffed.

Coat hangers clattered as he snapped through the outfits. He held up a bright blue satin shirt with short cap sleeves, fitted tight and buttoned low. 'This a fab thirties look. See? You knot this little matching tie around your neck, bow to one side. Very jaunty. Very Amelia Earhart adventuress chic. I'm sure we could find some wide-legged pants to go with it.'

'It's a great shirt,' I agreed. 'But I really think I'd rather have a dress.'

Truth was, I wanted to look as sexy and gorgeous as possible for Marcus. Pants were not going to cut it, no matter how chic.

'Well, then. Fancy being Miss Joan Hunter Dunn?'

Ambrose held up the cutest tennis dress. White pleats, sleeveless, a grey knit tie slung low on the hips as a belt. It was wonderful. But it was very, very short.

'Knees, Ambrose. Terrible. Remember—?'

He sighed. 'So demanding . . .'

'You know—' I ventured tentatively. 'Glam could be all right. If the skirt wasn't trailing along behind me. Risk of wet grass and all that . . .'

Ambrose raised a speculative eyebrow. 'And why this sudden reversal?'

I blushed. 'Well, it is a posh party. And I'll be meeting most people there for the first time. Plus, my partner looks spectacular no matter what he's wearing.' I made an apologetic face. 'In short, I think I'd rather be over-glammed than under-.'

There was a short pause, as Ambrose stared at me. 'Hmm,' he said.

Then he turned back to the racks. Hangers clattered and in a trice, he was holding up two dresses.

'Oh . . .' I breathed. 'Wow.'

One was pale creamy gold satin, sleeveless with a smooth bodice but the most amazing skirt that dropped in inverted herringbone triangles from hip to ankle. The neckline was high but adorned with a sparkling *thing* — like an upside-down tiara tipped with an art deco star. The other dress, also sleeveless, had layers of pale pink chiffon falling softly over crêpe panels, with one wide, pink-beaded stripe along the straight neckline and another under the bustline that accentuated the boobs. I could not decide which dress I lusted after more.

'Of course, neither may fit,' Ambrose added crushingly.

He held both up to me in turn. 'The pink does less for your colouring. But the shade is more "day", if you know what I mean. Here—' He handed it to me. 'Try it on.'

I glanced around. 'Er . . .'

Ambrose's eyebrow shot up again. 'I have seen more naked people than a Berlin bathhouse attendant. Believe me, nothing about your anatomy could possibly shock, or for that matter, interest me. Come along. Whip it off.'

The pink dress did fit. So did the gold satin.

'Which one?' I demanded.

'Which one feels more like you?' Ambrose asked.

I gazed at him. 'I don't know,' I admitted. 'Neither, I suppose.'

'Hmm. What will your spectacular partner be wearing?'

I didn't know that, either. And I found that embarrassed me more than getting down to my smalls in front of a man I'd only just met.

'Oh — um,' I invented. 'Something to do with cricket? I don't think we have to match,' I added, hastily.

Ambrose nodded. 'Go with the satin,' he ordered. 'You wear its simplicity better.'

I changed back into my clothes. Ambrose found a bag and folded the dress into it. He handed me the bag along with a pair of shoes. They were cream leather with a small heel and a thin strap across the front at ankle height.

'They'll fit. I checked the size of the shoes you're wearing. They're not a perfect match with the dress but very suitable for treading on aristocratic lawns.'

'Thank you so much,' I said. 'You've been a lifesaver.'

He picked up his jacket and hooked it on his finger over one shoulder. He gave me another speculative look.

'Let me know how it turns out,' he said. 'That kind of thing always intrigues me.'

I realised later that I wasn't entirely sure what he was referring to.

Swear to God, the sheer relief of having found a pretty dress temporarily unhinged me. By the time I turned down my street, I was entirely lost in a nineteen thirties fantasyland. Marcus and I were in a white and chrome Bugatti convertible, roaring down the country lanes. It was right out of a Marjory Allingham novel, or possibly Georgette Heyer. I swear that Marcus may actually have been about to say 'Happy, darling?' when I collided with something that knocked the breath out of me.

It was Anselo. Or, more accurately, the big load of wood he had in his arms. He stayed upright. I fell smack on my backside. I sat there on the footpath, my legs splayed straight out in front of me like a wooden doll, clutching my bag and gasping at the pain in my tailbone.

Anselo stood over me, scowling. 'I'm carrying half a fucking house. How could you not see me?'

I could hardly reply 'because I was driving flat out in an imaginary Bugatti'. As it was, I was barely able to wheeze out a 'Sorry . . .'

Anselo dumped the wood back in the van, and bent down to me.

'You all right?'

I shook my head. 'I think I broke my bum. You'd think there'd be enough padding for it not to hurt like this, but no.'

Anselo grinned. He took the bag from me, held out his other hand and helped me up.

Gingerly, I felt the base of my spine. 'Ouch! Bloody, bloody *ouch*!'

'I'd offer to rub it better, but—'

His smile was hesitant, as if he was testing the ground. I had a sudden hunch that this might be his way of apologising for the sulks of the past week. He was holding my bag in a slightly defensive manner, in front of a t-shirt so old and ripped and covered in sawdust, I could only just make out the image on it. It was a Stranglers album — The Raven. Tom liked the Stranglers. *Peaches. Duchess.* "No more heroes any more . . ."

Anselo was speaking to me. I tuned back in to hear '—a drink.'

'I'm sorry,' I said. 'I was made momentarily deaf by the pain in my arse.'

He gave me that half grin again. 'I said — I could apologise by buying you a drink. At five, maybe? I've got to, um, head away by six-thirty, but if that's OK?'

It wasn't the most articulate invitation, but it was quite sweet, nonetheless. I had *no* idea what we'd talk about for an hour and a half, but I could hardy refuse—

'Thanks,' I said. 'I'd like that.' I nodded at his sawdusty t-shirt. 'And if we go to that Queen's Head pub I've seen up the road, you won't even have to change.'

He handed me back my bag. 'If we go to the Queen's Head, we may not come out again.'

Tyso appeared in the open doorway. He saw my bag and grinned. 'Shopping?'

I shook my head. 'Borrowing.'

The second dress, in fact, that I'd borrowed in order to go

out with Marcus. Not that I was counting. And not that I had any bloody choice.

Anselo hooked his thumb at the load of wood. 'Take this lot in, Tyso.'

'Thought you were doing—'

One look from his boss and Tyso's protest died mid-whinge. Muttering, he gathered up the wood and carried it none too gracefully into the house.

Anselo leaned against the side of the van and folded his arms. There was a slight smile on his face as he watched Tyso disappear down the hall.

'You're hard,' I remarked.

'He needs it,' Anselo replied. 'He's got three older sisters, who've done every bloody thing for him since he emerged from the womb.'

'Why did he take up building, then? If manual labour wasn't his thing?'

Anselo's eyes shifted my way. 'Because his father told him he had to work with me.'

'Did *you* have any say in the matter?'

He gave a short shrug. 'I needed an apprentice. I had more work than I could handle. Good contract labour is hard to find.'

He unfolded his arms and stepped away from the van. 'Speaking of work—' and with a quick, slightly wary look of enquiry, added, 'Meet you here at five?'

'Five is good,' I nodded, and headed inside.

Even better, I thought as I hung the satin dress carefully in my wardrobe. I won't have to worry about what to wear.

Chapter Seventeen

I WATCHED Anselo navigate his way around the tables to the bar. He'd exchanged his Stranglers t-shirt for a brand-new-looking polo shirt. Pale blue. Lacoste. I wasn't sure it suited him. Maybe his girlfriend bought it for him? She sounded like the Lacoste type.

We were at the pub down the road. It was on the verge of closing down, the stakeholder brewery having withdrawn its interest. The owner was keeping it alive as long as he could, perhaps in the hope that a new financial partner would arrive out of the blue. A shame, because it was a nice pub. Cosy, friendly, and with comfortable couches that I'd made a beeline for, feeling they'd be more forgiving on my still aching rear.

Anselo came back with, to my surprise, two glasses of wine. Well, I wasn't surprised about the one he put in front of me, as it was exactly what I'd asked for. I was surprised at his. The fact he had one, that is.

'Not a beer man?'

He shrugged. 'Depends.'

I took a sip of my wine. My only request had been that it be white, dryish and not too nasty. My usual experience of pub wine didn't make me too hopeful about the latter. But I was wrong—

'That's really good!'

'Should be. Your country does sauvignon blanc better than anyone.'

I gaped at him, until I became aware I was doing so and stopped. 'Don't tell me you're a wine buff?'

'All right,' he said. 'I won't.'

He swirled his glass of red under his nose and then drank a little. He made a face. 'Could be worse.'

'I can tell the difference between red and white,' I told him.

He nodded slowly. 'Good start.'

'I also make a mean margarita.'

'All margaritas are mean if you make them right. Underhanded, too.'

'You speak from experience?'

'If I could remember, I'd tell you.'

I smiled, and for a nanosecond was treated to one of his sparkling grins in return. Then his natural state of discomfort took over and he turned his head to stare out the window. He had a fine profile, I observed. It would be even better if he didn't look so discontented all the time.

I sat back in the couch and sipped my wine. I didn't really mind if he wasn't keen on talking. My mind was still in panic mode about the coming weekend. I wondered what on earth Marcus and Claude's mother was like. There were two possibilities, I'd decided. She'd either be brisk and horsy and order me repeatedly to speak up. Or she'd be languidly arranged on a couch, clutching a champagne flute and a Pekingese.

My brain connected to my ears in time to hear Anselo say '—family.'

Fortunately, I knew I hadn't missed much. His sentences were never more than a few words long.

'Sorry?' I made a face. 'Again.'

'*A secret life*,' he said. '*It becomes what you'd most protect if the government said you can protect one thing, all else is ours*.'

This time, I didn't even try to shut my mouth.

'Stephen Dunn,' he said. 'American poet. And no, I'm not a poetry buff. I just read it somewhere and remembered it.'

'I can see why . . .' I shook myself. 'What were you asking me? About family?'

'How many others? In yours?'

'Oh . . .' I made a glum face. 'Just me, Mum and Dad and my half-brother, Simon. He's heaps older,' I added. 'He's a scientist. Studies waves.'

'As in — waving goodbye?'

'As in tidal.'

Anselo frowned. 'How do you hold a wave still long enough to study it?'

'You can ask him,' I grinned. 'He's coming to stay soon.'

'That'll be cosy. We might have to occupy the house in shifts.'

'Are *you* from a big family?' I ventured.

He gave me a look. 'We're Roma. There's no such thing as a small family. I've got two older brothers, two younger sisters, and four hundred and fifty million cousins.'

I laughed. 'Don't you like being Roma?'

'Not really.' Then he shook his head, as if irritated with himself. 'No, I do. I like it that I'm something. I like the stories . . .'

'I have to confess I've always associated Romani people with brightly painted caravans, and songs that go "Ah de do, ah dee dady".' I decided not to mention the hedgehogs.

Anselo pursed his mouth. 'Yeah, well, most people associate us with grotty bunches of heather and poaching. And marrying thirteen-year-old girls.'

'From what I've seen of your family,' I said, 'that doesn't strike me as all that accurate.'

He avoided my eye. 'We bettered ourselves. Some of us better than others . . .'

'How?' I could see he was uncomfortable with the subject, but too bad. I loved other people's stories.

He sighed. But to his credit he didn't refuse to answer. 'In the sixties, before I was born, the persecution got pretty bad. My grandfather, who's Tyso's granddad, too, decided enough was enough. He and his brothers all had a real gift with horses, and Granddad persuaded them — ordered them, really — to stay in one place, get proper houses and jobs in stables that paid good money. So thanks to horse training, our family got a leg up financially and socially. Excuse the pun.'

'Your grandfather sounds like a force to be reckoned with.'

Anselo sighed. 'My family is full of men to be reckoned with.'

'Your dad?'

He hesitated. 'My dad died when I was twelve.'

My heart clutched. 'Oh, I'm so sorry!'

He made a non-committal face, as if it wasn't a big deal. 'Tyso's dad looked out for us. And, later on, Patrick . . .'

A certain ambiguity in his tone made me curious. 'Don't you like Patrick?'

'Who couldn't like Patrick?' His voice was even enough, but I could practically *see* the sarcasm.

'I think Patrick's amazing. He's open, funny, generous—' It was the truth, but I said it more to provoke Anselo. His attitude was puzzling, and slightly irritating.

'Yeah, well, he ought to be!'

'What's that supposed to mean?' I frowned. 'Are you suggesting he doesn't deserve his money?'

Anselo scowled down at the last of his wine. 'Forget it,' he said shortly. 'You're right. Patrick deserves everything he has. Including his trophy wife.'

'Oh, come on! Clare's no trophy wife!' I was really cross now. 'What is your problem?'

He didn't answer. His face was tense with anger and more than a hint of shame. But suddenly, his shoulders slumped and he blew out a long breath.

'My problem . . .' he said to his shoes, 'is me.' He lifted his head to stare at me. 'And I have no idea what to do about it.'

'But—' I was honestly quite perplexed. 'What's wrong with you? You're really good-looking, you're your own boss, you've got a gorgeous girlfriend—'

He scowled. 'How do you know *that?*' Then he rolled his eyes. 'Tyso. Jesus. The kid is his own media channel.'

He hung his head again, but when he lifted it to face me this time, it was with a small, wry grin.

'Yeah, you're right. What could be wrong?'

My anger had gone. Now I felt sorry for him. I knew exactly what it was like to be reluctant to look too closely.

'Perhaps you need to be a bit easier on yourself?' I suggested. And for just a *fraction* of a second, his mouth went quite square, like he was going to cry.

Abruptly, he stood. 'I have to go.'

Surprised, I checked my watch. 'But it's not—'

I stopped. Let the poor man beat a dignified retreat, Darrell.

'OK,' I smiled. 'I'll see you tomorrow.'

He hesitated. 'Do you want me to walk you home?'

'No, no.' I shook my head. 'I'll stay and finish my glass.' I patted the couch. 'I quite like it here.'

He nodded. When he was at the door, he glanced back at me. I held up my hand to wave goodbye. He hesitated again, and for a moment, I thought he was going to change his mind and come back. But then he gave me a quick, curt wave in return, and the door swung shut behind him.

I decided to cut through the small park that would take me to the end of my street. It probably wasn't the smartest idea;

although it had barely gone dark, there was still a high chance of bumping into what my mother would refer to as 'undesirables'.

As it was, I saw no one until I reached the gate at the end. A figure I recognised immediately was crossing the road from the estate. Big Man. Where was he going? If it was time for a can shop at Tesco's, he was heading in quite the wrong direction.

I hid behind the gate pillar and peered out from between the bars of the iron fence. Good Lord! He'd stopped outside my house! I saw him peer through my front window, as if trying to work out if I was home or not. I hadn't left a single light on — *must* get more security-minded — so it was pretty clear the house was empty.

He moved back to the door and, to my astonishment, lifted the flap on my letterbox and slotted in what looked like an envelope. My heart sank. I could just imagine what the letter inside said. Oh, well. No one could say I hadn't tried . . .

Big Man glanced up and down the street, turned on his heel and strode back across to the estate. After he'd disappeared from view, I waited a few more minutes, just to make sure he hadn't bent down to tie a shoelace or something. Opening my front door, I found the envelope on the mat, glowing a noxious yellow with reflected streetlight. For a second, I considered binning it — why be needlessly depressed? With a brief muttered curse, I snatched it up and ripped it open.

There was money in it. And I knew, without counting, that it would be exactly enough to cover the coffees I had delivered to him. I sighed. Yet more proof that Big Man was the most ornery, most cussedly proud individual on the face of the planet.

I was about to screw up the envelope, when I thought I'd better double-check there was no note. And lo, there was indeed a slip of paper inside. It was an old till receipt from the newsagent. Big Man had bought two packets of cigarettes and a paper. Did he feel I needed to know that? Oh. Right. I turned it over—

The note said: *Bring some fucking sugar next time*

My first reaction was one of hot, unreserved shame. I was prying into this man's private life and he had no idea. The nice, equally unsuspecting woman at the register office had promised to go through the records to see if a child had been born to Michael James Hogan and his wife, Elizabeth Marie. The woman thought she'd probably have a result by mid next week.

However — and this was important — Big Man *did* have no idea. And there was no reason that should change. My guilty heart started to pound less. The reality was that Big Man had actually begun to trust me. He'd opened up his life the merest crack, that was true. Still, it was a start.

Tomorrow, I would bring some fucking sugar.

'Look at this.'

I shoved the note under Claude's nose.

He began to read. 'Ranjit's Magazines and More—'

'Oh! No—' I turned it over.

'Is that a special type?' he asked. 'Like muscovado?'

'Fool,' I grinned. 'Good news, though, don't you think?'

'A small but significant breakthrough . . .'

Claude's voice tailed off, as his line of sight shifted towards the door. Miss Flaky had arrived and was at the counter. She was wearing her maroon cardigan over a long skirt of multi-coloured crocheted squares, as if it had once been the kind of blanket your sight-impaired grandmother insisted on making out of leftover wool. And she was studiously ignoring us.

Curious, I watched Claude watching Miss Flaky. His expression seemed to be equal parts resignation and resolve, like that of a man who knows the final showdown with his mortal enemy can no longer be avoided. High noon at the Italian café.

'Excuse me—'

Claude was on his feet and moving purposefully towards the counter. He approached Miss Flaky and — my God, was the man insane? — touched her lightly on her arm! I saw her whole body tense as she averted herself to shut Claude out. But he bent his head and murmured a few words in her ear. I could see Mario's cheerful, beaming face behind the counter, a complete contrast to Claude's resolute profile and Miss Flaky's rigid back. What on earth was he saying to her? And why?

Claude lifted his head and saw me staring. He murmured one last word to Miss Flaky and left her standing at the counter. His face, as he walked back to our table, gave nothing away. By the time he sat back down, I was hopping with curiosity.

'What did you *say?*' I hissed.

'Say?' Claude was all wide-eyed innocence.

'Stop winding me up, curse you!'

Claude smiled. 'I said what needed to be said.'

I was seriously considering giving him a dead arm, when I heard a throat clear. Fortunately, the sound of Claude leaping to his feet obscured my gasp of dismay.

'Please—' Claude gestured to the chair he'd pulled out for her.

Miss Flaky sat and placed her tray of tea things in front of her. I became aware that my face was screwed up as if I'd smelled something bad. I did my best to smooth it out.

'Darrell,' said Claude, 'this is Ruth.'

'Harper,' she added, with reluctance. 'Ruth Harper.'

'Darrell Kincaid,' I said.

'Darrell is a writer,' said Claude.

'Really?' Miss Flaky invested the word with bored disdain.

'I write romance novels,' I said in a way that could also be translated as 'fuck you'.

'I never read fiction,' said Miss Flaky, dismissively. Which I thought was a bit rich, considering the books she *did* read.

'Ruth is studying at the London Homeopathic Centre. Or so I gather—' Claude added hastily, as Miss Flaky skewered him with a look.

'How'd you know?' she demanded.

'I confess I deduced it from a glimpse at some papers you were perusing one morning.'

Miss Flaky regarded him. 'Do you always talk like you have a Victorian bureaucrat's speech notes shoved up your ass?'

'Yes,' replied Claude, without hesitating. 'Will that be a problem?'

To my amazement, Miss Flaky burst out laughing.

'I can't get to grips with this English class shit,' she said. 'Are you top of the tree, or just putting it on?'

'Am I, in other words, nothing but an English fuck?' said Claude. 'Or the real thing?'

'You forgot spineless,' she told him.

'So I did.' Claude nodded. 'I can't imagine how that slipped my mind, when it was the most accurate of your assertions.'

Miss Flaky grinned. 'So? Are you the real thing or what?'

'My father was a duke, until he chose no longer to be. The title has not been reclaimed. Therefore, I am, and am not, "the real thing".'

'No shit. What kind of duke doesn't want to stick it out?'

'One who aspires to the House of Commons.'

Miss Flaky eyed him over her steaming cup of pungent tea. 'And did he get there?'

'He did not.'

'Ouch.' Miss Flaky paused to sip her tea. 'Why didn't he grab back the title? Seems like kind of a waste of a good wicket.'

Claude replied evenly, 'At the end, I suppose it seemed the least of his losses.'

For a long moment, they stared at each other. So long that I began to feel quite a lot like a third wheel.

So I stood up. 'Got to go,' I said. 'Coffee run.'

Miss Flaky gave me such a dark look, I wondered if she thought it was a euphemism for clubbing baby seals.

But then she said, 'You can tell Mr Michael Hogan that I'm going to clean that shit-hole apartment of his if it fucking kills me.'

I almost fell over. 'How did—? When—?'

'I did some checking of my own,' she replied. 'If even that asshole doctor followed up, I figured I ought to do something. I know you bring him coffee. He told me.'

'He *told* you?' I echoed.

I have to confess I was seriously put out by this. Why would Big Man talk to Miss Flaky when all he'd told me was to sod off?

'I—' Miss Flaky screwed up her mouth. 'Yeah, well, let's use the word visit, why not? I visited him.'

My sense of being hard done by increased. 'And he let you in just like that?'

'Hell no! I knocked until my knuckles were black and blue but there was no answer. I *knew* he was in there, though — I could hear the damn TV. So I yelled and yelled until he finally opened the damn door. And then I just shouldered my way on in. Jesus fuck. Only a man could live like that.'

'I can't imagine he was too happy with you?' I ventured.

Miss Flaky smiled grimly. 'Yeah, he was pretty pissed all right. One stage, I thought he was going to pick me up and toss me out bodily, but then I threatened to kick him in the balls and he backed right off.'

I gave a gasp of shocked laughter. I'd have to remember that even Big Man caved in when his nuts were threatened. It could come in handy.

'You're going over there now?' Miss Flaky's speculative look made me uneasy.

Hastily, I said, 'Yes, but I'm sure he told you I only leave the coffee outside his door. I don't go in.'

Claude, who had been witnessing our exchange much a like a spectator at Wimbledon, finally spoke. 'What exactly is, er, wrong with Mr Hogan's abode'

'You don't wanna know.' Miss Flaky shook her head. 'The shock could kill you.'

Claude's mouth went all sulky, but he didn't press it. Instead, he turned to me. 'Does our arrangement for tomorrow still stand? I will come to collect you at ten?'

Oh, God. Thanks for reminding me.

'Still stands,' I said. 'What kind of car do you have? So I can keep an eye out.'

'An old one,' he replied, with a faint smile. 'But it should get us there and back.'

As I was leaving, Miss Flaky called to me, 'I meant it, you know. You tell him!'

I had absolutely no intention at all of doing so until I got to Big Man's flat. And then I thought — why not?

There was a paper napkin wrapped around the cup to make it cooler for me to hold. I put down the cup and plastic bag full of sugar sachets, removed the napkin and retrieved a pen from my bag.

I wrote that I wouldn't be at the café Saturday morning (no need to mention the garden party; Big Man's eyes might roll so far back they dropped into his skull), so the next coffee delivery would be Monday. And then I wrote down Miss Flaky's promise — or threat, I suppose — word for word.

I slid the napkin under the door, knocked once, loudly, and walked away as fast as I could without actually breaking into a run.

Chapter Eighteen

I WAS IN A LATHER. It was a quarter past ten and there was no sign of Marcus or Claude. I'd been ready since nine, worried that I wouldn't look as good in the dress as I'd hoped. But the dress was still pretty, the shoes fitted and I'd found a very nice costume art deco hair-clip for fifty pence at Camden Passage. I wasn't at all sure I would pass muster in Claude's mother's eyes, but it was too late to change anything now. The weather wasn't helping. For the past fortnight, it had been grey, chilly and murky. But this morning, the sky was crisply blue and there was a shimmer in the air that portended real heat. My satin dress was already feeling clingy and heavy. I could only be grateful it didn't have sleeves. Ambrose's tennis dress, knees or not, suddenly seemed like a much better idea.

Thank God! There was the knock—

I opened the door, smiling and expectant, to find only Claude. He was wearing in a navy blazer, worn over white wide-legged, square-cuffed trousers and a white shirt, collar open. He would have looked very handsome had his face not been tight with irritation.

'I am so sorry we are late,' he said. Then he blinked. 'Goodness. What a lovely dress.'

I would have been flattered if I'd not been so distracted by the lack of Marcus. But then I caught a whiff of nicotine and he stepped into view. He was wearing what appeared to be cricket gear — how *had* I known? — a striped red and white blazer over trousers and shirt not dissimilar to Claude's. I was overwhelmed both by relief and by how astonishingly attractive he was. It was one thing to talk to him over the phone, quite another to have him here in the flesh. I had forgotten just what an impact he made on me. It was knee weakening.

He wasn't paying the same attention to me, however, being busy sucking the last out of a cigarette, which he then dropped onto the footpath and ground under his heel.

'Sorry, sorry,' he grinned as he approached. 'Can't smoke in Claudie's car—' His eyes widened as he caught his first proper look of me. 'Good Lord!'

'Is that a good good Lord?' I asked, nervous. 'Looking at you two, I'm afraid I'm a bit over the top.'

Marcus stepped up to me. He surveyed me slowly, down and up, and met my still anxious gaze. The light in his brown eyes was somewhere between amused and triumphant. I felt a second surge of relief. He liked what he saw.

'Glorious dress,' he murmured.

He placed his hands on my waist, causing me to shiver. He bent his head and kissed me lightly on the mouth. Then he kissed my jaw, my cheek and, with his lips against my ear, whispered, 'And I intend to have you out of it at the first available opportunity.'

Behind us, Claude coughed meaningfully. 'Marcus, we are already running late. Let's not compound the situation.'

Marcus rolled his eyes, as if we were teenagers being reprimanded by a parent.

'Do you have everything you need?' he grinned at me. 'Purse? Lipstick? AA card?'

'The car is in perfect order,' said Claude, irritated. 'And as long as you are prevented from driving it, it should remain so. Shut that door and come *along*—'

When Claude had said he had an old car, I'd immediately formed a picture of the banjaxed Austin Princess parked in my street. Claude's car was as much like an Austin Princess as I was like Princess Diana.

'Is that a Mark IX Jaguar?' I asked, in surprise. 'How lovely!'

'God,' Marcus grimaced. 'Please tell me you're not a car enthusiast?'

'My father had a Mark II,' I explained. 'He thought it was the epitome of English taste, until someone pointed out that it had been the getaway car of choice for bank robbers in the nineteen sixties. He sold it straight away, to my everlasting regret.'

Claude had the passenger door open for me. 'This car was our father's also. It seemed a waste to let it go.'

Marcus had slid into the back seat. 'You haemorrhage money on this damn thing, Claude. It's more of a waste to hang onto it.'

Claude ignored him, started up and pulled away from the curb. I'd adored my father's Mark II, hence my interest in the breed. Dad's car had been winter white with a red leather and walnut interior. It looked and smelled, I always imagined, like an exclusive London's gentleman's club. Claude's Jaguar was green, with moss green leather upholstery and *acres* of walnut.

'Does it have the fold-down picnic tables in the back?' I murmured to Claude.

He laughed. 'Two. Twin veneered.'

'God, how wonderful.'

Marcus muttered something I didn't catch. I looked over my shoulder at him. He had his phone out, and was checking the screen.

'I thought everyone had an expensive car where you live?' I said.

'Almost everyone has a garden with a palm tree, too,' he replied, without looking up. 'I don't think much of those, either.'

Something he was reading made him smile. 'Gus says she'll be late,' he said to Claude. 'But we're to start being obnoxious and disreputable without her.'

Claude frowned. 'I thought she had declined?'

'Mother exerted eleventh-hour pressure on her, apparently,' said Marcus. 'Probably threatened to slash her wrists or something.'

'I hardly think—' Claude was irritated.

'Don't blow a valve. I'm kidding. But you have to admit — she does rather put the "ma" into "drama".'

Their mother was definitely sounding more Peke than pony. I wasn't sure if that was better or worse. Less risk of coming after me with a riding crop, I supposed.

My neck was starting to hurt. I'd been craning it around the whole time, watching Marcus. Which was proving not only painful but also somewhat embarrassingly pointless, as he seemed to have eyes only for his phone.

And now said phone rang, causing Claude to direct a dark look into the rear-view mirror and tut in disapproval.

'Must he—?'

'*Allo*—'

Marcus began to speak rapidly and fluently in what I assumed was French. I suppose I shouldn't have been surprised, but all the same, I was. It was a sharp and not exactly pleasant reminder of the distance between our lives.

I glanced at Claude. If Marcus was that fluent, I assumed he must be, too. He wasn't reacting to anything Marcus said, so I guessed it was all pretty banal. Not that it had anything to do with me. Marcus would do whatever he pleased, and I could accept that or not. That was my choice.

Marcus ended the call, and blew out a breath. 'Why do

other people make everything more complicated than it needs to be?' he said to neither of us in particular.

'Would it be too much to ask for you to allow us to drive in peace?' said Claude.

'Fine,' snapped Marcus. And he shoved the phone into his jacket pocket, slumped back in the seat and proceeded to stare out the window.

We drove on in, if not peace, exactly, then at least in silence. Claude exited the motorway after about forty-five minutes and I was on my first trip into the English countryside. On this clear blue day, it glowed like the real versions of the Constable prints my parents insisted on hanging on their walls. They would never buy original art; it was far too threatening. Prints came pre-approved as safe and tasteful, like the *Concise Oxford English Dictionary* and Axminster carpets.

The villages we passed through suggested we were among wealth. Not gaudy wealth — no high-gated mock-pillared mansions and flashy cars. The people here were comfortably, a little smugly, well off. Even in this rural area, everything was clean and neat. There didn't appear to be a real farm in sight. I got quite excited when I saw an actual cow.

'Welcome to our little slice of the Home Counties,' said Claude, 'about which the best thing you can say is that it's not Cheshire.'

'Is this where you grew up?' I asked him.

'Heaven forbid. The family seat was in Wiltshire.'

'It still is, of course.' Marcus had decided to re-join us. 'It's just minus the family.'

I glanced back at him. 'Do you miss it?'

Marcus stared at Claude's profile. 'What do you think, brother dear? Do we miss it?'

But all Claude said was, 'Here we are . . .'

And as he slowed, and turned down a long gravel driveway, panic made me forget I'd ever asked the question.

By golly. If this was a trade-down from the family seat, I was even more out of my league than I had previously feared.

The house wasn't that large compared to, say, the whole of Lichtenstein. My parents' house was about the size of the garage. That is to say, the garage right at the end of the string of garages. Or were they stables? All my years of Nancy and *Tatler* had prepared me not a jot for the real thing. Claude and Marcus had no reaction at all, and I realised this was everyday for them. But I could not imagine a life for me in which this would ever be the norm.

The vast circular area that marked the end of the driveway was already chock-full of cars.

'Christ,' said Marcus. 'How many millions of people has she invited?'

Claude parked on the grass. 'I'll take the consequences,' he sighed.

It was Claude who opened my door for me. Marcus had his phone out again, and was checking messages. I saw him frown briefly, but when he looked up and saw me, he smiled and came to take my arm.

'If there is another woman here today to rival you,' he said, 'I will eat Claude's blazer.'

'You will not,' said Claude. 'I borrowed it. And it's a jacket. Blazer is common, as you well know.'

My heart gave a small clutch of dread. I didn't know that one. What other class faux pas was I likely to unknowingly commit?

'Why the hell,' muttered Marcus, as we crunched our way across the gravel to the house, 'did she insist upon this ridiculous dress-up nonsense, anyway? Why couldn't she have a common or garden party like everyone else?'

'She told me it was because the majority of the people she knows dress in clothes that have been rejected even by Oxfam. She hoped that, this way, they might turn up in something if not less old, then at least with fewer holes. That was her reason,' Claude replied. 'Personally, I think she's done it purely because it amuses her.' He gave Marcus a sideways glance. 'In that regard, you and she are very similar.'

Marcus looked furious. 'I'm not related to the woman. We have nothing in common whatsoever.'

The front door of the house was open. At least, I assumed it was the front door — hard to imagine there'd be a bigger door somewhere else. Inside, I had the impression of vast ceilings, primrose and cream and apricot walls, dark wood floorboards and a double staircase that swept upwards from two sides of the lobby and met at the floor above.

Claude led us along a hallway and through a series of airy rooms into one last, spacious one. Two sets of French doors along the back wall were wide open and as we stepped through onto the paved area outside, I almost gasped. The view was breathtaking. Standing on what I wanted to call the patio but suspected I shouldn't, we looked down a series of broad stone steps that emerged onto a vast sloping lawn that in its turn ended at the bank of a narrow, curving, willow-edged river. To either side of us were the gardens proper. The magnolias stood tall above box-bordered flowerbeds, and I could see why Marcus and Claude's mother wanted to show them off. They were luminous, in shades of pink, purple and white. There was a pergola to our far left, smothered in clematis and wisteria. Through it, I glimpsed what looked like a swimming pool. The thought of cool water was extraordinarily enticing. I'd have to find an excuse to take a walk over there . . .

I'd been so struck by the view that I'd failed to really register how many people were standing around. And how well they were dressed. And how posh they sounded. They yocked and haw-hawed all around me. I began to shrink inside.

Marcus' voice made me jump. 'Brace yourself. Claude has foolishly attracted the attention of our mother.'

'Well, it is her party,' I said.

'No excuse—'

'My dears!'

The woman who walked towards us was neither horsey nor Pekey, and she looked, I swear, no older than Claude. She had dark red hair and beautiful pale skin, faintly specked with freckles like brown sugar dusted on cream. She was wearing a green dress with enormous puffed sleeves, not unlike the one Ambrose had rejected. On her, it looked sensational. She had a superb figure, all high breasts and great legs. She could have worn a sack and looked terrific.

She kissed Claude, who kissed her back, and Marcus, who did not, and fixed me with gimlet stare.

'That's a very lovely dress,' she pronounced.

I felt, somehow, her tone held a note of censure. Should I have worn something less lovely?

I heard Claude give a small, prompting cough. 'Marcus—'

'Yes, yes!' Marcus said. 'Mother, this is Darrell. Darrell, this is my mother.'

'She can hardly call me that, can she?' Marcus' mother held out a hand. I took it and squeezed it gingerly. Her own grip was firm. 'Anne,' she said.

I *just* managed to stop myself saying, 'Pleased to meet you.' Instead I said, 'Your magnolias are magnificent.' Inwardly, I cringed, but it was a better than 'Pleased to meet you.'

Her eyes flickered briefly in the direction of the trees. 'Yes, I know. Felix and Elizabeth are in particularly good form at the moment.'

Had she given her trees names? Or were they actual varieties of magnolia? I didn't dare ask.

'There's Gus!' Marcus sounded pleased.

'So I see.' Marcus' mother did not. 'Dear God, what *has* she brought with her?'

Stepping through the French doors were two women. One was tall and willowy, with short, gamine-cut dark hair. She was extremely beautiful in a slightly mannish way, reminding me of the eighties supermodel Erin O'Connor. She was wearing a boy's school uniform, which only just fitted her: grey shorts, a grey and yellow striped blazer and a matching Billy Bunter cap. Under the blazer, she appeared to have nothing on at all.

The second woman reminded me of someone, too, but I couldn't put my finger on who. She was shorter and more athletic-looking than her companion. On her lower half was a pair of plaid plus fours that managed to look sexy rather than ridiculous. On her upper half was a tight-fitting Argyle-patterned vest. She wore no bra. Her dark hair was so close-cropped as to be almost shaved, and she had a barbed wire bracelet tattooed on her upper arm. She had sultry kohl-rimmed eyes and bright red lipstick on full, pouty lips.

Both women were utterly gorgeous, effortlessly glamorous and stratospherically more sophisticated than I was. As they approached, I was filled with a sort of crawling dread. It was like I'd been flung right back to the third form, to one of those moments where I'd come around the corner and bumped smack into the mean girls. Like evil robots, their eyes would scan me up and down, registering every chubby inch, oozing fear and lack of cool. And that was all they needed to do to inflict maximum damage. They might decide to also then dead-arm me for fun, but that didn't matter — they had already stripped me bare of any delusion that I was anything but a tragic goober.

Fairly obviously, I was no longer thirteen. But while I knew now that I was pretty enough, I also knew I wasn't more than that. I lacked that refinement, that sheen of true class and beauty. Marcus had it, and so did his mother. Claude almost had it; what he lacked was the sexual spark that gave energy to physical beauty. His sister and her friend also had it. In spades.

Oh well. I could hardly run for the hills. I wondered which one was Gus. I rather assumed, from Marcus' mother's comment, that it was not the one with the tattoo.

Never assume. As Adam always said: It makes an ass out of you and umption.

The tattooed one spied Marcus, broke into the broadest grin and came running over to throw her arms around him. She kissed him soundly and a little too fully on the lips for my personal comfort. But then, they weren't blood brother and sister. If that made it any better.

She broke away and beamed up at Claude. 'Don't panic,' she said. 'I know you hate it when I do that. Here—' She pecked him lightly on the cheek, and then beamed at both of them. 'How are you, my darlings?'

'Top hole,' replied Marcus. 'Or is that an expression better reserved for your kind?'

'Fuckwit,' said Gus, with affection. Then her smile vanished. 'Hello, Mother,' she said.

'I was wondering when you'd notice,' said her mother mildly, tilting her head to receive a desultory kiss on the cheek. 'You look well. Unfettered as usual.'

The willowy blazer-wearer wandered up, a glass of champagne in her hand.

'Where did you get that?' demanded Gus.

The blazer-wearer blinked and then glanced vaguely around, as if the source of champagne had been right behind her only a minute ago.

Marcus' mother made a brisk exasperated noise and snapped her fingers. A waiter appeared like magic. The blazer-wearer picked up a second glass with her free hand.

'This is Jules,' said Gus. 'Jules, these are my beautiful brothers, Claude and Marcus, and this, God help you, is my mother.' She stared at me. 'I have no idea who this is.'

'She can't be called Jules, Gus,' said Marcus. 'All lesbians are called Jules. It's like a Spaniard being called Jose, or a Scotsman being called Jock.'

Winning my undying gratitude, Claude put his hand on

my shoulder and drew me closer. 'This is Darrell,' he said, firmly. 'Darrell, this is my sister, Augusta.'

She took a very brief second look at me. 'Hello.'

'I thought you were going to be late?' Marcus asked her.

Gus screwed up her nose. 'I tried. Believe me. But Jules wanted to make sure we got here before the liquor ran out. I warned her how notoriously cheap our mother is.'

I was furious at how rude she'd been to me, but I was *gobsmacked* at how rude she was to her mother.

Anne, however, seemed to be not bothered in the slightest. Without any change in expression or tone, she said, 'Well, I must circulate. Do try to leave things as you found them. My insurance premiums become more crippling every year.'

Gus directed a one-fingered salute at her mother's departing back.

'Why did you bother to come, Gus?' Claude asked quietly.

His sister had the grace to look embarrassed. 'Oh, you're right,' she sighed. 'When there's half a continent between us, I feel quite relaxed about the old trout. But as soon as we're face to face, I want to slap her.'

Marcus had finally noticed that I was silently steaming. He put his arm around my shoulders and gave me an apologetic squeeze. 'Sorry, angel. Our mother tends to bring out the worst in us.'

'I don't know why,' I said stiffly. 'She seems perfectly all right to me.'

'She's got great legs, your mother,' said Jules, the blazer-wearer, unexpectedly. 'Great hair, too.'

'And you have no dick,' snapped Gus. 'So bad luck.'

Jules offered her scowling companion a lazy smile. 'Show me round,' she said. 'Before it gets too hot to move.'

She was right. It hadn't yet gone midday and the heat was already becoming oppressive. Guests were shedding jackets and clustering under the shade canopies that stretched part-way across the paved area. Most faces were acquiring that reddened sheen that results from too many glasses of champagne quaffed to quell a thirst caused by too high a temperature. The waiters, in black shirts and trousers, were clearly dying to roll up their sleeves and undo a few buttons. Both Marcus and Claude had removed their jackets. Marcus had thrown his onto the nearest chair. Claude had draped his neatly over the back. I wondered what Jules would do if hers became too hot? Instinct told me I already knew the answer.

'My God, is there anyone here under five thousand years' old?' Gus' face was wrinkled in disdain.

'These *are* mother's friends,' Claude pointed out. 'And she is sixty-eight.'

'Wow.' Jules' eyelids lifted a fraction. 'Has she had work?'

'Course not,' scowled Gus. 'She's preserved by inner bile.'

She drained her glass in one go, and clattered it down carelessly on the nearby table. 'Come on. Let's do the grand tour of the old bat's estate.'

Without saying goodbye to any of us, she started to jog down the stone steps that led to the gardens and lawn. Jules blinked vaguely after her, and began to follow, two glasses still in hand, in an unhurried fashion. I had a hunch that her leisurely response was quite deliberate. Fair enough. Trying to keep up with Gus and all her bundled angry energy would be exhausting.

Marcus was watching after them, grinning. His grin died immediately when he caught the look on Claude's face.

'Would it kill you to be polite?' Claude asked. 'Mother has gone to a great deal of effort and—'

'Have I been rude to her?' Marcus demanded. 'I don't recall that I have.'

'You and Gus—'

'Oh, leave it, Claude,' Marcus snapped. 'Just leave it.'

In gesture that exactly echoed his sister's, he lifted and drained his glass, dumped it on the table and snatched another from the tray of a passing, sweating waiter.

He waved the glass at his brother. 'Have a drink, Claude. Lighten up. I promise you I will behave around Mother, but what Gus and I do or say together is none of your business. I think that's fair, don't you?'

'Yes,' said Claude, after a pause. 'Yes, that's fair.'

Marcus narrowed his eyes, but Claude seemed to have meant it. Marcus then shifted his gaze outwards to the expanse of lawn. I could see Gus had almost made it to the river. Jules was only halfway. She had stopped under a tree and was showing no inclination to go any further. She leaned against the tree trunk and sipped from one glass, then from the other. I decided I quite liked Jules.

But Marcus wasn't looking at Jules. Gus was at the river now, and was standing on one leg, taking off her shoes. As she started to wade into the water, Marcus put down his glass, and I knew he planned to join her. In the same instant, I knew I could never go with him. My insides began once more to crawl with a sick despair.

'Well, I don't know about you,' said Claude, 'but I am retreating indoors. This heat is starting to become absurd.'

Marcus seemed not to hear. Claude gave me an inquiring look, but I smiled and shook my head. I saw that he wasn't the only one to have abandoned the patio. Marcus and I were now, in fact, alone. And suddenly, I was overwhelmed with a sense that if I didn't do something drastic right now, right this second, I'd lose my chance with him for good.

For the second time in our acquaintance, I placed my hand on his crotch.

His head swivelled frantically, first to me, and then behind him to see who might be witness. When he realised everyone had gone, he expelled a relieved breath.

'Christ,' he said. 'I thought for one minute we were about to become the floorshow.'

'No, I'm more subtle than that,' I said. 'Not *much* more, but still—'

He moved up to me, slid his arms around my waist and pulled me to him. I put my hand on him again, just to leave no stone unturned as it were, and he cupped my face with one hand and kissed me hard.

'I believe,' he murmured against my mouth, 'that it may be time for a tour of the house.'

In my overheated state, the cool, airy interior was a blessed relief. We walked quickly back the way we'd come, through high-ceilinged, pale-walled rooms, sparsely and tastefully decorated with simple but obviously very good pieces of furniture. Nothing I would actually dare touch, of course, but very nice nonetheless.

'The house is Queen Anne,' said Marcus. 'It was restored by the previous owners, a married couple whom the whole nightmare renovation process drove to divorce. Mother bought it lock, stock and period-perfect barrel. Neither husband nor wife wanted any reminder of the place.'

'Does your mother like it here? It's a big place for one woman on her own.'

'What makes you think she's on her own?'

When we reached the big double staircase, Marcus paused. The front door was still open, and the sun glinted off the cars parked outside, their metal shells pinking in the heat. Marcus nodded towards the side of the house we hadn't yet seen.

'Yonder lies Mother's library. Again, it came with the house. I'm not sure she's read a decent book in her life.'

Marcus gestured at the staircase. 'And up there are the bedrooms—'

He met my eyes and pure lust shivered through me from top to toe. With a knowing grin, he took my hand and led me up the stairs.

We wound through several corridors and came to a halt outside a partly open door, through which I glimpsed a neat, white bed. Marcus pushed me up against the hallway panelling and ran his thumbs under my breasts and down to my waist. I could feel the blood rushing in my ears. His own breathing had quickened.

'God,' he murmured. 'How much do I want you . . .'

He cupped the side of my face again and kissed me. His tongue touched mine and I gave a small moan. He grabbed my hips and pulled me into him. His erection pressed the satin of my dress onto my bare skin. It was the most erotic sensation; I realised I may have been too quick to dismiss satin sheets as tacky.

With a short, muttered oath, he lifted himself away from me.

'Come on,' he said, 'before I am never again able to take these trousers to the dry-cleaners.'

The bedroom floorboards were the same dark-stained wood as downstairs, but everything else was white on white. I dimly registered a pretty watercolour of a girl in a wild-flower meadow (undoubtedly *not* a print), but then Marcus had tipped me onto the bed and was running his hands urgently up under my skirt. I felt the seams of my dress tighten and strain, and I sat up in panic.

'Be careful of the dress! I have to give it back.'

Marcus grinned at me. 'I'll take it off then, shall I?'

And he did. Quickly and efficiently. Then he took off my bra, pressed me back down onto the bed and slid his hands into my knickers. I arched my back at the sheer unadulterated pleasure of his touch. And came in about thirty-two seconds.

'Christ!' He was propped up on his elbow, staring down at me, open-mouthed. 'Do you always come that quickly?'

I grinned, lazy with bliss. 'Only with you, apparently.'

'Right. Well. I'll get—' He hooked his legs over the side of the bed and glanced around. 'Damn!'

'What?'

'They're in my what is commonly called a blazer.'

'Ah.'

'Yes. Hell—' He glanced down. 'I can hardly go back out there in this condition.'

I shuffled over to sit next to him. He'd taken off his shoes but nothing else, and I snaked my arms underneath his shirt to find his bare skin. I pressed my lips against his shoulder and murmured, 'There are other things we can do.'

'True . . .'

'Take your clothes off.'

He turned his head and smiled. 'Your wish is my command.'

It was a rather frenzied and sweaty doing of other things. He brought me to the brink with fingers and tongue, but this time, I couldn't quite get over. Then he coaxed me up onto my knees and slid himself between my legs from behind.

'Press your thighs together,' he ordered. 'Christ, yes. That's it—'

He had his hand on me, touching me, and I was so close, it was agonising. But then his hand shifted to grasp my hip, and I heard him say breathlessly, 'God, I'm going to—' and I almost sobbed in frustration. Not yet!

As he reached around to prevent the bed getting the worst of it, and came with a stifled shout, I felt my orgasm start. He was pulling away, which was fair enough, I suppose, given what he was trying to keep contained in his hand, but I gasped, 'No, don't!' Startled, he stayed where he was. And I proceeded to come in intense shuddering waves, oblivious to all else.

After who knows how long, I heard, 'Um, angel? Would you mind? My knees are about to give in, and I have what resembles week-old vichyssoise leaking out between my fingers.'

'Oh!' I realised I was leaning back against him, and he was supporting my whole weight. He was right about the knees; I could feel them shaking. He was right about the handful, too.

'Ick!'

'Indeed.' He shuffled carefully to the side of the bed and, with a slight trembling at the knee, stood up. He glanced down at his closed fist and grimaced. 'I now have complete sympathy with all those woman who are reluctant to swallow.'

He opened a door with his free hand, and I saw that the bedroom had an ensuite. Probably not a period feature, but welcome all the same. I heard the tap run, a muffled curse, more running water, the squeak of a towel rail. And then he'd emerged and was leaning against the doorframe, grinning at me.

'All well?'

By now, I was lying full length on the bed, on my back, limbs deliciously heavy in the afterglow. I smiled. 'What do *you* think?'

He flopped down on the bed beside me. 'I think, unfortunately, that we'd better be getting back.'

'Oh . . .'

My heart sank. I knew he wasn't going back out of politeness to his mother. It was only his sister he wanted to see. I'd played the only card I had, and had temporarily been the winner. Now, I had nothing left. All I could do was delay for a few moments longer.

'It's all about the now for you, isn't it?' I asked him.

He raised an eyebrow, more amused than surprised. 'What else do we have but now?'

'The future?'

'There's no point in worrying what the future will bring,' he said. 'Because it will bring it despite us. And we can't relive the past. So now has to be all that matters.'

I sighed. 'I wish I could be like that.'

Marcus grinned. 'Chin up,' he said. 'I think you've got a mild case of post-coital depression. Come and get stinking drunk with me. Then you won't care about anything.'

My heart sank further. 'Are you going to get stinking drunk?'

'Have you any better suggestions for surviving this hell?'

I replied, without any real hope. 'We could stay here—?'

He gave me a look. 'Do you think I have more in me? After that?'

'It seemed a lot, didn't it?'

Marcus grinned and sat up. 'And who says romance is dead?'

He shuffled off the bed and started to pull on his shirt. I had no inclination to move whatsoever. But if I didn't, he would leave without me. With a sigh, I sat up. And in ten minutes, we were back out on the patio.

Chapter Nineteen

THE HEAT WAS SCORCHING NOW. The patio was still abandoned, but from the distant sounds of splashing and female laughter, I guessed that Gus and Jules had migrated from the river to the pool. In our absence, lunch had arrived in the adjoining room and it seemed people had set upon it like wolves because all that was left were sprigs of parsley and one squashed maraschino cherry, which I despise. I cursed silently, and ate the cherry anyway. It didn't even touch the sides.

Marcus didn't seem hungry. He, too, had guessed that Gus was at the pool. He started immediately down the steps.

I wasn't even sure he realised I was still there, but then he looked back over his shoulder. 'Coming?'

'I have to find some food.' I was pleased it sounded so plausible. 'I'll be there soon.'

But I stayed to I watch him walk away. He had his hands in his pockets, creating a slight tautness across his admirable rear. His shoulders were strong and broad under the soft drape of the white shirt. His gait was leisurely, a confident saunter that just bordered on a swagger. I relived his kiss and his touch with a hot, vivid intensity and as I watched him go, I suddenly felt as if he was pulling part of me with him, unravelling me as he went. It was if I was losing definition, like a cloud in the sky, stretching, thinning and eventually disappearing.

I heard a gleeful shout of greeting from the pool. And I turned away and walked back into the house.

As I did, I almost bumped into a blonde girl striding purposefully towards the door. She was wearing a serving uniform, and a pissed-off expression.

'Sorry, ma'am,' she said, meaning the opposite.

I'm no ma'am, I wanted to tell her. Just an ordinary Joe.

She began to gather up the last of the serving plates. When she was fully laden, she paused and took a breath, as if preparing for an ordeal. 'Fuck's sake,' I heard her mutter. 'Sherpa sodding guides don't even have to go this far.'

'Here.' I stepped towards her. 'Let me help.'

'Jesus!' She almost dropped her armload.

'Sorry.' I reached for a platter. 'Want to hand me those?'

She scowled at me. 'Are you winding me up?'

'No. I'm hoping you'll lead me to the kitchen,' I told her. 'I missed lunch.'

'OK,' she shrugged, and let me take a few of the big plates. 'Whatever.'

As we were walking, she said, 'Are you from Australia?'

'New Zealand.'

'What are you doing here?'

For a second, I thought she meant here, in the house. But then I realised.

'Long story.'

She eyed me beadily. 'Bloke?'

'Well, yes. In a way—'

Thank God. We'd made it to the kitchen. She'd been right about the Sherpa guides. We'd been walking so long, my arms were trembling from the effort of holding the stack of plates. I dumped them on a bench with relief.

'Thanks,' she said. 'I dunno if there's any food left, but I'll do what I can.'

The kitchen, even given my limited posh-kitchen experience, was vast. There was a scrubbed table that would seat at least twenty, a single Aga but also a wall oven, and a gleaming brushed stainless double-door refrigerator. I sat down at one end of the table, keeping out of the way of the catering staff, who were washing dishes and scrubbing down benches.

'Here—'

The blonde girl was back with a plate of cold meat and salad. I noticed she had a tiny diamond stud in her nostril, no more than a shiny speck against, I also noticed, her very good skin. She looked not unlike Princess Anne's daughter, Zara Phillips. But everything else about her showed she did not belong here. Not that she seemed to have any desire to. She was glancing around the room, as if she only now had time to notice it properly. Her lip was curling.

'Fuck's sake,' she said again. 'You could fit my whole house in here.'

I laughed. 'Mine, too.'

'Why would you, though?' She stared at me in such a challenging fashion, I wondered what I'd done wrong. 'Want to live here? Be one of this lot?'

Personally, I could think of many, many reasons. But before I could begin to list them, she went on. 'It's like you're just passing through, just one in a whole string of people with the same sodding name. I mean, why live your life so all you can do is hand all this over to the next in line and become another mark on a mouldy old family tree? I might not make anything of my life, but at least I get the fucking choice to do it all my way.'

A gesture from across the room caught her eye. She sighed. 'Gotta go. More sodding dishes.' She glanced down at my plate. 'You done?'

'Oh—' Hastily, I salvaged the last piece of bread as she

grabbed the plate from me. 'And thanks—' I said. But she was already clattering dishes at the sink.

I sat at the table and wondered what to do next. Find Marcus? I was longing to see him, but I just couldn't face that special humiliation that comes with being an outsider in a group of people who are all so very intimate and familiar with each other.

Find Claude? But again, who would he be with? And what would they have in common with me — we both breathed in and out? Even then, that couldn't be guaranteed.

I sighed. It would have to be Claude. At least he would be polite to me.

I ventured out into the house. But having blindly followed the blonde girl to the kitchen, I found I now had no idea how to get back. I wandered in what I thought was the right general direction, but ended up opening door upon door that led to empty rooms. Who *needed* this many rooms? Marcus had hinted that his mother wasn't on her own. But who was she with? The Mormon Tabernacle Choir?

I was starting to breathe in that rapid, shallow way that precedes a small fit of hysterics. I stopped, and tried to get it under control. Be Zen, I told myself. This is not the Gobi Desert. Your bleached bones will not be found months later, a skeletal hand clutching yet another doorknob.

'What are you doing?' said a voice behind me that I recognised instantly as belonging to Marcus' mother. It wasn't exactly an accusation, but there was a distinct note of impatience.

'I got lost.' I made an apologetic face that I immediately regretted.

'Lost?' The note of impatience was heightened. 'Isn't Marcus with you?'

'Not at the moment . . .'

She sighed. 'He really is the limit,' she murmured, more to herself than me. 'Well, then. Come along—'

She extended her hand to me in an almost imperious gesture. I felt like a dog ordered to heel. Which, I suppose, was not so far from the truth.

I followed her to a drawing room where groups of people were clustered in separate arrangements of sofas and chairs. They were all quite old, I observed. This was a relief. Old people were much less likely to make me feel like something scraped off the bottom of a shoe.

Anne led me to a group in the far corner, where one woman was speaking loudly and authoritatively to the others. Anne gestured that I should take a seat on a small, hard sofa and then, to my mild alarm, sat down next to me.

Our arrival had not broken the loud woman's stride even for a second. She was in her late fifties, I guessed, red-haired and strong-boned, like a cross between Sarah Ferguson and Penelope Keith. Her voice was the carrying kind common to wealthy English people abroad.

I heard Anne sigh. 'I will introduce you later,' she murmured to me. 'This may take some time.'

'And the new pack of Henry's,' the woman was saying. 'Sparky little bitches!'

'Eh? Eh? What did she say? Sparky what?'

A very old man was leaning forward. He had a large grey moustache stained with nicotine, and was wearing white trousers and a navy blazer. If he were an Agatha Christie character, I decided, he would have to be a retired military man.

'Bitches, Major!' Anne said, loudly.

Bingo. I glanced at Anne, and to my surprise thought I caught a fleeting smile. But I couldn't be sure.

'It was my first ride on Stubby for ages,' the woman went on. 'He was terrific. Such a pleasure. Went on and on. Brilliant to be mounted on something that reliable.'

'What'd she say?'

'Mounted, Major!'

'And then it all built thrillingly to a tremendous climax—'

'Eh? What?'

'Climax!'

'At one point, we had to get airborne!'

There was no doubt now. I could feel Anne's shoulders shaking.

'Thank God for Stubby,' the woman concluded. 'Though at one stage, I thought he was never going to get his head out of the bush!'

'What? Out of what?'

'No, I can't,' Anne murmured. 'I simply can't—' She clapped her hands. 'Everyone! This is Darrell.'

'What? Cheryl, did you say?'

'Darrell!'

I was introduced to the loud woman, whose name was Sally; to the Major, whose last name I could swear was Blunderbuss; to a smiling, nodding woman named Bitsy, who appeared to not know where she was; and to a woman who was in her eighties at a minimum, and who was wearing a blue wig, bright orange leggings and a pink sparkly t-shirt sporting the words 'Daddy's little girl'.

'Marjorie rather got the wrong end of the stick about the party theme,' said Anne.

'I knew a fella once like that,' said the Major. 'Took to pig-sticking in quite the wrong way.'

'That's a song, Major!' said Anne. 'Written by Noel Coward!'

'Isn't he the one who wrote filth?'

'No, that's Oscar Wilde! Or possibly D.H. Lawrence!'

'Thought that was the fella in the desert? With all the wogs?'

'We don't say "wogs" these days, Major!' shouted Sally.

'Don't we? Why not?'

'Oh Lord, that's quite enough,' Anne whispered in my ear. 'I must escape again. Come with me.'

She stood, and said, firmly, 'Darrell and I are going to visit the library. I promised to show her my first-edition Audens.'

'Goodbye, Cheryl!' the Major yelled after me. Then I heard him demand, 'When are we eating?'

'We've eaten, Major!' bellowed Sally.

In the library, Anne sank down immediately into a chair. 'Dear God,' she sighed. 'They are my dear friends, but sometimes I would prefer them to be at least forty years younger.' She gave me a look. 'Not that the young people I invite are any more rewarding.'

I was fairly sure she didn't mean me. But I decided to stay quiet, just in case.

Anne gestured impatiently to a second chair. 'Sit, sit!'

I sat. 'Do you, er,' I began, 'actually have first-edition Audens?'

She glanced around. 'God knows. That was the first excuse I could think of.' She shook her head. 'You can certainly see why they call it a double entendre. One would simply not be enough. Not that dear Sally has a clue. It's hard to imagine that she was once Debutante of the Year in *Horse and Hound* magazine.'

'Really?'

'Yes,' said Anne. 'I've never been entirely sure to which species she was most meant to appeal.'

I laughed until I realised Anne was fixing me with her gimlet stare. She said, 'Please don't tell me you are in love with my son.'

My whole face flamed. 'Well, I . . .'

'I wouldn't object, personally,' she went on. 'You seem a pleasant girl. But for your sake, I couldn't in all conscience recommend it.'

'No . . .' I knew she was almost certainly right. But it felt like a hole was opening in the ground in front of me.

'Oh, dear.' Anne had seen my face. 'If it's any consolation, it could be worse. You could be in love with Claude. At least

Marcus knows how to show affection. Well, not to me, of course.' She sighed. 'I suppose it's my fault. I should have put the record straight much earlier. Now, of course, they won't believe me.'

I had no idea what she meant. What record? I was just wondering if I dare ask her, when she frowned and fixed me with another gimlet stare. 'Darrell. Unusual name. You're not a writer, by any chance?'

I blinked at her, astonished. 'Actually, I am.'

'I knew it!' And with the alacrity of a much younger woman, she bounced up out of her chair, strode to a pile of books on a side table and began to fossick through them.

'There!' She brandished a book in triumph, strode back and handed it to me. It was my third book, *Bound by the Billionaire's Secret Contract.* 'Darrell Kincaid. Is that you?'

I stared at the cover. The artist never quite got the hero to look as I imagined him.

'Yes,' I said. 'That's me . . .'

As soon as I said it, I knew it was true. The books *were* me. They defined me, shaped me. Tom had done the same. With him, I'd been complete, intact. When he went, I'd lost more than a husband. I'd lost myself. Without Tom, I was a fragment, a partial person. And now even that fragment was at risk. If my books went, what on earth would be left?

The hole in front of me was yawning wider and wider. And I knew that if I looked any further down into it, I was doomed.

'Oh dear . . . '

I heard Anne's concerned murmur, but there was nothing I could do. I could not speak. I could not move. My fingers were locked onto the book so tight that it creaked under the strain.

Footsteps. There were footsteps approaching.

'What on earth?' Claude was beside his mother. 'What happened to her?'

'I'm not sure,' Anne replied. 'But I've certainly seen this reaction before.'

'What is it?'

'Grief.'

'Well—' Claude sounded at a loss. 'What should I do?'

'What do you think?' snapped his mother. 'Comfort her, you silly ass!'

'But—'

'I'll fetch some brandy.'

'But—'

The fading of brisk footsteps confirmed his mother's departure. Claude sank down into the chair she'd left vacant.

'My mother just called me an ass.'

I managed to suck in a deep breath, which caused him to glance at me in alarm. I had some sympathy for him. Here he'd been, quietly minding his own business and avoiding company, when he'd been flung headlong into an emotional maelstrom.

'Silly ass,' I said.

He gazed at me, bewildered. 'What?'

'She called you a silly ass.'

His mouth twitched. 'I stand corrected. As well as insulted.'

Then he frowned, reached out and placed his hand over mine. At his touch, my fingers released their limpet grip on the book. One by one, wincing, I stretched them out.

'What on earth happened to you just now?' he asked.

'Oh . . .' I was back to being embarrassed. 'It's — hard to explain.'

'My mother said it was grief. Was she correct?'

I nodded.

'May I ask for whom?'

'My husband.'

Claude's eyes widened. 'I see. I'm so very sorry. Was it recent?'

'Recent enough.'

'Yes. Clearly.' Claude screwed up his mouth. 'Apologies. Stupid question.'

Brisk footsteps again. Anne was back.

'Here. Drink this.' She handed me a glass of brandy. 'Chair, Claude,' she said to her son.

'Oh! Of course!' He hopped up obediently, ensured she was seated comfortably and then stood behind her, one hand on the chair back.

'Better?' There was an irritation in Anne's expression that encouraged me to nod.

But then she said, 'Not that I imagine this will help in the slightest, but it does get a little less — acute.'

I was puzzled. Marcus had implied that his parents' marriage was far from happy.

Anne was on her feet again, smoothing down the front of her dress. 'I must go. Doesn't pay to sit still for too long.' She gave Claude a look. 'I suggest you take her home.'

He blinked at her. 'Oh. Yes. All right—'

She made a tchah sound. 'And for God's sake, find someone to marry! Then there'll be some point to you wearing that bloody ring!'

Claude's other hand stole immediately to said ring. He twisted it while he watched his mother leave the room.

'Is it hers?' I asked him, softly.

'Yes. She gave it to me when he died.'

'Your father?'

'No . . .'

He let go of the ring, turned to me and smiled. 'Shall we go?'

'What about Marcus?'

He made a face. 'Must we?'

Inside me, panic began to rise. The thought that I might not see Marcus again today was appalling. I needed him.

Needed his touch, his laughter, his energy. Needed him to bring me back from the abyss.

'How else will he get home?' I insisted. 'We *have* to take him.'

'Very well.' Claude held up his hands in surrender. 'But you do realise that means we will also have to take Gus?'

Now, that I did *not* want. But if it meant I left with Marcus, it was a price I was prepared to pay.

I stood up. 'Come on. They're down by the pool.'

I'm not sure quite what kind of debauchery I was expecting, but when we arrived, my first impression was that it could hardly have been more quiet and sedate. Marcus was slouched in a chair, at a table under the shade of a big umbrella. He had a white terry-towelling sun hat over his face and if weren't for the lit cigarette in one hand, I'd have guessed he was asleep. Gus was next to him, but her chair was facing Jules, who was sitting on the side of the pool, her bare feet paddling idly in the water. I counted only three empty champagne bottles. There was an ashtray on the table in front of Marcus. In it were numerous cigarette butts and something I was fairly sure was a roach. I was not about to sniff it to find out.

I walked up to Marcus and gently lifted the hat. He wrinkled his face in protest and opened one eye. 'Mmph—'

He sat up and pouted at me, like a cross child awoken early from a nap. 'Where have you *been*?'

I pulled up a chair. 'Talking with your mother.'

'Christ, really? Poor you.'

'And what have you been up to?'

His eyes shifted guiltily to the cigarette. 'Breaking my two-a-day rule, as you can see.' He stubbed it out, and made a face. 'I also tried to get drunk, but my heart wasn't in it. I *am* quite nicely stoned, though, so the afternoon hasn't been a complete loss.'

'Claude wants to leave,' I told him.

'Thank God!'

This came from Gus. I hadn't thought she'd even noticed we'd arrived. She called to Jules. 'Dry your feet, sweets. We're about to take a ride in the green beast.'

'A ride that is leaving now,' said Claude. 'I don't intend to wait.'

But to Claude's obvious irritation, Gus flopped right back in her chair, and said, 'What are you up to tonight, Marcus?' The 'you' was unmistakably singular; it did not include me. 'Shall we hit the town?'

'I fly out tomorrow after lunch,' he said.

My heart lurched. But then, he did have a job. And we'd at least have the morning together . . .

'So do I. What does that matter?' Gus turned her head towards the pool. 'What do you want to do, Jules? Shall we go out?'

Jules had stood up and was shaking the water from her feet. Her shoulders lifted in a languid shrug.

'Come on,' Gus urged her brother. 'We haven't been out together for ages. And this afternoon's been *useless*. I really need to let off steam.'

Marcus met my eye, and I knew, before he even asked, what I had to say.

'You go,' I told him.

'Without you?' he frowned.

I was poleaxed by disappointment but I had no choice. All I could do was put a brave face on it. I was getting quite good at those.

'Clubbing's not my thing.'

Nor is your sister, I didn't add. Nor are the places you and she will choose to go. Places where I simply would not fit in.

'Then I'll come to you afterwards,' he said. 'I'll make sure it's not too late—'

My heart leapt.

'Gus!' Claude's patience was at an end. 'Marcus! Now!'

'*Jawohl, mein Standartenführer!*' Gus leapt up and saluted. Then she dashed up and kissed him on his rigid cheek. 'Drop us the hotel?' she wheedled.

'Absolutely not! You can take a taxi from my house.'

Unabashed, Gus grinned. Then she dashed back up to Marcus, grabbed his hand and tried to yank him up out of his chair.

'Ouch!' he protested, but he let himself be pulled to his feet.

Smiling, he bent towards her, as if intending to kiss her, and jammed the sun hat down over her ears. For a minute, they were nose to nose.

'Wow.'

Jules was behind me, her shoes in her hand, her feet trailing damp pools on the paving. Her one syllable was matter-of-fact rather than impressed. As I stared up at her, she gave me a brief glance from under her heavy, almost bored lids.

'Don't they know?'

I blinked at her. What on earth did she mean? I considered asking, but even though Jules was way less intimidating than Gus, I still hesitated.

I lost my chance. Jules turned away and, swinging her shoes, began to stroll towards the pool gate, where Claude was waiting for us, car keys in hand, foot tapping impatiently.

Chapter Twenty

AS I WAS BENDING to put the coffee cup down outside Big Man's flat, the door was yanked open. Wide-eyed, I stared upwards. From this angle, Big Man loomed huge and menacing. I felt like Jack at the top of the beanstalk. Only in my case, there was no escape.

'You tell that blonde harridan,' he said, 'that if she comes anywhere *near* me, God help me, I'll fucking shoot her!'

'With what?' I was upright now, which meant my eyes were at his chest height. It was a slight improvement.

'You think there's any shortage of weaponry around here?' he yelled.

I made a face. 'I'm not sure that would stop her, you know.'

He stood there, glowering, breathing heavily. Then he pointed downwards. 'That mine—?'

With a sigh, I picked the cup up off the ground and handed it to him. He took it with one hand and began to close the door with the other.

I was outraged 'Oi! Don't you shut that door on me!'

He paused. 'You've done what you came to do. Now—'

'Listen!' I jabbed a finger in his face. 'I have had a *very* trying weekend! I am sick of this stupid heat and sick of rude people giving me grief! Would it kill you to be polite for ten fucking seconds!'

He stared at me. 'Yes,' he said, and shut the door.

I was enraged. So enraged, a red mist actually rose in front of my eyes. I lifted both my fists and began to pound on the door for all I was worth. All my fury, all my disappointed, frustrated, helpless fury, came out with every blow. Big Man's door was getting the thumping of its life . . .

Marcus hadn't come back to my place on Saturday night. He rang me at two o'clock on Sunday afternoon.

'Angel, I'm so bloody sorry.'

He sounded genuinely contrite. He also sounded like he'd smoked a thousand fags and stayed up all night. Which I could only assume he had.

'I'm so sorry,' he said again. 'I *swear* to you that I was getting ready to leave at about one, and then, I don't know, somehow, it all went horribly wrong. I'm sorry.'

'Where are you now?'

'At the airport. Slumped in a chair staring at the ceiling, because if I sit up, I'm afraid my eyeballs will slide right out of my head. Christ knows how I'm going to get to the plane. I may have to blag a wheelchair.'

He gave a short laugh, and then had to hold the phone away as he descended into a coughing fit. 'Oh my fucking Lord,' he croaked. 'Never again. I'm far too old.'

Then he said, 'I'll make it up to you. I'll check my diary and let you know when I'm next over. I promise.'

Suddenly, I wasn't angry any more. I clutched the phone as if, somehow, that could bring me closer to him. I wanted to see him so badly, I felt faint.

'All right . . .'

There was a bustle and beeping in the background. He said, 'God, I have to go. Wish me luck. At least there'll be a sick bag within reach once I'm on board.' I heard him breathe into the phone. 'Angel, I'm sorry—'

'Don't miss your flight,' I said.

Then I hung up because I did not trust myself to say anything more…

'Fuck's *sake!*' Big Man wrenched open his door so fast, I almost pounded his chest. 'What the *fuck* are you doing?'

I gazed at him, panting with the exertion. As my breath came under control, it began to dawn on me that my hands were really quite sore. I checked. My knuckles were bruised and raw. One was bleeding.

'For fuck's sake,' said Big Man again, but without the rancour. 'Here—'

He handed me the napkin that had been wrapped around the coffee cup. I dabbed my bleeding knuckle and winced. 'Ouch.'

Big Man made a quick, exasperated noise, as if he knew he'd regret what he was about to do. 'Come on,' he said. 'Let's go for a walk.'

We walked slowly and in silence all the way down to the canal, where Big Man sank down onto the nearest seat in the shade.

'If this is global warming,' he said, 'we're all fucked.'

'Is it not usually this hot in May?'

'It's not usually this hot in midsummer! This is England! Not fucking Qatar!'

'Are you all right?' I asked. 'You're not going to keel over, are you?'

I saw the ghost of a smile. 'If I do, just roll me in the canal. Round here, no one'll notice.'

He leaned against the bench's hard back and closed his eyes. I took the opportunity to have a good, long stare. He looked better than he had the last time I saw him in daylight. He was less heavy around the waist and chin. His colouring had improved, though he could do with a shave. His hair was still military short; I wondered if he cut it himself? Due to the heat, he'd not brought the nasty blue bomber jacket. Instead, he had on a frayed polyester shirt with a singularly hideous abstract pattern in shades of brown. His pants were cotton drill, which at least would breathe, but they looked as if they'd once belonged to someone at least six inches shorter.

I studied his face. He had excellent bone structure — high, Tartar-sharp cheekbones, a firm jawline and a straight, strong nose. If you ignored the excess weight and the awful clothes, you could say that Big Man was handsome. He had been very handsome at one stage, I guessed. Until circumstances, or his own will, had brought him down.

'Didn't your mother tell you it's rude to stare?'

I was sure he hadn't opened his eyes. He must have just sensed it.

'She did,' I sighed. 'She also told me that "hey" was for horses not people. I never really understood that one.'

'My mother used to say things like "You'll put that down right now if you know what's good for you!" Trouble is, I didn't know. She never explained that bit. So I got a clip round the ear-hole and was none the wiser.'

I laughed. Big Man opened his eyes a fraction, and slid his glance my way.

'I meant it you know,' he said. 'About the harridan. You tell her to keep away.'

'Why?'

Big Man's eyes snapped fully open. He scowled in disbelief. '*Why*?'

'Yes, why? What are you afraid of?'

Personally speaking, right at that moment, I was a little afraid of Big Man. He sat bolt upright, with a face like thunder, one giant fist clenching and unclenching by his side.

'If I say I don't want her near, then I don't want her near! Get it?'

Then I was just pissed off. How *dare* he try to bully me?

'What are you going to do?' I retorted. 'Thump me one?'

His eyes widened, and he gazed down at his clenched fist, as if it he'd never seen it before in his life.

'No, I'd—! I'd never—!'

I watched, astonished, as he stopped and stammered. He'd been completely thrown. With a stilted, jerky movement, he balled both his hands and buried them in his lap, and sat hunched over staring out at the canal.

After a moment, I placed a tentative hand on his shoulder.

'I didn't really think you would—'

He flicked his shoulder to dislodge my hand. 'What would you know?'

'I think I know when someone means me harm,' I replied gently.

He grunted. 'You mean I'm full of piss and wind instead.'

But his fists were no longer balled in his lap.

I was taking a huge risk. But if I didn't do it now, I never would. 'I know what happened to you. Dr Flynn told me.'

Slowly, his head turned. 'And what could *Dr* Flynn tell you about me?'

'That you did time in jail. But that you were innocent.'

The pause as he stared at me was possibly the most uncomfortable I'd ever experienced. He didn't scowl, or glower, or even narrow his eyes. He just stared, without blinking, for far too long.

'Is that what you're here for?'

I frowned, confused. 'What do you mean?'

'I had letters, you know. From women on the outside.'

'Oh! God! No!' I felt my face burn. 'No, I'm not like that! I just want to—'

'Look after me?' His voice was ominously calm. 'Make sure I'm OK?'

And it came to me, clear as day, that I was never going to get anywhere with this man. I had no hope. None at all.

'All right,' I sighed. 'I'll stop. I won't come any more. You win.'

I got to my feet. 'The coffee's on me. Don't bother paying me back.'

And I walked off and left him.

I came back home to an argument. As I opened the front door, I heard Tyso yelling in the courtyard. 'You bloody promised! How can you do that to her?'

'I did *not* promise!' Anselo wasn't yelling, but he wasn't exactly calm, either. 'She took it for granted, like she and you and the whole bloody lot of them always do!'

'She went off and cried all last night.'

'She cries when she breaks a nail, for Christ's sake!'

'You *wanker*!'

Tyso must have taken a swing, because Anselo said, '*Don't* do it—' There was a strain to his voice that suggested he had a firm hold on Tyso's arm.

'Wanker.' Tyso's voice jerked, as if he was on the verge of tears.

'Tys, give it a rest.'

Anselo sounded weary. I pictured Tyso sunk down on the floor, Anselo standing over him, the reluctant conqueror.

'You promised her,' I only just heard Tyso mumble.

'I didn't. I never said I'd be there. She assumed. You all did.'

'It's *family*!'

'Yeah, it always is.'

There was a pause. Anselo said, 'Come on—' I pictured him holding out his hand to the boy on the ground.

'Fuck *off*!' I heard Tyso snap.

And then he came running towards me down the hall. He didn't see me till the last minute and startled, pulled up short. His face was screwed tight, boiled red with anger and humiliation. With one embarrassed, resentful glance at me, he yanked open the door and ran out.

I shut the door myself, and turned to see Anselo at the end of the hall.

'Sorry,' he said, when I reached the kitchen.

'Has he gone for good?'

He grimaced. 'Not if his father has anything to do with it.'

I held the kettle under the tap. Seemed like a good time to make tea, despite the fact the house was like a sauna. 'What was it about? Can I ask, or is it none of my business?'

'His sister's getting married. She expected me to come. And bring Vee.'

'Vee?'

'Vivienne. My girlfriend.'

Vivienne. The blonde goddess. I suppose it was too much to hope that she'd be called Edna or Mavis.

I set down the kettle and flicked it on. 'And you have other plans?'

He leaned against the kitchen bench and folded his arms. 'Vee's got some dinner party we have to go to.'

Telling way of phrasing it. But probably best to keep that thought to myself.

'And I never said I'd go!' Anselo was finally allowing himself to sound aggrieved. 'Fuck's sake! My family drives me fucking nuts sometimes. There'll be at least a million bloody people there! Why the hell does she need *me*?'

'Because you're her cousin?'

He threw up a hand. 'The million people are *all* cousins! We're *all* fucking related!'

'Well — because she likes you?'

'Jesus. Don't *you* start!'

'She'll only have one wedding.'

He gave me a look. 'You met her?'

I handed him a cup of tea. 'I think you should go.'

He blew out a long breath. 'Yeah. I know . . . '

LADY MO: Why silence re latest writing effort?? By now I'd expect to be regaled with outlandish plots and hilarious names no real man possesses!

DARRELL: Have had hitch. My editor done gone.

LADY MO: Is editor the one with the hilarious name no real woman possesses?

DARRELL: Same. She's gone to another firm. Left me in lurch.

LADY MO: Surely your megacorp grubby book publisher has more than one editor?

DARRELL: Not one assigned to me yet. My book is in limbo. May never emerge.

LADY MO: This you know, or this you only fear?

DARRELL: Are you psychic? How do you know I am too scared to find out what's going on?

LADY MO: Dr Phil. He knows everything. Call them, you fool!!!!

DARRELL: Sigh. Will do, as otherwise I won't hear the end of it from you.

LADY MO: Do you have plots in mind, anyway? Who is the model for the stinky rich sexual athlete this time? Pierce or Henry? Or — hint, hint —sexy new ducal boyfriend???

DARRELL: Not really my boyfriend.

LADY MO: Then how come all that shagging?

DARRELL: It's complicated.

LADY MO: Darrell. Sweetie. That's not good. You are not the sort to cope with shag-around shenanigans. You need commitment.

DARRELL: Maybe. But doubt I'll get it. Not sure I want it, anyway. I hate his sister.

LADY MO: Let me guess. Sexy thinks his sister is the duck's nuts? Believes sun shines out of bottom? Is blind to her utter bitchness?

DARRELL: How do you KNOW?? No, don't tell me . . .

LADY MO: Phil knows everything.

DARRELL: I did start a new book. A real book. Confess shamingly that I have not got far.

LADY MO: Maybe you need a new model for rich sexy hero? Why not go blonde for once. Oo! How about using Chad?!!

DARRELL: No!!! Ick!!!

LADY MO: You saying Chad is ick?! Chad is perfect and you know it!

DARRELL: Chad is not ick! Is ick to use best friend's

husband as model! Model must be someone you can fantasise about freely!

LADY MO: I see. You are right. We could not stay best friends if you did that. Would have to hunt you down and cut off your fingers with the play-dough knife. Anyone else? Builder? Builders can be super studly. I would add that they are also another romance cliché. Has he offered to mitre your joints?

DARRELL: Builders never turn up in romance novels. You're thinking of porn movies.

LADY MO: I have never seen a porn movie in my life! But that is no reason why such scenarios should not pop up in my mind. So is he studly, or beer-bellied with hairy butt crack? Latter not conducive to porn-style fantasy, let me tell you.

DARRELL: He is quite studly. But is also surly, though confess has lately improved. Not blonde though.

LADY MO: What about Mr Perfect? You don't need to go out with him to fantasise about him. As you well know.

DARRELL: Mr Perfect behaving slightly strangely.

LADY MO: Strange like a man who has women caged in his cellar torture chamber?

DARRELL: No!!! What on earth are you watching when Dr Phil's not on??

LADY MO: Best not to ask. How is he strange then?

DARRELL: Unhappy, I think, but I don't know why. Bit worried to tell the truth.

LADY MO: Is he giving away possessions? Ringing up distant relatives and saying goodbye? That's what suiciders do. Before, obviously. Not after.

DARRELL: That is a horrible, horrible thought. May not forgive you.

LADY MO: Why not ask him? If he's unhappy, he may be dying to tell. Do not mean dying like suicide of course.

DARRELL: Man is bordering on paranoicly private. But yes. That's a good idea. Hope he is at café tomorrow, as he wasn't there this morning.

LADY MO: Not saying a word. Especially not one starting with 's'.

DARRELL: Thank you very bloody much! I won't sleep a wink tonight!

LADY MO: Call non-boyfriend then. Have phone sex. You'll drop off right away.

I had never phoned Marcus. I was desperate not to seem needy. Even though, of course, that's what I desperately was.

But when I went to bed, I couldn't sleep. It was too hot, and my mind was too full of gremlin thoughts. They bickered and whispered and insinuated until I was tempted to yell out loud.

I sat up and switched on the light. Twelve-fifteen. Which made it eleven-fifteen in Paris . . .

'Marcus Reynolds,' said his voice. 'Leave a message. *Partir un message.*'

I had no idea what that last bit meant.

I didn't leave a message, but I did hope he'd see my number. I listened to my phone failing to ring until past three, when I finally sank into a fitful, clammy sleep.

Chapter Twenty-One

CLAUDE WASN'T at the café again. But Miss Flaky was.

'Jesus fuck.' She slumped into a chair at my table. 'What happened to mists and mellow fruitiness?'

'I think Keats was talking about autumn,' I told her.

'No shit.'

'And it's fruit*ful*ness, by the way.'

'My version's better,' she replied.

I glanced at her properly and did a double take. She was wearing a sleeveless sundress! Admittedly, it was down to her ankles and buttoned high at the neck, and in a red and white gingham pattern that made her look like she should be on a table in an Italian restaurant. But it was most definitely an improvement.

I also noticed that Miss Flaky did not shave her armpits, nor, I caught a glimpse of calf as she sat down, her legs. White blonde hair sprouted out all over. I wondered what obsessively neat Claude would make of that? If he turned up, of course.

'And why is it—' Miss Flaky continued '—that the English have radiators even in the john, but seem to have never heard of air conditioning? My apartment is like a Turkish prison. I could crawl into the oven and sweat less!'

I grinned. 'I think the English consider it somehow un-British to be comfortable.'

'Speaking of which—' Miss Flaky craned her head towards the entrance. 'Where's Lord Fauntleroy?'

I felt a brief clutch of unease. 'I don't know.'

But Miss Flaky seemed unconcerned. 'Most likely can't come out,' she sniffed. 'They haven't made a suit light enough for this heat.' She turned back to me. 'So. Did you tell him?'

It took a second to work out whom she meant. 'I did,' I nodded. 'He said if you came anywhere near, he'd shoot you.'

'Ha! Right. That's gonna happen. He's full of shit. Just like his fucking apartment. But not for long.' Her mouth tightened determinedly. 'Oh, no. Not for long.'

'Do you think,' I ventured, 'that it might be better to let him be?'

Miss Flaky regarded me as if I were a stain on a mattress.

'What kind of lame idea is that?'

'I think Big Man has the right to choose how he lives.'

Then I realised what I'd said. And cringed.

'*Big Man*?' Miss Flaky's grin was wide and genuinely amused. She nodded thoughtfully. 'Good name. What do you call me?'

'Nothing!' But my voice squeaked treacherously.

'Right.'

But her knowing grin was quickly overtaken by a scowl. 'The man needs serious help,' she announced. 'He's just too damn proud to take it. So I intend to give it to him, pride or no pride.'

I felt a pang of envy that she could be so undeterred. Perhaps I *had* given up too easily?

'Know any cops?' she asked unexpectedly.

I shook my head.

'Pity,' she said. 'I would love to get my hands on a Taser.'

. . .

I opened my front door to once more hear voices in the courtyard. This time, though, they weren't raised.

I wandered down to find Anselo flanked by two truly huge men. They were standing, arms akimbo, in such a way that if I hadn't recognised one of them, I'd have been quietly reaching for the bread knife.

'Darrell,' said Patrick. 'How's it going?' He gestured to huge man number two. 'This is Jenico Herne. Tyso's dad.'

Jenico Herne had clearly been the origin of his son's dark red hair. But the rest of him was nothing like Tyso. He was Patrick's height, at least six five, but with the barrel chest and arms of a grizzly bear. He wore an outfit that was exactly how I'd imagined a Romani should dress. A pineapple yellow shirt, undone at the throat, with a yellow and red patterned kerchief knotted around his tree-trunk neck. His trousers were chocolate brown and made of a soft fabric, roomy but well cut. He wore less jewellery than I expected. Just two gold earrings and one ornately carved gold ring on his little finger, with an engraved red stone that I guessed was a carnelian. His features were broad but not soft, and his eyes a startling hazel-green. Although the rest of his expression was forbiddingly stern, I detected a glint of something else. I really hoped it was amusement.

'I apologise to you on behalf of my son.' His voice rumbled like a passing train. 'He will, of course, also apologise in person.'

I bet he will, I thought. If I were Tyso, I'd want to keep those giant feet well clear of my backside.

'It was no problem,' I said. 'Most of the time, your son is a delight.'

'And I am sure he will continue to be a delight from now on.'

Amazing how he could make such innocuous words so softly threatening. I glanced at Anselo. His expression was neutral enough, but I sensed he was not entirely enjoying this visit.

'Jenico's oldest daughter, Talaitha, is getting married this weekend,' Patrick informed me, even though he must have known I knew.

'Congratulations.' As I met Jenico Herne's sphinx-like gaze, I felt my smile waver.

'Why don't you come?' Patrick asked.

'Me?' I replied, startled.

'Yeah, why not? Clare's refusing to move and I don't blame her. She's the size of a fucking house now, not that I'd ever say that within earshot. You can come with me instead.' He looked across at his giant companion. 'All right?'

'I would be honoured.'

'Good,' said Patrick, ignoring the fact I'd not actually said yes. 'It's an evening wedding. Saturday at five. I'll pick you up at four.'

Then he nodded to Anselo. And the two huge men made their way to the front door. When it shut behind them, it suddenly felt like there was a lot more air in the house.

'I'm going to your cousin's wedding,' I said to Anselo.

'Well, there's a coincidence,' he said. 'So am I.'

Up in my bedroom, I picked up the phone to ring the publishers, but bottled out before the call was connected. To punish myself, I decided to knuckle down and write. The heat inside the house wasn't actually as bad as it was outside, but I had to strip off down to my faded Kate singlet and a pair of old shorts before I felt remotely comfortable.

Anselo was hammering away downstairs as if possessed by the god of hardware. I didn't know how he could exert himself like that in this heat, but sensed that it was probably more to let off steam than for any practical building purpose. I stuck my earbuds in and turned it up just loud enough to drown him out.

It didn't help much; I just couldn't get into it. And for the first time, I wondered whether it was more than doubt about my ability stopping me. After all, I *could* write; I'd written eight published books! God willing, soon to be nine! True, they wouldn't be earning me a shot at the Pulitzer, but they were competently crafted, enjoyable reads. I knew how to plot and pace and create believable, likeable characters. So why couldn't I do that now?

It was as if I'd found myself on a path that should have been utterly familiar, but on which, all of a sudden, I recognised nothing. I'd come to a halt, bewildered, unsure not only of where I was but also where I'd been headed. The destination I knew so well, the place my books had always, inevitably, reached was as indistinct as vapour. I could no longer imagine a happy ending . . .

I was startled by a sharp rap on my door. I tugged free the earbuds just as Anselo's face appeared in the gap. He didn't look too happy. But then, when did he ever?

'Someone here to see you,' he said.

For a split second, my heart leapt. But Anselo knew who Marcus was. He wouldn't have called him 'someone'. What he *would* have called him was probably best left to the imagination.

'Who?'

He shrugged. 'Tall? Suit? Sounds like he's swallowed *Burke's Peerage*?'

'*Claude*?'

Hurriedly, I shoved back my chair. Anselo stepped back to let me through the door.

'New boyfriend?'

There was an edge to his voice. From which I gathered Claude had not made the best first impression.

'Just a friend,' I replied.

'Yeah, right,' I heard him mutter, as I ran on down the stairs.

Claude was by the bookshelf in the living room, flicking through a volume of *Dance to the Music of Time*. I came up behind him.

'Anyone you know in there?' I smiled.

'No, but I suspect the occasional character may be familiar to my mother.'

He slotted the book back on the shelf and his glance slid in the direction of the kitchen, where Anselo had resumed hammering, louder and more aggressively than before, if that were possible.

Claude offered me an apologetic half-smile. 'I hope you don't mind me intruding?'

'No! It's lovely to see you!' I didn't mention that it was also a big relief.

Then I frowned. He'd begun buttoning and rebuttoning his jacket. It only had two buttons. 'Are you all right?'

'Yes! Yes . . .'

But then he gave a terse, irritated tut. 'I'm sorry. I shouldn't have come.' And he pushed past me, heading back towards the door.

'Claude!' I followed him, and put my hand on his arm.

He stopped, but kept his face averted.

'Claude, what's wrong? Can I help—?'

For a moment, he stared down at me, his face tense with what looked like disgust — for me or for himself, I couldn't tell. And then he grabbed me roughly behind the neck, pulled me to him and kissed me hard on the mouth.

It was over in a second. He let me go, and I gazed up at him, my mouth and eyes three wide, astonished Os. I wasn't sure what had shocked me more — that he'd kissed me, or that there had been so much anger in it.

'Why did you do that?' I managed to ask him.

'Oh, you know—' His voice was flat, distant. 'Just to see.'

'To see what?'

His eyes were looking over my shoulder now. 'Anything.'

He glanced back at me ever so briefly. 'I'm sorry,' he said. 'I'll go now.'

And he opened and closed the door so swiftly, I didn't have the chance to say a word.

I wandered down to the kitchen in a bit of a daze. Anselo popped immediately out of the courtyard, almost as if he'd been waiting for me.

'You all right?'

'Sort of.'

Anselo scowled. 'Did he upset you?'

'No!' He was starting to irritate me.

I unplugged the kettle in order to fill it, but struggled to get the lid off. I wrenched and wriggled it with growing exasperation. 'Sod it!'

'Here—'

Gently, Anselo removed the kettle from my hands and tugged off the lid first go. Then he filled the kettle at the tap, replaced it on the bench and switched it on.

'So, he didn't upset you, then?' he said.

I sank back against the bench and slid my hands up and over my face. My hands were clammy. And now my cheeks felt sticky, too. I craved a bath.

'I don't know what he did,' I replied.

'But you let him anyway.'

The kettle was building up to its big finale. Steam was cascading from the spout. It didn't help the atmosphere in the tiny kitchen one bit. Why on earth do we feel compelled to drink tea in times of crisis?

'I didn't let him do anything!' I protested crossly.

Anselo's expression was challenging, if not outright aggressive. I suspected that he was still smarting from his earlier encounter with his huge male relations — and that I might be a convenient outlet.

'Why do you do it?' he demanded. 'Why do you hang round with arrogant sons of bitches like that? All they do is treat you badly. You've looked like hell for days now! Why do it to yourself?'

I was taken aback. 'I do *not* look like hell—'

'You do! You've got black bloody rings under your eyes! You wander around like you're barely in the land of the living!'

'I've got things on my mind!'

'You've got an arrogant bastard boyfriend who thinks he can treat you any way he likes! And then you've got *that* bastard—' Anselo stabbed a finger towards the front door '—who's just as bloody bad! What the hell? Are they *related?*'

My face instantly gave him the answer.

'Oh well, that figures.' He threw up one hand. 'The Brothers Arsehole. But that's OK, isn't it?' His voice went all sing-songy with sarcasm. 'Because they're posh. And posh people can do whatever the fuck they like to anyone, can't they?'

Now, I was furious. 'You don't know *anything* about them! *Or* me!' I jabbed a finger in his face. 'Just because you got put in your place by bigger men, don't take your wounded bloody pride out on *me*!'

He jerked back as if I'd slapped him. His face flushed briefly red, and then lost every bit of colour. I could see his jaw moving, as if he was testing out words and rejecting them. I regretted being so harsh, but I was still far too furious to apologise.

In the end, he ran a hand over the back of his head and stared off into the courtyard. I saw the corner of his mouth lift in a small, wry smile.

'Yeah, well,' he murmured. 'You'd think I'd know my place by now, wouldn't you?'

Oh God. I should never have said it.

'I'm sorry—' I began.

The look he threw back at me was one of pure, cold hostility. 'No, you're not.'

'Anselo, come on—'

But he held up one hand, as if to ward me off, and strode back into the courtyard. There, he immediately grabbed hold of the circular saw and, without stopping to put on earmuffs, wound it up so that it screeched like a banshee on attack.

I could have stood there and shouted at him. But what was the point?

I made a cup of tea and took it upstairs. Where I sat on my bed and stared into it until it was too cold and nasty to drink.

Chapter Twenty-Two

I'D FORGOTTEN — until the phone call from the nice woman at the Registry Office reminded me. Now, I was sitting on a bench in Islington Green, staring at a brown envelope on my lap. The woman hadn't given me any details, but the fact she had an envelope for me told me enough. With a sense that I was about to be damned for all eternity, I ripped it open.

Her name was Lydia Jane. Born to Michael James Hogan and Elizabeth Marie Hogan, née Walsh. I did a quick calculation. If she were alive, and please let that be the case, Lydia Jane would now be twenty-eight.

What now? I suppose I could see if her name was on a marriage certificate. But to be honest, I'd run out of steam. I simply couldn't bring myself to pry any more. What earthly use would it be for me to know more about Big Man's daughter? I slipped the certificate back in the envelope and schlepped home.

Where I sat round, stewing, until I couldn't bear it any more.

'He has a daughter.'

'And you're telling me this why?' Gabriel Flynn enquired.

'I had to tell someone. Or I'd burst.'

'Have you ever seen someone burst? I have. One of my patients. They'd died in the bath and when I found them, they'd been there three weeks. When the ambulance crew tried to lift—'

'Please stop.'

'You started it!'

'I'd given up on him,' I confessed. 'But now, I don't know. It's just that I have a hunch he hasn't seen his daughter since he came out of jail. Possibly not even since he went in—'

'His choice, I'd bet.'

'Are you telling me I shouldn't interfere?'

'Jesus, Mary and Joseph! What would be the use of that?'

'But where to from here?' I almost wailed.

'Ah!' he said, suddenly. 'Yes! I knew I had something to tell you. Not that I was going to make an effort to actually phone you or anything. But now that you're on the line—'

'Jeepers! What?'

'The other week, I was invited to testify at the murder trial of a man who, as I stated in my professional opinion, was an unhinged sicko—'

'You phrased it differently, of course.'

'I did not, don't interrupt. His lawyer, despite clearly having come to the same conclusion as myself, did a remarkably fine job of defending him. Not fine enough to get his client off the charge, for which nine year-old girls everywhere can breathe a sigh of relief, but enough to interest me in engaging him in discussion afterwards.'

I waited. 'And—?'

'His name is Desmond Richards. He was one who fought to have Michael Hogan acquitted.'

Desmond Richards lived in Holland Park, in the penthouse apartment of an imposing grey brick building.

'My late wife had money,' he informed me. 'I've done well enough in my career. But not this well.'

We decided that it was, alas, too hot to sit out on the roof terrace and opted for the kitchen. I watched as he made me a lime and soda. He was not that much older than Big Man, around fifty-five, I guessed, and of average height with a lean, stringy build that reminded me a little of Tom. I wondered if Desmond Richards was a runner, too?

'I haven't seen Michael for years,' he told me as he joined me at the kitchen table. 'I saw him regularly, of course, while he was in jail. But once he was released — well, I was given the distinct impression he'd prefer me not to contact him.'

'After all you did for him?' I frowned.

'I suspect he was embarrassed. I think he felt, somehow, that he was obliged to repay me. And he was at a loss to know how.'

'Still—'

Desmond Richards offered me a small smile. 'Well. As you've met him, you'll have some idea that he is an intensely proud man. And, dear God, a stubborn one. He always reminded me of that P.G. Wodehouse story, where Lord Emsworth describes his Scottish head gardener as having all the ingredients of a first-class mule. Lord Emsworth decides that he would have liked the gardener better had he, in fact, been a mule. I confess I often felt the same way about Michael.'

'You must have been very young when you defended him?'

'Thank you for suggesting that I may look young now,' he smiled. 'I *was* young. It was not my first case, but it was my first big one.'

'Did you know then that he was innocent?'

'It was my job to assume that he was until proven otherwise. The evidence against him was mostly circumstantial. He was found in possession of the murder weapon. His fingerprints were on it. Whether he had been holding it at the time of the murder was never proven. But then, it didn't really have to be. His manner on the stand was what damned him. Lord knows I tried to work around it, bring the jury back to the facts. But to no avail.'

My hunch had been right. 'I'd already suspected he wasn't the most sympathetic defendant—'

Desmond Richards gave a shout of laughter. 'Dear God, no! I think the Nuremberg judiciary had more sympathy for Reichsmarschall Göring than that jury had for Michael!' He shook his head. 'I lost my temper with him so many times. I simply could not understand why he would not help himself. I may as well have bashed my head repeatedly on the prison wall for all the good it did me.'

His shoulders slumped. I well understood why. Big Man made head bashing seem like quite a good option. Certainly a less painful one.

'So how did you find out he hadn't done it? If he never spoke to you?'

'It was his daughter—'

My heart gave a guilty lurch. But I kept quiet.

'She was seven at the time. A very bright, very articulate little girl. Her mother, Michael's wife, Beth, had been a school teacher. I think Lydia benefited from that.' He frowned. 'Not to say that Michael lacks intelligence, as he most certainly does not. But he was also a man of his time — and place, I suppose. More liable to settle arguments with his fists than with words.'

'So he *was* violent?' I broke in. 'Did he hit his wife?'

Desmond Richards looked shocked. 'No! Never! I apologise — that was a careless sentence. Michael never lifted his hand to a woman. However, his size did make him a target for other men who wanted to, let's say, prove themselves. By all accounts, he usually refused to react. Unfortunately, the night before the murder was one of the few occasions when he did.'

I recalled that the alleged motivation for the murder had been a sexual assault on Big Man's wife.

'He had a fight with the victim?'

'In the local pub. The victim, a crawling low-life by all accounts, received a broken nose and a fractured jaw before Michael was pulled off him. The jury decided Michael wasn't satisfied to leave it at that, and that he went to the victim's flat the following night to finish it.'

'But he didn't. And his daughter knew that?'

'As I said, she was a very bright and articulate young lady. It was a shame that she did not choose to speak up until after the trial…'

He placed both his hands around the glass in front of him, as if its cool, dewy surface was comforting.

'The day after the verdict had been pronounced, Lydia and her mother came to my chambers,' he continued. 'Beth had come to thank me for all I'd done. It had not been easy for her. She and Michael had separated; the trial proved too much for their marriage. I know she regretted deeply what had happened, and indeed felt partially responsible—'

Something like embarrassment crossed his face. 'Beth Hogan was a smart, good-hearted woman. I liked her immensely. She confided that she intended to take Lydia away for a fresh start, and wanted to know what I thought of that. I told her I thought Michael would agree that their daughter was the first priority.'

How did Lydia feel about that decision now, I wondered suddenly? Did she regret she'd never had a say in the matter? Or was she glad of the distance put between her and her convict father?

I tuned back in, as Desmond Richards continued with his story. 'Beth left Lydia with me for a few minutes, while she went to the bathroom. Lydia picked up a picture book that was lying on my desk, which I'd intended as a present for my niece. She said, "That's the book Daddy was reading that night. He fell asleep, the silly. *I'm* the one who's supposed to fall asleep." I asked her what night. I was simply making childish conversation, but she replied, "The night before the police came." I must admit, I jumped as if she'd stuck me with a pin. I asked her what time she went to bed and she told me seven-thirty. I asked if she could remember how long her father had slept for. I knew I was grasping at straws, but, my God, she said, "He was squashing me, so I woke up. I went to get some water. I saw the clock. It said twelve-oh-oh. That's midnight!"

'She was so proud of herself. I, on the other hand, was so agitated, I could barely bring myself to ask the next question: had he been asleep the whole time? She answered without hesitation. Yes. Because he wasn't allowed to sleep on her bed any more. He'd done it once when he was drunk, she told me, and her mother had given him such what-for that if he'd woken up he wouldn't dare come back to her bed; he'd go to his own. He was asleep the whole time. She was sure of it.'

'And the murder was committed—?'

'Between eleven and twelve.'

We were both silent, locked in our thoughts.

'She could have been mistaken?' I ventured. 'She *was* only seven.'

'I know. I kept telling myself that. But on the day Michael was sentenced, I finally summoned the courage to repeat to him what his daughter had said. To my shock, he grabbed me two-handed by my collar and slammed me into the wall. "You leave her out of this", he demanded. "You don't talk to her, you don't go near her! Understand?" All I could do was nod.'

That sounded like Big Man, I thought. Subtle. Considered.

Desmond Richards met my eye. 'And it was then I decided to re-examine the evidence against him.'

'Even though he'd slammed you against a wall?'

'*Because* he'd slammed me against a wall.' He made a wry

face. 'As a lawyer, I am averse to hunches. But I saw, in his eyes . . .'

'What did you see?'

'Fear. That his secret had been revealed.'

I threw up my hands. 'But *why*? Why did he take the blame? Who did he take it for?'

'I've never found the answer to that question. The acquittal was on the grounds that the conviction was unsafe, that the judge and jury had ignored vital evidence. Forensic testing had found fingerprints on the murder weapon — a golf club, if you're wondering — that were not Michael's. The same fingerprints were in the victim's flat. At the flat, there had clearly been a struggle and there was blood present that was neither the victim's nor Michael's. The prosecution had argued that the victim was a known felon, who consorted with other felons not averse to casual violence. That was potentially true. What tipped the balance was that there was not a trace of blood on Michael when they arrested him in the morning. At the time, this was put down to the fact he'd changed his clothes and showered. I was able to prove that he had not. I was also able to prove that it is nigh-on impossible to beat someone to death with a golf club and escape unmarked.'

'And you never found out whose blood, or whose fingerprints?'

'There was no match found in the police database. And before you ask — they were not Beth's, either.'

A thought struck me. 'But where was she that night? Why wasn't she at home, too?'

Desmond Richards shot me a look. 'I don't know,' he said. 'But let's be clear. I have also never wanted to find out.'

This time, Mick Jagger's was the only voice I heard as I opened my front door. *Brown Sugar* was rocking out loud from the courtyard. Normally, the boys kept the volume down. But I guessed they knew I was out—

Drawn partly by curiosity and mostly by a strong need for the comfort of tea, I headed straight down to the kitchen.

'*I'm* no schoolb—' Tyso bustled out, saw me, and halted in mid-not-very-tuneful song. His gaze dropped immediately to his scuffed boots.

''m sorry,' he muttered.

I'm not sure his father would have considered it an entirely adequate apology, but I wasn't so mean as to make the boy squirm any longer than necessary.

'No problem.'

I nodded towards the speaker. 'So some of the old music's not too bad then?'

Tyso's eyes widened. 'Is this *old*?'

Smiling, I shook my head. 'There is no hope for you.'

Then Anselo moved into view. I took a deep breath and stood in his way.

'Hi,' I said. 'I'm sorry about yesterday. I didn't mean it. I was angry.'

He stopped, his stance and expression wary.

'I didn't mean it,' I said again. 'Truly.'

'Yeah, well.' Now, he looked embarrassed. 'I'm sorry I gave you such hard time.'

It was only then that I noticed he was gripping his finger and wincing. And that there seemed to be really quite a lot of blood. 'God! What did you do?'

'Sliced it against the saw.' He saw my face. 'It wasn't going. Blade's still sharp enough, though.'

'Let me see—?'

It wasn't such a deep cut that it needed stitches, but it was bleeding like the blood had been waiting for just this chance to make a break for freedom.

'Run it under the cold tap,' I instructed. 'I'll grab the first aid kit.'

I was fastening the gauze bandage around his finger when I noticed his shirt. 'Oh my God, it's everywhere! Are you sure the saw wasn't going?'

'Splatter!' said Tyso, who was in the doorway, grinning. 'Chainsaw massacre!'

Anselo glanced down. 'It's not that bad.'

I made a face. 'It is. You look like you've been slaughtering a pig.'

'I don't have a spare,' he told me. 'It's in the wash.'

'I have one—' And in two minutes, I was back with Captain Awesome.

Anselo saw the shirt and gave me a faint smile. 'You were wearing this that morning.'

My cheeks flushed bright pink. If he recalled the t-shirt, he probably also recalled the underwear. And the knees—

Anselo's smile widened. 'Thanks,' he said. And with a single, swift, one-handed movement, he took his own blood-stained shirt up over his head and off.

I have to confess, I had a little moment. His upper body was quite simply spectacular. I don't know if it was a result of time at the gym or the physical nature of his work, but every single muscle was taut and defined. Not in that glistening meat-pack way you see in the ab machine infomercials. Just nicely firm, and set off by flawlessly smooth olive skin.

In my head, I was Roger Rabbit — eyeballs bugging on springs accompanied by a horn going 'A-*ooo*-ga!' But, and boy, was I proud of myself, I managed to look him in the eye and breathe normally, as if half-naked, ripped Romani men were ten a penny.

There was a knock on the door.

'Tys—' Anselo nodded.

'What?'

'The door!'

'Did he just mutter "I'm not your slave"?' I grinned at Anselo.

'If he did, he's dead wrong.'

Voices at the door shifted Anselo's gaze over my shoulder. He face fell. 'Shit—'

I swivelled round and almost hit the ceiling. 'My God!'

It was Marcus. My heart began to pound, and I couldn't tell whether it was joy or nerves. Was he really here? Was he staying—?

Marcus' gaze travelled between me and the half-naked Anselo, and then rested on my hand, still clutching Captain Awesome.

'Bad moment?' he asked.

Anselo, without haste, took the t-shirt from my grasp. 'Thanks,' he said again. And with barely a passing glance at Marcus, he strolled back into the courtyard.

Marcus' eyes lingered a fraction too long on Anselo's shirtless, well-muscled back. There was a touch of the sulks around his mouth, from which I concluded that in the Marcus–Anselo macho-off, it was now one-all.

'Next time,' he said, 'I'll give you some warning.'

'No!'

The reality of his presence had sunk in. He really *was* here!

'No warning required!' I wrapped my arms around his neck. 'It's brilliant to see you! You've made my day!'

'Well—' He grinned, clearly chuffed by the eagerness of my response. 'In that case . . .'

He pulled me to him and kissed me deeply and with an overt use of tongue. Suddenly, I became aware that Anselo would almost certainly be watching, and that Marcus without any doubt knew that and was showing off. The thought made me very uncomfortable. So I broke away.

'Come along—' I took his hand. 'Privacy's not *that* overrated.'

'Aren't we going upstairs?' he frowned, as I led him towards the living room.

'There are *people* in the house!' I was blushing, which made me even more uncomfortable.

'So? There were over fifty people in my mother's house, and I don't recall you letting that constrain you.'

'It was a big house,' I muttered. 'The people weren't directly below.'

He blew out a breath. 'Darrell, I managed to find this *tiny* window of opportunity. If I have to take you to a hotel, that window will shrink to the point where I may as well kiss you goodbye now and be done with it.'

I could almost *hear* Anselo. Why do you do it? Why do you let them treat you any way they like?

But what could I do? What choice did I have? If I refused, Marcus would leave—

'All right. But can you try not to make it bloody obvious where we're going?'

He grinned. 'What *do* you take me for?'

In the bedroom, he wasted no time. I would have preferred a little more lead-up, but I suppose he was working to a schedule. As it happened, we ended with time to spare. Less than three minutes into it, he abruptly withdrew and, grimacing, reached down to grab the base of his erection.

'Oh, Christ—' he muttered. 'Sorry—'

And he shoved himself back inside me and came.

'Shit . . .' He rolled off and sank onto his back. 'Well, that will teach me.'

I spooned into him. 'Teach you?'

'Not to fantasise compulsively about having sex with you.' He offered me an apologetic smile.

'Do you?' I was insanely flattered.

'Then again,' he sighed, 'it's really your fault. You shouldn't write such exciting little books.'

I sat up so fast, I almost took his eye out with my elbow. 'What? What do you mean?'

He smiled, amused. He was enjoying teasing me.

'Seems we have a mutual friend. Well—' He made a face. 'Friend is overstating it. A mutual acquaintance.'

I gazed at him, dumbly. I had no idea who he could possibly mean. Unless—

'Hippolyte McManus,' he announced. 'Name ring a bell? Don't deny it. There can hardly be two of them. Thank Christ.'

Oh my God. 'How did you—?'

'Meet her? I haven't yet; we've only spoken by phone. She works for the publishing house that has now bought the English language rights to my little French star's book.'

He worked his jaw. 'I have to negotiate with them as well, now. The fuckers are pushing the price up, which is making me very, very displeased.'

I felt my breathing start to go haywire with panic. 'Does that mean you'll be going to New York?' New York was a *lot* further away than Paris.

'Absolutely not! That would suggest I was desperate! No, at this stage, phone calls only. Though I swear,' he added darkly, 'if she employs the phrase "It's been real" one more time, I *will* be on a plane to New York. And I will go to her office, take her down to the Hudson and hold her head under until the bubbles stop.'

I frowned. 'But — how on earth did you and she get to talking about *me*?'

'Oh, I was buttering her up,' he said, casually. 'Flattering her into believing I thought her intelligent. Somehow we got onto women authors with male-sounding names. I was able to list quite a swag of them. George Eliot. Richmal Crompton. Carson McCullers. Harper Lee. Hippolyte listed you.'

He hauled himself into a sitting position next to me. 'Why didn't you *tell* me?' he demanded. 'I almost fell off my bloody chair when she said your name!'

'I don't know . . .'

He began to nuzzle my neck. 'Were you embarrassed?'

'Maybe.'

'You should be. My God. Silken hardness? Nipple-biting?'

I shoved him off me. 'Did you *read* one?'

He grinned at me, unabashed. 'Of course! I went and hunted one down as soon as I got off the phone!'

'Oh . . .' I grabbed a pillow and held it over my flaming face.

'There was moaning in it,' I heard the bastard continue. 'And sobbing with need. Not to mention feverish, demanding writhing—'

He prised one hand off the pillow and placed it on himself. 'As you see, it had a terrible effect on my towering male strength.'

My voice was muffled by the pillow. 'I thought you didn't have much time?'

He jumped. 'Shit!' He reached across me and grabbed his watch. 'Shit, shit, shit!'

And he leapt out of bed and began to throw on his clothes.

I didn't bother to get up. What was the point?

Shirt still partly unbuttoned, tie in hand, he leaned down and brushed a hasty kiss across my mouth.

'Sorry, angel. That was a poor show on my part. Promise I'll make it up to you.'

He blew a kiss from the bedroom doorway. 'Thank you,' he said. 'Again, more generous than I deserve—'

I heard him clatter down the stairs, and slam the front door. His footsteps clipped quickly along the path below my window, and I listened as they faded up the street until I was absolutely sure I could no longer hear them.

Chapter Twenty-Three

WHAT TO WEAR to a Romani wedding?

I asked Michelle and she emailed me a photo of Gypsy Rose Lee in suspenders and a giant ostrich-feather hat.

I asked Adam and he sent me the exact same picture as Michelle.

Even if I'd wanted to ask Claude, I couldn't. He wasn't at the café. Again.

I couldn't ask Miss Flaky because the woman wore blankets and tablecloths.

Anselo gave me a look like I'd asked him to drink freshly squeezed badger juice and replied, 'Some kind of dress—?'

And then I remembered Tyso had sisters . . .

'I've got a red halter-neck,' I told him. 'It's my only posh frock. It's got a long skirt but it's a bit, um, low in the neckline. And it's — red.'

'Sounds perfect. We like colour. Brighter the better.'

'Isn't there a risk of upstaging the bride?'

He grinned. 'No risk,' he replied. 'Trust me.'

Patrick looked imposing but wonderful in a formal dark grey suit and white shirt. The only touch of colour was a scarlet tie and small red rosebud in his buttonhole.

I was beginning to wonder if Tyso had led me astray, but Patrick looked me up and down with brisk appreciation and said, 'Just as long as no photos of you get back to Clare, I can safely say that's a great dress.'

I blushed. 'Thank you. You look pretty excellent yourself.'

He made a face. 'I'm going to fucking die in this heat, though. Come on—'

He gestured to his car. He was driving a Mercedes. I couldn't tell you which model but it was a big, silver two-door coupe with shark fin grille bits. It looked as if it might take your arm off.

As Patrick was opening the passenger door for me, the man on the bike wheeled past and yelled, 'Garn! Gizza blow job!'

Patrick, with really quite startling speed, stepped out into the road, grabbed the bloke by the scruff of his neck and hauled him off his bike. Then, apparently with no effort at all, he dangled him a few inches off the ground.

'That—' said Patrick, as the bloke struggled fruitlessly in his grip, '—is no way to talk to a lady.'

'Lemme darn!' the bloke whinged.

'When you apologise to the lady.'

''m choking!'

Patrick tilted his head to one side and smiled. 'Apologise,' he said in a gentle sing-song manner that was deeply, primordially threatening.

'Fuck! Sorry!'

'There now—' Patrick put him back down. 'That wasn't so hard, was it?'

Muttering evilly, the bloke scuttled off to pick up his bike. When he'd ridden a safe distance, he started to hurl obscenities back over his shoulder.

Patrick ignored him. When we were both in the car, he said, 'If you ever have any trouble—'

The scenarios that leapt to mind to complete his sentence

were, to be frank, a tad unsettling. I gave him a sidelong glance, and wondered anew how *exactly* he had made his money.

A faint smile appeared on his face, as if he'd guessed what was on my mind.

'I haven't had a real scrap since I was nineteen,' he said. 'That was when I finally learned that my brains were in my head, not my fists.'

I recalled what Desmond Richards had said about Big Man. It sounded as if he'd also done his best to avoid fights, but to his ultimate detriment hadn't quite been able to manage it. I suspected that he and Patrick weren't a million miles apart in many ways. But here was Patrick in a souped-up silver Mercedes, and there was Big Man in a crappy blue jacket. Was it down to the choices they'd made? Or just luck?

Oh well, in for a penny. So to speak—

'How *did* you make your money?' I asked.

'I stumbled across the stolen haul of Lefty Barnes, notorious East End gangster, who'd fallen foul of the even more notorious Slasher Briggs and taken the secret location of his stash with him.'

'Ha, ha.'

He grinned. 'You'd be amazed how many people would actually buy that.'

I waited. 'Well, go on!'

'It's not exciting,' he warned. 'Dead boring, in fact.'

'I've never found a story boring yet,' I told him.

And it wasn't. Young Patrick, pre his brains-versus-fists epiphany, had been a parent's worst nightmare. Dropping out of school at fourteen, he had fought, thieved and vandalised his way in and out of juvenile court. To start with, he served mainly community sentences, but the older he got, the more jaundiced became the eye of the judiciary. Being, as he put it, ten foot fucking tall and bulletproof, young Patrick ignored the warnings, and it was to his shock and amazement that at nineteen, he was banged up for six months in an adult prison.

'Fuck me, that was terrifying,' he said. 'I'd always fancied myself as a fighter, but fisticuffs with a few boys my own age is cat-lick compared to what a bunch of hard grown men can dish up. I was convinced, every single day, that I was going to die. So when I got out, I decided enough was enough.'

Trouble was, work opportunities for an uneducated nineteen year old with a criminal record didn't exactly abound. And Patrick's family, by this time, had reached the end of their tether.

'Uncle Jenico took me aside and told me that they were tired of my arrogance, and had decided to let me sink or swim on my own. As I recall, I did quite a bit of snivelling. But as you can imagine, Jenico's not a man who's easily swayed.'

I could imagine. Tyso's dad could hold up one hand and stop a freight train.

'I moped for ages until I got sick of being broke and started to put some real effort into job hunting. Which is when I had my first bit of luck. I got a job working for an old bloke who owned a cleaning firm. Cleaned office blocks. We got on well. He was struggling with the paperwork, and though I never finished school, I had a head for figures. I helped him make that business ten times more profitable. He had no family and so when he died, he left it all to me. I built it up, sold it for what seemed a shitload at the time, and bought my first commercial property.'

He slid me a glance. 'See? Told you it was boring.'

I smiled. 'And now you're going to be a dad.'

'Yeah,' he replied. 'And that, let me tell you, is a fucking sight more terrifying prospect than having the shit kicked out of me by psycho crims.'

. . .

The wedding venue was a listed mansion, set in the middle of an expansive deer park. Both setting and decoration were standard wedding fare, attractive enough, neutral and tasteful, nothing to offend. If it had not been for a little too much sequinage among the women and ear jewellery among the men, it could have been the wedding of any well-to-do British family.

'This is quite posh, isn't it?' I said to Patrick, as we walked up to the main cluster of relatives on the lawn. I could see Jenico. But then, satellites in space could probably see Jenico Herne.

Patrick gave me a sideways look. 'You mean for a bunch of thieving Gyppos?'

'Ugh. Sorry—'

'I'm not offended. You're right. My family has made good.'

'Anselo told me about his grandfather—'

'Did he?' Patrick grinned. 'The boy must like you.'

'Why must he like me?'

'He talked to you,' Patrick replied. 'Anselo doesn't talk to anyone if he can help it.'

Jenico was moving towards us, beaming, arms outstretched. He was wearing the same dark kind of suit as Patrick but with a waistcoat and tie that gleamed so brightly in the sun that they looked woven from pure gold. He greeted both of us with a robust embrace and a smacking kiss on both cheeks.

'Welcome!' He threw wide his arms, as if not only the venue but also the whole world belonged to him. And, I suppose, in a way it did.

Then he grasped my hand in both of his huge ones, and said, 'We are so glad to have you part of our family!'

'Don't worry,' Patrick murmured in my ear, as led me away to make room for the next lot of greetees. 'I'm pretty sure he's not expecting you to get hitched to one my cousins. Not today, anyway.'

Speaking of which . . .

I looked around, but while I spotted young Tyso in the midst of a gaggle of girls — he grinned and gave my dress the thumbs up — I could not see Anselo. Perhaps he was coming later? After his girlfriend's dinner party?

A champagne flute was thrust into my hand, and Patrick steered me towards the group around Tyso.

'Meet the Tyso fan club. His sisters, Nadya and Myfanwy. And his cousins, Mirela . . .'

I lost track as he reeled off a list of exotic names. The girls were all delightful, and doted on Tyso so much that he practically purred. No wonder he was a naturally happy boy. He received more positive affirmation in ten minutes than Miss Flaky could read in a year.

'I love your dress,' one of the girls said to me.

'I was worried it would be a bit over the top,' I replied.

Every one of the girls laughed, like I'd cracked the best joke in years. Fair enough. I'd been so self-conscious about my dress that I hadn't really stopped to compare. These girls were all decked out in variations on the theme of short, tight and sparkly. Next to them, I looked about as risqué as Mrs Thatcher.

'People give us Romani shit about being trashy,' said one of Tyso's cousins. 'But fuck 'em, I say. What girl doesn't want to wear rhinestones and glitter and fuck-me shoes?'

Her sisterhood loudly expressed agreement.

'Yeah, why choose a dress just because you're worried about offending people?' added another. 'Every woman I've met who wanted to look *tasteful* —' She made inverted commas with her fingers in the air '— fuck me, you couldn't pull a needle out of their arse with a tractor! When I wear a dress,' she went on, 'I want to feel like the fucking queen of the May!'

Tyso, glancing anxiously around, said, 'You shouldn't swear so much, Nady. If Dad catches you—'

'I'd smile sweetly,' replied his sister. 'And he'd let me off with a warning, cos I'm his little girl.'

'Personally, I'd put you over my knee,' remarked Patrick.

'Oo-oo!' wolf-whistled all the girls.

Nadya gave him a look from under her eyelids. 'Promises, promises.'

'Jesus,' Patrick muttered as he steered me away towards the chapel. 'I bloody well hope Clare and I are having a boy.'

I looked around again for Anselo. Still absent. The blonde goddess must have put her foot down. Blood, in this case, was obviously not thicker than viognier.

And then, there he was. He'd been roped in as an usher. His expression seemed to suggest that he was taking it exceptionally seriously, or that he was dying to be somewhere else. He didn't see me until Patrick and I were right in front of him.

He and Patrick were in almost identical outfits. Anselo's tie was also scarlet, but the fabric a smart weave rather than Patrick's glossy silk. His dark grey suit was beautifully cut, wide on the shoulders and narrow at the waist. I had a sudden vision of the muscled torso I knew was underneath, which caused me nearly to stand on Patrick's foot.

Anselo, in return, gave me only a cursory glance. 'You're in here.' He gestured to the middle of the row of chairs. And then he looked quickly past us to the people behind.

'Man with a mission,' murmured Patrick, as we sat. 'He really should learn to lighten up. He'll have a fucking stroke.'

The ceremony was wonderful. And Tyso was right — the only person at risk of upstaging the bride was Elton John in his 'Crocodile Rock' days. Or Lady Gaga in one of her less restrained moments. The dress must have cost Jenico a bomb.

'Fuck's sake,' muttered Patrick. 'I can feel my retinas sizzling.'

'It's glorious.' I nudged him with my elbow. 'Shut up and enjoy.'

When the groom, a handsome young man who looked terrified from start to finish, as well he might, kissed his new bride, I heard Patrick sniff. This time, it was me who was able to offer him a handkerchief.

'Thanks,' he said.

'Sentimental fool,' I grinned.

'Guilty.' He made a face. 'Thank fuck Clare's not here. Place'd be awash.'

The reception was in an outdoor pavilion lined with white silk. By now, it was early evening, but the heat was still punishing. Every man had his jacket off. Women were fanning themselves with menu cards. I was at a table with Patrick; Patrick's mother, Consuela, who had obviously been a stunning glamour puss in her day; Anselo's equally striking mother, Adrienne; and five middle-aged cousins, whose names I instantly forgot. Anselo was at top table, right next to Jenico. I grinned to myself. Poor bastard. He certainly had been soundly punished for his attempted betrayal.

During dinner I drifted away, content to let the buzz of family-centric conversation wash over me. Anselo's mother brought me back with a thump.

'You know *mi chava*, my boy, I gather?' she said. 'How do you find him?'

I just stopped myself saying: I follow the sound of hammering. Instead, I replied, 'I like him.' Then I frowned. 'Is that what you meant?'

Anselo's mother fixed me with such a penetrating glance, I could understand why people believed in the evil eye. 'My two older sons — they are content with their lot in life. I am not so sure about my middle boy.'

'Oh!' was the best I could manage. 'I'm afraid I don't know him *that* well . . .'

'Don't grill the poor girl, *Beebee* Adie,' said Patrick. 'Anselo always was a sulky little bastard, pardon my French. But he's hardly a boy now. If he's not content, that's his choice.'

'*Si covar ajaw.* So it is. I know. But—' Anselo's mother wagged a finger at Patrick '—and you will learn this for yourself very soon. They are our children *ever-komi!* They will forever cut us here—' She slapped a hand on her heart.

Patrick rolled his eyes at me and grinned. 'Romani melodrama. You have to love it.'

'You speak the language?' I was fascinated.

'Not really. The older ones do, so you pick up words here and there. Anyway—' He grinned. 'I'm not a full *Romano rye.* My father was a Traveller. In fact, I come from a fine long line of *chories*, thieves. The Kings weren't the most law-abiding family. Suppose that's where I got it from.'

'Yes, Tyso told me you were nothing but pikey tinkers,' I said slyly.

'Did he now?' Patrick raised an eyebrow. 'I'll be having words with young Tyso.'

'Oh, don't!' I pleaded. 'One big man on his case is enough.'

Patrick laughed. 'Did you know that's exactly what Jenico is called? *Rom baro.* Literally: "big man". The leader. The head of our *familiya.*'

He was interrupted by the ding of a spoon on a glass. The speeches had begun. Most of it I didn't understand. There was a lot of crying and kissing — mainly between the men — and it was clear that the unity of the family was all-important, particularly to Jenico. Coming from a family that was about as emotionally demonstrative as a dead spider, I revelled in the seemingly boundless warmth and affection. I could sympathise with Anselo, though. Too much of this would be like having your head held down inside a lava lamp. You'd suffocate slowly and very brightly.

My gaze travelled towards the top table. While the rest of the group was laughing and animated, Anselo was leaning back in his chair, staring into the middle distance. Probably wondering how the goddess's dinner party was going. And wishing he was there.

At nine, the dance floor lit up. The music kicked in. The bride and groom did their thing, and then the floor was open to all.

'D'you dance?' Patrick asked me.

I made a face. 'Very, *very* badly.'

Tom was a superb dancer. I used to try to imitate his moves but he had a limber, natural grace that I simply did not. But he never laughed at me . . .

Patrick was on his feet and holding out a hand. 'That makes two of us. Clare insisted we take ballroom dancing lessons once. I tell you, if that DJ bloke plays any Chris de Burgh tonight, I'll have no choice but to rip his spine clean from his body.'

I'm not really a small girl, but up against Patrick, I felt like Tinkerbell. He was mildly pissed, so we kept treading on each other's toes and getting the giggles.

'Thanks so much for inviting me,' I smiled up at him. 'It's been so nice to just kick back and enjoy myself.'

'Yeah, well, this is the last bit of freedom I'm going to have for a while. So may as well make the most of it. Within limits, of course.'

'I'll drive you back if you like?' I offered. 'If you trust me with your car?'

'Yeah?' He was genuinely chuffed. 'Fucking fantastic!'

'I won't have a hope of lifting you, though. So if you pass out, I'm leaving you here.'

'Can't say fairer than that.'

The song came to an end. And up rose the unmistakeable opening of *The Lady in Red*.

'Fucking hell,' muttered Patrick. 'Right. That's it. I'm going out for a smoke.'

'I didn't know you smoked?'

'I don't. Chris de Burgh can drive a man to anything.'

Patrick had taken my elbow, to lead me back to the table, when I felt a touch on my other arm. It was Anselo.

'Do you — um—?'

'Yes,' said Patrick. 'She does.' And he left us together.

It was oddly nice, being in Anselo's arms. He had one hand in mine, one around my waist. He held himself a little apart, and his eyes would meet mine and then dart away again, as if he was expiring with embarrassment. We moved somewhat stiffly and uncomfortably. But, on the whole, it was nice.

Finally, he spoke. 'This really is a fucking awful song.'

I burst out laughing. And, suddenly, he grinned. 'Do you want to go outside?' he asked. 'It's stifling in here. I'm sick to death of the heat.'

Out on the front lawn, a path led down to an ornamental stone pool. We sat on its edge — not close, a good foot apart. There were no lights by the pool, but the lights blazing in the house meant we could just see each other's faces.

It soon became obvious it would have to be me who opened the conversation. Oh well. May as well go for broke—

'Your mother was grilling me about you.'

His eyes widened in alarm. 'Yeah? Jesus. What did she say?'

'She said she didn't think you were content with your lot in life.'

He blew out a breath. 'Did she . . .' Then he added, 'Oh well. Could have been worse. She could have grilled you about when I was going to get married.'

I felt a pang of — what? Regret? It shouldn't have come as a surprise to me. He was the ideal marrying age. He had a beautiful girlfriend. Somewhere.

'Did Vivienne not want to come?'

He shifted, as if uncomfortable. 'I didn't ask her.'

'Why ever not?' I frowned.

'Because . . .' He hesitated and then, quickly, defensively said, 'Because I haven't worked out how to get both parts of my life to gel. I still need to keep them separate.'

He sighed and leaned forward, propping his forearms on his knees. 'I don't know. With her, I suppose, I can pretend I *am* a big man.'

'Oh, sod it!' I poked crossly him in the shoulder. 'I didn't mean that! I was pissed off with you because you were saying things I didn't want to hear!'

He sat up. 'It's true, though! Jesus—!' He waved his hand towards the house. 'That fucking room there is packed with men who achieve more in a day than I've achieved in my whole life!'

'You mean Jenico? Patrick?' I challenged him. 'Why compare yourself?'

He stared at me. 'Wouldn't *you*?'

Oh dear. He did have a point. And who was I to berate him about feeling inadequate?

'When we were at the pub that evening,' I said, 'you seemed to dislike Patrick more than admire him. Did something happen between you?'

He bent his head and trailed his hand slowly along the surface of the water. 'When I was a kid, Patrick was my hero,' he began quietly. 'My whole family used to wail and wring their hands when he doing his "Wild One" impression. But I worshipped him. I wanted to be him. When he calmed down and started making money, I was in my teens. And I still worshipped him, for different reasons.' He shook his head, in admiring disbelief. 'It was incredible what he achieved. One day, he was this leather-clad hoodlum, the next he was wearing Armani and driving a Porsche.'

Pausing, he lifted his hand and watched the water drip off his fingers. 'When I was eighteen, I went to him and asked him to make me his apprentice. He listened — and then he asked me why. Why did I want to learn from him? What did I expect to gain? I said — money, of course. But it wasn't the truth. What I wanted most was to be close enough to him so that some of what made him rubbed off on me. I wanted to *be* him. But I couldn't tell him that—'

He offered me a quick, wry smile. 'What he did then is still clear as day. He stared at me for an age, and then he said: "You need to be more of a man". And he showed me the door.'

No wonder my gibe had hurt so much. My heart went out to him. 'That must have hurt. A lot.'

He met my eye briefly. 'Oh, yeah. I was devastated. But, as you do when you're young and a bloke, you never admit you're vulnerable. So instead, I got angry. Furious. I *burned* with hatred for him. What right had he to say that to me? Unlike him, I'd done well at school. I'd stayed out of trouble. I'd done right by my family. What the hell right had he to tell me how much of a man I was?'

'But you got over it?' I asked him. 'I mean, you're on speaking terms now, aren't you?'

'Yeah, I suppose.' He trailed his hand in the water again. 'Not exactly bosom buddies. If we weren't family . . .'

I had a sudden thought. 'Did you start going out with Vivienne to impress him?'

He bridled. 'You don't think I deserve a girlfriend like her?'

'No, no, no! God! You're super studly! You could get any girl you like! I just—' I hesitated. 'She just doesn't sound like you, I suppose. Like the kind of girl you'd like . . .'

I was *so* glad it was dark. My face was burning. How could I have even *thought* something that humiliatingly lame, let alone *uttered* it?

'Studly?' He was grinning. 'Never been called that before. At least, I'm assuming it's a compliment?'

'Mmph—' I had my hands momentarily over my face.

He laughed, and gave me a gentle shove in the shoulder. 'Too late. Can't take it back now.'

'Erghh—' I dropped my hands and shuddered. 'How mortifying.'

I grinned at him, but this time, he did not return it. He was shifting on the stone again, his expression tense, almost scowling.

'Darrell, why the fuck do you go out with that wanker?'

I couldn't look at him. 'It's not — serious . . .'

'Bullshit!'

Instantly, I was on the defensive.

'Oh? What makes you the expert?'

'Because I saw your face when he turned up that day!'

'I was surprised to see him!'

'You were *astonished* to see him, and then you were fucking ecstatic,' he said. 'It was like watching a kid so desperate for affection and attention, they'll take any shitty present going, just as long as it's from Dad!'

That *stung*. A tiny part of me knew that Anselo meant well, that he was concerned about me. The rest of me was hating him.

'You know *nothing* about this!' I yelled. 'You know *nothing*! Marcus *isn't* a wanker! He's kind! He's good to me!'

'Of course, he is!' Anselo waved his arm in the air. 'Anyone can behave well for five fucking minutes! And that's about as long as you can expect him to stick around!'

Suddenly, I couldn't breathe. A black haze buzzed behind my eyes, and I had to drop my head down onto my knees. My hands were damp and shaking, as I pressed them to my temples.

'Shit—' I felt Anselo's hand on my shoulder. 'Darrell, I'm sorry.'

Tentatively, gently, he rubbed my back, and stroked my hair, until I gathered myself together enough to sit back up.

'Here—' He placed one arm around my shoulders and

guided my head gently against his chest. 'Jesus,' he murmured. 'I'm sorry.' I felt his mouth brush my hair. 'You OK now?'

'I don't know what to do,' I whispered, 'but I can't let go.'

'I know,' he murmured. 'It's like you'll lose part of yourself. And you're terrified there's not enough of you as it is.'

I lifted my head and stared at him. 'How come you feel like that? I thought it was only me.'

He shrugged. 'Maybe it was losing my Dad?' He gave me an apologetic half-smile. 'Maybe it's just my winning personality.'

Way off in the distance, there was a faint but distinct rumble of thunder. A breeze brushed through, bringing with it a new smell, an ozone-laden crispness.

'It's going to rain,' Anselo remarked. 'Thank fuck for that.'

On impulse, I kissed his cheek. 'You should be happier,' I told him.

He dropped his head sharply, and for an instant, his mouth hovered over mine. But he pulled back, and gazed at me, unsmiling.

'So should you.'

Chapter Twenty-Four

MONDAY MORNING and I was sprinting to the café. I didn't know why; I was soaked the minute I stepped out my front door. Unless I actually managed to warp the space-time continuum, I would arrive no less wet, no matter how fast I ran.

Since the skies broke in the small hours of Sunday morning, it had poured so hard that when Marcus rang unexpectedly on Sunday night, the first thing he said was, 'Christ! What's that noise? Are you being besieged?'

'It's rain.'

'Incredible. Have you made friends lately with anyone named Noah? Because now might be the time to seek him out.'

Then he paused. It was the kind of pause that often precedes bad news, and I felt the cold, sick clutch of dread.

But then he said, 'So, tell me. How was your weekend?'

The question was exactly what any lover separated by distance would ask — the opener to a deeper connection through the exchange of comforting trivia, words of endearment and promises of affection to come. From Marcus, though, it came as such a surprise, I was unsure how to answer.

The irony was that, for once, I had so much to tell him. I'd been to a glorious wedding. I'd learned a few words of Romani. I'd driven a happily drunk London property magnate back to town in a car that made me feel like the queen of the world. I'd parked it outside his house and reluctantly handed him back the keys.

'I'll walk you home,' he said, swaying gently on the footpath.

'No need,' I grinned. 'I'm not sure you'll make it, anyway.'

'I'm not that bad.' He grimaced. 'Though I'd better head to the spare room. If I wake her, I'll be in the shit. The baby kicks like a bastard at night.' His face lit up. 'Maybe he'll play football and make millions and I can retire.'

'Patrick—?'

I wasn't sure if I should be telling him this. But you never knew what had been said or left unsaid up till now . . .

'You do know you were Anselo's hero, don't you?'

He blinked at me, bemused. 'Anselo?' Then he scowled. 'Bullshit.'

'Why do you say that?'

'He never had two minutes for me! Never said two words! The only time he came near me was to ask for a job. And he didn't even want that. He wanted a ticket on the King gravy train. Thought he'd get one foot on my ladder and then climb right over me. I could see it, plain as fucking day!'

Oh, dear . . .

'That's not what he told me—'

I had a sudden qualm that I really *was* betraying secrets. But I'd begun now. Might as well finish—

'He told me he'd hero-worshipped you, right from when he was a little boy. That's why he asked for a job. He didn't want the money. He wanted to be just like you.'

Patrick's face was truculent with suspicion. 'He never said that. Not once.'

'I don't think,' I ventured apologetically, 'that Anselo is terribly good at saying what he feels . . .'

I could see the possibility that he had been wrong all these years begin to dawn on Patrick's face.

'Shit . . .' Slowly, he nodded. 'That would explain a fair bit.' He screwed up his face. 'What an arsehole I've been.'

Then he stared down at me. 'Thanks,' he said. 'I'm glad you told me. And don't worry—' he broke into a grin '—I won't tell him you did. And I'll go softly-softly to make amends, too. Won't do anything to threaten his male fucking pride.'

I stood on my tiptoes and kissed his cheek. 'Thank you. What were the words for good luck, again? Bosht something—?'

'*Kosko bokht*,' Patrick replied. 'Take care on your way home, Darrell Kincaid.'

I could have told Marcus all that. But I didn't.

I said, 'My weekend? Well, the weather went from one extreme to the other.'

'Then I'd better bring a brolly on Friday.'

My heart lurched, as it always did at the prospect of being with him. 'You're coming over again so soon? I'm flattered!'

'Ah. Well—'

I could hear his sudden embarrassment, and I braced myself. Somehow I knew exactly what he was about to say.

'Gus is over again. She suggested we have dinner together. All three of us, of course,' he added quickly.

Thank God for phones. It's such a relief to know that the person on the other end can't see your face.

'Only three?' I managed to sound quite casual. 'No Jules?'

'Gus and Jules had a falling out. Gus refuses to speak to her.'

Well. There it was. I had a choice, I suppose. I didn't have to go . . .

'Where did you have in mind? Restaurant-wise?'

'Oh, some new place in the West End,' he replied vaguely. 'I'll find out the details. I'll also have to meet you there,' he added. 'I've run out of excuses to flit to and fro, so I've actually had to make meetings during the day. I won't have time to pick you up. Is that all right?'

He did sound genuinely apologetic. What else could I say, except: 'Yes. That's fine.'

'Angel, I really do want to see you.' Even though I'd done my best, he must have picked up something in my response. 'I find myself thinking about you quite a lot, you know. You're a beacon of sweetness and normality amongst this ridiculous grotesquery I laughingly call a career.'

Hope is extraordinary, isn't it? One little gleam is all it takes.

I heard chatter in the background behind him. A group of people. A woman's laugh.

'I'd better go,' he said. 'I'm about to be in demand. I'll text you about Friday.' His voice was fainter, as if he'd turned his head from the phone.

'Marcus—'

'Yes?'

I had no idea what to say to him. Hastily, I made something up.

'Have you talked to Claude lately?'

'Claude?' He sounded puzzled and mildly irritated. 'No. Why?'

'Oh, no reason. I was just—' I paused. 'No reason. Take care. See you Friday.'

'Bye, angel.' His voice was warm, affectionate. 'You take care of yourself, too.'

. . .

As I dashed, dripping, into the café, Miss Flaky glanced up immediately and beckoned me over. I suspected she wanted to talk about the still-absent Claude. The thought filled me with a vague dread but I wasn't sure whether said dread was related to Claude or to the prospect of being grilled by Miss Flaky. What I *was* sure about was that I was in truly desperate need of coffee. So I nodded and pointed at the counter, to indicate I'd come over once I'd ordered.

The café was quite full for this time of day — people keen for a bit of warmth and dryness, I guessed. So when one more person came through the door, I didn't take much notice.

Mario said, 'Two fifty, *grazie, signora*.' I reached out with my money, and almost expired when a voice said, 'I'll get that.'

He was standing a little behind me, hands stuffed rather defiantly in the pockets of his awful blue bomber jacket. He pulled out a fiver and handed it to Mario.

'*Signor!*' Mario spread his hands so wide he appeared to be trying to touch both walls of the café at once. '*Bentornato!* It is too long since we've seen you here! You are well?'

Big Man, I could tell, was finding this outpouring of Italian sentiment excruciating. But he rallied well.

'Yeah, I'm good,' he mumbled. 'Uh — double espresso.'

'*Bene! Bene!* I'll bring it to you right away!'

Big Man and I were left staring at each other. His expression said, clear as crystal, that if I uttered so much as a word, he'd be out the door, never to return. So I kept my mouth shut.

Which, of course, meant he was forced to speak first . . .

'Where are you sitting?'

My face must have shrieked guilty alarm, because he glanced quickly over his shoulder at the tables. He turned back, wide eyed.

'You're fucking kidding. Please tell me you're winding me up.'

'Hey, Michael!' Miss Flaky was waving her hand, and smirking evilly like a predator whose quarry has just made a wrong turn onto exposed ground. 'Over here!'

'Come on,' I said to him. 'I think you two might actually get along.'

'She threatened to kick me in the nuts!' he hissed.

'Exactly—'

I beckoned. And with a stream of muttered imprecations, he followed.

'You're not going within a mile of my fucking flat,' he said the instant he sat down.

'Yeah, you keep telling yourself that,' said Miss Flaky.

Big Man's face was a picture. 'What are *you* grinning at?' he demanded of me, indignant. 'Right. That's it—' He pushed back his chair.

'Sit back down, Tex,' Miss Flaky ordered in a bored voice. 'You're not going anywhere and you know it.'

'*Tex*?'

She gave him a sideways look. 'Shoot first. Aim later. If at all—'

'Espresso for *signor* and *signora*!' Mario's intervention was timely. 'Anything else you want, you just ask!'

'A bayonet?' Big Man muttered. But he pulled his chair back to the table.

'So—' Miss Flaky turned her attention to me. 'Lord Fauntleroy. Where do we think he's got to? Flown the coop for good, or just temporarily indisposed?'

She saw the look on my face. 'Whoa. You're worried? Why? What's up?'

I sighed. 'I don't know. Nothing. Probably—'

'Who're you talking about?' Big Man frowned. 'That posh bloke you were with the other night? Mr Well Hung?'

Miss Flaky's eyebrows shot up. 'Lord Fauntleroy's got a big johnson?'

'No!' I was red as a beet. 'I don't know! Jeepers!'

'You mean the bloke who comes *here*?' Big Man persisted. 'The one in the suit? Looks like he has a carrot shoved permanently up his jacksie?'

I waggled my head in helpless acknowledgement.

'How come you're worried about him?' Miss Flaky demanded.

I felt like I'd betrayed enough secrets lately. Anselo had greeted me this morning with a curt nod, as if to say he'd prefer me to forget we'd ever talked. Big Man's unexpected presence had vividly brought back my conversation with Desmond Richards. I was being prodded all over by sharp fingers of guilt and shame. I simply could *not* tell them what Claude had done.

'Just a hunch,' I said feebly.

Miss Flaky's mouth tightened. 'I think you're right. There's definitely a screw rattling round somewhere in there.'

She picked up her teacup and then put it straight back down. 'Come on,' she said. 'Let's go pay him a visit.'

I boggled at her. 'I don't know where he lives. Do you?'

'Nope. Do you?' she asked Michael.

'Course I fucking don't!'

She turned to face the counter. 'Hey! Mario! You know where Claude the suit guy lives?'

'*Sì.* I delivered to his house two, three weeks ago.'

'What kind of house has he got?' Miss Flaky asked.

Mario gave an expressive Italian shrug. 'Big. And very — how you say? *Ordinato.* Tidy.'

'He's gotta be OCD,' she muttered. Then to Mario, 'OK, gimme the address.'

And to Michael, 'You're coming too, Tex.'

He gave her a fierce, incredulous scowl. 'What the hell for?'

'Because I say so. You wanna argue with me?'

Big Man was around six four and by my guess well over sixteen stone. Miss Flaky was literally half his size. He could have snapped her like a twig. But, to my amazement, all he did was mutter sullenly, 'It's pouring.'

'No, it's stopped,' said Miss Flaky, peering out the café window. She grinned at him. 'How lucky is that?'

Claude's house was indeed big — a double-fronted end of a terrace, worth by my estimate several million quid. Miss Flaky knocked, and knocked again more loudly. But there was no response. A wrought-iron fence and a small but densely planted garden lay between us and the front window. We peered in but the curtains were drawn. Round the back was a high, impenetrable brick wall.

'Can you lift me over there?' Miss Flaky asked Big Man.

'No, I bloody can't!'

Lips pursed tight in annoyance, Miss Flaky stepped back and surveyed the street.

'Know any criminals?' she asked me.

I went beet red again. And despite my best efforts, my eyes slid to Big Man.

Who looked outraged. 'I was in jail for murder!' he protested. 'Not fucking house-breaking!'

'No shit?' Miss Flaky was staring at him with new appreciation. 'Who'd you bump off?'

'No one!'

'No shit?' she grinned. 'Well, there you go.'

She narrowed her eyes at the wall, as if she could bring it down through sheer force of will.

'You got any pals who could help us out?'

'No!'

She shrugged. 'Don't ask, don't get.'

I thought Big Man was going to have a stroke. And then I

was struck myself, with a sudden and not entirely comfortable thought.

'Um—' I began. 'I might know someone . . .'

I got out my phone, and scrolled through to 'P'.

'You have got to be fucking joking,' Patrick said.

'You don't actually have to do the deed,' I told him, clutching my phone a little tighter out of guilt. 'Just tell us how, and we'll do it.'

'Oh, my Lord.' Patrick sounded like he was rubbing a hand over his face. 'All right, I'll come. But I'm not promising a thing!'

Miss Flaky filled the waiting time by staring at Big Man so intently and for so long that I feared he'd pick her up and stuff her head first into Claude's bushes.

'So—' she said eventually. 'They got the wrong guy, huh?'

I didn't think Big Man would answer. But to my surprise, he said calmly, 'Guess that depends on how you look at it.'

Miss Flaky's eyebrow shot up again. But just then a big silver Mercedes growled around the corner and scorched to an impatient halt down the street.

Patrick emerged like Hades from the underworld, scowling thunderously.

He stuck a finger in my face. 'Remember! This is only because I like you!' Then he glowered at the others. 'Who are you?'

I said, 'This is Ruth. And this is Michael—'

It was a slightly surreal moment, Patrick and Big Man's first meeting. On the surface, apart from physical size, they had so little in common. But as they exchanged a curt nod, I saw a tiny spark of recognition leap between them.

Patrick said, 'So what's the deal?'

'We need to get in the house,' Miss Flaky replied.

'You know, if he's dead, we could save ourselves a lot of effort and just call the police?'

'He's not dead,' she said. 'You gonna help us or not?'

Patrick blew out a breath. He eyed up the front door. 'All right. But you *never* saw me do this!'

Up by the door, he took what looked like a leather pouch from his coat pocket, and extracted some sort of metal instrument from it. He bent down, stuck it in the lock and fiddled for less time than I expected. There was a click. Patrick stood up and stepped back.

'It's no wonder the burglary rate is so fucking high,' he said indignantly, as we clustered around. 'These locks are rubbish!'

He shoved the leather pouch back in his pocket. 'Don't forget.' He gave me a quick grin. 'I was never here.' And he strode back to his car.

Slowly, Miss Flaky pushed open the door. It didn't creak at all. I imagined even the smallest squeak would be anathema to Claude. He probably oiled its hinges every day.

'Hey!' Miss Flaky called out. 'Where are you?'

There was no response.

'Sure he's not dead?' Big Man asked. 'A crypt would have much the same cosy cheer as this place.'

He was right. As we walked from room to room on the ground floor, I started to goggle. Every wall and ceiling was painted white, and there was so little furniture, I initially wondered if the reason Claude wasn't here was because he'd moved out. But if you looked, you could see he had everything he needed. A couch. A desk. A chair. But no ornaments. No paintings. No books, even. I'd seen more cluttered ice-cube trays.

'Jesus,' said Miss Flaky. 'This is some serious disorder.'

'Looks pretty fucking ordered to me,' said Big Man, gazing around in dismay. 'It's like I'm his evil twin.'

'No, I meant the guy himself. I thought it might be OCD, but I dunno. Something else going on here. It's like he's trying to disappear—'

'Oh my God,' I said, suddenly struck. 'I think you're right.'

They both stared at me.

'What — you mean be like the Invisible Man?' Big Man asked.

'Yes. In a way.'

Miss Flaky folded her arms and frowned. 'He doesn't like who he is, does he? I mean he *really* doesn't like it.'

Big Man raised a sceptical eyebrow. 'The man is rich and a nob. What's he got to complain about?'

'Is he a fraud?' Miss Flaky suggested. 'Is he putting it on after all, and all that ex-duke shit is just that — shit?'

'He's a *duke*?' Big Man was gobsmacked.

'Ex-duke, Tex.'

'How the fuck do you become an ex-duke?' Big Man demanded. 'Shag a royal corgi?'

'He's definitely not a fraud,' I broke in. 'I've met his mother.'

'Then what the heck is it?' Miss Flaky tapped her foot impatiently. 'What's the deal?'

Big Man tilted his head to one side and regarded her. 'Why do you care?' He grinned slyly. 'Do you fancy him?'

'You know what?' Miss Flaky mused. 'I guess I do.'

'Really?' I couldn't help myself.

She gave me a look. 'Yeah, it's a mystery to me, too. But there you go.'

Big Man was frowning at her again in disbelief. 'Do you ever decide to keep your thoughts to yourself?'

Miss Flaky grinned. 'Where would be the fun in that, Tex?'

Big Man blew out a breath. 'Well, unless he's lost the power of speech or become really fucking small, I think it's safe to say he's not here.' He started to move towards the front door. 'I, for one, don't want to hang around until the cops come. Plus, I'm starving. Can't imagine there's so much as a water cracker in this sanitised hell hole.'

To Miss Flaky, he said, 'You should stay here. Leap on him when he comes home.'

She sniffed. 'That's not a bad plan, Tex. But you know what?' To his utter and somewhat comical dismay, she stepped up to him and slipped her arm through his. 'I'd rather tag along and annoy the living crap out of you.'

Chapter Twenty-Five

'NO.'

'No.'

'No.'

'Fuck's sake!' exploded Big Man. 'What wrong with *this* place?'

Miss Flaky sniffed. 'You want a side of faecal coliform with your bacon roll, you go right ahead.'

'Jesus,' Big Man muttered, but he let himself be led past.

'*This* place!' He gestured to a small Italian café tucked between a magazine shop and a real estate agent. 'Come on! *Surely*!'

Miss Flaky peered through the window. 'I dunno. Don't like the look of that refrigerator unit. The seals have a touch of mould.'

'*You're* the one who's touched!' said Big Man. 'You are fucking certifiable!'

He shook his arm loose of hers. 'I'm starving. I'm going in.'

But he got no further. The bell on the café's front door jingled as it was opened from the inside. And out stepped Claude.

His reaction was pretty composed, considering. The three of us were lined up in a row, rather like expectant policemen. I almost expected Big Man to place a hand on Claude's shoulder and say, 'You're nicked, sunshine.' But all any of us did was gape. And all Claude did was stop and then stand very, very still.

There was a short pause. Claude's glance darted back and forth between us. Finally, he said, 'What are you doing here?'

'We're stalking you.' Miss Flaky had recovered from her initial surprise and was now grinning. 'How d'you like them apples?'

Claude blinked at her, bewildered. 'But why? What do you want from me?'

'I dunno, champ,' Miss Flaky replied. 'An indication you actually possess a spine would be a start.'

Claude lifted his chin. 'I have absolutely no idea what you mean by that.'

'Well, it looks to me like you've run away,' Miss Flaky told him. 'Which is always the first resort of the spine-removed.'

'I have not in the least "run away"!' Claude fumed. 'I was — I simply felt in need of a change of scene!'

'Right,' said Miss Flaky. 'Yeah.' She glanced pointedly at the café. It was small, Italian and had a plastic awning over the front. 'Looks pretty much identical to the last scene if you ask me, champ.'

Claude stiffened. 'Really, this is none of your business! In fact, I feel it is a rather severe violation of my privacy!'

'Oh, stop clenching,' said Miss Flaky. 'You're tight enough as it is.'

I heard Big Man suppress a snort of laughter. Claude's eyes slid to him and me for the first time since we'd met in the doorway. His mouth went all tight and petulant.

'Enjoying ourselves, are we?' he asked us.

'Bloody am not,' retorted Big Man. 'Thanks to this nutbar here—' He gestured at Miss Flaky '—I'm half bloody starved!'

'Yeah, he could "kill" for a sandwich,' grinned Miss Flaky. 'Right, Tex?'

'*Tex*?' Claude's expression was a mix of disbelief and resentment. 'You've awarded him a *nickname*? You barely know the man!'

'I call you champ to your face and Fauntleroy behind your back,' Miss Flaky replied. 'What more do you want?'

Their eyes met and, just for a moment, Claude flushed beet red. He glanced away immediately, but it was too late.

Slowly, Miss Flaky's mouth turned upwards in a grin. 'Well, well—' she murmured. 'What do you know?'

'What *do* you know?' demanded Big Man.

'He fancies me,' said Miss Flaky.

'Terrific,' said Big Man. 'Can we eat now?'

Claude blushed again. 'Really!' he spluttered. 'This is absolutely—'

'That's why you ran away,' Miss Flaky said to him. 'Thought it might help stuff all those inconvenient urges back into their box.' She waved her hand dismissively. 'Fair enough. I mean, God forbid you should peel off any of those zillion layers of repression. Who knows what horrifying normality you might unleash?'

'It is *not* why I ran away!' Claude protested. 'If I ran away at all, which I did not!'

'Yeah?' Miss Flaky raised an eyebrow. 'What set you scuttling then? Farmer McGregor and his gun?'

Claude flushed again, but this time, his gaze slid ever so briefly to mine.

'Oh!' I said, as I realised why.

'Oh—?' Miss Flaky glanced between Claude and me, intrigued.

My expression in response was pleading. And, fairly obviously, ridden with guilt, because Miss Flaky twigged right away.

'You tried it on with Darrell here?' she grinned at Claude. 'How far'd you get?'

By this stage, the poor man was mortified down to a molecular level. I felt I had to rescue him.

'It was just a kiss,' I said, and added hastily, 'A very small one.'

Miss Flaky threw Claude a look. 'Yeah, that figures.' She shrugged her shoulders. 'What gives, champ? You may as well tell me now, because you know I'll only hound you till you do.'

I saw a number of expressions flit across Claude's face, but the one that finally settled was resignation.

'There have always been beautiful women in my life,' he said. 'They rather come with the territory. The trouble is, I have not been attracted to any of them. Not one. Ever. And before you ask,' he added, 'I am equally unattracted to men.'

He shot me a quick glance. 'When I met you, Darrell, I liked you tremendously. You are so sweet and so very pretty. But I simply could not find you desirable. Seeing you and Marcus connect so easily, so naturally — that was the last straw. I couldn't deceive myself any longer; I knew there must be something wrong with me. That's why I kissed you. I wanted to find out once and for all. And because I *have* found out, that's why I — ran away.'

'But you find *me* desirable?' Miss Flaky said to him.

Claude eyes slid frantically from side to side, but there was no escape. 'Well, er, since you insist, yes, I do.'

'Which must mean,' Miss Flaky continued slowly, 'that you don't find me beautiful.'

'Oops,' I heard Big Man mutter beside me.

'Well, no,' Claude replied, unthinking. Then his eyes widened in horror. 'No! I don't mean no! I mean— Oh Lord . . .' He ran his hand over his face, on which there was a distinct sheen of sweat.

Miss Flaky studied him narrowly. Big Man put a hand on my arm, as if readying us both to run for cover.

But then she lifted her fist and punched the air. 'Yes!'

'Look, I really must go—' Claude seemed not to have heard her. He was green with distress, and already moving away. 'I'll— We'll— Perhaps later—'

And he strode off briskly down the street, as fast as dignity would allow him.

'Well, would you look at that,' Miss Flaky said after a few moments. 'He's forgotten something.'

Both Big Man and I glanced around, frowning. 'What?'

'Me,' she said.

And we watched her speed like a mini blonde Exocet up the road, her gingham tablecloth dress flapping about her feet as she inexorably closed the distance between herself and the tall, straight figure further on.

Big Man and I walked in silence until we reached the high street. On the corner where we needed to turn, there was a kebab shop. A smell of old oil, boiled meat and onion sweat wafted outward. It was delicious.

'I still haven't fucking eaten,' Big Man muttered. 'God damn the pair of those nutters to hell.'

'I don't know if I want to eat or not,' I said. 'I'm so hungry I've stopped feeling hungry.'

'No excuse.' He eyed the kebab shop. 'But not here.' He hooked his thumb up the street. 'We could find somewhere nicer?'

I was touched. I doubted Big Man had been to a restaurant in over twenty-five years and the prospect was probably causing every atom of him to shriek with awkward embarrassment. Yet he still offered.

'Or we could get pizza and go back to my place?' I suggested.

His shoulders sagged with relief. 'Brilliant,' he said. 'Do they still make that one with pineapple on it?'

When we got home, there was a message on my phone.

'Hello, Darrell.' The voice was American. 'This is Ellen Price at—' She named my publisher, and I instantly felt like throwing up. Oh God. Here it comes . . .

'Could you give me a call whenever you're free? There are a few things I need to go over with you.' She rattled off her number. I wrote it down with numb fingers. And gazed at it, unseeing, until Big Man came over to me.

'You all right? You look like someone died.' Suddenly appalled, he said, 'Shit. Sorry. I didn't mean—'

My brain ground slowly back into gear. 'Are you referring to Tom?' I asked him. 'You remembered!'

'Yeah, well,' he said. 'My response to that little revelation earned me a slap in the face. Hard to forget that.'

I blushed. 'I'm sorry.'

He shook his head. 'Don't be. I deserved it.'

I grinned. 'Is this you apologising to *me*?'

He scowled down at his shoes. 'Yeah, well I've been doing a bit of that lately.'

I frowned. 'What do you mean?'

He hesitated and then in a rush said, 'Desmond came to see me.'

'Did he now?' Suddenly, I felt a tad happier.

'His wife died a few years back.'

'Yes. We talked about it.'

'I know.'

He met my eye. His expression was his usual defensive bordering on hostile. But I did detect a tiny note of entreaty. Don't ask me, it said. Let me tell you in my own good time . . .

'I've got beer in the fridge,' I said. After Marcus' surprise visit, I had decided to stock up.

'I haven't had a beer in years,' Big Man said.

'Health reasons?' I asked with a straight face. 'Given up the booze like you've given up smoking? You have given it up, haven't you?'

He gave me a look. 'Got to look after yourself,' he replied. 'After all, I'm not getting any younger.'

Halfway through my second slice of pizza, I started to flag. I dropped it onto the plate and leaned back in my chair.

'What's up?' Big Man asked. 'You still upset about earlier?'

'Oh . . .' I stared up at the ceiling and sighed. 'Not just that. A bunch of stuff.'

'The message on your phone?'

Seems Big Man was also Observant Man. I supposed if he hadn't been born that way, he would have had to become so in prison. I thought about Patrick's story. Patrick was only in jail for six months. I could not even *begin* to imagine how someone would survive twelve years.

'How did you get through it?' I asked Big Man. 'Prison, I mean. When you knew you shouldn't be there?'

'Who said I shouldn't have been there?'

His voice was quiet, calm, but there was a warning in his eyes that told me not to push it. I couldn't help thinking about it, though. Our time was so short, so precious. It seemed inexcusable to waste even a minute.

Oh, damn it. I needed to talk to him. I needed to hear his voice, hear him laugh. I needed the tonic of his self-confidence and his capacity for joy.

'Who are you calling? That American bird?' Big Man asked me.

I held up a finger as the call was connected.

'Allo?'

It was a woman's voice. No, not even a woman. A girl.

'Is Marcus there?' I managed to keep my voice steady.

'Marcus—?' In any other circumstances, her accent would have been delightful. '*Non.* No, he eez not 'ere. Who eez thees?'

'It doesn't matter,' I said dully. 'Thank you.' And I hung up.

Big Man was watching me, but I couldn't bring myself to meet his eye.

My phone ringing made me jump—

'Darrell.' Marcus sounded slightly out of breath. 'You called me.'

'Yes—' I girded myself. 'Your secretary answered.'

He actually laughed!

'No, that's Berenice. My little French writer.' I could tell from the smile in his voice that she was still there with him. Wherever they were. 'Who has a terrible habit of answering my phone. She thinks it's amusing, curse her. Next time I go to the bathroom, I will take the damn thing with me.'

My mind was churning furiously. He simply would *not* be this relaxed if there was anything going on between them.

'What did you want, angel? Are you all right?'

And he wouldn't call me angel in front of her, either.

Or maybe he would. Marcus did whatever pleased him most at the time . . .

I needed to get off the phone. Now.

'Yes, I'm fine,' I lied. 'I just wanted to let you know that I, um, finished my latest book.'

'Ha! Excellent!' He sounded genuinely amused. 'Were you planning to read it out to me?'

I lied some more. 'I was. But — some other time?'

'It would certainly add a further element of excitement to Friday night,' he said. 'You're brilliant, angel. I look forward to it with eager anticipation.'

I hung up. And threw the phone across the room. It clattered against the bookshelf. The *Dance* quartet toppled over like fat, dusty dominoes.

'Want to get it off your chest?' Big Man asked, eventually.

'No.'

'Want the last of this pizza?'

'No.'

'Want me to go?'

I didn't answer. He left the table, and sank his hand briefly down on my shoulder.

'Come on over to the sofa,' he said. 'I'll tell you a story.'

Big Man's story. I wanted to weep. I wanted to yell, too. *Why*? Why did you think you had to punish yourself like that? What good did it do *anyone*?

But it was too late for yelling. And I couldn't cry in front of him; it would have destroyed him. So I listened, and didn't utter a word.

Big Man's story: Strong, handsome, twenty-two year-old Michael Hogan, welder, and pretty young schoolteacher, Beth Walsh, meet and fall crashingly in love. They are from opposite sides of the tracks. But Michael has a steady job, so when Beth accidentally falls pregnant, it's not a crisis — Michael can support them. They get married. Six months later, Lydia is born. Ten months later, the number of unemployed in Britain reaches unprecedented levels. Michael Hogan is now one of them.

He tries. But there is no work. Beth suggests that *she* goes back to work and he looks after Lydia. But he's having none of it. That isn't what men do. Not real men like Michael Hogan, anyway. Proud, stubborn men.

After an age on the waiting list, they get a council flat. Although it is a step up from the squalid fleapit they've been forced to rent up till then, Beth hates it. Hates it with every fibre of her being. They have no money. They have a baby. They fight. A lot.

Beth *insists* that she returns to work, and this time, her husband gives in. She gets work on and off as a relief teacher. He becomes increasingly surly and withdrawn. The only person he responds to is Lydia. He loves her fiercely and she adores him. He stops looking for any kind of job.

Michael goes to the pub. A lot. Beth stays home. There are

dry spells between teaching jobs. In the next-door flat is a man named Terry Sheen. He is unemployed, a recovering junkie. But he's been well educated and, until his habit brought him low, was a moderately successful writer. He has started writing again. He wants to know what Beth thinks of his work. They start an affair. Michael has no idea.

Also living in the estate is a petty thief named Jimmy Dale. He is a repellent man, a slimy little perv, fond of stealthy gropes and odious, suggestive comments. One day, Jimmy Dale gropes Beth Hogan in the lift. She remonstrates him severely. For God's sake! She has her daughter with her! The child is seven years old! Beth leaves Jimmy cringing in the lift and forgets all about it. But Lydia doesn't forget. And she tells her father.

Michael finds Jimmy at the pub. Terry Sheen is also at the pub. He hears what happened. He sees Jimmy pounded into a bloody pulp until Michael is pulled off and thrown out. Michael goes home. In his mind, retribution has been exacted. In Terry Sheen's mind, the red mist rises. He seethes for a day, and then the next night, he retrieves his mouldy golf bag from the wardrobe and extracts a club.

Beth is away that night. Her elderly mother is very ill. She is uneasy about leaving Michael and Lydia alone, and he responds badly to her lack of trust and tells her to fuck off and go. He reads Lydia a book and falls asleep on her bed. He is woken at three a.m. by urgent knocking. He opens the door to a blood-spattered Terry Sheen. Who, sobbing with delayed shock and fear, tells him what he's done. And why.

Michael tells Terry to go home. He orders him to get rid of his clothes, somewhere a long way away. He prises the golf club out of Terry's fingers, and props it up in a corner of the living room. Terry leaves. Michael has made him swear never to tell a soul. Terry won't. He is far, far too afraid.

The police arrive at eight in the morning. Michael puts up no resistance. Beth hurries back to find him in a cell, charged with murder. She runs to Terry, who hears her story and is aghast, amazed. It's all right, he tells her. I'll look after you . . .

'She never knew?' I finally spoke.

'She's a smart woman,' he said. 'She may have suspected. But she loved Terry. I knew that as soon as he told me about them. The signs were all there; I just refused to see. I doubt she questioned him too thoroughly.'

'But why?' I had to ask. 'Why did you take the blame? Because she loved someone else?'

'Because I failed her. And I failed Lydia. I'd been a failure for years, as a husband, a father and a man. I deserved all I got.'

'Where are they now?' I asked, after another silence.

'Australia. Sydney.'

'You know for sure?'

'Beth sends me a Christmas card every year. With photos of Lydia.'

I pictured his flat. There could well be twenty-one years of Christmas cards buried somewhere in there.

I had a sudden insight. 'Did you go back to the same flat?'

He was silent for a moment. 'Desmond wanted compensation. For my wrongful imprisonment. I asked for the flat—'

'Good grief . . .'

'It isn't.'

'What?'

'Grief,' he said. 'It isn't good.'

'No,' I agreed. 'No, it isn't good at all.'

Big Man — Michael, as I now thought of him — and I kept each other company for the rest of the day, and then I made him stay the night in the spare room. He didn't protest; I think we both knew he'd get no sleep at his flat. Too many ghosts.

Mind you, I'm not sure he slept at my place, either. He was up well before me, and when the builders arrived at seven, they were perturbed to find a gaunt-eyed, unshaven giant in my kitchen, making himself yet another cup of strong, black tea.

'Is he a relative down on his luck?' Anselo muttered, having cornered me in the hallway. 'Or have you started taking in the homeless?'

'His name's Michael,' I told him. 'Come on. I'll introduce you.'

'I should go back home now,' said Michael.

He'd shaken the hands of Anselo and a wide-eyed Tyso, who, I observed, was now whispering urgently in his boss's ear and casting furtive looks our way.

'I need a shower.' Michael rasped his hand along his chin. 'And a shave.'

'You need some new clothes, too,' I pointed out. 'Shall we go get some?'

He looked at me as if I was mad. 'You mean — shopping?'

'Well, we could steal them,' I replied, 'but I imagine you're probably not that keen to be slung back in jail.'

His shoulders sagged, and in a tired voice, he said, 'One step at a time, Darrell. Can you do that for me?'

I must have moved towards him, because immediately he added, 'And for fuck's sake don't hug me, either. That'll finish me off completely.'

'How about I meet you at the café in an hour?' I said. 'We could—'

The expression on his face stopped me.

'I can't,' he told me, apologetically. 'Not yet.'

I felt a sudden lurch of despair but I wasn't exactly sure why. Too much emotion, too little sleep, I supposed. Still, I couldn't shake the sense that whatever had bound us together, even if only for yesterday and last night, was slackening. Michael was drifting away. I did my best to hide it, but—

'One step at a time,' he said gently. 'You can understand that, can't you?'

I managed a nod.

'Good girl.' He lifted his jacket from a chair. 'You're a good girl.'

I don't think he could get out the door fast enough.

'You all right?' Anselo was at my shoulder.

I had no idea how to answer him.

'Who *is* he?' Anselo scowled. 'Looks like he's crawled out from an underpass.'

'It's a long story.'

'You're not in any trouble, are you?'

'No, no . . .'

Anselo did not look convinced. Suddenly, I was filled with gratitude for his indignation and concern on my behalf.

'Thanks—' I slipped my hand around his waist and rested my cheek on his chest. It was the briefest of hugs, barely a touch, but even so, I felt Anselo flinch. As I let him go, he was pulling away just as fast.

I did him a favour by grabbing my bag and leaving the house. Neither of us said goodbye.

I didn't head straight for the café. At this time of the morning, it was always busy and I simply couldn't face the thought of being surrounded by bustle and chat and laughter.

But what option did I have? The only other thing I could do was to go back home and hang around til I could ring the woman at my publisher and find out the worst.

I went to the café. I picked up a Patricia Cornwell from the newsagent and sat and read for two hours, until the boisterously happy mothers and babies drove me away.

Even then, I didn't go back home. I topped up my Oyster card and went into the city. I went to the National Gallery and the National Portrait Gallery. I spent time in every room, looked at every painting, every photograph. But to be honest, I'm not sure I could describe to you a single thing that I saw.

Chapter Twenty-Six

LADY MO: Why not ask him outright if he's shagging the teen porn queen?

DARRELL: Because the answer is almost certainly 'yes'.

LADY MO: There is logic in that approach. Twisted in-denial logic of the 'no news is good news' kind, but still. Speaking of which – have you womaned up and called your publisher?

DARRELL: Publisher and I have had contact, yes.

LADY MO: Detect weaselness in that answer! Messages left on answerphones do not count as contact!

DARRELL: Can we change the subject?

LADY MO: To what? Would you prefer to discuss the odds of your non-boyfriend hooking up with the nubile pubescent shag-ee?

DARRELL: . . .

LADY MO: Sigh. I suppose your latest romance-writing attempt is also off the table?

DARRELL: I'm stuck. Storyline is not forming properly. The ending is remaining blurry and indistinct.

LADY MO: Ending = happy ever after, surely? Same as always?

DARRELL: Has lost its lustre. Is no longer the end point to dash to with winged heels. Feet are dragging.

LADY MO: No great shock that, though, wouldn't you say?

DARRELL: Why wouldn't you?
LADY MO: Well — rose-tinted view of romance is not really possible when one is attached to an absent rake?

DARRELL: Has it occurred to you that you are an insensitive cow?

LADY MO: Cannot read tone of voice on screen — was that said lightly and with affection or with white knuckles and lemony lips?

DARRELL: Has it occurred to you not to rub it in?

LADY MO: Rub what? Knuckles?

DARRELL: The fact that my life sucks and yours is effing perfect!

LADY MO: Cannot help how the cards have fallen.

DARRELL: Can help patronising smugness though!

LADY MO: Has it occurred to <u>you</u> that we don't really have much in common anymore?

DARRELL: It has, yes! I cannot contribute to discussion on potty training, apple porridge preparation or pregnant sex positions. I'd sooner pluck out eyeballs than watch Dr Phil! And I wonder if Chad is really that perfect or you just see what you want to see!

LADY MO: Have a nice life, Darrell. I certainly will. Lady Mo signing off . . .

'YOU GOT A JOB OR SOMETHING?'

Tyso handed me a cup of tea. His boss was nowhere to be seen. I took the tea, even though I did not want it; I was grateful that he'd thought to make me one.

'A job?'

'You've been out whole time we've been here this week. Thought you might be going to work.'

I had been out all day, that was true. But no one was paying me a wage. I'd been to the British Museum and the V&A. I'd been to the Tate Modern and the Tower. I'd even trooped around HMS *Belfast*. I'd sat on a lot of benches and stared at a lot of nothing.

'No job,' I told Tyso. 'I've been out doing — research. For my writing.'

And now I intended to change the subject. 'Where's your boss?' I asked.

Tyso made a face. 'Psyching himself up, probably.'

'Psyching for what?'

'Tonight.'

Really, I could get information faster and more lucidly by draining my cup and reading the tea leaves.

'And what's happening tonight?'

Tyso glanced over his shoulder into the courtyard, just to make sure Anselo hadn't beamed himself in during the last thirty seconds.

'I dunno, exactly,' he said. 'But I've overheard phone calls, haven't I? Between him and that cow.'

'The girlfriend cow? Or a whole new cow?'

'No, just her.' Tyso's face darkened. 'He said he had something important to say to her. Can only be one thing, can't it?'

Personally, I felt that all depended on your definition of important. For example, 'I forgive you' from a friend might seem like the only thing worth hearing right now. Much, *much* more important, in fact, than 'I love you' from even the most desirable man.

But we weren't talking about me. 'One thing?'

Tyso looked at me as if I was backward. 'He's going to pop the question.'

You know, that made a lot of sense. And it was probably me who'd been the spur. At the wedding. I'd questioned why he hadn't brought her, which I think made him question his commitment. So now he'd come to a decision.

'If it's any consolation,' I told Tyso, 'you won't have to work with her. I don't think she's the steel-capped boot type.'

My cup was still full of tea and there was a skin forming on the top. I reached past Tyso and poured it down the sink.

'Was it crap?' Tyso asked me. 'I make it too strong sometimes. Sorry.'

He was so sweet. A truly nice boy. One day he'd make some lucky girl a wonderful husband.

'I have to go.' I put on a bright smile. 'I'll be back after you've gone, so enjoy the weekend.'

'OK . . .'

Tyso was frowning. I did not intend to wait and see if he was about to ask me if I was all right.

Outside, I was relieved to see that Anselo's van was parked down the street in the opposite direction to the way I was headed. I would congratulate him. I really would. But later. Not today.

Marcus had texted me tell me the name of the new place in the West End. It was already super-fashionable, a place to be seen. Gus had scored a booking through some contact she had in the art world. I knew that I should have looked for something to wear during the week, but I hadn't. By the time Friday came, all I had in my wardrobe was my red halterneck. It wasn't as fresh as it should be — I hadn't got round to taking it to the dry-cleaners. But I had no choice.

I took a taxi and when I arrived, I was horrified. There was a queue of people, waiting for tables to become free, or waiting to be permitted entrance — I didn't know which. I made the driver go past and drop me further down the street; I had no wish to announce my arrival to all those people. I stood outside a closed-up antique dealer's shop and tried to work out what I should do.

I had purposefully arrived fifteen minutes late, but that did not mean Marcus would already be there. I did not know whether to wait outside for him, or whether to jump the queue and persuade the doorman I was legit. But Marcus had not said whose name the booking was under, and after seeing the people in the queue I'd lost all confidence. They were so beautiful. So skinny. So cool. Their clothes were the height of smart fashion. My red dress was out of date and ridiculous. My hair was all wrong. I was too big, too unfashionable, too much of a nobody.

And then I saw them. They were getting out of a cab right outside, laughing at some shared joke. They had not seen me.

I ducked back, into the shadowy doorway of the antique shop. Gus took Marcus' arm and they walked straight inside, without even a passing glance at the waiting queue. Their poise and beauty shrieked privilege. They were so alike, twinned in elitist cool.

I knew then that I would never make it into that restaurant. I also knew that I had just seen Marcus for the very last time. And the loss struck me so hard that I could not breathe.

'Darrell—?'

I didn't recognise him right away. He was in a suit that made him look like a million dollars. He'd have no trouble fitting in to the queue.

He touched me lightly on the arm. 'You all right?'

I became aware there was someone with him. Anselo stepped a little to one side and said, 'Darrell, this is Vivienne.'

Tyso was right. Vivienne looked just like Grace Kelly, with a touch of Ingrid Bergman around the mouth. She was wearing a black dress that was immensely stylish and very short. Her legs were amazing. I thought what a beautiful couple they made. I only hoped Anselo had not bought her a ring he couldn't afford.

'Are you not well?' Vivienne asked me. Her face was kind, concerned. She was a nice person. 'You're very pale.'

I was finding it hard to speak. 'Just — migraine . . .'

'Oh God, they can be appalling,' she said. 'We should get a cab to take you home. Anselo, can you—?'

Anselo stood out into the street and hailed the next cab. He helped me in and said, 'Will you be OK?'

I nodded. I could not look him in the eye.

The cab driver wanted to get going. Anselo held the door open a bit longer, frowning at me. But all he said was, 'Take care.' And then he shut the door, and the cab grumbled off.

I don't remember paying the driver, although I must have. I don't remember opening my front door. I do remember not having the strength to go upstairs. I made it as far as the sofa and, still in my red dress, curled up tight. It wasn't cold inside, but I wrapped my arms around myself and shook for ages, until I fell into something black that passed for sleep.

Chapter Twenty-Seven

I COULD HEAR SINGING. A man's voice. Baritone. Pleasant.

The song was something about some fields in a place called Athenry. Where someone was lonely . . .

Then it faded out.

Spoken words this time. The same man? Another?

'She can't bloody well stay like this forever, can she? We need to do something.'

'She's fine.'

'*Fine*? She's hardly fucking fine!'

'Put another blanket on her if you insist. I, myself, am going to make a cup of tea . . .'

Tea. How nice.

More blackness . . .

More singing. About young Willie McBride this time. Who, it transpired, was dead . . .

Snippets of conversation . . .

'I should never have let her go home on her own—'

'Tip when buying a hair shirt: pick a smaller size. It chafes more effectively.'

'Is he always this obnoxious?'

'Fucking hell. You have no idea . . .'

Was that toast I could smell—?

What was this song about? A veil. A long black one. Walking on a grave . . .

'Whatever happened to fucking *Danny Boy*?'

'They die in that one, too, you know.'

'They don't all die. Just the singer.'

'I thought Danny ended up taking the low road back home?'

'I think you'll find that lyric in fact pertains to the Scottish song, *Loch Lomond*.'

'Yeah? Where'd you find that marmalade—?'

It sounded like a knock. The door had been opening and closing so often . . .

A to and fro of voices. And then—

'Dear, oh dear. This isn't the best time, is it? And it had been going so well. No screaming infants on the plane. And a pleasant "Welcome to Heathrow" instead of a "Sir, could you step this way".'

Simon . . . ?

There he was, kneeling beside the sofa in front of me. And I sat up and hugged him so hard I heard his bones creak.

'Oh, *Simon*—'

I burst into tears. Tears that came from the centre of my being, where they had been caged up for far, far too long.

'Dear, oh dear,' I heard him murmur. 'My dear sweet girl.'

I wanted to stop but I simply could not. Though it must have been agony for him, there on his knees, Simon's hold didn't slacken at all.

'That's it,' he said. 'It's about time you let it out.'

Finally, and it was an *age*, the onslaught began to dwindle into those hiccoughing sobs that are the coda of any prolonged crying jag. As they eased, I started, bit by bit, to become aware of things around me. Simon's arms holding me, the sinewy strength in his shoulders as I clung to him, his chin pressed against my temple—

I sat back and blinked at him. 'Where's your beard?' I blinked at him again. 'Goodness! When did you suddenly become this handsome?'

His expression was only mildly affronted. 'Decent haircut and a shave. Made a bit of a difference, hasn't it?'

'You're fifty-three! Why now?'

He shrugged. 'Why not? No harm in reinventing yourself at least once in a lifetime.'

From his pocket, he drew out a handkerchief. 'Here.' Gently, he wiped my eyes and held it under my nose. 'I used to do this when you were little. Go on. Blow—'

I blew. And wiped and blew again. And looked up to find five people staring at me.

'How long have you all been here?' I frowned.

They exchanged glances.

'How long d'you think you've been on that sofa?' Michael asked.

I gazed at him, wide-eyed. 'I don't know,' I admitted. 'How long?'

'Two and a half days.'

'Two *days*—?'

Simon, wincing slightly, got up off his knees and plumped down on the sofa next to me. He had on new jeans, a t-shirt and a very fashionable corduroy jacket. His glasses looked new, too. Dolce and Gabbana, I saw written on the side. I didn't think Simon had ever even had *heard* of Dolce and Gabbana.

'Did you introduce yourself?' I asked him.

He smiled fondly at me. 'They were hardly going to admit a perfect stranger.'

I leaned my head against his shoulder. 'I'm *so* glad you're here.'

Michael harrumphed. 'There's gratitude for you. Here's us keeping a bedside vigil for fucking days and he waltzes in at the eleventh hour and gets all the credit.'

'You told me not to hug you,' I reminded him.

'Yeah, well,' he muttered. 'That was then . . . '

I stretched out a hand. 'Help me up first—'

He rolled his eyes. 'Pathetic.'

But he hauled me to my feet and let me hug him.

'Is this a new shirt?' My voice was muffled against it.

'Maybe.'

I stood with my arm around him and, with growing embarrassment, stared at the others. Miss Flaky — I suppose I should now call her Ruth — was next to Claude, who apart from being a little pinched in the face, looked much the same as usual, suit and all. Ruth was shaking her head, smiling. Gabriel Flynn was smiling, too. Well, it was more of a smirk, really. Anselo wasn't smiling at all.

I counted two and half days forward from Friday night. 'God, I'm sorry,' I said to Anselo. 'I've stopped you from working!'

'It's all right,' he said. 'Tyso's got flu, anyway.'

He dropped his eyes. 'I'd better go—'

'I'm sorry,' I said again. I glanced around the group. 'I've put you *all* to so much trouble.'

'No trouble,' said Ruth.

'Speak for yourself!' objected Gabriel Flynn. 'I've rarely made such an enormous sacrifice!' He glared at me. 'Why in the good Lord's name do you not have cable TV?'

I made a face. 'Can't afford it.'

'I missed *Naked Wild On: Buxom Beauties*. It may well have featured one of my very good friends.'

Anselo was at the door, van keys in his hand. 'I'll — um—' He darted a glance my way. 'I'll be back tomorrow.'

With a start, I remembered that Anselo was probably engaged! But I had no time to find out for sure, because with some speed, he stepped through and shut the door.

'And now that the young Lochinvar has departed, I, too, should be on my way.' To my surprise Gabriel Flynn bent and kissed me on the cheek. 'It is about time I did *some* work that I'm actually paid for.'

'Thank you.' I kissed him back. 'For everything.'

'Ah, to be sure, as unfortunately we do say far too often. It was a pleasure. Even more of a pleasure to see you in that racy if now somewhat crumpled dress.'

Gabriel Flynn winked at me. Then he turned and nodded to the others. 'Claude. Ruth. Michael. Whatever your name is — the brother.'

Hands stuck in his pockets, he strolled out, whistling *Whisky in the Jar*.

'Well—' Ruth took a deep breath. 'I don't know about you but I could do with a cup of coffee. Who's with me?'

'I thought you only drank tea?' I frowned.

'So did I,' she replied. 'But right now, I need a bigger boost than I'm going to get from a raspberry fucking zinger.'

Ruth roped in Michael to help her get the coffees. While they were gone, I showered and changed. And came down to find Simon asleep on the sofa.

'Jet-lag,' I said to Claude, who had seated himself at my table.

'Indeed . . .'

That was it from both of us. We sat in silence until Ruth and Michael returned.

'Here.' Michael handed me a paper bag. Inside was a piping-hot buttery croissant, stuffed with ham and oozing cheese. I've never been so glad to see an item of food.

'Oh, my God,' I said indistinctly. '*Thank* you!'

Michael glanced over at the sofa. 'I got one for him, too—'

'I'll have it!' I pulled the bag towards me.

'Your body's a temple, I see,' he said drily.

'Indeed it is,' I replied, licking buttery grease off my fingers. 'To St Jude. The patron saint of lost causes.'

Ruth finished her coffee. She gave herself a little shake. 'Whoa! Rocket fuel!' Then she said to me, 'You gonna be OK?'

I thought about it. 'Probably.'

Claude was shifting around as if embarrassed. 'Darrell, I would like to offer you an apology,' he began. 'My behaviour to you has not been all that it should.'

'Yeah, you should never stick your tongue down a woman's throat without her permission,' said Ruth. 'It's — what's that limey stuffed-shirt expression? Damned poor form!'

'Must you be so coarse?' Claude protested.

'Yeah, champ, I must. It comes, as you like to say, with the territory.'

To Michael and I, she added, conversationally, 'Boy, you've gotta say it for years of pent-up sexual frustration.' She pulled on the string of an imaginary train whistle. 'Mercy!'

Michael's coffee went down the wrong way, and he began to cough violently.

'Ruth, *please*!' protested Claude. 'There is a *limit*!'

'Oh, don't get all puffed up.' Ruth waved a dismissive hand. 'You love it.'

'I do *not*—'

'Yeah, you do. You love it even more than when I do that thing with—'

'Jesus!' Michael had returned from the kitchen, where he'd gone for a glass of water. He thumped back down onto his chair. 'Give the poor guy a break!'

'*Thank* you,' said Claude, somewhat stiffly.

Michael slid Ruth a baleful glance. 'Not that she'll listen to me.'

The two men eyed each other for a moment across the table. Class, breeding and comparative bank balances all went out the window in a brief exchange of male bonding.

Ruth caught *my* eye and grinned. 'So you said you met his mother? What's she like?'

I blinked, surprised. 'She's great,' I replied. 'A little short-tempered, but—'

'Wouldn't you be?' said Ruth. 'I mean, the shit she's had to put up with!'

'Has she?'

'Ruth—' Claude's warning was more of a formality; he clearly had no real hope of a result.

'The family myth was that *she* was the big adulterer,' Ruth told us. 'And she did have a lover for years, but he died. Skied into a tree, apparently. Sounds like a bit of a bonehead if you ask me. But as we who sit here today all know, love ain't picky.'

Ruth leaned forward. 'So the two other kids think Mummy was a slut. But she only ever had that one affair. And in fact, it was *Daddy* who was spreading it around town. Seems like he'd flop his johnson out for anything—'

'Ruth, if you insist on telling everyone, which clearly you do,' sighed Claude. 'I'd appreciate it if you could leave me with at least a *scrap* of dignity.'

'Sure, yeah,' Ruth replied. 'Whatever. So—' She went on. 'Daddy the duke was banging anything with a pulse and he wasn't always too careful. Let's just say there were at least a couple of accidents—'

'Oh my God—' It all fell into place. 'Marcus and Gus! They really *are* brother and sister! Jules and I both saw it but only she worked it out!' I gazed at Claude in astonishment. 'Your father adopted his own children!'

Ruth was shaking her head. 'And all the while pretending to be this earnest politician, dedicated to social good. What a shit-heel.'

I frowned at Claude. 'But what about—?'

'Me?' He said the word lightly. But his eyes shifted away, towards the window. 'Well, there's the question . . .'

'Claude thinks he's the odd one out,' said Ruth. 'That he's the result of some other shit-heel's wayward sperm.'

'So?' said Michael.

'My reaction exactly!' Ruth grinned. 'But apparently with this English class shit, it's the blood that's all important. It's way thicker than adoption-certificate ink. So Claude here feels like a fraud. Claudius Fraudius.'

'And Marcus and Gus have no idea?' I asked him.

'Not as far as I'm aware,' Claude replied. 'But then, they are the ones who are close. They would not necessarily tell me.'

'That must be hard for you,' I said. 'Knowing they share a bond that you don't.'

'Nonetheless,' he said quietly, 'I do wish that I liked them better.'

'Don't feel bad about that, champ,' Ruth told him. 'I don't like your jerk-off brother one bit. Can't imagine Gus and I are going to be bosom pals, either. I like the sound of your mother, though. Can't wait to meet her.'

I saw Claude give a small shudder.

'Wait, wait wait!' Michael held up his hand. 'Are you saying you've decided you're not your father's son because you don't look like him? And your brothers do?'

'Brother and sister,' I reminded him. 'Gus is a girl.'

Claude bridled. 'It seems the obvious conclusion.'

'Jesus—' Michael reached for his wallet, pulled out a photo and slapped it on the table in front of Claude. 'That's my ex-wife. That's my daughter. You tell me who looks like who.'

Ruth and I craned our heads to see it, too. The photo must have been taken about ten years ago; Lydia looked no more than eighteen. And she looked nothing, absolutely nothing like either Michael or her mother. Michael had brown hair and brown eyes. In the photo, Beth Hogan was a redhead, the gorgeous Pre-Raphaelite kind with grey eyes, luminous skin and not a trace of a freckle. But her daughter's hair was blonde, and she had hazel-green eyes not unlike Jenico Herne's. Lydia Hogan could not have looked more unlike her parents if she had tried.

'And before you say a word, she looks exactly like my mother's mother.' Michael replaced the photo in his wallet. 'So there you go.'

He said to Claude, 'If I were you, I'd find out for sure, so you can stop moaning and start living. And I'd paint that unspeakable fucking house, too.'

He saw my face. 'Don't say a word.' Then he aimed a warning finger at Ruth. 'And don't you get any ideas, either!'

'Too late,' she said. 'Already working on a plan. Gonna reroute the Thames. If it worked for Hercules—'

Michael sat back in his chair and folded his arms. He had a small, dangerous smile on his face. 'And what's *your* story?' he asked her.

'Story?'

He gestured with one hand at her blanket skirt and cardigan. 'Why d'you dress like that? You get fiddled with as a kiddie? First boyfriend dump you for your mother?'

'What is this?' Ruth's lip was curling in disbelief. 'The Sigmund Freud hour?'

'Don't much like the tables being turned, do you?' said Michael triumphantly.

'Stick it back in the holster, Tex,' she said in her bored drawl. 'There's no story. I just got sick and tired of being beautiful.'

There was a pause.

'Sorry?' Someone had to say it. May as well be me.

'I got tired of being beautiful. It was a fucking burden. I was always expected to look good. Can I tell you how great it is not to have to wax anymore?' She sat back and sighed. 'And I got sick of men seeing nothing but my tits and ass. I mean I've got a degree from Brown, for Christ's sake! And the intelligent ones were the worst! I'd be at dinner talking about Keynesian microfoundations and they'd have this glazed fucking look as they fixated on my cleavage. I'd wanna snap my fingers in front of their face and yell "Hello? Anyone home?".' She shook her head. 'Fuckers.'

Then she glanced down at her skirt, with a smile that could only be described as affectionate. 'I saw one of these babies for sale in some crappy hippy store and that's when I decided. No more beautiful Ruth Harper. I'm going feral.'

I couldn't help it. I burst out laughing.

Ruth grinned at me. 'Look at him,' she said, nodding at an astonished Michael. 'You could throw a ball in his mouth and win a prize.'

'You still make an effort with the hair,' Michael finally managed to say.

Ruth screwed up her face. 'Yeah okay, Tex, I'll give you that. I came *this* close to doing a Britney once, but I chickened out.' She sniffed. 'I like my hair. So sue me.'

The phone pealed. We all jumped. I retrieved the handset from the bookshelf.

'Hello?'

'Is that Darrell Kincaid?'

It was an American voice. A woman. Suddenly, my heart clutched with dread.

'Yes.'

'Hello, Darrell. It's Ellen Price. Did you get my message?'

'I did. I'm sorry. I've been — flat out.'

'Oh, no problem. I'm glad I caught you. Listen—'

She talked for no more than five minutes. I hung up the phone and burst into tears.

'Oh, my sweet fucking Lord,' said Michael. 'What the hell's gone wrong *now*?'

'No—' I flapped one hand at him, and tried to stem the flow with the other. 'No, it's all good. I'm just so *relieved*—'

On impulse, I rushed up and gave Michael a fierce, damp hug.

'Ouch! Jesus! What's that in aid of?'

'Nothing! Everything! I've no idea!'

Over on the sofa, my darling Simon began to snore. I checked my watch. 'It'll be eleven o'clock at night,' I said to Michael. 'Will that be too late?'

'Too late for what?'

'For you to call,' I replied. 'You do know the number, don't you?'

Michael stared at me. 'I can't call. It's far too late. And I don't mean that in a middle-of-the-night sense, either.'

'How do you know?'

'Darrell, I haven't spoken to her for twenty-one fucking years!'

'Chicken,' said Ruth.

He whirled round and brandished a finger. 'Don't you start!'

As soon as he'd turned back to me, Ruth murmured, 'Bo-ok, bok, bok.'

Michael's shoulders sagged. 'I hate her,' he said to me. 'I really fucking hate her.'

'I just tell it like it is, Tex.'

'I'm sorry?' Claude finally spoke. 'Who, er, exactly are we contemplating phoning?'

'I've no idea,' Ruth replied. 'All I know is he's being a big chicken about it.'

'It's his daughter,' I explained. 'He hasn't see her for a while.'

'Twenty-one years!' Michael protested. 'I haven't spoken to her for twenty-one fucking years!'

'Change is as good as a rest,' said Ruth. 'That's a rest, not arrest, of course.'

'I can't call her.' Michael was barely audible. His face had lost all colour, and I could see sweat forming on his forehead. 'Not now. Not yet . . .'

Ruth stared at him. 'You know what? I'm feeling lenient. Must be the result of all the sex—'

'Do you *mi*—' Claude pinched the bridge of his nose, and sighed. 'Why do I bother?'

'OK, you can call her when you're ready,' Ruth told Michael. 'But you will call her.'

'Why do I have to do what you say?' Michael had recovered some of his belligerence.

'Because if you don't I'll plague you to the end of your days. And you haven't even *begun* to see what I'm capable of.'

'I hate you,' he muttered.

Ruth grinned, delighted. 'Yeah, you keep on telling yourself that, Tex. You just keep right on.'

Chapter Twenty-Eight

ANSELO TURNED up the next morning alone. He dumped his gear in the courtyard, and came to stand in the kitchen doorway. I got the feeling he had something to say to me. I was pretty sure it was his big announcement, and not at all sure it was what I wanted to hear.

Anselo opened his mouth to speak. So I got in first—

'Apprentice still sick?'

Anselo nodded. 'Yeah, but don't feel too bad for him. He has more women at his beck and call than the late Hugh Hefner.'

I smiled. He almost smiled. And that was it. When Simon arrived in the kitchen, I think I was even happier to see him than I was the day before.

'Hello. Anselo, wasn't it?'

Simon was squinting through his Dolce and Gabbana spectacles. He had on another new shirt and a very smart pair of Lee jeans. I hadn't had a chance to grill him further about his transformation. My guess was a woman was involved. But then again, perhaps I shouldn't be so quick to assume?

I smiled fondly at my elder brother. 'Poor Simon. He was

up at one in the morning making sandwiches. New Zealand's twelve hours ahead,' I explained.

Simon was checking his watch. 'It's time for *Coronation Street* back home.'

'Tea?' I asked him.

'Yes, please.'

I raised an eyebrow to Anselo. He shook his head. Fair enough. Judging by the greatly reduced number of teabags left in the box, he and the others must have drunk gallons of it over the weekend.

I handed Simon his cup. 'When do you head to the Faroes?'

'Thursday morning.' He gave me a look. 'Is it all right if I stay till then?'

'Of course!'

'As in — Egyptian?' Anselo asked.

'As in Islands,' Simon explained. 'They're about halfway between Iceland and Scotland, but are in fact an autonomous province of Denmark.'

'And about to be invaded by wave scientists,' I added.

I didn't add, 'And why on earth are you still hovering in the doorway?' It was most un-Anselo-like behaviour. Usually, when there was work to do, he got on with it without delay. I doubted that the lack of apprentice was the reason; I suspected Anselo got more done without Tyso than with him.

No, the reason had to be that he wanted to tell me his news. I suppose there was no point putting it off, although I still felt that tactic was not entirely without merit.

Plate of toast in one hand and cup in the other, Simon said, 'Do you get the paper?'

'No, I'm too cheap. I read it for free at the café.'

'I might check the news online, then. Do you mind if use your computer?'

'As long as you don't mind the sight of my unmade bed.'

Anselo waited until Simon was all the way upstairs before

speaking. 'I'm sorry I had to leave yesterday. I had to—' He made a face. 'Well, doesn't matter. How are you?'

'Surprisingly OK,' I told him, truthfully.

He frowned. 'Are you staying home today?'

I hadn't thought about it. I found I had no inclination to roam the streets. Simon might want to go to Greenwich, but I'm sure he wouldn't force me to go with him.

'I'll be here,' I replied.

'Do you want to go for a drink later?'

Oh God, here it comes. The moment of truth will occur at five twenty-two at the pub on the corner.

Anselo was frowning again. 'Don't take this the wrong way, but I'd like it to be — well, just you and me—'

There was no doubt now. His Big News. I might as well be resigned to it.

'All right,' I nodded. 'Simon will probably be asleep by then, anyway.'

'Leave here at five?'

'Five it is.'

'Great—'

This time, Anselo did smile. I wished he hadn't; it made him depressingly handsome. But I supposed he had quite a lot to smile about.

He hooked his thumb towards the courtyard. 'I'd better get to work. Got to earn a living.'

I remembered that, in my delight in hearing my book had been accepted, I'd promised my publisher another one in four months. Could be worse. In my relief, I'd have promised her another book in four hours.

'Yes, I'd better go earn my living too,' I said. 'I hope Simon hasn't dropped jam in my keyboard.'

At five, Anselo was waiting for me at the front door. He was wearing the same light blue polo shirt he'd worn last time we went to the pub. I still felt it didn't suit him that well, but I imagined he didn't think much about that; it was simply the one he kept in the van to change into if required.

'Want to go where we went before?' he asked.

'I thought it was going out of business?'

'It got a last-minute reprieve, did you know that? Some wealthy Russian who'd always wanted to own an English pub. Had clout with the brewery. Or something that resembles clout.'

'A Cinderella pub.' The thought made me smile. 'Rescued by a black prince.'

'Yeah.' Anselo held the door open for me. 'Be careful what you wish for.'

As before, he chose the wine. As before, it was very good. I settled back into the couch. Anselo did not settle, but sat perched on the edge. He turned his wine glass in his hand but did not drink.

'Darrell—' he began.

And, suddenly, I knew I did *not* want to hear it. Not yet, at least.

'Tell me,' I said, quickly. 'I never asked. Who found me? Who got in touch with everyone else?'

Anselo blinked at me, taken aback. 'Um. It was me.'

'*You*?'

'Yeah.' He frowned, as if embarrassed. 'I was coming to — well—'

Coming to tell me, I bet. I was making hasty plans to divert him once again, but mercifully, he stuck with the story.

'I didn't know what to do,' he said. 'Didn't know whether to call an ambulance. I was *this* close to getting your phone and finding the number of the posh arsehole—'

'That would have been interesting,' I murmured.

He gave me a sideways look. 'But then I remembered the big bloke, Michael. Thought he'd be a better bet. I had no idea how to find him, but I figured he lived around here because he'd walked home from your place that day. So I went to the café, to ask them if they knew him — and there he was. He called that Irish shrink—' He shook his head. 'Who is completely fucking nuts, by the way. Though he does know his stuff.'

'So when did Claude and Ruth turn up? And how on earth did they find out?'

'Dunno. Blokes at the café again, perhaps? All I remember is one minute they weren't anywhere; next minute it's like we were in a Noel Coward play.'

'Did they fight?'

'Not exactly fought, more hurled insults at each other across the room. The Irish shrink thought it was hilarious. Egged them on.'

'I don't recall any insults. Only singing. And something about marmalade.'

'Yeah, I think we ate all your bread. And drank most of your tea. Sorry.'

I blushed, embarrassed. 'I can't believe you were there for two days.'

'Well, we took turns, watching you.'

'Lying there in my red dress . . .' I made a face. 'It gets worse and worse.'

'It's a great dress,' he said. 'You looked incredible in it at the wedding. Beautiful.'

Now it was his turn to blush. Fair enough, I *was* gazing at him in frank astonishment.

'Wasn't enough to make you like *The Lady in Red*'

I had only wanted to break the uncomfortable silence, but then I had the horrible thought that he might interpret it as fishing for more compliments.

But, Lord love him, he said, 'Not even the promise of being able to lick hot chocolate off a naked Emilia Clarke would make me like *The Lady in Red*.'

'Emilia Clarke,' I grinned. 'Interesting choice.'

'Is it?' He gave me half a smile. 'And who would you choose to have lick hot chocolate off you?'

'Hmm. Tough decision. Pierce Brosnan and Henry Cavill are currently the hot favourites. Can I have both of them? Or is that just plain selfish?'

'Pierce Brosnan's a bit old, isn't he?'

'Well, a) the mental image I have of him is straight out of the 1990s, and b) that doesn't matter with men.'

'No, guess not.' He made a face. 'Her nibs is at least ten years younger than Patrick.'

He frowned. 'But then,' he went on, 'I think you're right. They are happy, aren't they? They chose well.'

Oh God. Quick! Dive! Dive!

'Look, I don't mean to be rude,' I said, 'but I'm not really feeling up to talking about relationships. If that's OK?'

I cringed inwardly at his expression of shock. Brilliant, Darrell. Subtle. Restrained.

'Sure. Yeah—'

He was staring at his feet now, poor man. I'd ruined his moment and humiliated him in one fell swoop. I felt so bad, I almost decided to be brave and change the subject back.

But then he looked up and gave me a quick, resigned smile. 'Timing has never been my strong suit,' he said. 'Nor has subtlety, for that matter.'

'Sorry,' I told him sincerely. 'I didn't mean to be so abrupt. It's just that—'

'No, I understand. I do.'

We sat again in uneasy silence. Then I saw Anselo frown, and take a deep breath.

'Can I just ask you one thing?' he said, and without waiting for me to confirm, 'Was your boyfriend the reason you —?' He ground to a halt.

'What? Melted down?'

He flushed. 'Told you subtlety wasn't my strong suit.'

'No. I mean — no, he wasn't the reason. Well,' I amended,

'he obviously played a part. But I think it would have happened eventually, whether he'd been there or not.'

'Has he called you at *all*?' he scowled.

'Yes,' I nodded. 'Yes, he has . . .'

He'd called me several times. There were two messages left that night, the first puzzled, the second concerned. After that, I found out he'd rung Claude. The messages from then on were all concerned. Finally, I'd summoned the courage to call him back. And tell him the truth.

'You know,' he'd said after a short silence, 'I have to say I mind that a great deal. The prospect of not seeing you again is surprisingly unpleasant.' He'd paused. 'Is there anything I can do to change your mind?'

I was touched. But I was no longer delusional. 'I just think you're more used to being the dumper than the dumpee.'

'Ouch,' he'd said. 'And that's not true. I have certainly done my fair share of grovelling. I'm quite prepared to grovel now, if you wish?'

'You'll be perfectly happy without me.'

'That's not true, either. I'll miss you. You were good for me.'

'You'll be home soon.'

'Back to the solace of sunshine and large-breasted women, you mean?'

'Yes,' I'd grinned. 'Exactly.'

'I'll still miss you.'

'Send me a postcard, then. With palm trees on it.'

He'd sighed. 'We both know how unlikely that is, don't we?'

'We do,' I'd replied. 'Take care, Marcus.'

'You, too, angel. You, too . . . '

Anselo didn't look at all pleased that Marcus had been in touch. But then his complete and fundamental loathing of him made it impossible to look otherwise.

'Anyway,' I sighed. 'That's not the worst thing that's happened to me lately.'

Anselo's eyes widened in genuine alarm. To reassure him, if not myself, I began to explain about Michelle—

'. . . and I did send her one message to say I was sorry. But she didn't reply. And then, what with everything over the last few days . . .'

'Why don't you phone her?'

It had occurred to me. But—

'I'm too chicken.'

'Why? What's the worst that can happen? She hangs up on you?'

'That would be the worst, yes.'

Anselo gave me a look. 'Do you think she's right, and you no longer have anything in common?'

'Well . . .' I said, reluctantly. 'She's married and I'm obviously not anymore. She's a mother and pregnant again, and I'm not likely to have even one baby any time soon. She seems happy not to have a paying job whereas I'd go nuts.' I stared at him. 'Does that make it a big fat yes?'

'Depends,' he replied. 'What matters more? What you talk about? Or staying friends?'

I hadn't actually asked myself that question. Did I want to stay friends with Michelle for the same reason I'd have done anything to stick with Marcus — because the prospect of letting go was simply too terrifying?

'I adore Michelle,' I told him. 'I adore everything about her — her humour, her loyalty; she's been a staunch, good friend to me all these years. I even adore her constant bragging. I find it somehow comforting. As if the world's a better place because everything's worked out so well for her. I don't really want her life, but I do want her friendship. In fact, I can't bear to think of my life without her—'

I'd started to cry. Again. Seemed now that the floodgates had been opened, there was no stopping me.

Anselo set down his glass, moved up to my end of the couch and placed his arm lightly around my shoulder. I leaned into him, resting my cheek on his chest. He smelled good. He *felt* wonderful. My arm was across him, my hand on his hip. It was so comforting, so familiar, so *right*—

I tried not to sit bolt upright, but I still managed to startle him.

'Sorry,' I said. 'I just — didn't want to get your shirt all damp.'

He glanced down. 'I'm not that fond of this shirt, as it happens. But, it was a gift.'

I was trying to stop sniffing. He pulled a handkerchief out of his pocket and offered it to me, along with a brief smile.

'For what it's worth,' he said, 'I think friendship's a fine thing. Sometimes, it's the best thing.'

I got the message. In the nicest possible way, he was hinting at what I'd so far prevented him from saying out loud — that he was now committed.

But that was OK. Being friends with Anselo would be perfectly fine.

Perfectly.

I tuned back in to find he was looking at me slightly askance. 'Do you, um, want another drink?' he asked me. 'Or do you want to head home?'

Another hint. Again, nicely given—

'Home, I think. I should probably make a phone call . . .'

Chapter Twenty-Nine

WHEN ANSELO ARRIVED the next morning, I was surprised to see he wasn't wearing his work clothes. Instead he had on a peacock blue shirt, which looked incredible against his dark skin.

'Nice shirt!' I told him. 'Another gift?'

He blushed furiously. 'Thanks,' he muttered. 'And no — I bought this one.'

I was oddly pleased to find that he'd bought it and not his girlfriend. And then I remembered that she was no longer his girlfriend, but his fiancée, and I was pleased no more. But I'd better get used to it. This was how things were to be from now on.

'No Tyso again?' I smiled. 'Must be a bad flu.'

'I gave him a day off.' Anselo's reply was rather short. 'Look, Darrell,' he said. 'Can we—?'

The stairs creaked. Simon rounded the corner into the hallway. Anselo stepped back and ran his hand roughly over his head, the gesture of a man resigned to frustration. I looked at him, curious, and he offered me a quick shake of his head and a small, wry smile.

'Hello again,' Simon said to Anselo. 'I'm off your computer,' he said to me. 'Apparently, there is a plague of cluster flies back home, thanks to a wet summer.'

'Ick!' I made a face. 'Our mother will be appalled.'

'I doubt she'll be wasting time on unnecessary emotion,' said Simon, 'but will instead be arming herself with a can of super-strength, fast-knockdown fly spray. Probably one in each hand. Your father would be wise not to make any sudden moves.'

I noticed Anselo had that antsiness about him which usually heralded his intention to leave. I found I really didn't want him to, so I put my hand on his arm.

'Why don't you come with us to the café? I suspect Michael will be there. And probably Ruth. Which means Claude will be there, too.' I screwed up my face in apology; this was sounding worse and worse. 'But you're welcome to join us.'

Anselo's face suggested he'd rather swim naked to join the wave scientists on the Faroes. But then he sighed and said, 'Yeah, why not?'

Plunging starkers into the Norwegian Sea seemed exponentially more attractive to Anselo, I could tell, when we arrived at the café and found gathered together at an outside table not only Michael, Claude and Ruth but also Patrick and Clare.

It took every ounce of my effort not to goggle. Clare was *enormous*!

'Yes, go on, say it,' she muttered, bitterly. 'Is she giving birth to a baby? Or to a mid-sized family sedan?'

'We think labour may have started,' said Patrick. 'That's why I'm not letting her out of my sight.'

'What's this "we" business?' said his wife. '*We* are not having labour pains. *I* am.' She grimaced. 'My back is *killing* me.'

'*Kali Carbonicum* can be good for lower back pain,' said Ruth. 'Your baby could be posterior.'

Clare gave her a look. 'You mean it's a pain in the arse?'

'Yeah.' Ruth grinned. 'I can go home and get some drops?'

'No, that's fine,' said Patrick, a little too quickly.

Ruth shook her head. 'Men. Jesus. It isn't *you* about to push a head the size of a watermelon out your—'

'I think it's their decision,' Claude interjected swiftly. 'As you are always saying — it is about personal choice.'

'It's about *informed* choice,' said Ruth. She jabbed a finger onto the tabletop. 'The system—'

I stood up. 'Who's for coffee? My shout.'

'I'll come with you,' said Anselo.

At the counter, we were behind two people. Then we were behind one. Suddenly, Anselo said, 'Darrell, I *have* to talk to you!'

Startled, I turned, just as Mario said, '*Signora*! What can I get for you?'

Anselo held up a hand to him. 'Please. Just — wait—'

He glanced around inside the café. The table tucked in the corner beside the gelato freezer was empty.

'Give him the order,' he told me. 'Then come over here. Before I fucking expire.'

'Oh! Okay . . .' So I did.

He was on the edge of the chair, leaning forward, his forearms propped on the table, his fingers knotted together.

'What's the—?'

'Don't,' he said. 'Please. Just listen. Or I'll never get it out.'

He stared down at his knotted fingers for a moment. Then he gave a sharp intake of breath—

'Darrell, I'm pretty sure I love you—'

If he'd been worried about me interrupting, there was no prospect of it now. I'd been robbed of all ability to speak.

'I was knocked for six by you the first instant we met,' he went on. 'You opened the door and I felt like someone had smacked me round the head. A little voice, clear as fucking day, said: "This is the woman you want to spend the rest of your life with". I could hardly get two words out. What you must have thought of me—'

His mouth twisted wryly. 'No, I *know* what you thought of me. But there was no way I could explain. I couldn't even figure out what to do. I had Vee, and I didn't want to hurt her, and I wasn't even sure if I did leave her that you would—' He ran his hand over his head again. 'But that was being unfair to Vee, so I had to decide *something*.'

He paused, a little breathless, but immediately resumed what was, I suspected, the longest speech he'd made in his life.

'I was almost there. I'd almost decided. And then—' His mouth compressed into a grim line '—*he* came along. Mr Arsehole. I was furious. I thought I was angry with you for falling for him. But I was only angry with myself. Because I'd missed my chance. Maybe forever—'

He took a deep breath. My own heart was still pounding so hard, I could hear the blood thumping in my ears.

'I couldn't let it end there, though,' he went on. 'I had to make a decision once and for all or I'd go fucking mad. So I did. That's why I came to your place on Saturday. I wanted to tell you, once and for all, how I felt.'

'But—' I began. I'm not sure he even heard me.

'Darrell, I've no idea how you feel about me,' he said. 'No idea at all. And I know it's not fair for me to spring this on you. You said it last night, it's too soon. But—'

I could see him wrestling with himself. Desperation versus discretion, I guessed. I knew how *that* felt.

'But please—' Desperation had won out. The look he gave me was nakedly beseeching. 'Please put me out of my misery. Is there any hope? Or have I blown my chance yet again?'

'But—'

'But what?' he said warily.

'Aren't you getting married?'

'*What?* Who on earth told you *that*?'

'I thought *you* had! Or you were trying to—'

He shook his head. 'No! I ended it with Vee that Friday! The night we saw you!' He frowned. 'That's why I had to leave early, after you'd — come round. She was really upset, wanted us to try again. But I had to tell her there was no chance.' His expression became shamefaced. 'I should have done it much earlier, I know. I just — I wasn't sure . . .'

Truly, I did not know what to say. I barely knew what to *think*—

He slumped back in the chair. 'I've blown it, haven't I?'

'Anselo, I—'

Outside the café, there erupted a godalmighty commotion. Yelling. Clattering. Swearing. Both of us wheeled around to see Patrick stalking in, grim-faced and tense.

'Where's the nearest fucking doctor around here?' he demanded of Mario.

'It's okay!' Ruth was in the doorway. 'Claude's gone to get him!'

Without a word, Patrick pushed past her and strode back outside.

'What the hell's going on?'

Anselo and I rushed up to Ruth. There was *serious* yelling coming from outside.

'She's having the baby!' Ruth was wide-eyed. 'Right now! I can see the goddamn head!'

'Surely, it's not supposed to be *that* quick!' Anselo looked aghast.

'You wanna tell the baby that?'

'What should we do?' I asked her.

'Keep out of the way, I guess.' Ruth, for the first time ever, seemed at a loss. 'I dunno. Let's go back outside at least. Be there if they need us.'

Clare was on her knees, bent over a chair, clutching onto it for grim death. She was yelling at the top of her lungs. Swear words, mainly. The air around her was blue.

Michael and Simon had backed right off and were

perched gingerly on the low wall that bounded the disused patch of grass next door.

Patrick was striding to and fro, hands on his hips, face taut and anxious. At one point, he bent down and touched Clare lightly on the shoulder.

'Don't *touch* me!' she bellowed.

He lifted his hand like a shot. 'OK, OK!'

Then he yelled, 'Where the hell's that doctor?'

'Here he comes,' said Ruth.

Alastair came running up, Claude jogging behind.

'We've called an ambulance,' he told us breathlessly.

Alastair bent down and inspected the situation. 'Right,' he said to Clare. 'I'd like to move you inside.'

'I'm not going *anywhere*!' she yelled at him.

'All right. OK—'

Suddenly, she doubled over and gave an almighty bellow. '*Fuck!*' she said through gritted teeth. 'It's *coming*—'

And my God, it was. Alastair barely had time to roll up his sleeves before, accompanied by one long, deafening yell from his mother, the baby King shot into the world and was caught by the doctor's waiting arms.

The baby was startlingly big, and *covered* with ooze and blood. Claude's legs folded like a marionette beneath him and he sank to the ground, completely out for the count.

'Shit!' Ruth's quick reflexes managed to prevent his head smacking like a dropped pumpkin onto the concrete. But she was too slight to move his dead weight.

'Tex!' she yelled. 'Help!'

Simon came too, and he and Michael took an arm each and dragged Claude over to where no one would tread on him.

Alastair was still on his knees, looking slightly amazed. Gently, he massaged the baby's chest. 'Come on, you.' And there it was. That unmistakable new-born cry.

Clare was collapsed on the chair, panting. 'Fuck,' she gasped. 'I can't move.'

'Here—' As Alastair deftly shifted the baby, Patrick gently, tenderly helped Clare off her knees, and sat her on the ground. He dropped down next to her, and buried his face in her neck.

'My heroine.' He kissed her sweaty cheek. 'What a fucking star.'

Alastair saw Mario and Vincente in the doorway. 'Clean dishtowels! Now!'

In a trice, they were back, and Alastair wiped the baby in one striped cloth, and wrapped him best he could in another. With a smile, he placed the baby in the lap of its exhausted mother.

'It's a boy,' he smiled. 'Congratulations.'

'Oh . . .' Clare gazed down at the little face. 'My God . . . Where did you come from?'

Then she grimaced. '*Fuck!* Why's it still hurting?' she demanded of Alastair.

'I'm afraid you still need to pass the placenta. And I should clamp that cord—'

'Jesus Christ—' Clare bent her head to the baby. 'Good thing you're worth it.'

Alastair dashed back to his surgery, and brought back a sterile clamp and a scalpel. 'Would you like to cut the cord?' he asked Patrick.

Patrick's face was answer enough. 'Wimp,' said his wife.

'Too right!' he said. 'It took all my courage just to watch you shove him out!'

Alastair cut the cord. 'Here,' he said to Patrick. 'All yours—'

Patrick took his son and cradled him as if he was made of eggshells.

Clare saw that her husband was crying. 'Soppy git,' she grinned. 'What shall we call him? How about Tom?'

I jumped like I'd been stung. But after the first shock faded, I realised there had been no grief bomb. I did the mental equivalent of patting myself down to check for injury. There was none. I was, for the first time in forever, intact.

'Tom King,' said Patrick. 'Good name.'

'Oh my *God*!' Clare suddenly exclaimed. She had been drying off her son's small crop of matted hair. 'He's *ginger*!'

Patrick peered and grinned. 'So he is!'

'That's *your* fault!' Clare accused.

'Mine?' said Patrick, bewildered. 'I'm dark!'

'Hidden ginger! It's *rampant* in your family!'

Then she grimaced again. 'Ow! *Fuck!* How long is this hell going to *last*!'

Up the street came the wail of an ambulance. It screeched to a halt.

'Hmph.' Michael was behind me. 'Like déjà vu all over again.'

I hugged him quickly. The last time an ambulance pulled up at the café it had been to take Michael to hospital. I didn't need to say how glad I was that he was with us today.

The ambulance crew helped a truculent, swearing Clare onto a stretcher. Claude was still on the ground, but conscious now. His head was in Ruth's lap. He didn't seem in a hurry to move.

'He's fine,' Ruth said, when one of the ambulance crew came over. She ran her fingers through Claude's hair and smiled down. 'I'll look after him.'

He stared up at her. 'You're so lovely,' he murmured.

'Yeah?' she grinned. 'Boy, you *have* got it bad.'

Patrick still had the baby in his arms. He was about to join Clare in the back of the ambulance.

'Come on—' I took hold of Anselo's hand. 'Let's go say hello.'

Patrick couldn't stop grinning. 'Look!' he said as we approached. 'Will you fucking look at this!'

Anselo and I peered down at the red, screwed-up little face. I still had Anselo's hand in mine. I squeezed it. 'Wow.'

'Yeah,' Anselo agreed. 'Wow.'

'By the way,' Patrick said to Anselo, as he readied to climb in the back of the ambulance, 'you're godfather.'

Anselo's face was a picture. 'What—?'

'Godfather,' repeated Patrick. 'You.' And the ambulance door closed.

Anselo blinked as it pulled away. 'Wow . . .'

I vowed to thank Patrick later. That was a *very* good thing to have done.

Anselo then, to his apparent surprise, found that we were still holding hands. He gazed at me with a slightly manic look in his eye.

'Darrell—' he began.

But I needed no encouragement. We launched ourselves at each other, and kissed and kissed until I had absolutely no idea where I was. It was bliss. Delicious and passionate and perfectly right. I was so happy, I could hardly stand it.

'You're laughing!' he murmured against my mouth. 'Have you *any* idea how wound up I've been about this? And for how long?'

'I'm sorry,' I told him. 'How could I not have known? It was completely bloody obvious that it was you all along. What a moron I am.'

I kissed him again. It was even better. In fact, it was astonishing. All other recent kisses paled against it.

'Wow,' I said, after what was really a very long time.

'Yeah,' Anselo agreed. 'Wow.'

'Do you mind if I do this?' I asked him. And I ran my hand up under his shirt.

'Jesus,' he breathed. 'You can do it, but you'll have to deal with the consequences.'

'I might suggest Simon takes a second trip to Greenwich this afternoon—'

He kissed me again, and said, 'I'm sure I love you. And I'm warning you now that I may want to marry you. And have a ton of babies—'

'I dunno.' I made a face. 'Today's kind of put me off.'

'You'll soon forget,' he grinned. 'Just think about how cute he was. And that's despite Patrick being an ugly spud, really. We'd have *beautiful* babies.'

'Would you settle for a dog in the meantime?'

He shrugged. 'Sure. Why not? I've always liked black Labradors.'

A black Labrador? Close enough . . .

'Hey! You two!'

Ruth was waving to us from the café doorway. 'Mario's cracked opened the prosecco! If you can stop face-sucking for a half second, let's celebrate!'

'To the *bambino*!' Mario was first to raise his glass.

'To us!' was Ruth's toast.

'And all who sail in us!' added Michael. 'The ship of loons!'

'To Michael!' I said, to his acute embarrassment. 'And to his excellent daughter who told him it was about fucking time!'

'Why don't you broadcast it to the world, Darrell?' he said. 'Go on. Don't you worry about me.'

'Oh, lighten up Tex,' said Ruth. 'You know we would have found out that you'd ponied up. Correction. *I* would have found out. Your daughter sounds OK by the way. Can't wait to meet her.'

'To Darrell's upcoming book!' said Claude, quickly, as Michael turned a dangerous shade of red. 'My mother will be thrilled.'

'To Darrell!' said Simon. 'May she be head girl forever!'

'What *are* you on about?' I frowned.

He blinked at me. 'Darrell was head girl, wasn't she? Or am I mixing her up with Angela Brazil?'

Bewildered, I looked to Anselo for help. He only shrugged.

'Simon,' I said firmly. 'Explain!'

'Oh. Right. They were your mother's favourite books. About a girls' school. What was it called again—?' He snapped his fingers. '*Malory Towers*! Enid Blyton! The head girl was called Darrell.'

'My mother named me after a character in an Enid Blyton book?'

'Yes!' He saw my face. 'She was a good character. Strong-willed, clever, courageous, all that fine plucky British stuff.'

'Good grief . . .'

'She had a sister called Felicity, as I recall.'

I shuddered. 'I'm glad she didn't name me that.'

Anselo was chuckling. The bastard.

'Why didn't you ever ask her?' he grinned.

'Too chicken,' I replied. 'You'd know something about that,' I added tartly.

He wrapped his arm around my shoulder and kissed me on the temple. 'I love you, Darrell the head girl.'

'Oh my God,' I said to no one in particular. 'And I really thought I would never be happy again.'

Epilogue

'YOU KNOW,' I said to the top of Anselo's head. 'We really are having a mad amount of sex.'

'Mm . . .'

'I mean, it's OK at this kind of time. But I really don't think there are any more errands you can send Tyso on during the day.'

Anselo finally lifted his head from where it was nestled between my breasts. 'And the kitchen bench is due for demolition tomorrow,' he grinned at me. 'So unless you want to perch on the oven?'

I thought about it. 'No. Those gas elements are too pointy.' I tweaked his ear. 'You're getting heavy, by the way.'

With considerable reluctance, Anselo rolled off me and flopped onto his back. He hooked one arm behind his head and stared at the ceiling.

I spooned against him and rested one arm over his perfect chest. 'Don't get me wrong,' I murmured. 'I'm not complaining.'

There was no reply. I propped myself up on one elbow and frowned down at him. 'What's up?'

His eyes darted to me and then away again. His mouth was screwed up tight.

'What's up?' I said, more gently. Confessions could only ever be elicited from Anselo through patient coaxing.

He sighed. 'Fuck it,' he said. 'I swore I'd never ask this question. But I can't *not* ask it. I'm too fucking paranoid and insecure.'

'Do you want to know if you're better in bed than you-know-who?'

'No!' His head jerked up off the pillow, rigid with outrage. 'No, I bloody don't! That wasn't what I was going to ask at all!'

'Sorry.' I made an apologetic face. 'Jumped the gun.'

Scowling, still affronted, he lowered his head back down. Then he muttered quickly, 'So? Am I?'

I smiled. '*Much* better. And I'm not just saying that because I adore you. With you, it's — transporting.'

'You make me sound like a Ford Transit,' he muttered.

But he let me kiss him.

'What did you want to ask me if it wasn't that?' I murmured when I'd finished.

'I wanted to ask—' He paused, and blew out a quick, nerve-girding breath. 'Would he have approved of me? Your husband, I mean—'

What a question. No wonder he had to work up the courage to ask.

'He would have.' I nodded. 'But he'd say you need to lighten up a bit. Have more faith in yourself, and don't take everything so seriously. He had no problem ever being happy, Tom.'

I rolled on my back beside Anselo, and stared upwards. The last of the evening light was filtering in through the crack in the curtains, and forming a thin, glowing stripe on the ceiling.

'I never realised how much I depended on him for that,' I

continued. 'I let myself be pulled along in the slipstream of his boundlessly positive outlook on life. And when it was gone . . .'

'I'm not sure I can offer you that,' Anselo said quietly.

'Oh God, no!' I turned my head to meet his eye. 'I don't want it! I mean, I want us both to be happy. But that should be down to us. You and me. On our own, as well as together. Don't you think?'

'Yeah . . .' He moved his head closer, so he could kiss me. 'Yeah, I do.'

Then he moved his whole body closer.

I grinned at him. 'More mad sex time?'

'I must be a diesel Transit,' he grinned back. 'Extra mileage—'

Suddenly there was a weird sound. Like the mass gasp of some distant audience.

Anselo blinked and looked around. 'What the fuck was that?'

Then a tiny, tiny voice said. 'Hello?'

Anselo glanced across to the desk tucked next to the bed. 'A very small live woman has appeared on your computer screen.'

'Oh my God—' I put a hand to my mouth. 'It's Michelle! On Skype!'

'Hello?' said the voice again. 'I can see something there. Is it you?'

'Can she see *us*?' Anselo hissed.

I nodded. 'Quick,' I whispered. 'Shuffle off. And keep your head down.'

Hastily, keeping low, I retrieved Anselo's t-shirt from the floor and pulled it on. Then I sat up on the edge of the bed and faced the computer.

'Hi!' I said, brightly.

'Where did you pop up from?' demanded Michelle. 'Were you doing yoga or something?'

'Yes! Definitely or something.'

A movement behind me caused Michelle's eyes to widen. 'Whoa! Chihuahua! There's a naked man in your room! A totally studly naked man!'

Quickly, I checked. 'He's got pants on!'

'But no shirt! He was fully naked from the waist up!' Then her eyes narrowed. 'Were you *doing* it?' She checked her watch. 'It's only — what, eight o'clock! You're at it at eight o'clock in the evening! Don't you have television over there?'

She waved her hands frantically. 'He's coming back! Shift your head, shift your head! Oh—' Her shoulders slumped. 'He's got his shirt on now.'

She pouted for a moment. 'Could he take it off again?'

'No! I am not making the poor man strip for you! He hasn't even been introduced!'

Anselo sat on the bed beside me. He leaned his chin on my shoulder, and then kissed my neck.

'Anselo, this is my best friend Michelle—'

'Hello,' he said to the tiny Michelle on my screen.

I smiled. 'Michelle has the perfect life.'

'I know!' Michelle was beside herself with delight. 'Isn't it *wonderful*?'

THE END

Want more?
Sign up for my Newsletter!

Read Michelle's story in Book 2 of the Imperfect Lives series:

The Not So Perfect Life of Mo Lawrence

#1 New Zealand best-seller!

The Sweet Second Life of Darrell Kincaid

"Intelligent, complex, forthright and hilarious."
"An empowering read with strong female characters - fun from the first page to the last."

Michelle 'Mo' Lawrence's life is just as she's designed it – perfect – and she can see no good reason why this should change. But then her husband, Chad, takes a job all the way across the country and change is upon her, whether she likes it or not.

As if building a new life with two small children in a place filled with cat-eating coyotes isn't enough, Michelle's husband Chad is becoming increasingly distant, her oldest friend, Darrell, is getting wedding jitters and her newest, Connie, is a little too obsessed with clean taps.

And down the street, there's Aishe Herne, a woman who could pick a fight with a silent order of nuns. In Aishe's own life there's room for her, her teenage son and no one else. But when cousin Patrick lands in town like a Cockney nemesis, both Aishe and Michelle are forced to look more closely at what it is that *actually* makes their lives perfect.

Read an excerpt...

'Hello?'

'Is he there?'

Forty years of living in the South had taken most of the clip out of Virginia Lawrence's Boston vowels, and while she would never go so far as to adopt the languid formality of a Blanche Dubois, she always spoke with a scrupulous courtesy. She would never, ever, under normal circumstances begin a conversation without a reciprocal hello.

'Virginia?' Michelle frowned. 'What's up?'

Normally, too, her mother-in-law would protest at the use of the expression 'What's up?', classifying it with others she deemed irretrievably vulgar, such as 'How's it hanging?', 'Where y'at?' and 'Gimme five!' When Harry was first learning to talk, Michelle had considered teaching him to greet his grandmother, just once, with ''Sup, G?' but had reluctantly decided against it.

But Virginia seemed not even to have heard her. 'Is he there?' she said again, with a breathless urgency. 'Is he home?'

'Who? Chad?' Michelle glanced at the clock on the wall. 'It's only quarter to six.'

'He left here ten minutes ago.'

Michelle felt a prickle of dread. The soles of her feet began to tingle, as if the ground she was standing on was no longer stable.

'He left *your* place? What was he doing there? He always comes straight home—'

She heard the click of the front door opening. It was a sound that she subconsciously waited for every weeknight. Usually it released a small but vital bubble of happiness, which flitted upwards from her gut to her heart. Usually that click meant Michelle could be sure all was right with her world.

'Daddy!'

Seemed she wasn't the only one who listened for it. Harry scrambled down off his chair, ruddy face alight with joy, and stood bouncing up and down on his tiptoes, ready to race forward at the first sight of his father.

'Virginia!' Michelle hissed urgently. 'What was Chad doing at your place?'

'It will *kill* him. Really, you *must* talk to him!'

'Kill *who*? Jesus!'

'Dad-*eeee!*'

Harry had spied his father in the kitchen doorway and was racing towards him. Michelle watched as her tall, blonde husband bent to scoop his son up into his arms. She heard Rosie in her highchair grunt and gurgle with excitement, knowing that Daddy would soon stride over and chuck her cheek with his finger and kiss the top of her dark, downy head. That was Chad's routine — a bear hug and a 'Hey, big guy!' for Harry, a quick kiss and a 'Hey, gorgeous' for Rosie, then a fuller kiss on the mouth for Michelle and a brief, silent exchange of amusement mixed with disbelief, as if neither of them was entirely sure how all this had come about but it seemed only right to count their blessings.

This Wednesday evening, however, at ten to six, there was no 'Hey, big guy!' Chad scooped up Harry and hugged him. But his eyes were on Michelle. The prickle of dread crept up her spine and insinuated itself everywhere. She felt suspended, in that nauseating instant when you realise you've stepped out onto nothing and are about to fall.

A muted squawking reminded Michelle that her mother-in-law was still on the line. She held out the receiver to her husband.

'It's your mother.' Chad nodded. 'Shall I put her on speaker?'

Her husband reached out for the phone. 'Mom, I'll call you back.'

The answering squawk was abruptly terminated.

Rosie, outraged at being deprived of her kiss, began to yell. Michelle saw Harry's face crumple and knew he, too, was about to cry. If Michelle didn't do something fast, there'd be three people bawling in the kitchen.

'It would be a very good idea if you got our children into their bath and then put them to bed,' she informed her husband. 'You will then find me in the living room, drinking a large glass of wine, and you will tell me what the be-jeepers is going on.'

Find out more about Catherine here

Also by Catherine Robertson

The Not So Perfect Life of Mo Lawrence (Book 2 in the Imperfect Lives series)

The Misplaced Affections of Charlotte Fforbes (Book 3 in the Imperfect Lives series)

The Midlife Misgivings of Edward Marsh (Book 4 in the Imperfect Lives series)

About the Author

Catherine Robertson's novels have all been #1 New Zealand bestsellers, and she's thrilled to send her first three (plus bonus novella) out into the wider world as the *Imperfect Lives* series. Catherine writes contemporary fiction for smart readers, who like to be entertained and who don't object to occasional swears. Catherine has lived in the US and the UK, and currently divides her time between New Zealand's capital city, Wellington, and the province of Hawke's Bay. She has one husband, two grown sons, four Burmese cats two rescue dogs and co-owns a very cool bookshop called GOOD BOOKS.

Printed in Great Britain
by Amazon

45738096R00223